Girls of Salt and Sea

GIRLS OF SALT AND SEA

HALCYON BAY BOOK ONE

NATALIA MACIAS LUCIA

Published by Lightkeeper Press LLC

www.nataliamlucia.com

Cover Design by Maria Spada

ISBN: HB: 979-8-9863441-8-8; PB: 979-8-9863441-7-1; eBook: 979-8-9863441-2-6

Library of Congress Control Number: 2022910938

First Edition: August 2022

To those who look out at the sea and wonder.

CHAPTER ONE

The swirling waters of Halcyon Bay greet me like a monster roused from a long sleep. An angry rush of waves surge atop a frothy sea, licking up the sides of the old ferryboat, tossing it up and back. Each swell threatens to drag it down to a sunken graveyard, to that final port of call reserved for wrecks and cursed sailors.

I press my palm to the salt-drenched glass, gulping down a breath as a spit of land comes into view…a distant island shrouded in mist, rising ghost-like from the sea.

The sky above the island is alight with electricity. Crackling yellow veins weave through the clouds, chased by low rumblings of thunder. The wind whirrs and whooshes in frustrated spurts as a starless night devours the last morsel of sunlight. Mom's words drift to the surface of my mind—

"Don't go back to Halcyon Bay."

I shiver against the tense edges of her warning, pushing it down to a quieter place. Try as I may to silence the noise, to ignore her words and the threat of the howling storm, it all feels like a menacing omen as

I blow into town.

The passenger cabin is packed with other anxious commuters like me, sardined into tight benches in tight rows behind the captain's bridge. The air in the space is dank, oozing with the unmistakable punch of brine and armpit. My bench mate—a gangly man who's spent the last hour puking into a paper bag—doubles over again, this time missing his target and dousing the crotch of his gym shorts instead, along with the seat, his feet, and, most regrettably, *me*.

The spatter of vomit hits my right calf, and I nearly lose my shit.

Gritting my teeth, I inch as far from the man as possible, curling my body into the crevice of the window. I swipe at my leg with the sole of my sneaker and suck in a sharp, revolted breath. Going nuclear on his swampy ass won't help my situation any, but I'd still like to hollow out his eyeballs with a spork.

The ferry is rocked by a massive wave that strikes out like a fist. We veer rightward and I brace myself, determined not to slide into upchuck territory, my nails digging little half moons into the underside of the wooden bench. The world outside our confines is a dizzying, blue-black whirlwind, but I swallow down my nausea and fix my gaze on that widening strip of land ahead.

Halcyon Bay.

Something unusual seizes my attention, fluttering in my periphery along the fringes of the island. Amid the tendrils of lightning, a streak of pale white shoots across the landscape. It's a milky blur, nearly translucent, like a phantom born of storms, nightmares, and darkness. *A night like this begs for a ghost,* I think. If only I believed in such ridiculous things. Even still, the sight of it sends an icy drip coursing through me, despite the trickle of summer-sweat slipping down my spine.

As the ferry staggers closer, I find—to my relief and subsequent horror—that the figure is not a ghost at all, but a girl in a white nightgown. She sprints across a dilapidated pier perched high above the sea, jutting from the island like a gnarled arm before reaching an abrupt, crumbling end. The nightgown clings to the girl's tiny body, as sopping wet as the hair plastered to her cheeks. Its sweeping train trails her like an eager spectator, urging her away from the safety of land and into the intensifying storm. Though she isn't wearing any shoes, she moves with alarming precision, her steps confident and unhesitating, as if she's rehearsed every single one.

The girl pauses near the end of the pier and glances back to land. I sense a flicker of panic in her, a split second of indecision, and she begins to sway. One little foot slips from the slick beams, the gown's train dripping treacherously from the railing, and a bolt of terror scorches up my neck. *I must be dreaming this.*

I squeeze my eyes shut and open them again, snap the hairband at my wrist, rub my cheeks raw, anything to try to wake myself up. But then—

"Oh my God. There's a girl on that pier!"

The shriek comes from a woman on the bench in front of mine. She whips her head around, eyes bulging, startling the newborn nuzzled into her chest. "Look!" she screams again. "She's going to jump!"

Confusion swoops through the cabin as the other passengers scramble to see. They press close together, craning their necks, tension packing the air. A loud groan explodes from Swamp Ass' lips as he spews a fresh puddle of chunks over the floor.

The girl on the pier spreads her skinny arms wide, stretching out into the shape of a cross. She leans her body to the wind like a fledgling bird readying for flight…and the clouds yawn open as if by command. Rivers of rain gush over the ferry windows, obscuring the island, the girl, and the pier, until all of it is swallowed up in chaos.

A cacophony of cries erupt within the cabin, the growl of our captain rising above the rest. "Where is she?" he yells, knuckles white on the wheel as he battles the twisting, seething tides.

"She was right there!" The woman in front of me raps her finger on the glass while her newborn wails at an earsplitting pitch.

Pops of lightning flicker across the sky once more, and I'm just able to make out the pier through the deluge. We're almost beneath the monstrous structure now, and I scan the length of it, desperate, needing to lay eyes on her again. But there are no signs of life, no streaks of white. The pier stands alone in the darkness, the girl gone. Nothing more than a haunting memory.

The cabin breaks into utter pandemonium, one terrified scream clambering over the next.

"She jumped!"

"Check the water!"

"I can't see anything!"

"Call nine-one-one!"

"Someone save her!"

"Someone save *us!*"

Frantic, I search the sea for a bobbing head or hand, but there's only the crashing foam of waves, the endless, brutal downpour, and the lingering echoes of my mother's grim warning—

"*Don't go back to Halcyon Bay.*"

"Mayday, mayday!" the captain spits into his radio. "This is Captain Dave McCormick for the Coast Guard. Can anybody hear me?" His panicked voice sounds miles away and gravelly, like I'm hearing it from somewhere deep below ground. "Mayday, mayday! Captain Dave McCormick here, of Cyprus Ferry Four. Can anybody hear me—"

His voice is extinguished by a roaring thunderclap that makes the whole world shudder. I duck instinctively, squinting up at the roof, half expecting to see a smoking hole ripped through the fiberglass. The other passengers are equally distraught, dropping to their knees in fear, heads bowed under arms for shelter. Someone recites an anguished prayer. The newborn's face goes purple as he tests his baby lungs. Swamp Ass—with nothing left in him to regurgitate—resorts to weeping into his lap.

The captain presses the radio to his mouth again. "Mayday, mayday! This is Captain Dave McCormick of Cyprus Ferry Four. We've lost global positioning due to the storm, but our vessel's approximately two nautical miles from Halcyon Seaport." His breath catches, all color draining from his face. He grits his teeth. "And we've...spotted a jumper...off old Prospero Pier."

The only response to his distress call is the deafening hum of static.

Seconds tick painfully by as the captain wipes the sheen of sweat from his lip. "Can anybody hear me? I repeat, there is a girl in the water in Halcyon Bay, somewhere beneath Prospero Pier. Send a rescue crew! Mayday, mayday!"

A bitter feeling nips at my limbs like frostbite. I squeeze my eyes tight, imagining the girl's slender body slamming against a blanket of unyielding water and rock, her ribs shattered, organs punctured, choking on her own blood.

"Don't go back to Halcyon Bay."

The ferry nosedives and the captain grips the wheel, spinning it sharply to the right. My temple collides against the window—an instant, jarring crack that reverberates to my toes. My vision explodes in inky black spots as something warm and wet flows down my face.

I collapse onto the vomit-pooled floor.

As everything dims to black, I think only of the girl in the pale nightgown, falling ever to strange, unknown depths.

CHAPTER TWO

"Name?"

I swallow hard before answering, my mouth as dry as the trickle of blood caked to my neck. "My name's Dell Costa."

"What day of the week is it, Dell?"

"It's Thursday…Thursday night."

"Do you know where you are?"

"H-halcyon Bay."

"Good. Now follow the light with your eyes, please."

Wrapped in a thermal blanket, I lie board-stiff on an ambulance gurney, a harsh beam of fluorescent light aimed at my face. A team of industrious EMTs hover above me, fussing over the state of my brain, poking and prodding my skull for fractures. I insist that I'm fine, but they don't spare a moment to listen. They have tests to conduct, procedures to execute, so I'm left with no choice but to lie still and wait.

My surroundings slowly come into focus. I see all sorts of boats littering a buzzing marina. A cheesy welcome sign anointing Halcyon Bay as *Florida's Last Unspoiled Paradise!* Swarms of police officers, Coast

Guard, and divers flitting from emergency vehicles to the docks and back. There's a sinister haze in the post-storm atmosphere, flashing blue and red lights, the scramble and rush of people. A horrible sense of doom, thick as molasses, clinging to the sultry air.

I knew that coming back to Halcyon Bay—dipping my toes in the murky pool of my past—would be unpleasant, but never in my most dismal thoughts could I have predicted this. When we received that bit of unexpected correspondence, when Mom got sicker and I made the choice to return to this godforsaken place, how in the world was I to know what was to come?

Would knowing have changed anything at all?

When the letter arrived last week announcing the death of Virginia Klyne, I felt nothing. Not because I'm insensitive to death, or to grandmothers for that matter, but because my mother's mother was hardly a grandmother to me.

Grandmothers are known for being familial, warm, and welcoming. They knit cable sweaters, bake pastries, attend church three times a week, and sneak candies into your pockets. At least that's what I hear. It all sounds quite nice, objectively, but I can't attest to any of it myself. I don't know what kind of grandmother mine was, other than the absent kind.

To me, Virginia Klyne was more of a myth than a flesh-and-blood person, a vague and indistinct figure from my memories, like a fairytale character from an old storybook. And since Mom didn't shed a single tear upon receiving word of her passing, I couldn't feel too guilty for my own lack of emotion.

Still, it was a veritable surprise that Virginia had included us both in her will, despite having spent two decades apart with endless miles to separate us.

When I was four, my parents moved us away from Halcyon Bay, a small island off the west coast of Florida, and the place where I was born. I grew up instead in a log cabin nestled into the highlands of

Woodbridge, Maine, about as far as you can get from Halcyon Bay without crossing the Canadian border. My parents never spoke of our island home again, and what little I knew of my time there retreated to the depths of my soupy memory pot. It all turned flavorless in my mind, utterly distant and unrecognizable. And that's exactly how they wanted it.

Woodbridge was a sort of promised land for my parents, free from whatever troubles we'd endured on the island—troubles that were never revealed to me, no matter how often or passionately I asked.

As a kid, I tried to remember the grandparents I'd left behind, to picture their aging faces or the glint of silver in their hair. But they always evaded me, fleeting as the caress of wind on my cheek, a game of slippery elusion I was destined to lose.

I heard their names uttered once, one bitterly cold Christmas Eve. I'd been startled awake by the drumming of rain on the roof, and, when I heard my parents arguing, crept from my bedroom. An orange glow emanated from beneath their door, the troubled pacing of feet breaking the light with a rhythm of shadows. Rain consumed much of their conversation, but when I dared to sneak closer, ear pressed to the door, I heard my father whisper their names at long last.

Ambrose and Virginia.

The recognition was immediate, like someone had wrenched open a curtain on my past, spilling daylight over every forgotten corner. I remember the sinking weight of my body that night, how I clung to the wall for support, as if my whole world momentarily teetered off its axis.

They had offered to send us money, and plenty of it, from what I could gather. Mom had had a difficult year—the first of many, we'd come to find—and their charity was meant to alleviate her mounting pile of medical bills. Dad wanted to accept my grandparents' help, if only while we got our finances in order, but Mom quickly shut him down.

"Over my dead body," she whispered in the night. "And even then, I'd roll over from the grave to stop you."

Just like that, their light went out, case unequivocally closed, and I remember tiptoeing back to bed feeling innately robbed of something, wondering what could've caused such an irrevocable fracture in our family.

More of my questions went unanswered over time, and I grew tired of waiting for reasons that never seemed to materialize. Life did its job of steering me forward, and Halcyon Bay eroded from my thoughts like a closed box I shoved to the back of my mind's attic. I let the dust settle over it, let the years pile up, and moved along.

But something shifted with the arrival of Virginia's death notice.

My parents agreed that my father was to travel alone to the island for the reading of her Last Will and Testament, and at first, I didn't care enough to protest their decision. But that same night, Mom had an episode, the first in months since being admitted to Hopewell Psychiatric Center. Nurses found her roaming the halls in the darkest hours of morning, whispering about something dead in the water. She rubbed her face viciously, pressed her fingers to a phantom wound at her temple, and repeated a name over and over in her half-sleep. One name, one syllable, on a loop like a curse.

Lo.

According to Mom's rotating panel of doctors, Lo is the product of some crippling, undisclosed memory, eating her up inside, bit by scraping bit. It's a demon wreaking havoc on her traumatized mind, a tell-tale sign of her deteriorating mental health.

Whenever Lo appeared, Mom slid in and out of reality like a ghost slid through walls—here one moment, solid and present, then gone the next, haunted and absent. She'd see Lo molded to the shadows of her medical suite, gaping at her across the landscaped grounds, hovering above her as she lay sleeping. She'd stop eating, slipping into a state of near-catatonic depression, riding a steady carousel of prescribed drugs and psychotherapy. Like a lifelong plague, Lo crushed Mom's body, mind, and spirit to splinters. I knew the dismal pattern like I knew my face in a mirror. Only this time, for the first time, I could pinpoint a trigger.

I knew in my heart it was the news from Halcyon Bay—the news of Virginia Klyne's passing—that compelled Lo to resurface. This was the spring from which my mother's torment flowed, the source of her affliction. And something stirred within me for the first time since childhood, like wildfire catching in the marrow of my bones. Something fierce and protective and sick of my own helplessness, of watching Mom fade to a corpse before my eyes. Something fearful of what might've happened to make her this way, fearful more than anything that it had something to do with me. Whether she'd fallen into this state of disrepair by my hand, or by some failure or lacking on my part...

For days, I dwelled on our long-forgotten island home, on the history we'd rejected and the grandparents I never knew. There was so much I'd been shielded from as a child, so many inconvenient truths I'd avoided as an adult. But now, with Mom dancing on a deadly precipice, I had to do something drastic, something *unthinkable,* to keep her from plunging off this cliff's edge. And I knew exactly what that something was.

A few nights back, Dad and I were coaxing Mom to nibble at her hospital-provided dinner. She'd barely spoken in days, hardly reacted to anything we said, but she reached over and squeezed my hand three times unexpectedly. It was our thing, a private *I love you* that no one else heard but we both could feel. Her skin was pale and paper thin, and I could see the constellation of blue veins thrumming underneath. Exhausted violet circles were all that kept her eyes from sliding down her cheeks.

"You know, Dell," she said quietly, the first I'd heard her voice in far too long. "Halcyon Bay is not like the mainland."

I froze. Talk of *that place* was not something we did, the past never a subject we dared to explore.

Dad cleared his throat, looking as shocked as I felt. He never spoke of his family either. His parents had died in their native Spain when he was an infant, and his great-aunt, who'd brought him to the United States as a kid, who'd raised and educated him, had long since passed. These were tidbits I'd pieced together over the course of twenty years. We'd been on our own for so long. My parents liked it that way.

"Uh, Laurel," Dad began, "I don't think that—"

"Tomás. Please." Her voice was a tired breath that gripped my father, making him stop dead in his tracks.

She turned back to me with eyes like deep wells of grief. "That place…it changes you. There's this enduring darkness in it, something cruel and unnatural woven onto its shores." She winced at some painful memory I couldn't share or comprehend. None of her rambling made any sense at all.

"I see that it calls to you, Dell, and it scares me," Mom added, whisper-soft. "I know that the island might seem alluring and strange, but it's dangerous for all of us."

She bowed her head then, eyelids fluttering, as if the few words she'd uttered had depleted her energy, siphoned her life force. That's when the warning dripped from her lips, pricking my heart with the sharp thorn of sadness—

"Don't go back to Halcyon Bay."

And so, subconsciously, she had to know what I had planned.

I squeezed her hand three times in return—an unspoken promise and a brazen lie, something I hated doing and was pathetically unpracticed at. She peered at me sadly, threatening to unravel all my plans, but my decision was made, my mind resolved. I could only hope she'd understand someday.

It wasn't a choice I made lightly.

I snuck into Dad's room that night while he slept, a duffel bag slung across my back. I snatched the notice letter from his nightstand with all the details I needed for the trip, and slipped from the house like a thief, leaving a brief note in my wake: *Please don't tell her where I am. I love you. I'm sorry.*

I traveled the 1,600 miles south over two sleepless summer days, stopping only for fuel-ups, bathroom breaks, and crappy fast-food runs in Podunk towns. The entire time I was driving, I had this nagging pinch in my back that had more to do with a guilt-ridden conscience than with hours cramped in a bucket seat.

But that curiosity within me, that stirring in my bones, would not be ignored any longer. I had to understand this island steeped in magic and woe, to learn the context of Mom's condition, and expose whatever drove us across the country.

All of which I never knew.

Now I would.

After an hour or so, the EMTs begrudgingly concede that my brain is not swelling up in my cranium, and consent to let me go free.

"Could've been much worse, hon," one of them says with shrewd eyes, as if to emphasize my incredible good fortune. "You're lucky the trauma was minimal."

I don't respond, deciding it best not to discuss the true depths of my trauma.

They send me off with an armful of dressings, gauze, and bandages, and I stumble from the ambulance with my duffel in tow, swept into neon-lit, caution-taped mayhem, into the heart of the recovery search for the girl in the white nightgown.

Mom's words remain a deafening ring in my mind, as constant and reverberant as the toll of a ship's bell.

"*Don't go back to Halcyon Bay.*"

Her warning never leaves me, though I try my damnedest to shake it off as I approach the roundabout in the parking lot and flag down the first taxi I see.

Sorry, Mom, I think. For better or worse, I've arrived.

CHAPTER THREE

The taxi driver that collects me pinches his nose when I shimmy into the backseat. The sight of me is nasty, but the smell is far worse. Apart from the puke-crust coating my jeans and the blood-soaked t-shirt sticking indecently to my bra, he pulled around the curb like a race car driver perfecting his drifting technique, sliding through a pocket of suspicious brown water and drenching me in filth.

He cranes his neck around, swollen eyes drinking me in, and gripes under his breath about my appearance, my stench—something about my smelling like a walking sewage drain. I shake the remnant sludge from my hair onto his floor. *Prick.*

"Where to?" the driver grumbles.

"Cliffmoor House," I respond. "Address is 330 White Magnolia Cour—"

"I know where it is." He lowers all four windows and loops an air freshener over the rear view before finally putting the car in drive.

Our ride through town is quiet and swift as the rain wanes to a drizzle. The streets are devoid of cars and people, riddled instead with silver wisps of fog and the lingering promise of stormy weather. We pass quaint neighborhoods speckled in yellow lamplight, flower-potted storefronts awash in faded shades of coral, and buildings erected from chalky Florida limestone. I try to soak it all in—to commit every misty crook and bend to memory, the scents, the scenery—but it's hard to focus when I reek *this bad*.

Searching my duffel for a change of clothes, I dangle a wadded-up twenty-dollar bill by the driver's face. "A little something extra for your trouble, if you promise to keep your eyes on the road."

He grunts his acknowledgment and plucks the bill from my fingers, still venturing to meet my gaze in the mirror—just once to push his luck—but when I shoot him a harsh scowl, his eyes flick back to the road and stay there.

I shake into fresh clothes, balling up the sticky ones I peeled from my body, holding them at arm's length like relics from the Bubonic plague. I cram them into a plastic baggie I find abandoned in the backseat, and the air in the taxi clears up quickly, freed from that acrid funk I'd dragged in with me. The driver exhales with relief. I still need a shower, but at least now I can stand being inside my own skin.

We turn down a winding road in Halcyon Bay's Old Town district while I trace our route on a map I grabbed back at the seaport. The street is lined on both sides with towering oak trees, their ancient black trunks poking up from the ground like bodies rising in the dark. Twisting branches stretch upwards into an ominous canopy. Beyond the line of oaks are sprawling manors with manicured lawns, every one of them dotted with shiny foreign sports cars glinting through the night. Each estate is a testament to the established affluence of Old Town, all of them stunning, but equally pretentious. Gratuitous displays of inherited wealth.

"So Cliffmoor House, eh?" the driver spits over his shoulder. "You a relative of the Klynes or something?"

I guess now that I don't stink, he thinks me worthy of small talk. Either that, or the guy's just a nosy schmuck. "Yeah. Do you know them?"

He snorts crudely, like I've made an inadvertent joke. "Everyone 'round here knows the Klynes."

I'm not sure what he means by that. Not sure I want to know, either.

We curve left onto a wide cul-de-sac—White Magnolia Court—and roll to a stop in the deepest part of the street. Beyond a vine-wrapped gate looms a magnificent gray mansion surrounded by lush landscaping. I hear the crashing tumult of waves in the distance, and breathe in the perfume of beach on the breeze.

"Home sweet home," the driver says, his shifty eyes sliding my way.

With a murmured "Thank you," I hand over a few more bills and shuffle out of the taxi, dragging my duffel behind me. As soon as I shut the door, he lead-foots the gas pedal, tires screeching on asphalt as he peels through the fog, leaving me alone in the thick, humid night to survey my grandparents' home for the very first time.

The enormous, three-story beach house before me is jaw-dropping, to put it bluntly. A true Victorian beauty, complete with gingerbread accents, steep gabled roofs, and grand half-moon bay windows. A tower soars as high as a church steeple from the far right wing, keeping a watchful eye over the ample grounds beneath. It's as I'd always pictured it in my childhood fairy-dreams—vast and beautiful, brimming with mystery, like it might exist on the border between our world and a more magical one. But the house seems far less like a fairytale to me now. More like an oppressive, impenetrable maze poised to test my resolve.

I approach the silver intercom box by the gate, my heart battering my chest like a caged bird demanding to be set free. The flicker of a television screen leaks through the curtains of a second-story window. Already, I'm questioning this half-baked plan of mine. I should just turn back, run home, and forget the whole idea.

No, I think firmly. *No turning back now.*

I press the call button and wait, fingers fidgeting at my sides.

Several moments later, an elderly male voice blares from the speaker. "Yes? May I help you?"

My breath hitches. "H-hello. I'm here to see Finley O'Hare."

Finley O'Hare is the Klyne family attorney and executor of Virginia's will. Earlier this afternoon, I'd called Finley from Cyprus, the mainland town from where I caught the ferry, but his office and mobile phones both went straight to voicemail. I meant to inform Finley that Dad's work schedule had changed and that I would be taking his place this weekend—more lies, of course, but Finley didn't have to know that. Unfortunately for me, I never got a call back, and thus am totally unprepared for what I may encounter tonight.

"Mr. O'Hare is gone for the evening," the man says curtly. My duffel bag sinks to my feet at this news, hope sliding like rainwater down the curve of my shoulders. "Moreover, miss," his sneering tone rings clear through the intercom, "this is a private residence, not a place of business. You may reach Mr. O'Hare at his office during regular operating hours. Please vacate the premises, or else I will be forced to call the authorities. Good evening."

The speaker goes dead.

Without thinking twice, I click the button again, trying to control the wave of panic washing over me.

"Yes?" the man replies.

Uneasy words rush from my lips like a bursting dam. "I'm sorry to bother you at this late hour, sir, but there must be some mistake. I'm sure Mr. O'Hare was expecting me. I had a bit of a delay getting to the island, but the letter I received from him…it said I'd been invited to stay at Cliffmoor House this weekend. I'm a beneficiary of Virginia Klyne's will."

I pause for a breath, reflecting on what I've said. I must have read Finley's letter at least a dozen times since leaving Woodbridge, thumbing over each of the fine creases, folding it carefully into my wallet.

As regrettable an occasion as this is, we invite you and yours, with tender hopefulness, to make Cliffmoor House your home while in Halcyon Bay, in honor of the late Mrs. Virginia, who would undoubtedly wish to see her daughters and grandchildren reunited at long last…

"I see," the man says, interrupting the script playing out in my head. "How did you know the late missus?"

"I didn't know her exactly, but I'm Virginia's…Virginia's my…um…" I struggle to say that anomalous word—*grandmother*. It dies on my lips, too clunky and unfamiliar to verbalize, as if my own tongue were rebelling against it. I settle on something easier. "I'm Dell. Dell Costa. Laurel's daughter."

There's pin-drop silence for a moment, and then, "Meridel?" An incredulous whisper. "Is that really you?"

Heat pushes into my cheeks. "Yes."

"My word, Miss Meridel!" he sputters. "I do apologize. We weren't expecting you this evening. I'd been awaiting your father's arrival, but I didn't realize you'd be joining him."

"It's just me, actually. My dad couldn't make it."

"Ah, well, we're pleased to have you, miss. Just a moment, please. I'll let you right in."

The speaker goes silent as the iron gate shudders to life, swinging wide with a grating creak. I plant my feet and wait for it to come to a stop, arming myself for what I'm about to do.

There's no doubt in my mind that Mom would hate my being here, undoing years of conscious disconnection from our family in one fell swoop, one impulsive decision. But Mom also raised me to be bold, courageous, and loyal, so I have to wonder whether somewhere down the line, she could ever be a little proud of me for coming back.

I straighten my shoulders, filling my lungs with a deep breath. The answer to my every question lies inside that house, a lifetime of truths waiting to be unearthed. All I have to do is take one step, then another, and another after that, all the way up the mossy brick driveway to Cliffmoor House.

CHAPTER FOUR

An elderly man opens the door, flicking on a porch light as he steps into the night. His attire is that of a butler: a simple, impeccably tailored black blazer, trousers, and polished dress shoes. He tucks his chin to better appraise me over his spectacles, perched low on a hooked nose.

I draw nearer to the house and glance up at the second-story window where the television had been turned on moments ago. The room is dark now, but the curtains at the open window shift faintly, as if by the nudging of the breeze or the breath of someone pressed against them—someone watching me. A shiver spider-crawls up my spine.

Get a grip, I command myself as I ascend the steps to the porch.

"Miss Meridel, welcome back to Cliffmoor House." The butler regards me with a formal bow, examining my appearance through steely gray eyes. I squirm when they land on the mass of gauze taped across my forehead. "Are you all right?"

My fingers fly to the bandage, briefly considering flinging it into the nearest rosebush. "Yes, I'm fine. Just a scratch."

Convinced or not, the man steps aside. With a flourish of his white-gloved hand and a polite "Please, come in," he ushers me through the door.

Hugging my duffel like a security blanket, I step into a lavish foyer abounding with art and priceless baroque wonders, a collection so remarkable it would put any museum to shame. The room is anchored by a dramatic central staircase and a magnificent chandelier swaying from high above. The fixture sends a kaleidoscope of rippling light across the space, an effect like undulating waves beneath an amber sky, drizzling the stairwell, the walls, and decor in flecks of gold. Classical sculptures and marble busts gleam from every corner, seeming to come alive in the shifting chandelier light. They scowl at my presence, turning up their chiseled faces, vacant eyes flashing their contempt.

Even the goddamn statues know I don't belong here.

The door clicks shut behind me. The old butler smiles. "I'm so thrilled to have you back in our neck of the woods, Miss Meridel."

I meet his wrinkled eyes, surprised to find affection in his gaze. A genuine kindness, despite the austere decorum he dons like a second uniform.

I extend my hand to him, a subtle offering of goodwill. "Please, call me Dell." I'll need a friend at Cliffmoor House, after all, and maybe this old butler is the keeper of all the Klyne's secrets, the map that points to where buried skeletons lie.

He seems to appreciate the gesture, his mouth curving into a wider smile when we shake. "Of course, Miss *Dell*. I'm sure you don't remember me, but I've been serving your family for nearly half a century. My name is Colin Briggs."

"No, I'm sorry. I don't recall."

Mr. Briggs swats the air with long, tapered fingers. "Ah, well. You were only a child when your parents left. And now look at you, grown up and lovely as ever." He shakes his head in disbelief. "Amazing how time flies. How is your mother doing?"

"She's well," I lie, wondering how much Mr. Briggs knows of Mom's condition.

"I'm so glad to hear that. I think of her often, and of you as well,

Miss Meri—*ahem*—Miss Dell. Now, please, if you would follow me, I'll show you to your accommodations."

I trail Mr. Briggs down a wide hallway, passing a series of dimly lit rooms as we go. A rich, olive-green study stretches before me, teeming with antlers, rifles, and wall-to-wall shelves stocked in leather-bound books. Then, a crimson dining hall inhabited by an impressive redwood table and twelve chairs, with a bronze effigy of Poseidon wielding his trident at its center. We move on past a mustard music room with a golden harp shining from one corner and a sleek grand piano flashing from the other. I peer into each of the rooms as we walk, doing my best to sponge up every minute detail, all the while keeping steady pace with the butler. But when we arrive at the parlor and Mr. Briggs continues in stride, I'm compelled to pause for a longer moment to consider the unsettling face staring back at me.

The luxurious, peacock-blue space is home to plush couches, wingback chairs, and a grand fireplace. Floating above the marble mantel, observing me from a gilded pedestal, is the portrait of a beautiful young woman in repose.

I linger in the room's archway, lost in the exquisite rendering of every one of her features—her silken curls, beguiling blue eyes, full red lips, and high cheekbones. Bulbous emerald jewels sparkle from her neck, perfectly matching the vibrant gown draped to her figure while contrasting the creamy alabaster of her skin.

"Your grandmother," Mr. Briggs offers quietly from the hall. His words course through me like a lightning bolt, the truth of them confirmed by the engraved placard at the base of the frame: *Virginia Marigold Klyne.* My late grandmother, immortalized in a moment of youthful divinity.

I examine her closely, enthralled by her stunning visage, but also perplexed by it. I *know* this woman. I recognize her from somewhere, some separate place and time untouched by the swirl of childhood memory stirring within me. Her face is keenly familiar, not because she's my grandmother, nor by her resemblance to my mother, but for some unrelated and mystifying reason I cannot for the life of me pin down.

It's just the lack of sleep, I think, shaking off the eerie feeling settling over me like a dusting of snow. *Just my weary eyes playing strange tricks in the dark.*

I duck out of the parlor and hasten my steps.

Mr. Briggs awaits in the deepest bowels of the mansion, by three arched French doors leading onto the grounds. He unlatches one and wrenches it open, the sea breeze and spray of rain rushing forward to lap at my face.

A sprawling turquoise pool winks at me from a distance, flanked by a gazebo wreathed in hundreds of twinkling lights. Tropical plants and palms coat the gardens in lavish bursts of green, red, and orange. A guest house the size of our cabin back in Woodbridge occupies the farthest edge of the property, and beyond that, past an expanse of sand dunes and sea oats, is a long dock stretching over an unilluminated beach.

"Master Ambrose had the guest cottage equipped for your father's arrival," Mr. Briggs says, opening an umbrella for me and another for himself. "Had he known you were coming, miss, he might've made other arrangements. But seeing as how the master has retired for the evening, and doesn't much like to be disturbed after hours—"

"The guest house is perfect," I pipe up quickly, my thoughts tossing back to that second-story window and the uncanny sensation of being watched. Nothing would make me happier than to sleep far away from this oppressive house and its elusive master.

Mr. Briggs leads me down a paved path across the lawn, speaking in a raised voice so as to be heard over the rain. "You'll have your own entrance through the gardens out here, so you can come and go as you please. It's private and quite peaceful. I hope you'll find it suitable."

We reach the guest house, and Mr. Briggs pulls a key with spiral embellishments from his pocket. He unlocks the door and we shake inside, collapsing our umbrellas as he flips on a switch, breathing life into the vacant rooms.

"The missus used this as her studio," he remarks, as I take in the countless painted canvases spanning the cottage.

Grand, earthy landscapes occupy every square-inch of wall space. Even more lean up against the white wicker furniture or rest atop an array of paint-spattered easels. Oils, acrylics, and gessoes, all marked by broad, confident brushstrokes and rich pigments. Delicate botanical studies in pale watercolor hues. Notes and sketches piled and pinned in every corner, scrawled along the edges of cocktail napkins and tissue paper, as if Virginia had left them here moments ago.

"She was an artist," I say without meaning to, my eyes feasting on the buffet of fine art spread before me, flitting hungrily from piece to piece.

"Heartwork," he replies, a knowing glint in his gaze. "That was her word for it. Art from the heart, and, boy, did she love it."

He takes me on a brief tour of the house, showing me where I can find fresh linens, how to adjust the air conditioning, and an unusual kink in the shower knob where hot is cold, cold is hot, and somewhere in the middle can vacillate anywhere between lukewarm and hell fire. I follow along attentively, heeding his direction like a student in grade school. Until I catch a glimpse of myself in the bathroom mirror, that is, and nearly fall over from the grim sight.

My dark hair, normally a mass of thick, lively waves, hangs stringy and lifeless by the sides of my face. Stress-induced hives snake up my left cheek, while the bandage strapped to my forehead diaper-sags over my brow. My hazel eyes are flat, my cheeks gaunt as a corpse, and an offensive amount of blood is still caked up the length of my neck. I flush red-hot in an instant, my eyes widening with humiliation.

Gratefully, Mr. Briggs—paragon of butlery discretion—pretends not to see my little meltdown. "I noticed you didn't bring a car with you, miss."

I tear my eyes from the mirror. "I left my car back in Cyprus. The vehicle transport ferry was being serviced, so I took a passenger boat over. Otherwise, I would've been stuck there until morning."

"Not to worry." He points out the bedroom window to an adjacent shed camouflaged in climbing vines. "There's a bicycle in there that belonged to the late missus. You may use it during your stay, should you wish to get around the island. The tires should have plenty of air in them."

"Thank you, Mr. Briggs."

"Goodness me! Briggs will do just fine, or Colin, if you prefer. Mr. Briggs is a title reserved for my father." The butler chuckles. "Besides, you'll soon find I'm not nearly as stuffy as I appear."

I smile, and at the same time, my stomach groans loudly, to which Briggs raises one bushy, silver eyebrow.

"You must be starving, miss."

"Oh, no. I'm all right."

"Are you sure you don't want a bite to eat? I can have Cook prepare anything you'd like."

I frown at the thought of more indentured servants waiting on me. "No, no. That's all right, thanks. I'll find something to eat in town."

"As you wish. Just be wary of inclement weather. The worst of the storm has passed, but there may still be showers well into the night."

I follow him back to the main living space. He says, "Mr. O'Hare will arrive at ten o'clock tomorrow morning for the reading of Mrs. Klyne's will. I'll instruct him to come check in with you before commencing. The family will gather in the parlor room. That's just inside the house and to the right."

As if there's a chance I could ever forget.

"The spreading of Mrs. Klyne's ashes will take place Saturday evening at seven o'clock. A limousine will come to collect the family at six and deliver you to the seaport for a sunset sail."

A sunset sail to dump Virginia's ashes? Where the hell was *that* in Finley's stupid letter?

"And finally, the missus' celebration of life will take place here, at the house, on Sunday at eleven. She was quite beloved among the islanders, so we're expecting a rather large turnout—"

I clear my throat to stop him, my exhausted brain plodding through this onslaught of information. I hadn't realized that by showing up tonight, I'd committed myself to an *entire weekend* of scheduled family functions. The thought alone is worrisome, not to mention draining.

How can I make good on my purpose here—riddling out some truth about my mother's strange affliction—if I can't get a second to myself?

Briggs' eyes scan mine. "Perhaps we'll shelf this conversation for tomorrow? You must be tired after so much travel."

He sets the key on the breakfast table, reaching for the doorknob, but just before leaving, he hesitates and turns back. He has a faraway look about him, like he's been transported to a distant past. "You look so much like her, you know." His voice is tight with emotion, eyes cloaked in a haze of memory.

Who? I wonder. My mother, Virginia, or someone else entirely?

Briggs coughs, snapping out of his bizarre reverie. "Your mother, of course. So very much like Laurel, way back when…"

I've always loved hearing that I look like Mom. Despite the obvious differences—our hair and eye color, for instance—our subtler features are uncannily similar. We share the same rainbow arch of our brows, our swan necks and plump lips, that little crinkle that digs into the space between our eyes when we're angry. Looking like Mom makes me feel like we're connected, tethered in the most basic way. Like she's always with me, always close, even in times we're apart.

But something tells me this is not what Briggs means.

"I get that a lot," I say, wanting to press him more on the subject, but the butler has already composed himself, smoothed out his emotions with practiced finesse.

"One last thing, miss," he adds, reverting to business matters. "You may find that cellular service on the island is a bit sparse…"

I pull my cell phone from my pocket, and sure enough, I have no service and no internet connection.

"A pesky disadvantage of island life." He exhales a weary sigh. "You'll find a landline phone on the bedside table. Dial zero-one to reach me at the main house anytime. Cell service is mostly limited to downtown areas, I'm afraid. Places where the tourists congregate, government buildings, that sort of thing. Old Town hasn't quite ushered in the era of modernity yet."

"Okay. Thanks for the heads up."

The butler dips his chin before grabbing his umbrella. "Sleep well, Miss Dell. We'll speak again in the morning. Please don't hesitate to ring me if you need anything at all." With a flutter of his gloved fingers, he disappears through the door and into the night.

My stomach groans again, reverberating across the silent house as stabbing hunger pierces my belly. I bite my lip, surprised by the sharp tang of salt that bites me right back.

CHAPTER FIVE

I'm hunched over the bar at Barracuda's Teeth—a downtown tavern a few blocks off the main strip of chain restaurants, clubs, and tourist traps—plowing through a pile of curly fries and a burger the size of my face.

The place is a dumpy watering hole, built of strong liquor and questionable hygiene, sandwiched between a run-down strip joint and a children's day care advertised as *For Lease*. The neighborhood's a little shifty, but the kitchen is open past midnight, the unsavory haze of cooking grease sizzling in the air, and right now, that's more than good enough for me.

The walls of the tavern are flocked with the miscellany of island life. Vintage photographs of sunscreened lifeguards, rescue buoys and vests faded pale-pink by the sun, expired Florida license plates coated in decades-old road dust. Swimming above my head among the moldy rafters is a hodge-podge of fishing paraphernalia and strings of half-lit Christmas lights. The focal point is a giant taxidermy barracuda, dangling haphazardly over the U-shaped bar, scales gleaming silver through its layers of grime.

Beyond the bar, past rows of vinyl dining booths, a trio of surf dudes with unkempt hair and board shorts bounce around onstage with various instruments in hand, performing for a small sea of dancing patrons. A blond girl in the audience springs up and tugs at the singer's shorts. He drops to his knees, wraps an arm around her waist, and proceeds to leech-suck on her neck. The drunken crowd roars their approval, beer cans and cigarettes pumped high in the smoky atmosphere.

Distracted by their PDA, I almost miss Dad's name lighting up my cell phone screen. The device vibrates against the bar top, its incessant buzzing like an angry scolding. I'd sent him a message hours ago from the seaport, assuring him that I'd arrived and was doing fine, having the good sense to omit any mention of tempests, drowning victims, or possible brain damage. I promised he'd hear from me soon. Then I lost cell service.

When the call drops and the phone stills, I watch a flood of delayed notifications pour in. Sixteen missed calls, four voicemails, seven texts, all in the last hour. The phone begins to vibrate again, but I quickly punch the decline button.

Glancing up, I lock eyes with the bartender who took my dinner order. She leans against the draft beer dispenser, a lip ring shining from her red-tinted mouth. Her hair is chopped short with frosted silver tips, and she wears a black tank-top with a series of strategic holes slashed across it, no doubt to accentuate her better assets. The chipped name tag on her chest reads *Lira*.

"How's the food?" Lira asks as she files her nails into knife-sharp points.

By the amount of dust flying in every direction, I'm sure that Lira could not care less about food quality, but I try not to dwell on this too much as I cram fistfuls of fries in my mouth.

"Food's good," I mumble, staring at my basket of clumped batter and grease drippings like it's the most interesting thing in the world. I hope she gets the hint. Socializing with the locals is not on my itinerary.

My cell phone *dings* with yet another frantic voicemail from my father. I flip the phone over, screen-side down, in obvious frustration.

"Looks like you could use a drink," Lira tries again, fiddling with her lip ring. She flicks it with her tongue like a frog might do to catch a fly, dropping a white cocktail napkin before me. Printed on the napkin is a caricature of a barracuda in sunglasses, flashing a set of spiky teeth. *'Cuda's—Hooking You Up Since '55,* boasts the napkin in groovy black lettering, with the C in 'Cuda's curled into the shape of a fish hook.

I mumble a quick "No, thanks," but Lira swoops in to interrupt me, jumping into her script of Thursday night drink specials.

"We've got five-dollar well drinks till closing. Penny beers too, if Busch or Natty's tickle your taste buds. Two-for-one pitchers of our house margaritas, mojitos, and our sinfully sweet island rum punch. Or, if you're feeling a bit more adventurous, you can take a chance on Bartender's Choice for ten fifty a pop. Fair warning, though, we pour hard and strong in the bay. Untrained livers need not apply." Her black eyes flash at me. "So…what's your hangover *du jour?*"

"Sorry, hard pass." I point to the gash above my eyebrow, contoured by a throbbing flush of purple. "I've already got my hands full with one headache tonight."

I'd showered before leaving the guest house earlier, ripping off my saggy diaper bandage in glee, but forgetting to replace it with the butterfly closures given to me by the EMTs. The cut on my forehead gapes open now, ugly and accentuated by an ever-deepening bruise.

Lira shrugs, returning to her nail filing. "What's with the head wound, anyway? No offense, but you kind of look like a cracked-out Humpty Dumpty."

At this, I choke on my mouthful of fries. Lira pours me a glass of water and slides it across the counter, an undeniable smirk on her lips.

"Thanks," I croak, sucking back small sips, compelling myself to breathe until the fries dislodge and I'm able to explain. "I got caught in a storm tonight, coming in on the ferry. The boat was rocking pretty bad. Smacked my head against a window."

"Sounds messy."

"Well, I passed out and wound up fetal in some guy's puke, so messy's a polite way to put it."

She snorts. "Did you get hurt real bad? Like, skull fracture? Concussion? Internal bleeding?"

I've never seen anyone light up this much over talk of traumatic brain injury. "No, I'm all right, thankfully. Got my clean bill of health. Might've done some damage to that old ferry, though."

Lira grimaces. "Please. Anything you did would've been an improvement. Those tubs are all so broken-down and ancient. Cabin leaks, electrical issues, rust eating up the hull, you freaking name it." She leans forward onto her elbows. "I'm shocked every day a Cyprus ferry doesn't sink. Freaking deathtraps. I wouldn't be caught dead on any one of them."

"You'd rather fly?"

Confusion paints her face. "Fly?"

"Yeah. You know, when you leave the island?"

"Why would I leave the island?" She seems so puzzled by my question, I almost feel stupid for asking it.

"Um, I don't know…to travel?"

Lira breaks into awkward laughter, waving her hand dismissively. "Ha. Negative. I'm good on permanent island time, thanks."

"Oh. Okay."

I duck back into my dinner basket, contemplating her words. The residents of Halcyon Bay seem all too comfortable with their isolation, like they have no need for the outside world or any of its landlocked drudgery. This place is a world unto itself, encapsulated in nautical, rum-soaked bubble wrap. A place where people live in willful detachment, fueled by the sedate IV drip of island life—a medley of weed, saltwater, and reggae music thrumming in their communal vein.

Lira inspects her bird-talon nails one last time. Content with her work, she slips the emery board in her back pocket.

"So. Humpty." There's an expectant chirp in her tone. "This your first time on Halcyon Bay?"

"First time back, actually. I'm from here."

"A native? I freaking knew it. I'm Lira, by the way." She taps her name tag with a talon, as if I could have missed it popping off her chest.

"How could you know that?"

"Occupational hazard. I've got hawk eyes for tourists with deep pockets." She narrows her eyes at me and smiles thinly, as if I've got a sign on my forehead that reads, *Don't bother, I'm broke!*

Bitch, I think. I am broke. But still.

"You get a lot of tourists in here?" I ask, recalling how the bustling Main Street several blocks over had been crammed with well-dressed, sun-kissed travelers when I passed it. While the occasional straggler might meander off the beaten path in this direction—myself, for example—the Barracuda crowd seems predominantly local, rife with scruffy, sun-bleached hair and skin like bronzed leather, unbuttoned fishing shirts and bare, sandy feet.

"Sure do," Lira replies. "The ones in search of the real Halcyon Bay."

I raise my eyebrows. "And *this* is the real Halcyon Bay?" One act of condescending bitchiness deserves another.

"Real as it gets," Lira shoots back. "We may not be flashy enough for the spring break crowd, with their slushy drinks and their wet t-shirt contests, and we may not be fancy enough for folks with champagne tastes. But tourists come to 'Cuda's for the authentic island culture, the history! You think the likes of Clarence Pilot and Ginnie Gold hung out at Daiquiri Daze or Tarpon's Ale House in their heyday?"

"Sorry, who?"

"You've never heard of Clarence Pilot, the famous blues singer?" Lira blinks wildly. "Or legendary Hollywood actress, Ginnie Gold?"

I shake my head.

"Geez, Humpty, they're only freaking mega stars. Names that put us on the map, made us a real vacation destination."

She jolts upright, as if she's remembered something important. "Wait a sec! My boyfriend's in the Coast Guard, and he told me there was an incident involving one of the Cyprus ferries tonight. Something about a dead girl in the channel. You must've heard or seen something about that, right?"

My heart plummets as I take another drink of water, gulping down the icy feeling that accompanies the memory of the girl on the pier.

"Well?" she probes.

"No. I, uh…I didn't hear about that."

Lira pouts as I trace my fingers over my temple, probing the tender point of collision, a constant headache rolling in the back of my skull. I don't even know how to begin processing what I witnessed tonight.

"What do they think happened to her?" I ask, trying to sound casual. As casual as can be when discussing a dead child.

"All signs point to suicide," Lira says, her dark eyes dancing. "Word is, she jumped off Prospero Pier on the north side of the island, crashed on the rocks, and drowned right there in the bay. We won't know anything definite till the morning news, but if the whispers are true…"

I rub my hands down my arms, readjusting on the wooden barstool. My skin feels like it's suddenly crawling with fire ants. "Is that a fishing pier?"

"Used to be. It was originally supposed to be a highway stretching to the mainland, but locals hardcore protested the project. Funding was pulled, construction halted, and people started using the structure for fishing instead. Part of it collapsed a few years back though, so no one's allowed out there anymore."

The girl in the nightgown had thought out her plan carefully, going so far as to choose a remote location to minimize exposure. Had she also waited for the cover of a stormy night, or was that little detail just sick serendipity?

Lira eyes me as I sit with my thoughts. "I'm really surprised you didn't hear anything about this," she says again. "The seaport must've been crawling with cops. Shit like this never happens around here. It's major news."

I know she's goading me for some fresh gossip, hoping I'll give up something juicy to fuel the island rumor mill, but I'm less concerned with that than I am with depressurizing the slow-cooker of emotions in my chest. The next few days are crucial, and I need to keep focused. Mom's health is my mission—my *only* mission. Dwelling on what brought some poor little girl to her demise is not part of the equation. So maybe talking about it, unloading onto some random stranger, isn't such a bad idea.

"Hello?" Lira crosses her arms. "Earth to Humpty?"

But no. I can't. I can't bring myself to speak on what happened, no matter how much I'd like to. It's too awful, too fresh, and no amount of idle chit-chat will absolve me of that.

"Like I said, I knocked out on the ride over. I have no clue what went on around me, and I didn't hear a thing about any suicidal kid." I shrug with an indifference I certainly don't feel and stare off into the haze of the tavern, focusing on the band and the grinding crowd.

Lira grows antsy in the absence of conversation, drumming her nails on the counter, in need of some new distraction. As soon as another patron raises a hand for their check, she slinks away, calling over her shoulder, "Let me know if you need anything, Humpty!"

Relieved for the solitude, I look down at my basket, only to find that I've shredded my burger bun to bits, tossing pieces around my basket like sad confetti. A pity party for one.

Someone nearby begins to chuckle, reeling me back from my private bubble of misery. *Now what?* I think, glancing up to behold a man with the most striking green eyes I've ever seen.

The stranger watches me from a few seats over, his attention rapt, lips cast in an easy smile. My jaw goes slack when our eyes meet, his glinting like uncut emeralds in the dark. The rowdy bar ambience seems to mute around us, warmth unspooling in my stomach the longer I stare. I've never laid eyes on anyone quite so handsome, nor so keenly focused on me.

In a throbbing, fiery instant, I know my night just got far more interesting. And vastly more complicated.

CHAPTER SIX

The stranger has the kind of tan one only gets from working in the sun: deep, consistent, and golden. He wears a crisp white t-shirt with *Urban Fishing Company* printed across the chest and a pair of old blue jeans. His honey-brown hair is tucked into a frayed baseball cap. He can't be more than a couple of years older than me.

"Something funny?" I ask, irked by his scrutiny.

The stranger's smile widens at the pique in my voice. "Not really," he says melodically, spinning his amber beer bottle on the counter. "But, in case you couldn't tell, Lira's exhausting. Persistent as a horsefly, and about as pleasant too. Best to avoid her at all costs."

His quicksand eyes are steady on me—beckoning, enthralling, like pools of liquid jade—and I'm compelled to remind myself that it wouldn't behoove me to get tangled up with the locals.

"Duly noted," I mutter, averting my gaze.

Make no unnecessary ties to this island. That's the promise I made myself. My business on Halcyon Bay lies exclusively in the past, so I have no time to waste on this infuriatingly good-looking man.

What I need to do is climb in bed and get some real sleep. Let the last four hours of bleak reality dissipate into dreams. Let them fade from my mind like a Polaroid picture.

"You've really been put through the ringer, haven't you?" the stranger continues. He taps his forehead over his cap, right at the spot where my skin is slashed open. "Ferry ride from hell and all."

"You were eavesdropping? Really?"

"It wasn't all that hard." His arm muscles tighten when he raises the bottle to his lips. He's far too attractive, aggravatingly so.

"Your mother must be so proud."

The grin that breaks across his face sculpts a dimple into one cheek, causing my pulse to quicken. "Who do you think taught me to read lips? It's a learned skill, you know. Takes *years* of practice, dedication…"

"Sounds like real profound bonding material."

He laughs. "Think what you will, but eavesdropping, gossiping, and butting into other people's business is like our small town calling card. Gives us something to talk about other than fish harvests and weather forecasts."

I force a scowl. "That's precious."

"No," he admits. "But that's Halcyon Bay."

Without warning, the stranger stands and walks the several paces over, sliding onto the barstool beside me, his arm brushing mine when he plunks his beer on the counter. A summery warmth radiates from his skin, as do the scents of Coppertone lotion and salt.

I pop a handful of fries in my mouth, eager for something to do other than gawk at his face, but chewing proves impossible with him leaning in so close. My jaw moves excruciatingly slow, like a rusty machine on its last legs, until eventually, I venture to ask, "Can I help you with something?" I sound way more annoyed than I am, and I'm a tiny bit proud of myself for putting on a good show.

"I didn't mean to eavesdrop, love," he says, smiling all the more. "Guess I've been stuck on this damn island so long, I forget the outside world is a bit more—"

"Evolved?" I bristle with disapproval and thrill at being called *love*.

He scoffs and adjusts his baseball cap, sweaty locks of caramel hair jutting out over his ears. "I was going to say sophisticated, but evolved works too. A little harsh maybe, but…well…"

"Such is life," I quip.

"Such is life," he echoes.

My eyes lift to his, drawn to that sea green like it's my newfound center of gravity, only to find his gaze anchored on me too. I don't need a mirror to know that my cheeks are flushing. *Damn him.*

"Truthfully, I was just looking for a reason to talk to you." He says it like a spilled secret, though his grin is far from sheepish.

I take a careful sip of water before answering, my heartbeat skipping like a skimming stone in my chest. "Usually a simple hi will suffice."

"Just like that?" He sucks his teeth, squinting playfully. "Not into all this meandering, flirtatious nonsense? A simple hi does the trick?"

My gaze levels with his, dredging up courage enough to say, "I don't really see a point in pussyfooting around."

"Ah. A lady of decisive action." He drapes an arm loosely over the back of my seat. "Fine then, have it your way." I suck back a gasp when he leans in closer, his breath caressing my damp hair. "Hi."

Say hi back, idiot.

"Hi back."

The stranger offers me his hand. "Hatcher Seaborn, at your service." A mischievous twinkle glints in his eye, like starlight dipped in a bubbling tide pool. "You can call me Hatch."

Don't, I think urgently, remembering the promise I made myself. *Don't get sucked in. Don't get involved…*

But some inexplicable force pulls me to him anyway, and despite my better judgment, I find my fingers slipping into his. His hand is chapped and rough, as would belong to someone accustomed to manual labor. Calluses scrape my skin when we shake, a more pleasant sensation than I care to admit.

"This is the part where you tell me your name," he prompts.

Don't.

"Dell Costa." I spit it out before I can convince myself otherwise.

A contemplative expression blooms on Hatch's face, like he's trying to decide something essential about me. We hold each other's hand for a long moment—far longer than what's necessitated by standard handshaking protocol—and when I come to my senses and pull away, my palm tingles like maybe it's been scorched by fire.

"I like it," he says, sending an electric rush coursing through my bones. "Dell. *Dell.* It's unusual, in a good way."

My eyes narrow. "This from the guy whose name sounds like it came from some backwoods *Pirates of the Caribbean* movie?"

Hatch roars with laughter, nodding his approval. "Well, I'll be damned. Guilty as *chaarrrged.*"

I purse my lips to camouflage a smile. I'm not supposed to be having this much fun. "Are your jokes always so lame?"

"Afraid so, love." His eyes glisten, reminiscent of waves bathed in golden sun, and I wonder what it might be like to take a dip in that sea…and instantly recoil from the unwelcome thought.

"What brings you to our unevolved island, Dell Costa?"

This is precisely what I wanted to avoid. Unpacking the details of this heinous trip—of everything it means, and everything it's worth—is the absolute last thing I should be doing with this stranger.

When I don't answer, he follows up with a second question. "Are you here for summer vacation?"

"No." If this were a vacation, I'd be free from the scourge of sick mothers, dead grandmothers, and broken families.

"Work trip?"

"No." Though I've got the sense that my time here will be a monstrous piece of work.

Hatch crosses his arms over his chest. I bite my lip, doing my best to ignore the way his muscles tense beneath his shirt sleeves. *Stupid, stupid girl.*

"Family reunion?"

"No. Well…" I hadn't thought of it that way, but this is a reunion of sorts, albeit a dark and somber one. I nod absently, ready to move on from this topic. "Yes, sure. You could say that, I guess."

"So you've got relatives in town," he deduces. "Anyone I might know?"

"Oh, no. I doubt it." The last thing I need is anyone filling my mind with ideas about the Klynes before I meet them myself.

"You sure? Twenty-six years marooned on this island means I've got a pretty good lay of the land, you know."

"Trust me, I'm sure."

To his credit, Hatch doesn't pry. "Well, 'Cuda's is a great place to escape to when you've had too much family-togetherness. It's the best bar in town, with some of the best people around. Present company included, but that goes without saying."

That crooked smile returns to his face, devilish and sweet, but that's not what worries me. It's those eyes that tilt my world off-kilter. Like deep beds of seagrass, so lush and inviting, I'll sink right into them if I'm not careful.

From the way he's watching me, I think he knows it too.

"Your arrogance is astounding." I laugh despite myself, fighting back the tingly, champagne-fizz of nerves pumping through me like lifeblood.

"I always aim to astound." He edges a bit closer, the arm he has draped over my seat gently grazing my shoulder, sending a cascade of heat down my back. "Especially if it means getting you to smile again."

Another sprinkling of laughter bubbles up from my mouth, and Hatch averts his eyes, grinning to himself too—the first time he's shown a speck of shyness yet. Somehow that makes him all the more appealing.

I bite down hard on my lip, berating myself in silence.

Good Lord. Get it together.

"Bad jokes aside," Hatch says, his serious tone misaligned with that smirk, "'Cuda's is a classic island haunt, the quintessential feel-good spot for Halcyon Bay's working class, frequented by some of our quirkier characters."

"Quirkier than you, pirate man?"

The gleam in his eyes says he's up to my challenge. "Decide for yourself! Take that guy, for instance…"

I follow Hatch's gaze to an unlit corner of the tavern, where a decrepit old man sits at a hightop table, lifting a can of Pabst Blue Ribbon to his shriveled lips.

"That's Silas Masterson. Goes by Salty to those who know him."

Wrinkles and folds are etched across the ancient leather of Salty's skin. He moves slowly, as if it aches his joints to do so, the mechanics of his lean body badly worn by time, like he's a living artifact.

"How old is he?" I ask.

"Salty's one of our eldest. Pushing a hundred now, and he's earned every one of those years. Seen a lot of things. Tells *plenty* of stories."

"What kinds of stories?"

"How much time do you have?" Hatch chuckles lightly. "I'll give you his best. Salty's got this massive banyan tree growing in his backyard—the biggest banyan on all of Halcyon Bay—and he'll tell anyone willing to listen that the tree is the living reincarnation of his first wife, Lillian."

I scoff my disbelief. "Get out."

"I'm dead serious," he emphasizes. "The story goes that, in his younger years, Salty enrolled in a big sailing expedition. It was only meant to be a months-long excursion, but his new bride, Lillian, was convinced that Salty was abandoning her, leaving her destitute, pregnant, and alone. They had a blowout about it one night, and Lillian flung herself from their second-story window in a rage. The fall snapped her neck. She died right there in their yard."

I eye the old man again, his rough, wizened face cast in darkness, peering into the opening of his beer can like maybe it holds the entire world inside.

"After the funeral, Salty noticed a banyan sapling sprouting from the place where Lillian fell. He said that banyan trees were her favorite, that this must be a sign from *beyond*. And there she still stands, almost eighty years later."

Hatch absently rubs the stubble on his cheeks. I trail the motion with my eyes, mesmerized. "It's strange, actually. We've had some foul hurricanes take out countless banyan trees on the island, but none have even come close to bringing down Salty's banyan."

"That's quite the story."

His grin is as cryptic as the tale he weaves. "Pristine beaches and a tropical climate are all people think of when they think 'Halcyon Bay,' but that's not the full picture, just a tiny fraction of it. The rest of it, the real meat and bones, is built on ghost stories and folklore. Strange, inexplicable things stretch across every corner of this island. Stick around a while, you'll see what I mean."

I scan the bar crowd, my curiosity piqued. "All right. Who else?"

Hatch glimpses the span of the tavern discreetly while I memorize the angles of his jaw, his nose. "Look a few seats down from us." He swings his eyes left without turning his face. "The old Hemingway look-alike in the orange bucket hat."

I peer around him to get a better view of our target. There sits a man in his sixties with a beard like a nest, puffing on a pudgy cigar, sending trails of smoke twisting through the air. The man's grimy shirt is half-buttoned over a bulging potbelly, exposing his furry chest and the strands of gold chain around his neck. His shirt-sleeves are pushed up to the elbows, revealing a sun-checked anchor tattoo. An Old Fashioned glass rests before him, ice melting to water on the bar.

"That's Captain Patton Fortuna," Hatch whispers. "Sole survivor of a doomed treasure hunt. Some years ago, the captain and his crew sank along with their salvage tug, the *Westward Ho,* while trying to recover fifty million dollars worth of treasure from a sunken Spanish galleon off the coast of Halcyon Bay. None but the captain made it out of the water alive."

"What happened?"

"Bilge pump failure. The tug rolled onto her side in the dead of night, trapping everyone below deck. The captain and two divers were the only ones able to get free, pitching themselves into shark-infested waters. Unfortunately, the divers were ripped to shreds in the night—"

"That's horrible."

Hatch nods, wide-eyed. "Only the captain survived until morning. When the sun came up, a boat anchored nearby saw that the *Westward Ho* was gone. They managed to pull him from the water before it was too late."

"And?"

"Let's just say, he's been a bit off ever since."

The captain chuckles now, a hearty rumbling, turning his neck to glance at us sideways. No question, he must've heard us whispering about him.

Through the haze of smoke, I see that one of his eyes is a crystal-clear blue, like pristine spring water on a cloudless morning. His other eye is…gone. A tiny, puckered crevice with no eyeball in the socket. Just an empty hole, and black from tip to tip.

CHAPTER SEVEN

"If you got shit to talk 'bout a man, Seaborn, you may as well be loud 'n' clear 'bout it, so as to make sure he can hear you."

The captain's voice is gruff but not without humor, his words slipping into one another like bar soap through wet fingers. He takes another puff, the end of his cigar burning flame-red, the glow reflecting across his weatherworn face.

"I'm sorry, Cap'n," Hatch starts to say.

"Ain't me you gotta apologize to, son. For Neptune's sake, are you trying to show this girl a good time or bore her half to death with your inane conversation?" The captain hiccups emphatically, a glint of gold flashing from his mouth. "Worst pick-up I ever seen in my life." He slams his hand on the bar, howling with laughter. "If I told you once, I told you a thousand times, you'll never get a woman into bed unless you quit your ceaseless yammering."

Hatch's eyebrows shoot up at the captain's intimation, and I have to bite my lip to keep from cracking up. It's fun to watch him squirm a bit, a sweet reprieve from his singular, smoldering focus.

The captain runs a liver-spotted hand through his beard. "Well? Aren't you gonna introduce me to the poor, unsuspecting victim?"

Hatch sighs. "This is Dell Costa. Dell, this is Captain Patton Fortuna, number one ball-buster in all the bay."

The captain grins. "Don't get your knickers in a twist, son. Ain't nothing personal. This old sea dog's gotta get his kicks somehow." He barks into the depths of the bar, "Close me out, Lira, my girl!"

Perched nearby, the bartender shoots the captain a mock salute and begins tapping at an outdated computer screen.

The captain winks at me with his one, crystalline-blue eye. "Pleasure to meet you, Delly."

I dip my chin. "The pleasure's all mine."

"Sorry for interrupting your riveting conversation with my friend, Seaborn, here. Musta really had your pulse racing with all that talk of reincarnated trees 'n' sinking ships."

"You've made your point, Cap'n," Hatch interrupts, but I can tell he has a soft spot for the old seafarer. His eyes are warm, the edges of his lips hooked into a faint smile, undeniably amused.

"I damn well hope I have, son." The captain breathes in his cigar, blowing out a thick cloud. "Whereabouts are you visiting us from, Delly?"

"Up north. Maine."

"No shit," the captain cries. "Up north, indeed. Spent some time in Maine myself. Loved it there, but the winters are cold. Much too cold for these brittle bones." He rubs his forearms for added effect.

Lira drops a check and an ashtray in front of the captain. Hatch and I are silent as he reaches for his wallet, grunting as he leaves a couple crumpled-up twenties on the bar. He looks for a moment like he's going to stand, readying to leave, but then his mustached mouth does a strange little twitch, as if debating whether or not to divulge something more.

"You'll have to 'scuse my prying, Delly," he says, "but I overheard you got caught in that godforsaken storm today."

Does everyone on this island have advanced bat hearing or something?

"That's right."

"Nasty business 'bout that little girl," he says, darkness falling across his face. "The ocean's a real fickle bitch sometimes. Temperamental, impossible to trust. She don't discriminate, just takes 'n' takes. It's a tough pill to swallow when she claims the little ones, though. The girls especially."

The captain's countenance takes on an air of mystery, a curious curl on his tobacco-stained smile. "Tell me, Delly. Do you know what happens to the girls that drown in Halcyon Bay?"

Taken aback, I shake my head no, not sure I like this sudden shift in conversation. Hatch adjusts his baseball cap and sneaks a private glance my way. *Buckle your seatbelt,* his eyes seem to say.

The captain leans in, the barstool creaking under his weight, his fingers twisting in and out of his birds-nest beard. "The girls become sea spirits, water ghouls, devilfish. They drift along the coast like wisps beneath the surface, watching the fishermen work with their soulless, black-coal eyes."

Maybe it's the intoxicating island air, the smell of wet cigarettes and cheap beer, the sting of salt piercing my nose, or the bruise to my skull causing my brain waves to short circuit, but I break into a nervous fit of giggles. Hatch nudges me, and I force out a cough, attempting to cover for my hysterics.

"I've seen 'em," the captain insists. "Floating out there, skin a sick milky blue, hair like seaweed itself. Something changes in the air when the devilfish come. Everything goes real quiet, but not the peaceful kind. It's the quiet of a *terrible stillness,* as if the ocean 'n' all her fish have gone dead 'n' you're the only living thing for miles, your breath ringing out like a beacon to 'em."

His good eye shifts from me to somewhere beyond, transported to some lonely ship of his past on a distant sea coated in that terrible stillness. "Their song blows in with the wind. A banshee song, shrill 'n' mad. 'N' once that song worms into your ears, it's a matter of seconds before *they* appear...the ghosts with the gaping eyes, just beneath that water line."

The captain falls silent, his words lingering for a moment, suspended in the smoky air like a curse, until—

"Lira! Another whiskey, please."

A girl sweeps up to the bar, filling the empty space between us and the captain, breaking the spell cast by his haunting tale.

It's the blonde from the dance floor, the one sucking face with the singer. Her cheeks are flushed from all the dancing, and probably all the face-sucking, and she smiles to herself as she scrolls through her cell phone. Her rippling hair smells of coconut as she shakes it, hips swaying to the music in cutoff jean shorts.

Lira prepares a Jack Daniels on ice while the captain takes one final drag on his cigar. He smashes it into the waiting ashtray as Lira slides the drink to the girl. She blows her a multitude of air kisses before prancing back to her spot near the stage.

The captain pats his fluffy beard, but it springs back up stubbornly. "Of course, I ain't seen too many devilfish lately," he says, jumping right back into his strange train of thought. "Not since they dismantled the Brine 'n' burnt the sea trumpet fields to crisps. But this jumper, this little girl…I dunno. Smells like trouble might be starting up again."

I stare at him blankly, turning over each word in my mind—*devilfish, the brine, the sea trumpet fields*. None of it makes one drop of sense, but I remember what Hatch said about how the captain lost his crew and nearly his own life at sea…how he'd drifted alone in shark-ridden waters, certain he wouldn't survive the black night, praying that death would come swiftly and mercifully. Then, to be rescued, plucked from the darkness, while his men and his vessel were left to settle at the ocean's bottom. What does trauma like that do to a person? How long were the nights, and how filled with ghosts? The captain reminds me of Mom in this way, and so I stay quiet, deciding it best not to ask questions I might not want the answers to.

He tips his bucket hat, staggering off his stool and to his feet. "Evening, kiddos. Take care tonight. More screwy weather coming in this weekend, I hear. Waves whipping up a batch of fresh storms out there. The next bastard might just raise the damn dead."

He hobbles out of the bar, whistling a sailor's tune. We watch him limp across the street, enveloped in the drizzly mist of the evening.

"Good old Cap'n Pat," Hatch muses in his wake. "Always good for an unsolicited lesson on Halcyon Bay's resident sea spirits."

I stare at him, barely holding in another bout of anxious laughter.

"He means well," Hatch says, peeling back the sticker from his beer bottle. "But, like I said before, the man's a bit off."

Interesting, that Hatch can admit to the captain's eccentricities but won't deny the stories about the girls turned ghosts, their siren-like lore, and the sweeping tenor of mystery that looms over the island like a shroud.

"Have you ever seen one?" I ask tentatively.

His sea green eyes are on mine in an instant, the bar and the people and the noise around us dimming. "Seen what?"

"A water spirit. *Devilfish.*" I wiggle my fingers. "Any weird encounters you care to spook the mainlander with?"

Hatch cracks a smile. "No."

"No, you've never seen one? Or no, you won't cop to it for fear of sounding as mad as the captain?"

"No, I've never seen one. But that doesn't mean I'm not mad." He swishes his bottle so the last splash of beer clinks against the glass, tipping it back one last time before setting it down again. "I am, however, due for a refill. Care to join me for a drink? Give me a chance to learn a little more about you?"

His eyes are tempting as the sultry, summer night, and an electric charge courses between us, the thrill of mere possibility…

What the hell is wrong with me?

Letting some goo-goo-eyed fisherman distract me, after traveling so far and with so much at risk, would be as productive as having stayed back in Woodbridge, watching Mom worsen from the front lines. Despite the flush of heat crawling up my neck—my own body betraying me—I'm not interested in partaking in any whirlwind trysts. Hatch is nothing more than a fleeting fantasy, an attractive, temporary, physical diversion. And I'm not in the business of giving in to fantasy. I opted long ago to keep my heart rooted in stark reality.

Hatch's smile is utterly inviting. "What do you say?"

I'm about to make up some flimsy excuse, when—

"*Leeeraaa.*"

The blond girl is back, squeezing in beside us and flapping her hand to get the bartender's attention. Hatch stiffens.

"What. The. Hell," Lira huffs. "You're back already?"

The girl nods, batting her lashes. Her voice comes out whiny and apologetic. "The drink was for Mojo, but Finch grabbed it first! The little shit. Be a pal and make me another, pretty please?"

An irritated Lira pours out another whiskey. "Those dickheads run up a tab like no other, Palmer. No wonder they're broke! As the band's self-appointed manager, you should be more concerned."

The blond girl, Palmer, laughs easily, the sound like the peal of wind chimes on a breezy afternoon.

Lira slides over the fresh glass of Jack. "Anything for you?"

"No, thanks. I'm not drinking tonight."

Palmer cups the whiskey glass in both hands, turning to go, but when the smoky scent of liquor hits her, she pauses and begins to gag. She leans against the bar top to steady herself, her hand flying to her stomach as she doubles over.

"You all right?" Lira asks, her eyes discerning on her friend.

Palmer flashes a weak smile. "Just a bit hot, I guess." The pain in her eyes tells me that's a lie.

"Water." Lira pours a full glass from the tap and slides it to her. "Drink."

She quickly downs it, drawing in a few careful breaths after.

"Better?"

Palmer nods. "Thanks, Leer. What would I do without you?"

"Die a painful, dehydrated death."

The bartender winks and turns her attention to the computer screen just as Palmer readies to leave, recognition darkening her otherwise pretty face when her eyes land on Hatch.

"Oh. Hatcher."

She says his name like it's something detestable, with the same pinched tone one might reserve for words like *tarantula* and *terrorist*.

"Palmer." Hatch nods in the direction of the stage. "The boys are killing it tonight. Mojo must be thrilled."

"He is, thanks." Palmer's eyes are slits as she drinks in the sight of us, jumping from Hatch to me and back again. "Who's your friend?"

I never knew 'friend' could sound so dirty.

"This is Dell, a recent arrival from the mainland."

Palmer tilts her head, scanning me up and down with fluttering, mascaraed eyes. Clearly unimpressed with whatever she sees, Palmer says, "Lovely to meet you, Dell," with a heaping dose of contrived sweetness.

I wonder how the two of them know each other.

"Yeah, you too."

"Enjoying island life so far?" she asks, pursing her lips.

"It's all right. Nothing to write home about."

I don't intend the audible sting in my words, but a gratified smile steals across Hatch's lips, while Palmer's sugary expression falls away.

"Lucky for you, things can only get better from here," she replies coolly.

"Why's that?"

"It's all in the company you keep. And since you're scraping the bottom of the barrel right now…" Her glossy pink lip pulls into a sneer. "No offense, Hatch."

Hatch is unmoved. "None taken, Palm. I don't think Dell's all that impressed by my company either. Must be my brilliant repartee keeping her around."

I don't bother to curb my smile, which makes Palmer look all the more peeved.

"I should get this to Mojo." She shakes up the ice in the whiskey glass. "You two have *oodles* of fun tonight."

"We will," I toss back with a sleazy undertone. I'm not sure where all this animosity is sprouting from, but I've clearly found myself right in the middle of it, shots unquestionably fired.

Hatch throws in a sarcastic wave. "Give the boys my regards."

Palmer glares at us for a brief second before whipping her hair over her shoulder and slipping into the dancing throng.

I whistle low as she storms off.

"What?" Hatch asks.

"That just seemed kind of personal."

"Ah, well." He shrugs vaguely, as if to confirm that his issues with Palmer run far too deep to justify to some stranger he just met at a dive bar. "I haven't done anything to piss off the prom queen. Not lately, anyway."

I stop short of asking him if she's an ex-girlfriend, realizing I'd be crossing about a million lines and thoroughly embarrassing myself. Awkward silence fills the space between us that moments ago buzzed with heat and electricity. The easy cadence of our conversation, the hypnotizing pulse that held us both in its grasp, had been fractured, like a vinyl record skipping at its crescendo.

"So," Hatch says, trying to recover some of the momentum we'd lost, "back to that drink—"

"I'm going to have to pass." I think up a quick lie. "I…don't drink."

He pauses. "At all?"

"Never. And I should be going, anyway. Early day tomorrow."

"Okay, sure." Hatch nods as he stands, pulling several bills from his wallet and placing them under his empty beer bottle. "How about dinner tomorrow, then? You do eat, right?" he teases, glancing down at my basket and the stale remnants of my greasy meal.

"Yes."

"Well, if you can stand a little more of my insufferable company, I'd love to take you out. I think I owe you that much, for my uncivilized eavesdropping. What do you say?"

The magnetic green of his eyes compels me to say yes, but I shake my head firmly. *No, no, a thousand times no.* "I'm going to be pretty busy. Won't be able to get away. Family stuff and all."

"Right, right. Family stuff."

Hatch loops an arm over the bar top, plucking a nubby pencil from where Lira had abandoned it. He scrawls a phone number on a paper napkin, the action of it familiar, like something he's done hundreds of times before. The muggy heat of jealousy licks up my ears and neck.

"In case you change your mind, or if you decide you need a break from all the family stuff." He hands me the napkin, smirking. "Maybe I'll see you around?"

You won't.

Shrugging, I say, "Yeah, maybe."

I look pointedly at the stage and away from him, until eventually, he gives up and slips out of the bar. I watch him retreat into the night, taking in the easy swagger of his stride, the broad expanse of his back through that white t-shirt.

For the best, I think. *I'll never see that guy again.*

Lira comes my way and I hand her my credit card, ignoring the sensation of my heart deflating like a punctured tire. I had let myself get carried away with him, filled myself up with some reckless, hopeful feeling before jabbing in the harsh nail of reality. It was dumb. Weakness.

She returns with my receipt and starts clearing the area, but before she can dispose of the napkin with Hatch's number, I snatch it up and shove it into my pocket at the last second. I'll never call him, but I can't just leave it there for Lira to see and judge and whisper over. At least that's what I tell myself.

Sliding off my stool too fast, my legs soft as jelly, I quickly locate the restroom, tucked back in the deepest, smokiest part of the tavern. I wind through the drunken crowd while the singer announces the end of their set.

"We're The Knotty Talismen, and we love you naughty freaks! Let's do the dirty all over again next week, same time, same place!"

I trip through the bathroom threshold and catapult into a stall. Just as I'm locking the door behind me, someone else comes barging in, running for the next stall over. Immediately, there's the distinct sound of retching and the splashing of vomit. The soundtrack to my evening.

"Excuse me," comes a small, garbled voice. Through her sniffles, a girl whimpers, "Could you hand me some toilet paper?"

I wrap a wad of paper in my hand and slip it under the wall, not saying a word.

She takes it, uttering a soft "Thank you," before heaving into the bowl again.

I step out to wash my hands and, in the cracked mirror's reflection, see two espadrille wedges peeking out from the space beneath the girl's stall. Her body is slumped by the door, shaking out a series of desperate sobs.

I wash up quickly, hoping to make a swift exit, but all of my movements are clunky and plodding, like I'm moving through mucky water. Sure enough, when the girl unlocks her stall door, I'm still standing there, like a deer caught in the headlights. And when she steps into the humming white light, my stomach churns unhappily.

It's Palmer.

"Oh!" she says, startled, blinking back the tears weighing down on her like storm clouds. "I didn't realize it was you."

I turn off the faucet. "Surprise."

We're both quiet as she approaches the sink. She's several inches shorter than me, even with the added lift of her wedges, Rapunzel-blonde and golden-skinned with innocent blue eyes. A summer child, island-blessed. My antithesis in virtually every way.

I feel her eyes on me as I wipe my hands and head for the door.

"So how do you know Hatcher?"

Not good, I think. *Do not get mixed up in this.*

"We just met," I reply, glancing back at her over my shoulder.

"Hmm." She turns back to her own reflection. I slow my steps to hear what she says next. "Bit of advice?" she offers over the stream of running water. "Keep your guard up with that one."

All the emotions I've so carefully held in begin to bubble over, piping and feverish. I do not need this right now. "Why?"

Palmer chuckles at my tense expression in the mirror. "Don't get all bent out of shape about it. I'm just saying, girl to girl, watch who you rub elbows with around here. There are some shady characters in the bay, and that guy tops the list."

My blood seethes as I watch her apply lip gloss from a juicy pink tube. She doesn't give a blazing rat's ass what characters I rub elbows with. Her issue is with Hatch, and the fact that he'd been talking to me. Why? What insecurities, what secrets, is she concealing under that cherry-glazed façade?

Piecing together what I'd seen of Palmer this evening, a concept begins to form in my mind.

She'd just puked her guts up after nearly fainting at the bar, when, by her own admission, she hadn't been drinking, nor did she appear even the least bit intoxicated.

She'd held her belly when she complained of the heat, her bright eyes heavy, hedged in unspoken worry.

She'd exhaled dreadful sobs in that bathroom stall, the sound of them desperate and deeply afraid. Like someone utterly alone in the world, trapped by circumstances of their own making.

It's not a stretch to think that Palmer might be pregnant. And I'm not above using this presumption to hit her where it hurts in a moment of weakness and exhaustion.

I grit my teeth. "Thanks for the tip, Palmer, but I can take care of myself."

She rolls her eyes in response, popping her glossy lips together as if to say, *Your funeral.* But I'm not finished yet.

"You should try taking your own advice, though," I add. "Seems like a real rough-and-tumble crowd out there. Not the best environment for someone in your condition."

Her lips part a little, confusion registering in her eyes. "I'm sorry. My condition?"

"Don't get all bent out of shape," I quip, turning Palmer's own words against her like a loaded gun. "I just think you should put that wisdom of yours to good use, especially since you're looking out for two now."

She bristles visibly. "What are you talking about?"

"I think you know."

Palmer hands droop to her stomach, looking like I've slapped her across the face, but I don't stick around to relish in it. True or not, I'm not proud of what I've said, nor what I've likely made her feel.

Without another word, I burst from the bathroom and shove my way through the bar, not stopping until I get to Virginia's bike out front. Before leaving, I crush the napkin with Hatch's number in my fist and toss it into an overflowing trash can.

Screw this place and all these people.

I pedal out the rest of my anger on the road.

CHAPTER EIGHT

The dead girl floats face-up in the shallows of a desolate beach. She's an angel in the water, a halo of gossamer hair, white dress clinging to pale skin, a tinge of blue to the lips and fingers. The perfect portrait of childhood innocence, except for a gaping, bloody wound to her temple, deep enough to expose the soft matter beneath her skull.

The girl drifts near the shoreline, a smudge of white against the vast blue expanse. I'm standing on the sand some distance away, with a set of footprints beside me leading to the water—a trail I'm meant to follow.

Her eyes are open, misted over like the summer storm brewing overhead. They flick to me, watching me watching her. Her cold lips form a tiny smile, slender fingers twitching, inviting me in. I take a tentative step and the girl's smile widens. Each of her small, milky teeth come to a point.

I'm terrified, but filled with a strange desire to go to her, wrenched forward by some invisible rope, tethered to her from some raw place in my chest.

I move closer.

Blood drips down her porcelain face from the hole in her head, so much blood that it stains the ocean red. And when the bloody sea foam nips my toes, a ripple spreads far and wide, and the water grows wild. I watch in horror as the waves stir furiously, swallowing the girl's body beneath the surface.

A scream rips from my throat as I run to her, slicing through the whitecaps crashing angrily to shore. I plunge my arms into the water, grasping for her as if my own life depends on it. But the girl is nowhere to be found.

I dive beneath a wave and open my eyes, blinking fast in an attempt to distinguish shapes and shadows through the blur of red water. I stretch my arms and propel myself forward, swimming farther and farther, out, out, out, until all my breath is consumed and my muscles weak. Drained, I push up toward the orb of sunshine in the sky, reaching for the surface, for air.

Something brushes past my leg.

It circles me in the swirling water, as swift and fluid as water itself. Through the murk, there's a silhouette—long and slender with cavernous eyes. Tendrils of silver ripple from a nebulous head. In the bloodshot darkness, there's a knife-sharp smile.

I gasp for air that doesn't come, my lungs burning as they fill with water. I thrash, struggling to ascend, but the surface is somehow farther away now, the warm rays of sunlight fainter than before.

The creature is missile-fast, and in a sweeping flurry of bubbles, it's inches from my face. I can almost reach out and graze its pearly white skin, but my limbs are paralyzed. Those black, gaping eyes elongate like the mouths of two endless abysses. They yawn open, sucking me in.

I collapse into darkness and drown.

I wake to a persistent knocking, my eyes braced against the morning light filling up the unfamiliar bedroom.

At first I think it's the drumming in my skull that kept me tossing through the night—the same headache that brought me so many terrible dreams of the girl on the pier, of drowning, and of a strange creature lurking in the waters of Halcyon Bay. The old captain's ghost stories did wonders for my restless imagination.

I turn over in bed and shield my face with a pillow, trying to drown out that ceaseless knocking, but it only grows louder and more demanding.

I yank off the covers and pad into the kitchen. Through the curtains, I see a middle-aged man in a pressed, robin-egg blue suit and cotton candy tie, tapping his toe against the doorsill with a steaming cup in hand. He nearly spills it on his shiny leather oxfords when I finally open the door.

"Meridel!" the man gasps, giving me a disparaging once-over. "Briggs mentioned you were a bit shook up but, Lord Jesus, he didn't do you justice! What in God's green earth happened to you?"

I can't tell if his southern drawl is genuine or a put-on.

"Mr. O'Hare?" I ask, squinting against the sun and the man's unnatural, alien-white teeth.

He primps his Elvis-like pompadour hair. "In the flesh, sweet pea, and not a moment too soon! Please, call me Finley. May I come in?" He offers me the cup of coffee—a universal olive branch.

"Uh. Sure." I take it from his hands and he prances inside, not bothering to shut the door behind him.

"I just wanted to say how sorry I am that I didn't get a chance to return your call yesterday. My schedule was jam-packed. It was an absolute doozy of a day."

"That's okay."

He takes an inquisitive gander around the guest house. "You seem to have settled in all right, though, even without my bumbling two cents!"

"Yeah, um, Briggs helped me out."

"Mhm, mhm." Finley nods like an overzealous bobble head. "We're all positively tickled that you decided to join us. I know your grandmama would be so darn happy you came all this way just for her.

Why, I'm sure she's smiling down at us from the Great Beyond right now!"

"That's very"—terrifying? nauseating?—"*nice* of you to say."

"Now, Meridel, on a more serious note, I understand you haven't seen your family since you were quite young." He looks at me like I'm a flea-ridden puppy that's just been plucked from the gutter, with a sympathetic head tilt that makes me want to dump my coffee down his shirtfront. "If this proves to be too overwhelming for you, just give me a shout and I'll whisk you on out of there lickety-split. The last thing I want is for you to feel uncomfortable in any way, all right?"

I nod skeptically, and the lawyer's smile stretches from ear to ear. There's too many teeth inside his mouth, like a horse. If Mister Ed abused whitening strips, I imagine he'd look something like Finley.

"Wonderful!" he chirps, turning on his polished heel. He strides out of the house with a toodle-oo wave, calling over his tailored shoulder, "Twenty minutes in the parlor, sweet pea. Wear something pretty!"

I shut the door in Finley's wake, grateful to be away from him at last, and shuffle lifelessly to the bathroom. The pipes take a minute to start up the shower, but before long, it runs steamy and inviting. My mind whirrs with unease as I undress and step into the claw foot tub, resigned to the imminent, unsavory reality of my day.

I'm about to meet my mother's family, I think. People I would not recognize if I passed them on the street. Strangers, for all intents and purposes, and I never considered how those strangers might feel at seeing me again after all these years. Would they be surprised? Angry? Would they remember me at all?

I know what my presence here must look like from the outside, the story they might spin as to why I came back. It's reasonable and all too easy to deduce that I'm here for the money, to collect an inheritance I shouldn't even get, considering I never knew the woman who'd left it for me. The others might see my return as exploitive and heartless, but I can't concern myself too much with those optics. I have my own reasons for being back in Halcyon Bay, and they have nothing to do with making a power grab at Virginia's wealth.

The soapy water runs its course while I do all I can to relax my mind, to take this solitary, quiet moment for myself. I try more than anything not to think about Mom, riddled with terror at Hopewell, oblivious to my whereabouts. Or of Dad, who must be worried senseless, deceiving Mom to cushion the blow of my lies—a compounding shitstorm of untruths I've set into motion.

I reach for the shower gel, and in the reflective silver of the bottle cap, I see something that makes me freeze…

Someone else is in the bathroom.

They peer at me through the narrow slit in the shower curtain. I can't make out a face or any defining details in the tiny reflection, just an indistinct body with arms at its sides, neck twisted at an odd angle to better observe me.

With my heartbeat throbbing in my ears, I wrap my fingers around the bottle, yank the curtain aside, and, screaming, hurtle it at the intruder. The bottle hits the wall and cracks open, purple liquid drizzling over the vanity and wall. But the person I saw reflected in the bottle cap is gone, and the bathroom—despite being smothered in lavender-scented goo—is undisturbed.

I step out of the tub and wrap myself in a towel. The door is ajar though I'm certain I closed it, cold air drifting in from the bedroom, my wet skin crawling with goosebumps.

"Who's there?" I call, trying to mask the fear in my voice. But no one seems to be, and so no one responds.

I scour the guest house, checking behind each door, inside every closet, under the bed and the breakfast table. The windows are all shut and latched. The main door is locked, just as I'd left it. There's no adequate explanation for what I saw—what I *think* I saw—and so I decide to write the experience off as anxiety, my nightmares setting my nerves on a razor's edge.

I throw on a charcoal sheath and some ankle boots, working fast to cover the gash in my forehead with several butterfly bandages. The bump looks nasty this morning, the skin around it bursting a morbid purple, but I don't have time to fuss about my appearance. I give my lashes a quick swipe of mascara and pinch my cheeks for color, though I doubt any of it will match Finley's flashier standards. Grabbing my purse as I leave, I lock the door behind me and march across the grounds.

My heart is a rabid animal in my chest, thrashing so wildly I think it might crack a rib. Every fiber in me itches to run in the opposite direction, not stopping until I'm back at the seaport, boarding a ferry bound for the mainland.

There's muffled chatter as I approach the arched French doors on the backside of Cliffmoor House. Finley is there in the hall, along with Briggs and several others I don't recognize, awash in somber shades of black and gray.

They spot me through the glass and quiet down.

Retreat is not an option.

CHAPTER NINE

When I enter the hall, five pairs of eyes land on me.

"Meridel!" Finley flashes his creepy veneers as he pulls me into his arms. I wince, wrinkling my nose at the acrid stench of cologne and gin coming off him. "There you are, sweet pea."

I try to smile, try to act polite, but it's difficult to know what my expression betrays when I'm holding my breath and clenching my teeth at the same time.

Finley, of course, is oblivious to my repulsion, looking simply *tickled* at the sight of my smiling face. But Briggs isn't tricked so easily. He covers his mouth, faking a cough to shield his laughter. Phony smiles don't seem to fool the old butler, and I like him all the more for that.

A middle-aged woman approaches me, and I'm startled by how much she looks like Mom—the deep blue whirlpool eyes, the fair, thin skin, the sandy hair streaked in yellow from endless summers in the sun. It wouldn't be hard to mistake them for twins, except this woman's cheeks are plump and full, her breasts bulging over her lacy black dress.

Much healthier than Mom's rawboned, wilting figure.

"Oh, Meridel…" She swoops me into a hug.

I'm awkward and stiff where she's soft and warm, my arms hanging limp by my sides while she holds me, rubbing my back in a nurturing way that makes me homesick and nauseous all in one. Her hair smells of freshly-baked bread and cinnamon, but I'm also struck by the bitter scent of liquor on her breath. I wonder whether her morning buzz is a product of Virginia's death or a routine occurrence.

When she pulls back, eyes brimming with tears, she says, "I'm June. Juniper. Your mom's sister."

All at once, it hits me—Mom's sister, my aunt. A real blood relative. *Family.*

I'd been expecting this moment. I'd been mentally preparing for days. So why does it feel like such a sucker punch to the gut?

When June smiles, it's Mom's smile I see shining back, so a timid "Hello" is about all I can muster.

A small blond boy is perched nearby, peering up at me out of thick, black-rimmed glasses that are much too large for his face. He wears a charcoal gray suit with a tie to match his baby-blue eyes. A curious expression inches across his face.

June calls to him gently, "Come here, baby."

Obediently, he steps forward, hiding behind his mother's hip, clutching fistfuls of her black dress. She pats his gold-flecked head. "Leif, this is your cousin, Meridel."

The boy pinches his lip to one side as if in silent debate.

"You can call me Dell, if you want," I say, as a shock of nerves tingle up my neck.

"If you're my cousin, why haven't I ever seen you before?" he asks with a lisp.

"Because Dell lives very far away, honey," June responds, a deep sadness in her voice that sends a pang of guilt clanging through me.

Leif scratches his head as he squints up at me, gaining confidence enough to step out of his mother's shadow. "But we have an airport," he says precociously. "That's how my dad comes to visit us. Are you scared of flying, Dell?"

"No…though I don't care much for heights."

"I know what you mean." Leif nods animatedly. "Last summer, my best friend Jordan dared me to climb up a big palm tree, so I did, but an iguana was hiding in it, and it scared me half to death! I fell and had to have my arm in a cast for"—three little, pink fingers shoot into the air—"three whole months!"

"I'm sorry to hear that."

Leif shrugs. "It wasn't so bad. My cast was green and fat like a snake, so Mr. Pierson—that's my art teacher—drew a big *a-na-con-da* on it—that's how Mr. Pierson taught me to say it in class, *a-na-con-da*—and my friends liked my *a-na-con-da* so much, they all wanted casts on their arms too, but no one could get one but me!"

"Wow. That's lucky."

"It was wicked cool," the little boy cries. "And Mommy bought me lots of coloring books so I would be brave when it hurt, and I had to learn to color with my right hand, and it was the hardest thing I ever had to do."

"I bet." His eager eyes chip down at my walls a bit. "Maybe you can help me be brave like you."

Leif pushes his glasses up the bridge of his nose, but they promptly slide down again. "I know how you can be brave. You can try coloring, that always helps me. I brought all my books with me—"

June squeezes Leif's shoulder. "Maybe another time, baby. Remember we're here for an important reason, okay?" She whispers something in her son's ear as she leads him into the parlor. He squints back at me, shooting me a wide, toothy grin.

"Sweet pea, this is Sabine." Finley steers me toward the petite brunette in the corner, who jumps to attention as soon as he says her name. She skitters forward with a silver tablet in hand, her hair in a tight bun, lips a classic matte red, wearing a stylish black three-piece suit. Her pointed stilettos clatter on the hardwood floor as she walks up, reaching for my hand.

"Good to meet you, Meridel," she says, all polished professionality.

Her handshake is short and firm. "I was your grandmother's personal assistant. I'm very sorry for your loss."

"Um, thank you."

This is so incredibly awkward. I wonder whether Virginia's passing has left Sabine without a job. If so, my grandmother's death is a far greater loss for her than me.

Briggs clasps his gloved hands together. "Let's move into the parlor, shall we? It's just about ten, almost time to begin."

Like a mother duck corralling her brigade of clumsy ducklings, Briggs ushers us into the lush blue space. Morning light seeps through the curtains in long, lazy shafts, brightening the indigo walls and the heavy, velvet upholstery so they almost, *almost* feel bearable. Virginia's portrait is as stunning and baffling as I remember it, peering down at me with supernatural acuity. Leif and June are settled onto a wide tufted couch, and three other unfamiliar faces occupy various corners of the room.

A slick man in his sixties rises from his seat first, followed by a younger man right at his back.

"Meridel," the older man addresses me with a voice like rustling silk. He's tall and debonair, with hair so black it's blue. He wears a sleek suit that gives the impression of a businessman, his chest puffed up like an overinflated balloon animal, with a bold red tie that shines aggressively in the light.

He gives my hand an assertive shake, clapping my shoulder. "I'm your great-uncle, Florian, but you can call me Flip. Everyone does!" Almost as an afterthought, he adds, "And this is my son, Tristen."

Tristen is the sour-looking younger man in Florian's shadow, though he tops his father by at least a foot. He wears his hair long, his sallow cheeks stippled in acne scars. He's younger than Mom and Aunt June—by about ten years, if I had to guess—despite the three of them being first cousins. And that's just the way Tristen carries himself too, like he'd slipped in awkwardly between generations, barely making it, and with no comfortable place to land. Unlike his gregarious father, Tristen does not offer me his hand.

"Pleasure," he murmurs, his abrasive eyes piercing.

I muster a curt "Likewise" with equal enthusiasm.

Florian waves his son away and, like a mindless puppet, Tristen stalks off, settling on an armchair near the fireplace and burying his face in his cell phone. *Creep.*

"Oh, sweet pea," Finley coos in his syrupy drawl. "There's one more special someone left for you to meet." He pushes forward a hulking wheelchair, and seated in it is the final occupant of the room, the last family member left to be introduced. "Last but not least!"

My stomach springs into Olympic somersaults.

The well-dressed man in the chair is handsome, even in his old age. He has a strong cleft chin and a head full of peppered hair, parted smartly to one side. Deep folds cut along his forehead and cheeks, and a youthful grin stretches across his face. It's the smile of a winner, of someone accustomed to success.

The man laughs with a hearty energy, big enough to burst through the windows and ring out among the birds. His eyes are closed as he approaches, but I barely notice that. I'm too busy trying to keep last night's dinner from crawling up my throat, too consumed by the nervous swirling of acid in the pit of my stomach.

When Finley stops the wheelchair before me and the man snaps his eyes open at last, I recoil sharply at the sight. His eyeballs are swollen, bulging from their crevices in his skull, the pupils painted a sick glaucoma-gray, as though their natural appearance has been inverted— an eerie film negative brought to life.

"My lovely granddaughter, at long last." Ambrose stretches his arms to me, those two misty orbs boring holes into my face. "I can't tell you how long I've waited for this moment…my darling, Meridel."

He waits for me to come forward, and though I'm hesitant, I feel compelled to be well-mannered. I hold my breath and slip my fingers over his. He grasps them tightly and smiles to himself, closing those morbid eyes for a few brief seconds. I wish so much that he would keep them shut.

"You've brought an old man great joy today, my dear," he says as those dreadful gray spheres scan my face again.

"Isn't this beautiful?" Finley dabs the corner of his eye with a handkerchief. "I, for one, am so darn touched that some good has come of this devastating affair."

I slide my hands from Ambrose's just as soon as I am able, wrestling with the tangled mess of feelings waging war in my chest. My grandfather continues to watch me without quite watching me, gazing into my soul by some unearthly sight. I'm exposed as a specimen, pinned and wriggling under the microscope of these people, this strange club I'm bonded to by blood and history.

"Hungry?" Finley flourishes a hand above the mantel, where a basketful of puff pastries awaits, but I don't make a move toward it. I think I'm going to be sick.

By some cosmic mercy, the pendulum clock in the room begins to chime, announcing the top of the hour. "Ten o'clock," Briggs confirms. "Should we wait a few more minutes? We're still missing—"

"She'll get here when she gets here," June cuts in with an audible twinge of irritation. "Let's proceed."

I don't bother to ask who they aren't waiting on. I've lost all feeling in my tongue anyway, my capacity for speech woefully impaired.

Finley stands over the fireplace with an accordion portfolio in hand, pulling a stack of papers from it as Briggs directs me to an armchair across the way from Tristen. I sit silently, and the butler passes me a banana nut muffin wrapped in a silky white napkin.

Thank you, I mouth at him, still incapable of words. Briggs winks and floats away to linger by Ambrose. I take a cautious, preliminary bite.

Finley assumes center stage before the family, clearing his throat. He pulls the top document from his stack and begins to read.

"'I, Virginia Marigold Klyne of Halcyon Bay, Florida, being of sound mind and body, hereby declare that this is my Last Will and Testament, and set forth that my earthly estate be divided as follows...'"

He takes a short breath. My heartbeat ramps up in my ears.

"'To my husband, Ambrose Arthur Klyne III, I bequeath my half of all of our joint properties. These include the mansion in New

Orleans' Garden District, the villa on the Cote d'Azur, the penthouse in Upper West Side, Manhattan, and, of course, Cliffmoor House in Halcyon Bay, the beloved island home where our daughters were raised. Though trials and tribulations have pulled our family apart through the years, I hope that Cliffmoor House remains a testament to the deep-rooted, unending bond we all share.'"

A young woman enters the parlor wearing a simple black dress and a starched white apron—a maid's uniform. Her face is pink and free of makeup. She holds a steaming pot of coffee as she tiptoes around the room, keeping close to the walls so as not to distract, refilling mugs as she is beckoned.

"'To my brother-in-law, Florian Hamish Klyne, I confer my position as—'"

A sudden knock at the door brings Finley pause, and the maid slips out of the parlor as soundlessly as she came. The deafening silence in the room seems to stretch interminably. I take another careful bite of my muffin, unsure whether it's relieving my nausea or somehow making it worse.

When the maid returns, she's accompanied by a girl draped in a flowy black dress, with blond hair pulled into a wispy plait. She flies in with her head bowed low, murmuring a quick "Sorry, sorry I'm late," before dropping onto the couch beside Leif.

When she lifts her face to the light, I gasp, the muffin spilling from my fingers and onto the floor.

CHAPTER TEN

"Palmer!" Finley squeaks. "I was wondering when you'd be making a cameo this morning. We're tickled you're finally here, honey pie."

Palmer sinks deeper into the couch like she's trying to disappear into the overstuffed cushions. "Appreciate the shout out, Fin," she mutters, her cheeks blazing red, her blue eyes skimming the parlor.

In a flash, I duck to retrieve my rogue muffin, using my hair like a curtain in hopes of evading her sweeping gaze. But, inevitably—

"You!" she snaps from across the room, her face twisting with visceral appall. Blood rushes up my neck. "What are you doing here?"

I try to respond, but all that emerges from my mouth is a string of clumsy, brutish sounds. "Mm…ah…um…"

"You two know each other?" June asks, confused.

"I *don't* know her." Palmer's eyes are indignant, her tongue sharp. "Mojo's band played a late set at 'Cuda's last night. She was there, at the bar, and—"

"That's Meridel!" Leif exclaims, leaping to his knees. "She's our brand new cousin!" He bounces with excitement, the springs of the old couch groaning beneath him. "And we're gonna color together, Mommy even said so."

"Shoes off the furniture," June commands in his ear, yanking his stubby legs down from the upholstery.

"Our cousin?" A pained expression falls across Palmer's face. "But, but…I thought you said your name was—"

"*Dell.*" June's ornery gaze hones in on her daughter. I see the irrefutable likeness between them now, the resemblance I'd been blind to before. "Her name is Dell," she repeats.

"Which is short for Meridel," Leif chirps, not to be outdone.

Palmer's eyes are pleading as she scans the others' faces, looking for someone to come to her rescue, to deny the horrible news. "This is a joke, right?" she chokes out, asking no one in particular. "How can *she* be our…I mean, she can't be Laurel's *daughter*…is she?"

June's eyebrow spikes up as only a pissed-off mother's can. "What is so hard to understand about this, Palmer?"

Palmer's mouth gapes open like a hooked fish, shocked and utterly crestfallen. She leans into the couch, letting her head drop against the backrest, wallowing in this epic genealogical betrayal.

"Please continue, Finley," June instructs with a stern expression.

"Right then. Moving on…"

He shuffles his paperwork, while Briggs offers me a fresh muffin. I cup it in shaking hands.

"Ah, yes, here we are. 'To my brother-in-law, Florian Hamish Klyne, I confer my position as Chair of the Halcyon Bay Agricultural Committee. And to my nephew, Tristen Rolf Klyne, I bequeath my platinum membership to the local Garden and Botanicals Club. It is my hope that you both step down from the corporate rat race, and allow yourselves the time to savor some of the healthier, greener aspects of our island.'"

Tristen puckers his pale lips. Flip's face remains as fresh and unmarked as a sheet of writing paper.

"'To my granddaughter, Palmer Elizabeth Marin, I bequeath my wardrobe of couture and designer fashions, most notably the gown in which I myself was married, in hopes that it will inspire you to celebrate the great gift of love in your own life.'"

Palmer's eyes remain shut, her fingers twitching in her lap with restless energy. I'm not sure whether she heard any of what Finley said or if she's still stewing on the unfortunate revelation that the two of us share DNA.

"'To my granddaughter, Meridel Roslyn Costa'"—

I jump at hearing my full name said aloud, so formal, so unlike me. My heart pounds like a bass drum.

—"'I bequeath my compendium of prized first-edition novels, housed in my private stacks at the Halcyon Bay Island Library, in hopes that you will cherish the literary masterpieces as I have, making their characters and lessons your lifelong companions.'"

I feel the weight of everyone's eyes on me, gauging my reaction as I fight to keep my face still. A collection of first-edition books is a gift I could only dream of, but I remind myself that this transaction is meant to be melancholic, an unfortunate measure of time past and life lost. Planting a smile on my face would be profoundly inappropriate. Besides, I'd already made myself look like an inarticulate moron, I didn't need to add insensitive bitch to my repertoire.

"'To my grandson, Leif Simon Marin, I bequeath my beloved sailboat, in hopes that my passion for nature and exploration be carried on in you. The vessel will be entrusted to your mother until the eve of your sixteenth birthday, at which point, the title will be formally transferred to you.'"

Finley clears his throat and flips to the next page. "'Furthermore, each of my grandchildren shall also receive a sum of five hundred thousand dollars. In the case of Leif, a minor, distribution of these funds will begin upon his eighteenth birthday.'"

This time, there's no containing my reaction.

Five hundred thousand dollars?

My jaw drops, goosebumps crawling the length of my arms and neck. I feel a sudden, swift rush to the head, certain I've misheard or maybe had some sort of mild aneurysm.

Glancing around the parlor, no one else looks particularly ruffled, their expressions calm and almost bored, as if they're waiting in some mundane line for coffee. Is this kind of money *normal* for these people? Normal to the point of actual tedium?

Finley carries on. "'Finally, to my daughters, Laurel Anne Costa née Klyne and Juniper Elise Marin née Klyne, I bequeath each of you with exactly fifty percent of my assets, to be divided up via an independent audit conducted within the first year after my passing. These include the funds held in my various financial accounts, as well as personal heirlooms, like my assortment of jewelry and my collection of fine art. This assignation will be overseen by our trusted family financier, Mister Conrad E. Dorfmann, in collaboration with our dear friend and legal counsel, Mister Finley O'Hare.'"

My mind reels at the thought of how much those assets might amount to. If Palmer, Leif, and I are each to receive five hundred thousand bucks, I can only imagine how deep Virginia's money well actually runs.

I sneak a glance at Ambrose, who happens to be staring directly at me, or would be if his muddled eyes could see. An inexplicable shiver races through me, and I decide that I won't take their money, no matter how enticing. There's a reason Mom wouldn't accept her parents' charity years ago. Who knows what attachments—what strings—come along with it?

"'Additionally, to Laurel, I leave my most treasured family photo albums, in hopes that they, like a resolute lighthouse, help you navigate out of the darkness and guide you home.'" Finley lowers his stack of papers and shifts his horse-face to me. "Because Laurel could not be here today, Meridel, Mrs. Klyne's photo albums will be mailed to your family's residence at"—he flips several pages ahead—"622 Elk Road, Woodbridge County, Maine."

I nod back somewhat numbly. So much for keeping a low profile.

"'To Juniper, I bequeath my mother's handwritten book of recipes, in hopes that you recreate her concoctions for your own family and business, and assure that Mother's legacy in the kitchen lives on forevermore.'" Finley presents June with a worn linen book, crammed with torn bits of paper, ribbon, and popsicle sticks.

He flips to a fresh sheet from his stack and continues to read. "'As for the possessions that I amassed during my stint in the Hollywood limelight'"—

The Hollywood *what?*

—"'including all the memorabilia, movie posters, props, and scripts from such films as *Eight Nights in the Jungle*, *Alive and Living Well*, *Moroccan Sunset*, and *Dandy Girl*, as well as any other items related to my theatrical alias, Ginnie Gold'"—

I'd heard that name before. Lira had mentioned a Ginnie Gold at the bar last night. She was a popular local celebrity, an old Hollywood starlet.

My eyes snap up to the portrait of my grandmother, to the face I *knew* I recognized from somewhere. Virginia Marigold Klyne. Actress Ginnie Gold.

I feel like I've taken a baseball bat to the chest. I'd seen every single one of those old movies, curled up on the couch on wintry nights, never knowing exactly who I was watching, whose face I was seeing all along.

—"'I wish them all to be sold by private auction, and that the complete proceeds of those sales be dispersed among the various charities to which I regularly contribute.'" Finley meets eyes with Virginia's raven-haired assistant. "Sabine, the missus requested that this task be left in your capable hands."

Sabine nods once and taps something into her tablet.

Finley holds up a sleek ivory envelope. "Days before her passing, the missus also wrote this letter for me to share with you all."

He slides a slender finger across the flap and unfolds its contents— a brief, final message, scrawled across a creamy bit of parchment paper.

"'My life has been a full and long one,'" Finley reads. "'When the doctors informed me of the cancer prognosis, I was neither angry nor sad. I am an old woman, and these things are to be expected. I've been gifted far more in this life than most...more than I ever deserved. Many of you can attest to this, I am sure.'"

June coughs from her place on the couch, and my eyes flick to her. I'm surprised to find her round, pleasant face looking stony and tense. What was her life like in Halcyon Bay, living in the shadow of Ambrose and Virginia, in this towering castle by the sea? Did my aunt run from it too, in her own quiet way?

"'To my children and grandchildren, please know that I loved you with my full heart. So often that wasn't enough, and I am sorry for my many failures.'" Finley presses his handkerchief to his tear-streaked cheeks. "'But I've confessed my sins to our Lord and am ready to be relieved of my earthly regrets. I think I have been ready for a long, long while, and I look forward to doing things better next time around, when we all meet again in the afterlife.'"

Finley falls silent, carefully folding the letter up and returning it to his portfolio.

The reading of Virginia Klyne's will is over.

CHAPTER ELEVEN

I'm pressed against the far corner of the parlor, fidgeting into angst-ridden oblivion, while my irritatingly self-possessed family chatters quietly among themselves. What am I supposed to do now? Seek Briggs or Finley out for further instruction? Excuse myself to the guest house before someone inevitably corners me? I'm sure they all have tons of questions…about me, my mother, and our life half a world away.

An unexpected second knock comes at the front door, and Briggs bows out of the parlor to answer it. When he returns, he's accompanied by two solemn-looking policemen.

"Miss Dell," he says calmly. I jump at being singled out. "These officers would like a brief word, if you don't mind."

Everyone in the room gapes at me with identical expressions of shock and horror. *Perfect,* I think, my skin crawling with heat. *My role as the family pariah is secure.*

"Meridel Costa?" The shorter officer approaches, flashing me his badge. It catches the sunlight, glinting like a razor blade at his hip, nestled beside a sleek handgun. "I'm Officer Dash with the HBPD. This is my partner, Officer Parris."

The taller officer, Parris, nods at me tersely, before appraising the room and its black-clad inhabitants with flared nostrils. His icy-blue eyes remain on Tristen for a long, discerning moment.

"We're tracking down all the passengers that traveled aboard Cyprus Line Ferry Four last night," Dash continues. "The vessel in question disembarked from Cyprus Seaport at six thirty in the evening, and arrived in Halcyon Seaport just after eight o'clock. Your name was on the manifest. Can you confirm that you were, in fact, aboard that vessel, Miss Costa?"

"Yes, I was."

"We understand you witnessed an incident as you were arriving."

I nod, my mouth Sahara-dry.

"If you wouldn't mind, we'd like to get your account of the events that transpired. As you recall them, of course."

"Am I in some sort of trouble?"

Dash shakes his head. "Nothing like that, miss. We were only hoping that you would give us a statement. Unpleasant as the situation is, and I'm sure quite painful to revisit—"

"It would help in our investigation," Parris interrupts with a degree of finality, like he's used to having the last word on things.

"Okay."

Dash leads me to the tufted couch, as if sitting down might make me more comfortable and thus more cooperative. What Dash can't know is that here, surrounded by the family I've never known, dwarfed by a massive house harboring countless secrets, I will never, ever feel remotely comfortable. He may as well be guiding me onto a bed of pins and needles.

He settles down across from me, pulling a notepad and pen from his breast pocket, while his icier counterpart hovers somewhere behind me, pacing alongside the couch, his steps methodical.

"Now, Miss Costa," Dash begins, "describe the ferry ride for me, please."

I lick my lips, trying to determine where best to start. Not an easy feat with so many questioning eyes drilling into my face.

"It was a rough ride, to say the least. We got caught in a terrible storm. There was heavy rain, and the waves were brutal. The captain was fighting just to keep us afloat."

"Upon approaching, could you see the island clearly?" Dash asks.

"No. Honestly, it was difficult to see much of anything."

"But you did see *something?*" This question comes from Parris.

"Yes."

"And what did you see?" Dash asks. His brown eyes are kind, not yet hardened by the nature of his work, or maybe gentle in spite of it.

"A girl," I say, allowing the film reel of horror to unspool behind my eyes. "She was running...running in a long white dress. A nightgown, I think. That's what caught my eye in the first place."

"Her dress?"

I nod. "She was so out of place there. This glaring white spot, where everything else was darkness."

Dash nods, scribbling into his notepad. "Where was she running?"

"She was running across an old wooden pier—"

"Prospero Pier," interrupts Parris from behind me. "Yes, yes. We're aware of this, Dash. Move it along."

I turn to glance at Parris, repelled by his brusque disposition. "Was she alone?" he snaps at me.

"I think so, yes. I didn't see anyone else around."

"How did the girl look to you, Miss Costa?" Dash asks, his voice a soothing contrast to Parris' severity.

"What do you mean?"

"I mean, how did she seem? Was she calm? Panicked? Distressed?"

"Well, she looked—"

"Did she seem like she was being coerced in any way?" Parris interrupts again.

"She looked, um...uncertain."

Parris walks around the couch and stands face-to-face with me, eyes narrowed into slits. "Uncertain how?"

"Like she wasn't sure what she was doing," I explain. "I mean, at first, she seemed sure. Her movements were quick and precise. But then there was a moment where she turned back to land. Her foot slipped, and when she tried to correct herself, I saw her face. It was like, for a second, she was debating going back. She looked scared, and…" My voice trails off, the words growing heavier and harder to say.

Dash furrows his brow, as though he's sorry to have upset me. "And?" he prompts gently.

"I just thought maybe she was second-guessing her decision, that maybe she didn't want to be there."

Parris had asked if the girl appeared to have been coerced. I hadn't seen anyone else, but that doesn't mean someone else wasn't there, or that they hadn't threatened her in some other way.

"Do you think someone forced her to jump off that pier?" I ask.

"Not necessarily, but it's our job to consider all possibilities," Parris says, as if that would be his last word on the matter.

I ignore his harsh end-of-story tone. "Were you able to recover her body?"

"We did." Dash sighs.

"Can I ask who she was?"

Parris protests, but Dash sidesteps him. "A local girl," he says with soft-spoken reverence. "A twelve-year-old student from Halcyon Bay Middle. Her name was Callie Oxton."

The details from last night flit behind my eyes like sifting paper. I see her rust-red hair, wet and ropey by her face, her tiny, pale body, not yet shaped by womanhood, her little bare feet and ten soft toes. Everything that once made up Callie Oxton—dead. Gone.

"Is there anything more that you can tell us?" Parris asks, obviously finished with my statement, with me. "Any other details worth mentioning?"

"No, I'm sorry. That's all I remember."

Parris' glacial eyes settle on the bandaged cut on my forehead. "You're the passenger that needed the paramedics."

My hand shoots to my temple. "I had a little accident. I, um, hit my head on the windowpane…"

The officer's lips curve into a grimace. He lets out a frustrated breath and bows out of the parlor without so much as a goodbye, as if my head injury makes whatever I've said significantly less credible.

"Thank you for your time, Miss Costa," Dash says as he stands, folding his notepad back into his pocket. "You've been very helpful. We'll be in contact if we have any further questions."

He hands me a business card with a phone number splashed across it. *Get help now! Call the Halcyon Bay Crisis Counseling Hotline,* the card implores.

"What's this?" I ask, holding it like a hot coal I might fling into the fireplace.

"A program we offer for witness survivors," Dash says. "Oftentimes, after seeing a public suicide, many people experience bouts of PTSD. If you're feeling anxious or depressed, or if you're having bad dreams or thoughts of harming yourself, please be sure to get in touch with us."

I feel myself stiffen, my fingers curling into fists. Hell would freeze over before I'd go anywhere near a Halcyon Bay shrink ward.

"I know it sounds like the last thing you'd probably ever want to do," Dash admits, "but it is available if ever you need it. We don't want to compound tragedy with more tragedy. No one should have to suffer through that kind of trauma alone."

I can't help but think just how wrong he is. "Thank you, officer."

"Sorry for the interruption, folks." He ducks out of the room, with Briggs promptly following him into the hall.

The next few minutes pass by in a blur.

Low, agitated whispers are exchanged between the others while I close my eyes and lean back against the couch cushions, trying and failing to block out their noise. Before long, I feel a shifting weight when someone comes to settle beside me.

"Dell, honey?"

It's June, looking at me with that sad smile and sadder eyes— Mom's eyes. "Sounds like you've had quite the welcome back." She speaks quietly so as not to draw any additional attention my way.

"It hasn't been boring." My voice is ragged, hoarse, like the morning's events have aged me drastically.

June's tear-streaked eyes are hopeful when says, "It's been so long since you've been back, Dell. I'd love for us to catch up, even just for a few hours. How would you like to join us at my house for dinner tonight?"

"Oh, I wouldn't want to impose—"

"It's not an imposition," she insists. "You're family. We'd love to have you." Her eyes are even more beseeching than her words. She certainly shares my mother's innate ability to guilt trip me.

"Okay. Dinner would be…great."

June claps her hands, a rosy rush of delight brightening her face. "Wonderful! The address is 48 Anchorage Lane. How does seven o'clock sound?"

"Seven's great. Thanks."

My aunt beams at me while my stomach twists into knots. She puts her hands on my arms, rubbing the cold from my skin, and, to my surprise, I'm not inclined to jerk away. Something about her feels comforting and familiar, my heartstrings pulled by the slivers of my mother I see in her.

There's a *tug tug tug* on the edge of my dress, and Leif flashes me his signature toothy grin. "Tonight, we color," he says determinedly. It takes everything in me to return his smile.

Excusing myself for the bathroom, I slip out of the French doors and onto the expansive grounds, in desperate need of a reprieve. All I can think to do is put as much distance between myself and Cliffmoor House as possible, giving my lungs room to breathe, my mind space to process.

I've almost made it to the guest house when I hear my name being called from afar.

Palmer runs across the wide stretch of lawn, the black gauze of her dress rippling behind her like billows of smoke. When she reaches me, she takes a second to catch her breath. Her eyes are dewy and her cheeks flushed, her yellow braid gleaming in the warm sunlight. She's pretty without a stitch of makeup on.

"Hey, Meridel—"

"It's Dell," I remind her.

"Right, Dell." Palmer hastily glances back to Cliffmoor House, at the people still congregated inside, the family we both share. "Look, I know you're coming over to Mom's house for dinner tonight, so I want to clear the air before…you know."

Of course I know.

"About last night, what you said in the bathroom…" She looks as uncomfortable as the clumsy string of words fumbling from her lips. "I, um, haven't had the chance to share the news with anyone yet. It hasn't been the right time, what with planning Gram's funeral and all that, so…do you think you could just…I mean, could you *not*…you know…"

Shit. She really is pregnant. And I'm a lowdown, terrible person for making her worry about what I might do or say, what I might spill, given the proper nudging.

"I won't say anything," I mutter quickly, wishing I could erase everything I'd insinuated yesterday. "You don't have to worry."

"Really?" Palmer squints, unconvinced. "You won't?"

I shake my head. "Whatever's going on with you is none of my business. I was out of line last night. I won't bring it up again, promise."

"Oh." She nods, surely wondering whether she can trust me, then realizing she has no choice. "Okay."

"I can keep a secret."

Palmer exhales slowly, her shoulders loosening. A small wave of relief washes over her face. "Thank you."

"Don't mention it."

We stand awkwardly for a brief moment, until Palmer says, "Okay, so…great. I guess I'll see you later tonight, then."

With a swish of her braid, she prances back down the brick path to Cliffmoor House—a princess returning to her castle.

"I guess you will," I say to myself before disappearing into the guest house.

CHAPTER TWELVE

The Halcyon Bay Island Library is a grand, impressive sight, with towering marble pillars stretching up to frescoed ceilings, and sweeping shelves with stacks of books that seem to soar to the skies. Light floods the building through a multitude of tapered windows at each side, interspersed between wooden bookcases like alternating traffic lanes—light and books, books and light—creating a magical, cathedral-like effect, as if sunshine itself spills from the pages it houses.

I meander along the first floor, losing myself in endless titles and tomes, captivated by the dizzying scents of ink and weathered paper. There's no one around, or so I think, when I trip over a woman crouched by a low shelf. Half her body is hidden behind a mountain of paperbacks, and she lets out a yelp as my boots tangle up in her skirt. I nearly fall on top of her, sending several rogue books crashing down with me, but the woman scrambles to her feet, narrowly avoiding a collision.

I sprawl across the floor, the ache in my head reignited. "I'm so, so sorry. I didn't see you down there."

She grabs my hand in hers and tugs, yanking me to my feet in one swift and surprising motion. "Happens all the time, dearie," she says, collecting the spilled books in her rail-thin arms. "First visit?"

The woman resembles a pixie, with an upturned nose, hooded gray eyes, and tightly-curled black hair grazing her chin. From her earlobes dangle delicate copper earrings, long enough to dust her bony shoulders. She's wrapped in a shawl of clashing patterns and colors, and a pair of cat-eye glasses are nestled over her bangs.

I nod.

"Bit overwhelming, isn't it?" She sets her little hands on her hips and turns all the way around, her too-long skirt forming a twisted pool at her feet. "A book lover's paradise."

"Do you work here?"

"Nine hours a day, three hundred and sixty-five days a year," she chirps. "Can I help you with something?"

"Yes, please. My name's Dell Costa. I'm Virginia Klyne's, um, granddaughter." My voice gets all high and squeaky at 'granddaughter,' so it sounds more like a question than a statement of fact. That damn word will never feel natural to say. "She passed away recently and left me some first editions. Her attorney said I would find them here."

"Mrs. Klyne's granddaughter," the librarian repeats.

"Yes."

"You must be Laurel's daughter, then." An inquisitive gleam pokes through her dark eyes.

This town is a cesspool of busybodies and snoops.

"I am, yes."

"Splendid." She nods her little elfin head, satisfied. "Welcome back, dearie. I'd be happy to show you to Mrs. Klyne's private stacks. Do you have documentation corroborating the transfer of ownership?"

"Yes, right here." I unfold a signed affidavit from Finley. "And I've got this, too." I pull a small brass key from my pocket, tarnished and ancient, like an heirloom spanning the generations.

The librarian scans the document for a brief moment before giving it back to me, one discerning gray eye on the key. "Follow me," she says, shuffling away down the long marble hall.

For such a tiny person, she certainly moves fast. We pass hundreds of bookcases and ascend two flights of stairs until we reach the rafters, coming to stand before a hefty wooden door, carved and intricate, like something from a storybook.

"Key, please," she says, and I place it in her palm.

The door creaks open to reveal a small tent-shaped loft, so small that I can only stand up straight at the very middle. The elfin woman, however, easily maneuvers the narrow room, ushering me to the back.

Whereas the rest of the library is bright and airy, with plenty of sunlight pouring in, the loft is dim and at least ten degrees colder. As if reading my mind, the woman explains, "Natural light is bad for the books, as is the island humidity. We have a dedicated air conditioning unit up here to maintain ideal temperatures for our antiques. Ah! Here we are."

We reach a hulking glass case of eight shelves filled with hardback books in a rainbow of colors. Names like *The Great Gatsby*, *Don Quixote*, and *Jane Eyre* glint at me from the first shelf. The second boasts titles like *Frankenstein*, *Moby Dick*, and *Beloved*. Each one is full of new surprises, and I can't keep a smile from taking up residence on my face.

"Mrs. Klyne's private collection." The librarian runs a wistful finger along the edge of the case. "Beautiful, aren't they?"

"Can we open it?" I ask.

She nods, a glimmer in her gray eyes. "Of course, dearie. Just be sure not to crack the bindings, they can be quite sensitive. Try to keep the books flat so the pages don't warp. Now, let me find you a pair of gloves."

I spend what feels like hours perched in those cool, dusty stacks, poring over Virginia's assortment of classic literary treasures.

Plath and Salinger, Austen and García Márquez, Hurston and Woolf. I settle into their stories, cozy and familiar as sipping coffee with old friends, and for the briefest of moments, manage to forget about my familial melodrama.

Several chapters into a rereading of *To Kill a Mockingbird,* I find a photograph from a yellowed newspaper tucked within its pages.

It's a snapshot of my grandmother in the prime of her youth, her dark curls pinned back, stormy eyes glistening, waving coquettishly at the swarming paparazzi. The newspaper article itself is missing, but the tagline below the photograph reads, *A Star Shoots to the Skies: Ginnie Gold's Swift Rise to Fame.* The image plants an idea in my mind.

I return the book to its temperature-controlled home and venture down the stairs. The main room contains a smattering of wide wooden tables, each one dotted with a leather armchair and a shiny, silver computer screen. I sneak a swift glance around to make sure I'm alone, sink into one of the seats, and hit the power button. The computer before me jolts to life.

I've never researched the Klynes before. With my life so distanced from theirs, and my parents working overtime to keep it that way, I never saw a reason to, never cared enough to investigate a group of people who evidently wanted so little to do with me. But now that I'm here, mingling with this family of strangers, I'm undeniably intrigued.

Opening a private internet window, I type into the search box: *Ginnie Gold, Virginia Klyne.* Immediately, a long list of links appear, and I click through to one that directs me to a transcript of an old article from *L.A. Today.*

Burgeoning Film Star to Unexpectedly Retire

Virginia Marigold Aubuchon, famously known as mega-actress Ginnie Gold, has decided to retire from the glitz and glamour of show business.

On Monday evening, Ms. Aubuchon's agent made the whirlwind announcement that the actress and model would be leaving Hollywood in her rear view. Why? A new set of roles have piqued the great Ginnie Gold's interest—that of wife and mother.

The young Ms. Aubuchon, who recently became engaged to

renown financier and multi-millionaire Ambrose Klyne III, plans to relocate to the east coast to lead a quieter life with her soon-to-be husband and focus on growing their family.

In a statement released by her agent, the actress is quoted in saying that she hopes to "create a life apart from the fame of [her] name."

We will all miss the exquisite talents and sultry beauty possessed by Ms. Aubuchon, who has captivated cinema screens all over the world, making moviegoers of all ages swoon. Her beloved roles in films like *Dandy Girl, Eight Nights in the Jungle,* and *Moroccan Sunset* will live on in our hearts and minds, and we wish Ms. Aubuchon the best as she rides off toward her own happily ever after.

So Virginia's stint in Hollywood took place before she married Ambrose, before she even became pregnant with my mother. Maybe the secrets harbored by the Klynes have something to do with Virginia's celebrity?

I type in another search: *Ambrose and Virginia Klyne, Halcyon Bay.* Clicking through to one of the more recent articles, I'm directed to a medical journal centered on pathology and bioscience research.

Philanthropic Klynes Donate to Meaningful Cause

Prominent South Florida investor Ambrose Klyne and his wife Virginia, a respected horticulturist and former actress, are donating $1.2 million to the APM (Alzheimer's Purple Mission) in the name of deceased family member Georgia Aubuchon.

Revered and adored among their intimate Halcyon Bay community, the Klynes have made five other charitable donations this year to a range of disaster relief, environmental conservation, and educational reform organizations. According to the power couple, this latest offering is a much more personal one.

"It's a cause that touches us very deeply," Virginia said in a recent interview with HBTV Local 8 News. "My late sister Georgia's Alzheimer's diagnosis was devastating. The disease stole her from us in three short years."

The Klynes' generous efforts alongside the APM will help enhance the prospect of survival for those currently afflicted by the degenerative disease. Eventually, they aim to put an end to Alzheimer's altogether.

"The research conducted by the APM is indispensable," Ambrose said. "These funds will be allocated to advancing neuroimaging strategies and studies on brain chemistry that are crucial to our crusade to find a viable cure."

"We never gave up hope for Georgia, and we won't give up hope for the nearly six million Americans living with this deadly disease today," Virginia added.

The article carries on about the Klynes' legendary altruism. I skim through the majority of it, eager for something of interest to jump out at me, for some real clue as to what I'm doing here. But the article is extensive, bogged down with medical statistics and sympathetic quotes, all largely unhelpful for my purposes. I'm about to give up and skip to my next search query, when, all the way at the bottom, at the start of the last paragraph, I read a shocking sentence.

Having lost their youngest daughter in a drowning accident, the Klynes are no strangers to family tragedy.

Having lost their youngest daughter…

I reread it several more times to make sure I've understood. The words glare back at me defiantly, making my blood run bitter-cold.

I click back to the search engine, my fingers flying on the keys as I type: *Klyne drowning, Halcyon Bay.*

Pages upon pages of news links pop up, but I'm paralyzed, incapable of clicking on any of them.

My fingertips tingle with dread and anticipation, my vision blurring in and out of focus like a camera lens, as I skim headlines plucked straight out of a horror movie.

- **Beloved Halcyon Bay Teenager's Body Recovered from Sandspur Shallows**

- **Officials Investigate Suspicious Drowning of HBMS Swim Star**

- **Missing Girl Dies of Suspected Drowning on Sandspur Beach**

- **Community's Worst Fears Confirmed: 13-year-old Drowning Victim Identified by Coroner**

- **Accident or Homicide? Local Girl's Body Discovered Near Home**

My mind races, one thought crawling over the next. Mom doesn't have one sister…she has *two*. One of them is dead…dead at thirteen. It was a drowning accident…or homicide.

My heartbeat drums maddeningly in my ears. *What the hell have I stumbled upon?*

CHAPTER THIRTEEN

My fingers shudder on the mouse, hovering over the news links for a long, reluctant moment. The little arrow icon on my screen blinks incessantly, itching for me to click through, to peel off the bandage and examine the damage underneath.

The first link directs me to an article from a local newspaper, *The Halcyon Bay Beacon*, from two decades ago. Holding my breath, I read:

Beloved Halcyon Bay Teenager's Body Recovered from Sandspur Shallows

13-year-old Willow Klyne, daughter of local philanthropists Ambrose and Virginia Klyne, was found dead on Sandspur Beach early this morning. The suspected cause of death is drowning, however, significant injury to the girl's skull may suggest something more sinister.

The night prior, the Klyne family's annual summer solstice party was underway at their seaside estate, the historic Cliffmoor

House of Old Town, just inland of Sandspur Beach. The family noticed the girl was missing around one in the morning. Police were notified immediately, leading to an exhaustive search through the night. Her body was recovered at sunrise.

Commercial fisherman Abraham Urban has been taken into custody as a person of interest. Earlier this year, Mr. and Mrs. Klyne filed a restraining order against Urban for stalking and attempting to kidnap their youngest daughter from her middle school locker room after a swim meet. He was seen loitering in the vicinity of Cliffmoor House the night of the party, breaking his court-directed order. Security for the party apprehended Urban and had him removed from the grounds before midnight. His whereabouts for the remainder of the evening are still unknown.

At a press conference this afternoon, Halcyon Bay's Chief of Police, Captain Farlow Burn, had this to say: "We are waiting for the autopsy report to determine a definitive cause of death. We want to assure the entire island community that we are launching an extensive investigation. If Mr. Urban did, in fact, play a role in Willow Klyne's death, he will stand trial and be prosecuted to the fullest extent of the law. Until further details emerge, please join me in sending your love, prayers, and support to the Klyne family at this incredibly difficult time."

Klyne family attorney and friend, Finley O'Hare, Esq., added, "Willow was beloved by all who knew her. She was a luminary in the making, with Olympic aspirations and a huge heart. Her presence will forever mark this town. Her bright light will never fade."

Ms. Klyne's family members were not available for commentary. She is survived by her parents, two sisters, brothers-in-law, and two young nieces.

It feels like something foreign has lodged itself in the back of my throat, and as I read and reread those same unchanging sentences, the foreign thing swells, making it increasingly harder for me to breathe. A tingling sensation in my fingertips begins to spread too, crawling up my arms like a thousand needle-footed spiders.

I shake them out and promptly type: *Willow Klyne, Halcyon Bay.*

This time, I search for images.

Rows upon rows of photos pop up, agonizingly slow thanks to the patchy internet, and I'm bombarded by the same headshot over and over in neat little squares of a young girl resembling my mother and aunt.

The likeness is evident in her straw-gold hair, in the messy bangs spilling into her eyes…eyes an uncanny ocean-blue, deep and intense as a rolling storm. A pink, cloud-like birthmark snakes down the side of her neck. Her bright smile rivals the morning sun.

It's Willow's seventh-grade yearbook picture, I read. The one the papers ran after her death. The one used in her obituary, taken a year before her drowning.

Amid the rows of identical smiling headshots, another image catches my eye, different from all the rest. It's a stylish photograph of two young women and a girl, posing on a sandy stretch of beach—the Klyne sisters.

They stand barefoot in the sand, carefree and startlingly beautiful, wrapped around each other like the ocean breeze. Mom's sun-bleached hair is hippie-long and wild, and she wears a vibrant blue bathing suit with a sheer white sarong. June's hair is plaited to one side like Palmer's was this morning, and she dons a pair of unbuttoned Daisy Dukes over a teeny red bikini.

The young girl between them wears a purple suit, looking intently at the camera with those stormy eyes and a wide grin, her sunlit blond hair pulled into two spunky pigtails. She carries with her a green snorkeling mask and fins.

The three of them are devastatingly lovely—like the halcyon days of adolescence, the fairytale essence of summertime—but also…deeply sad to behold.

The photograph is accompanied by an article for *Style Savant,* a discontinued women's fashion and lifestyle magazine. It reads:

The Girls of Summer: An Inside Look at the Charmed Lives of Halcyon Bay's Golden Sisters

By Maureen Chagirin

When the Klyne girls step into the dingy coffeehouse where I'm tucked in a velvet armchair, forcing down a weak midday latte and struggling to keep my eyes open, the lazy, hum-drum energy in the room immediately shifts.

Laurel, 24, leads the charge, flashing a breezy smile before slipping into the upholstered couch beside me, dangling her tanned legs over the armrest. Her blond hair reaches down to her belly button, bared in a seersucker two-piece set. A faint layer of freckles dot her nose and cheeks, though her smile paints them over with a pretty rose flush. A white Birkenstock falls off one of her manicured feet, and Laurel promptly shakes off the other one, laughing melodiously.

Juniper, 21, who goes by June, sinks down onto the shabby Oriental rug. The whitewashed denim of her overalls is frayed, with several holes forming at the knees. This, paired with the vintage band sweatshirt hanging from one shoulder and those startling blue eyes lined in thick black pencil, evokes an effortless, seductive sort of cool. She nods at me in greeting, her lips forming a coy smile.

Willow, 9, plops onto the armchair across from mine, dropping her sandals and criss-crossing her legs. The youngest Klyne rests her chin in her palm, bangs held in place with several colorful clips. She sports a smart, if not roguish, grin that matches the amusing message on her tee, tucked into high-waisted plaid shorts. The shirt depicts a rain cloud wearing sunglasses, and at the top, across the chest, it reads: *Have a Nice Duh!*

I'm instantly captivated by all three of them.

The girls regale me with their plans for the summer. Laurel, recently married to realtor Tomás Costa, is working for her father while on respite from business school. June, an aspiring chef, is slinging pies and waitressing at downtown hot spot Pizza Nirvana (lovingly nicknamed 'Pizzana' by the local clientele). Willow has a coveted spot on the HB Rays swim team, and is practicing for a big inter-school swim meet at summer's end.

The girls giggle among themselves, sharing some unspoken memory or inside joke that I can't help but secretly wish I was part of. Because that's the thing about the Klyne girls—their aura is magnetic. You want to know them, and once you do, you want to be around them.

All I can say is, move over, Calvin. We've got some new Klynes breaking onto the scene!

The journalist goes on to describe the sisters in greater detail, their hobbies and passions, their travels and talents. Virginia is mentioned at one point as well, highlighting that undeniable *je ne sais quoi* that the Hollywood starlet passed on to her daughters. I find it difficult to focus much on the words. I keep getting pulled back to that photograph, to those smiling sisters on the cusp of tragedy.

No wonder Mom fled Halcyon Bay some twenty years ago. After Willow's death, she had to get away, had to shield herself from these painful memories and escape the oppressive small town where they all grew up, where every street and sidewalk harbored remembrances of a sister lost too soon.

No wonder her life became a merry-go-round of therapy, drugs, and institution living. No wonder her dreams are still plagued to this day...

Another mental puzzle piece snaps jarringly into place.

Up until this moment, I'd always thought of Lo as an *it*—a faceless nightmare or hallucination, engendered by Mom's worst fears and anxieties. But now, knowing this, Lo could just as easily be an actual person. A ghostly manifestation of someone she once knew.

A twisted-up version of her dead sister, Willow.

"Ms. Costa?"

The librarian's quiet voice startles me. She stands over my shoulder, a stack of books pressed to her chest, gray eyes trained on my computer screen. I quickly exit the search window, but I'm sure she saw enough.

"Closing time, dearie," the woman says levelly, her eyes dropping to meet mine. They suddenly seem cold and severe.

"Oh, sure thing. I was just wrapping up—"

"I'm going to have to turn the lights off now." She gives me a close-lipped smile, jaw taut. "You may return tomorrow, if you'd like."

I get the sense as I'm collecting my things that, for whatever reason, she'd rather I didn't.

Outside in the parking lot, I wrench Virginia's bike from the rack, while the librarian's orange coupe idles nearby.

She'd followed me out the front doors and briskly locked up behind us, scuttering away with that unnerving, narrowed smile. Now she watches me from behind the tinted windows of her clown car, refusing to pull out of the lot, like she's waiting for me to leave first.

I walk the bike down the sidewalk, keeping a peripheral eye on the coupe, until I reach a cluster of newspaper receptacles.

A photograph of Callie Oxton is splashed across the latest issue of *The Halcyon Bay Beacon,* and above her picture, the front page article reads:

Local Girl Jumps from Prospero Pier to her Death

Callie's face is heart-shaped and stippled in freckles. There's an air of mischief in her dark brown eyes, defiance in her smirk that strikes me as bold—daring, even. She's tough and strong and so unlike the fear-stricken girl I saw balancing on that pier last night.

I pop some change into the receptacle and pull out a copy.

Officials are still unpacking details from the horrible suicide of 12-year-old Callie Oxton, whose body was recovered from Halcyon Bay by the U.S. Coast Guard late Thursday evening.

Passengers commuting aboard the Cyprus Line Ferry reported that they saw the girl plunge from the inoperative Prospero Pier on the north side of the island at 7:45 at night. Ferryboat captain Dave McCormick made the mayday call to USCG.

Oxton's father was not available for commentary. When questioned, a neighbor and family friend mentioned that he'd noticed Oxton spending time with an older boy outside of her usual circle of friends. The girl was spotted on multiple occasions driving around town with the unidentified boy in an orange car.

Without lifting my head from the paper, my eyes flick up to the librarian's orange car. An odd coincidence, but I'm just being paranoid. Lots of people own brightly colored cars. This is Florida, after all. An eccentric island town inhabited by eccentric island people.

The neighbor, who would like to remain anonymous, said this: "They would peel out of the neighborhood at all hours of the night. I knew it was them from how the car brakes would squeak, waking me up every time. They sure were in a hurry to get somewhere."

Captain F.P. Burn, HBPD Chief of Police, implored the island community to keep their eyes open for any signs of this mystery boy, who officials believe may be able to provide further insight into Oxton's suicide.

Rumors have spread about a possible connection between Oxton and the disbanded cult of the Brine. Many locals will recall the homegrown movement that wreaked havoc on the island some years ago.

When questioned on the subject, Captain Burn said, "We are exploring all pertinent avenues and leads. At the moment, nothing

is confirmed, and nothing is off the table."

Oxton is survived by her father and three younger brothers.

My cell phone alarm chimes in my pocket, startling me to fast attention.

Time for dinner with June, my mother's one surviving sister.

I fold the newspaper into my bag and pull out my map of the island, mounting Virginia's bike while mentally planning my route. June's house isn't far, about a ten minute ride if I had to guess, but the clouds overhead are ominous. There's a good chance I'll arrive looking and smelling like a wet dog if I don't get a move on.

I pump my legs to gain speed, zipping around the giant roundabout in front of the library. I approach the intersection, about to take off down Plumbago Street, when the librarian speeds by in her little orange coupe and whips a quick left in the opposite direction.

Her brakes screech like a tea kettle as the vehicle hurtles, smoking, into the distance.

CHAPTER FOURTEEN

After thirty minutes of combing unfamiliar streets under a torrential rainstorm, I arrive at my aunt's house soaked to my underwear, feeling like a shivering, waterlogged mess, my map rendered useless in my hands. The downpour stops as soon as I lean the bike against a tree in the front yard, the clouds scattering swiftly as if to mock me. Within seconds, there's no trace of storm left at all, just the misty, orange-blue atmosphere of dusk. Only now I'm in need of an industrial-sized blow dryer, and maybe a Xanax to calm my nerves.

I climb the steps up to June's quaint stilt house. To the left of the door, a bench-swing hangs from salt-rusted chains, groaning complaints with each passing breeze. To the right is a large open window, the sounds of jazz music and conversation wafting outside. An array of sun-battered, overrun plants in cracked pots litter the porch in smears of green and brown. The house looks so normal—so lived-in and modest—that I find myself sighing with profound relief.

One knock at the door and it instantly flies open, revealing a smiling Leif in the doorway and a giant caramel dog panting with unbridled excitement. Neither of us has a chance to speak before I'm assailed by a pair of monster paws and a wet tongue lapping at my arms, licking raindrops from my skin. I teeter in place, barely staying on my feet.

"Bear, stop!" Leif yells, tugging on the dog's tail. "Leave her alone! You can't do that to company!"

June screeches from within the house, "Bear!" The dog whips his head, snapping to immediate attention. "Down!" He plops down at my feet, splaying onto his stomach, his tail slapping eagerly against the wooden floors.

"Dell, honey, come in!" June calls. "You'll have to forgive Bear, the ol' dope. Too excitable for his own good."

I wipe some lingering drool from my neck and step around the mammoth dog, his droopy eyes following each of my careful movements. "It smells great in here," I say to Leif, who shuts the door, taking me by the hand.

"Mommy's a chef," he replies matter-of-factly, leading me across the living room and into the kitchen.

June's busy at the stovetop, stirring a pot of something fragrant. A luscious medley of seafood and spice fills the air, a combination of scents that draw out the quiet, gnawing hunger I'd been ignoring for hours. My hand flies to my belly when it makes a mortifyingly loud rumble. "Sorry I'm late. I got turned around in the rain, and...well..."

June pivots, gasping when she sees me. If I wasn't embarrassed before, her dismayed expression does the trick. "Palmer!" she calls.

My cousin slips in from the hall without a word, cell phone in hand, her eyes widening at the sight of me. She almost smiles, almost laughs, but catches herself in time. Begrudgingly remembering that she should be nice to me, should placate me, for fear that I might reveal her secret.

"Go grab Dell a towel and some fresh clothes, will you?" June turns back to the stove. "Dinner's almost on."

Palmer rolls her eyes at her mother's back. "Follow me," she mumbles in my direction.

I trail her down a narrow hallway with a floor-length mirror at the far end, Bear plodding close behind us. From what I can see of myself at a distance, I realize I look a bit like I did last night—sheet-white, battered, and totally drenched. This time, my appearance is slightly improved by the lack of blood stains and puke chunks dripping off me.

Thank God for little miracles.

She enters a sunflower-yellow bedroom loaded down with cardboard boxes. Some are open with items spilling from the tops. Others are neatly stacked with sharpied categories scrawled along the sides. Books, electronics, shoes, miscellaneous—an entire life packed up and categorized.

Winding across the maze of boxes to a pretty armoire in the corner, Palmer pulls out a ratty t-shirt and a pair of biker shorts. "These are the best I can offer," she says with a shrug, handing them to me. "The rest of my crap is either boxed up or long gone."

The shirt is blue tie-dye with a melting smiley face on the chest—fitting for my current state. I take the clothes and ask no questions. "They're perfect. Thanks."

"Bathroom's two doors down on the left."

She turns back toward the kitchen while I shuffle down the hall. Bear scampers after me, and when I close the bathroom door, my heart twinges at the sight of his wagging tail and longing smile. "I'll be right back," I say gently, and the dog sinks onto his haunches to wait.

Within a couple of minutes, I get myself looking halfway decent, washing off the chunky tracks of mascara streaming down my cheeks, twisting my soggy hair into a bun at the nape of my neck, and slipping out of my wet clothes into Palmer's dry ones. I'm severely underdressed now, looking more like I'm ready to hop into bed than sit down to dinner. I hope I won't have to face any solicitous characters tonight. The thought of enduring Finley's horse-faced scrutiny or Ambrose's sickening gaze is enough to make me cringe.

Bear is still waiting when I step out of the bathroom, and I bury my fingers in his soft fur, letting him nuzzle into my arms. "Stay close, buddy," I whisper in his floppy ear. "I need all the help I can get." The dog's wise brown eyes peer into mine with quiet resolve. One of them closes sleepily—a little wink of reassurance.

I make my way back to the kitchen, stopping short when I hear the tense echoes of an argument unfolding.

"Of course he is!" June snaps. "Why am I not surprised?"

"He'll just be another minute, Mom," Palmer pleads. "Dell got here late too, so why is this such a big deal?"

"Dell is the reason for this dinner, Palmer. She doesn't know the island, all she's got is your grandmother's rusty old bike to get around, *and* the poor girl got caught in a rainstorm. You could have a little more compassion—"

"Compassion is what I'm asking you to have with Mojo!"

"Oh, please. Moises doesn't need my compassion," June huffs. "He's had plenty of chances to show us where his priorities lie."

"What do you know about Mojo's priorities?"

"Seeing as how he's never on time for my dinners, I can only assume that we don't rank very high on the list," June retorts. "Timeliness doesn't seem to suit his lifestyle. Neither does commitment, for that matter."

"What's that supposed to mean?" Palmer's words are shrill and offended. June goes silent, but I can feel the invisible heat waves radiating from the kitchen, and they aren't coming from the stove. "Goodness, Mom! Come out with it already!"

"I just find it so very comical," June says without even a shred of humor, "how content Moises is to shack up with you, yet he refuses to get serious about your relationship."

"*That's* what this is about?" Palmer shoots back, scathing. "You're pissed we're not getting married?"

"You've been dating the guy since high school, Palmer. If he's so serious about you, then why not propose?"

Now it's Palmer who grows quiet, while June begins chopping at something aggressively.

"The man runs full-speed from any sort of real, adult commitment, and you enable his behavior, chasing him through bars night after night like some lovesick groupie. Trust me, I did the emotional hamster wheel thing with your dad for years, and I want so much better for you—"

"That's not how it is with us," Palmer cuts in. "Mojo's nothing like Dad. And you're wrong about him running from commitment."

"Are you sure we're talking about the same person here?" June quips. "Because the Moises I know spends all his time goofing off with his friends, playing rock music, drinking and smoking and God knows what else, and you're right there with him, supporting his bad habits without so much as a basic plan for the future."

"He's trying to make something of his music, Mom. That is his future!"

"And where does that leave you, exactly? What about *your* future?"

Leif bounds out of the hallway and—rolling his eyes when he hears the bickering—grabs my hand, yanking me into the kitchen. June is flailing a wooden spoon in the air, while Palmer is pummeling a garden salad into submission. Both of them wear red, flustered faces. June manages a tight smile at the sight of Leif and I.

"We're ready to *eeeeat!*" he announces in a sing-songy voice.

"Great! So are we." June throws her daughter a look that says their argument is far from over. "Since the weather cleared up so nicely, I thought it'd be nice to sit outside. I've got everything ready. Show Dell to the table, will you please, Leify?"

He leads me through a sliding glass door and down a second set of stairs to June's back patio. The yard is moderate in size, but bursting with lush, exotic flowers, some of which I've never seen before. They tangle up trellises, undulate across tree limbs, and dangle from the mossy beams of a wooden pergola, all of them drizzled in tiny rain droplets, winking like diamonds in the night.

Beneath the pergola, under a canopy of fuchsia blooms, a round wicker table is set for five. Citronella candles are scattered over it, casting a lovely ambient glow. Leif climbs into one of the chairs and points to the seat beside him. "This one's for you, Dell," he lisps with a grin, peering at me through his too-big glasses.

I take my seat and Bear stomps over to me, wedging his snout underneath my hand. I rub the patch of fur between his eyes and he closes them lazily, drifting into a massage-induced trance.

According to the settings prepared at the table, the only person yet to arrive for dinner is Palmer's boyfriend, Mojo, one of the mop-headed musicians from Barracuda's Teeth and quite the polarizing figure in the Marin household. I silently thank my lucky stars that I won't have to suffer through a meal with any of the other Klynes tonight.

Palmer joins us outside, dropping the salad bowl at the center of the table before plopping into a chair and avoiding my eyes. I can't blame her for not wanting me around. Between our confrontation yesterday and the argument I'd just overheard, I know way more about my cousin's personal life than I should. I hope she knows this is as uncomfortable for me as it is for her. Maybe even more so.

I sit stiffly in my seat, a spastic pinch gnawing at my lower back. Leif hums a song and taps the beat against Bear's wet nose, making the dog's eyes flicker open sporadically. Palmer twists her fingers in her hair, stewing in her private discontent. For a long minute, we sit in awkward silence, with only the distant trill of cicadas to fill the night.

Eventually, Palmer's the first to disrupt the quiet, with a question directed at me. "So how long will you be in Halcyon Bay?" Blunt. To the point.

"Just for the weekend."

She nods, likely relieved by my answer. The sooner I leave, the better. "It's been, what, twenty years since you were last here?"

"Yeah, just about."

"That's a long time."

I nod.

"Do you remember much about the island?"

"No. I was pretty young when we left."

"How young?"

"Like, four."

"So you're twenty-four now?"

"Yep."

Our exchange feels as painful as having teeth extracted. I'd almost rather return to the silence, but then Palmer says, in an oddly genuine manner, "Guess we must've known each other when we were kids."

I meet her eyes and, surprisingly, find no pretense within them, no ulterior motive or swirl of catty acrimony. Just a sincere thought and honest expression. It's crazy to think that we once knew each other, maybe played together, maybe even cared for one another before circumstances drove our lives in vastly different directions.

"How old are you?" I ask her. She looks about my age, maybe a little older. Or maybe more sophisticated.

"Twenty-three."

"And I'm seven!" Leif chimes in.

"Not yet, you're not," Palmer says.

"Well, I'm *almost* seven…in two months!"

"Why're you in such a hurry to grow up, Shrimp? What's wrong with being six?"

Leif shoots his sister a judicious look. "Six is for babies. When I'm seven, I can do things."

"Here we are!" June's voice rings as she bounds down the stairs with a basket of dinner rolls and butter. "Some fresh bread to start…" She flies around the table, setting a piece on each plate before scurrying back up and inside the house.

"Hope you like bouillabaisse!" Leif licks his lips.

"I'm not sure I even know how to pronounce *bouillabaisse*," I say, butchering the word terribly. Leif cracks a toothy grin, and even Palmer manages a smile.

"It's like fish stew," she explains, "only better, because it's French. It's one of Mom's specialties."

"Cool. Leif tells me she's a chef."

Palmer nods. "She runs a local catering business called Gather. Works all sorts of corporate events, weddings, graduations…"

June shuffles out again with a large black pot in her gloved hands. The pot is smoking, bubbling like a cauldron, filling the yard with the fragrant aroma of cooked seafood. Bear pops his head up and sniffs the air, a dreamy glaze in his eyes.

"It smells delicious," I comment, and the dog barks his consent.

"Well, it should," June laughs, setting the pot down on a trivet. "Took me three years to get the recipe just right."

"Mommy says cooking is an art form," Leif informs me with an adorably serious expression. "Just like coloring."

"That's right, baby." June begins ladling stew onto each of our dishes. "Food is the finest of all the arts. If you've gotta eat it, it might as well be a damn masterpiece."

Leif chuckles in response.

"Do you cook, Dell?" June asks, spooning some bouillabaisse into my bowl. My stomach churns as shrimp, mussels, and clams slip out in a pool of spicy orange broth.

"Not well."

My aunt shakes her head, a nostalgic smile playing upon her face. "Funny…your mom didn't either."

This small observation cuts quick to my heart. "She still doesn't," I admit. "If it weren't for my dad and the godsend of takeout, we'd probably never eat at home."

Palmer snorts. "Takeout is sacrilege in this house."

June starts to say something, but is interrupted by a tanned young man prancing through the yard's side gate. He wears a short-sleeve button-down in a tropical flower print over a pair of tattered jeans and flip-flops. Several buttons at the top of his shirt are undone, exposing a chest tattoo and a woven leather necklace. The man flashes us a handsome grin, flipping his wavy black hair to one side. I recognize him as the singer from Barracuda's Teeth.

"Hi, Mojo," Leif calls excitedly, as Palmer bolts from the table to greet him.

Mojo holds up a bottle of white wine like a trophy, or maybe a peace offering, and flashes the table an apologetic smile. "Sorry for the delay, *familia*. Rehearsal ran late, but I come bearing provisions."

"Splendid," June murmurs.

"I'll pour." Palmer takes the bottle from Mojo's hands and runs upstairs to fetch wine glasses.

He doesn't know about the pregnancy, either, I realize, confounded by the depths of my cousin's secrecy. It's none of my business, and certainly not my place to say, but I can't help but hope that Palmer knows what she's doing, keeping this to herself.

Approaching the dinner table, Mojo musses Leif's hair as if he were his own little brother. He's more measured with June, kissing her modestly on the cheek. "Smells *delicioso*, Mrs. M. Thanks for having me."

"Thanks for showing up, Mojo," she responds with a forced smile, waving a hand at the table. "Please, have a seat."

"*¡Gracias!*" He slides into the open chair, smirking when his eyes land on me. "You must be the infamous cousin I've heard so much about."

"Her name is Dell," June responds testily.

Mojo's eyes widen as he lifts his hands in the air, like a bank robber caught mid-heist. "I was only fooling around, Mrs. M! Didn't mean anything by it, I swear. It's great to meet you, Dell. Really, really great."

"Same to you," I say, trying not to crack a smile. I'm not sure June would appreciate it.

While Palmer circles the table with wine, Leif leans in close to me, whispering loudly, "Mojo's such a funny dude. Mommy thinks so too. She even calls him a clown sometimes when—"

"All right!" June interjects. "Less talking, more eating. *Bon appétit.*"

I dig into my plate to keep from laughing, and find myself humming with delight from the first bite. I relish in that heaping mouthful, savoring every delicious flavor dancing upon my taste buds. "Wow. This is amazing."

My aunt beams. "Thank you! That's quite a compliment from a down-easter like yourself. The seafood in Maine is beyond compare."

I pause my chewing, intrigued by her cursory revelation. "You've been to Maine?"

"Uh…yes, I have. Once." Her smile pulls tight, eyes flitting around the table. She changes the subject. "What do you do back home, Dell?"

I clear my throat to stall for a moment, racking my brain for ways to make the truth sound more interesting than it is. "I work at an ad agency. I'm what they call a Junior Strategist." The others stare at me expectantly, awaiting some compelling detail or show of passion, but I have dismally little to impart. "It's just a temp job," I add lamely. "Not all that exciting."

"I work in retail," Palmer offers with a shrug. "Little tourist boutique downtown. Not all that exciting either."

This is…different. *Is Palmer being nice to me?*

"You know you always have a job at Gather, Palm," June tells her daughter. "Summer's our busiest season, and it's always helpful to have an extra pair of hands around—"

"Yes, Mom, I'm aware." Palmer taps her fingernails on her armrest. "But I need to figure out my own thing, you know? I can't just fall into yours because it's easy."

June glares at her and Mojo jumps in, likely in an attempt to cut some of the fast-growing tension. "So, Dell, Palmer tells me you caught our set last night. Any thoughts? Comments? Suggestions for the band?" He raises his dark eyebrows meaningfully, eager for my reaction.

I try to appear enthusiastic despite not having paid a lick of attention to the music. I'd been too wrapped in island folklore and a certain green-eyed fisherman to notice much else. "Yeah, you guys were great. The crowd was totally eating it up."

Mojo smiles, seemingly relieved to get a positive review no matter how bland or unimaginative. "Thanks! 'Cudas is one of our usual spots, and we've got a pretty solid local following. It's harder to book gigs at the bigger bars in town…or anywhere outside of Halcyon Bay."

"It'll happen," Palmer says encouragingly before turning to me. "The band's blowing up on streaming sites. They recorded an EP in one of our friends' garage-slash-studio, without any backing from a label, and the sound is *unreal*."

"That's great. I'll have to keep an ear out. What's your band's name again?"

"The Knotty Talismen," Mojo says proudly. Come to think of it, I do remember hearing that last night, right as I was running for the bathroom, before my fateful encounter with Palmer. "We're indie-psych meets surf rock—"

"And *I'm* an honorary Talisman," Leif interrupts with a cheeky smile. June snorts at this, and her son's little brow furrows. "What? It's true, Mojo said so."

"Please eat your dinner, Leify."

Our conversation fades, the night filled with the din of scraping spoons and sipped drinks. I swish my wine round and round in my glass, glancing at the others—these strangers, my family—memorizing their various quirks and peculiarities. Leif's low humming, his bulky glasses sliding down the ski-slope curve of his nose. Palmer's hair twirling, her eyes darting nervously at Mojo like she's desperate to say something but afraid she'll miss her chance. June nibbling her bottom lip, whirling her spoon in her bowl, distracted by some mysterious inner conflict.

Is my aunt thinking the same thing as me, wondering how to bring the conversation around to matters of importance? How to put words to the feelings bearing down on her heart? How to get to the crux of why I'm here?

"Why did my mother leave Halcyon Bay?"

My question slips out with little effort, slicing through the thick summer air and the quiet.

Everyone at the table gapes back at me, caught off guard by my unprecipitated outburst.

Awkward. So awkward.

"I'm sorry," I say. "I've just always wondered…"

June's response is careful, deliberate. "Well. There are many reasons for that, I think. At the time, things were complicated at home. And your mom…she just…needed a break."

I nod, deciding to ask yet another risky question, one with the potential to hijack June's family dinner and drive us straight into the ground.

"Was it because of Willow?"

CHAPTER FIFTEEN

Apart from the gentle stirring of wind and the far-off chirping of insects, the world is painfully still in the wake of my question. June's face runs pale with deep and utter shock, while my cheeks flush red with instant regret. I've wrecked the evening in one fell swoop, my words like a defibrillator to my poor aunt's heart, forever altering the comfortable rhythm of things.

"Your sister, Willow," I repeat softly, as if there's any chance June missed her name the first time. "I know she drowned on the beach behind Cliffmoor House."

My aunt opens her mouth, but all that comes out is a small choking sound, like a wounded animal.

"Is that what drove my mom away?" I ask.

June swallows, pushing past the tangled thickets of emotion within. When she speaks, her voice is a whispered rasp. "You know about Willow?"

I nod and she exhales, the hurt swimming in her watery eyes creating a sharp pressure in my chest. I feel compelled to explain.

"I was at the library today looking at Virginia's book collection, and while I was there, I did some research. There's a lot I don't know about the Klynes, and I just…wanted to make sense of things."

June stares down at her dish, pushing clams around without attempting another bite.

"Please," I say, my voice a fragile, quiet thing. I'm not even sure what I'm asking her for. Confirmation, denial, or something else entirely? "Is there anything, *anything* you can tell me?"

She shuts her eyes, shoulders rising as she draws in a breath. "Your mom took Willow's death particularly hard," she says faintly. I lean in to hear her over the hammering of my heartbeat. "We all struggled, but it was different for her."

She runs her palms along the cream-colored tablecloth, wrinkles digging into her eyes as she unearths the buried layers of her past. "If I have to pinpoint one singular reason why my sister left, then yes, I'd say it was because of Willow's accident."

"Accident?" Poking any further may be a harsh twist of the knife, but I'm too far gone by this point. I need to know the truth. "There was some debate about that in the articles I read."

"Yes, I imagine there would be." June sighs again. "We had our doubts for some time, but that's all it was in the end…a terrible accident."

A moment's silence comes over us like a thick woolen blanket— stifling, heavy, prickly—until I work up the nerve to ask, "Is she buried here, on the island? I'd like to pay my respects if I can."

My aunt nods. "She's buried at the Halcyon Bay Cemetery, in the family tomb."

"The family tomb?" I suppress an inner shudder, the Klynes seeming more ghoulish and antiquated by the second.

"My father commissioned it years ago. We're all meant to be buried there," June muses listlessly. "All except my mother, who chose to be cremated and have her remains spread at sea."

Palmer makes a tiny sound under her breath—a cross between a scoff and a grunt.

"What?" her mother asks.

"Nothing," Palmer replies innocently. "It's just that the Klyne tomb is *creep city*. I wouldn't want to be locked up there either, in this life or the next."

June doesn't disagree. "It was modeled after the mausoleums of Louisiana," she explains for my benefit. "My father expected it to be a new family tradition. Ambrose is big on his traditions." Her eyes meet mine. "Did you know that we lived in Louisiana for a short time? Back when we were schoolgirls?"

I didn't know that. "My mom too?"

"Yes." She smiles a little. "We were there a little less than a year while Cliffmoor House was being renovated. Our father remained on the island to oversee the remodel, while Mother went with us to live in New Orleans—her hometown. They bought this rambling estate in the Garden District, and that's where we stayed."

"How old was she?"

"Your mom? Let me think. I was…twelve, so that would've made Laurel fifteen."

"I had no idea."

"Oh, we loved it. The music, the people, the food. It's what inspired me to become a chef." After seconds of hesitation, she adds, "Willow was born there, actually."

"She was?"

"Mhm. By the time we moved back to Cliffmoor House, our family had a fifth member, and, to my father's dismay, a serious estrogen imbalance."

"I can't imagine living with so many women," Mojo chimes in, mashing a bread roll into his mouth.

Palmer shoots him a thorny look.

He gulps. "I just mean that I come from a family with a lot of men, you know? Brothers, uncles, cousins. It was testosterone overload twenty-four seven. A house full of girls is, like, a foreign concept to me. We were a rowdy bunch of *cabrones,* raising hell and running amok. Someone's balls were always in your face—"

Palmer rams her elbow into Mojo's ribcage so hard, I swear I hear it crack. He doubles over, groaning, while Leif giggles uncontrollably.

June closes her eyes and exhales in disapproval. She rises to her feet, muttering, "I'll be back with dessert," before stalking upstairs to the kitchen.

"What the—*ow!*" Mojo cries, rubbing his side as he peers at Palmer with wide, wounded eyes. "What'd I do?"

Palmer doesn't answer. Staring straight ahead, she grabs her water and takes a prudish sip. I notice she hasn't touched her wine all night.

"Great. The silent treatment. *No bueno.*" Mojo shifts his pained gaze to Leif. "What do you think, little man? What'd I do this time?"

"Well…" Leif laces his pudgy fingers together and sets them on the table in a judicious manner, as if he were a doctor preparing to diagnose some malady. "Maybe she's mad about the balls thing."

Palmer slams her hand on the table. "Leif!"

"What!" Leif yells back. "Mojo asked!"

"Babe, c'mon!" Mojo jumps in feebly. "I was only messing around with—"

His words are cut short by a second elbow to the ribs. This time, the cracking sound is even more discernible than the first, as are the explicit sputterings of pain erupting from his lips.

June returns with dessert and a pinched lip, taking in the scene— Leif, head tossed back wildly and cackling; Palmer, unperturbed, picking off a bit of lint from her shirt; Mojo, slumped over, forehead pressed to the tablecloth, groaning into the night like some hell-bent specter.

My aunt opts not to comment on any of it.

"So"—she swats a few stray hairs from her face—"who wants a slice of homemade key lime pie?"

Unsurprisingly, dessert is a quieter affair, with everyone mostly keeping to themselves and out of everyone else's way.

The second we finish and stand to clear the table, Leif plants himself before me, arms akimbo. He looks like a pint-sized superhero, with steely determination in his smile.

"Time for coloring!"

"Sure," I say, "but shouldn't we clean up first?"

"Go ahead, Dell," June says lightly, though there's a whirlwind brewing in her strained expression. "We'll take care of clean up."

Mojo's eyes widen as I retreat, mouthing a desperate plea for *Help!* But with Leif dragging me back inside the house at breakneck speed, there's nothing I can do about the verbal reaming he's sure to get from one or both of the Marin women in my absence.

Leif leads me to a midnight-blue bedroom decorated in an outer space theme. A three-dimensional model of the solar system dangles from the ceiling, the pillowcases and bed sheets bear a swirling pattern of planets and constellations, and the walls—speckled in glow-in-the-dark stars—are covered in Leif's artwork. As expected, some of the drawings are of various space-related objects, while others are of smiling people, turquoise waters, and fang-toothed animals.

"I drew this one for you," he says, handing me a colorful sheet of paper.

It's the two of us, our names scrawled across the top of the page in his childlike print. We're standing in a wide blue pool—the sea, if I had to guess—holding hands, with the sun shining down from a cloudy sky. He's drawn a wide smile across his face, curving up from cheek to cheek. But, strangely, my character isn't smiling. Instead, Leif has drawn me a large red O for lips, so I look perpetually terror-stricken, in a constant state of alarm.

He peers at me. "Do you like it?"

"Very much. Thank you." I can't stop staring at my startled face. Is this how he sees me? How *all* of them see me?

Leif instructs me to sit, and I sink to the floor, legs crossed. He pulls two unmarked sheets from a coloring book on jungle animals, and I begin filling in a tiger's stripes while he works diligently on a tree-scaling chimp.

While we color, he tells me about school, the classes he likes, and the girls who are mean to him. I listen mostly, nodding along until he runs out of things to say and begins humming the theme song to *SpongeBob SquarePants*.

Spending time with him is surprisingly easy, and that's saying a lot, because I'm not too comfortable around children. I have little experience with them, and minimal patience for their whims, moods, and prevailing whininess. But, to my relief, being around Leif is effortless, uncomplicated, even enjoyable. He's a sweet kid with an impressively honed wit. No wonder he's got the family wrapped around his little finger.

After about twenty minutes of coloring, Palmer appears in the doorway. "Break time, Shrimp. It's Mom's turn to hang with Dell."

Leif hangs his head, crushed by this news. "But we just started!"

"You know what they say, sharing is caring."

"Sharing sucks," Leif complains under his breath.

I hold up my tiger for him to see, hoping it might cheer him up. "What do you think? Do I pass the test?"

He turns his head this way and that, inspecting my work. "It's all right…" He takes the sheet to observe it more closely, holding it up to the light, closing one of his eyes. I get the sense that he's not overly impressed. "Don't worry, Dell," he says, shooting me a mischievous little grin. "I'll fix this up real nice for you."

Back in the kitchen, Mojo stands at the sink, drying the last of the dishes while June brews some coffee. "Would you like?" she asks when she spots me.

"Please."

She pours me a cup and another for herself, wrapping her shoulders in a soft knit blanket. "Come join me out on the porch."

We settle onto her rusty porch swing, neither of us speaking right away, but the silence is agreeable rather than awkward. Despite the borderline offensive mugginess of the day, the evening has grown oddly pleasant and breezy. I lean back as we swing in tandem, back and forth, back and forth, sinking into the calm and the quiet.

Palmer comes out to join us after a while, trailed loyally by Bear. She slumps down onto the porch deck, her back pressed to the nearest wall, and the dog crawls into her lap.

"You have a face full of questions," June says gently, studying me in the dim porch light. "If I'm honest, I have some too."

I sit up a little straighter.

"Please don't take this the wrong way," she says. "I'm thrilled to have you here, but I have to ask…why did you come? I know it wasn't for your grandmother. You wouldn't go to all this trouble for some woman you don't know."

June's eyes search my face for answers, a worried crease spreading over her brow. She looks more like Mom than ever before. "I guess what I really want to know is how Laurel is doing."

I don't answer right away, debating what to share and what to hold close. Last night, I'd told Briggs that Mom was fine. It was a knee-jerk response, an impulse to protect her the way I always have. And while I still don't want to get into the gritty details, I can't just lie to June, either.

My aunt asks again, tentatively, "Is she…all right? Getting the, um…the help she needs?"

I narrow my eyes. "How do you know—"

She sighs so despondently that my words turn to dust on my tongue. One look at her, and I know there's more to this story, far more than I know.

"I figured you probably wouldn't remember," she says.

An uneasy tingle climbs up my spine. "Remember what?"

"The time I visited you all in Woodbridge."

"I'm sorry, what?"

June bunches her shoulders around her ears. "It was a long time ago. I was only at your house for a couple of hours. Your mom set me up at an inn nearby so I wouldn't have to stay over."

"Why don't I know about this?" My mind reels, flicking from present to past, searching for June's face or voice in my memory, only to come up short. How is it possible that she'd come to visit and I'd had no idea?

"I don't think she wanted you to know," she says wistfully, "about me or anyone else from back home."

"But shouldn't I still remember *something?*" I insist. "How old was I, anyway?"

"You were little," June explains. "Six or seven, maybe. And your mom didn't tell you I was her sister. I think she called me…an old friend."

So she lied to me, I realize in silence, a simmering heat surging through my veins. She hadn't just omitted the painful bits, but outright *lied.* How many times was that now? How many lies had I been spoon-fed my entire life?

Those strange feelings of loss that I'd shouldered—the lack of family and sense of abandonment, the relentless uncertainty I could never shake—all rush back to me now. I'd spent years trying to sharpen the blurry edges of my memory, to remember a face or a name or *anything* from my past, only to fail miserably time after time. My own parents had doomed me to that hazy labyrinth of questions, misleading me at each turn, condemning me to darkness.

"She had her reasons, and I understood," June continues. "Laurel had to do what was best for you, but I was in a rotten place. I'd been having problems with Drake, my ex-husband. He'd decided to move out—the first of many times. I'd just suffered a miscarriage. Willow was dead. Your mom was gone. Just like that, I'd lost two sisters, a child, and my husband." June breathes heavily, leadened by a sadness too fierce for words. "So one night, on a whim, I left Palmer with my parents and booked a red eye to Maine. I didn't have a plan. I just wanted to see my sister. Bizarre as it may sound, we were very close once."

"And she didn't turn you away?" It's a stupid question to ask, after all that June had said, but I can't wrap my head around my mother blatantly lying to me. Why would she do that? What, or who, was she keeping me from?

June shakes her head. "Granted, she was surprised to see me. Worried that you might become confused by my being there. Worried you might…get the wrong impression."

"The wrong impression of what?"

"I suppose she didn't want you knowing that you'd left people behind here. People that still loved you, and wanted to know you," she says sadly. "I think she was afraid that you might come looking for us someday. Kind of like you did now."

There's an earnestness in June's face that makes me want to spill everything, to nick a proverbial vein and bleed out for her, extending my trust like a warm embrace. But I *can't*. I can't go into detail about Mom, or the pain we'd all been living with for so long. I can't afford to break down that far, that deep.

Keeping my voice steady, I muster a morsel of truth. Small, but honest. She deserves that much.

"We admitted Mom to a treatment center recently. It's only a temporary arrangement, but they're helping her better than we can at home."

June nods, absorbing the blow of this information. "It's hard to imagine her in a place like that," she whispers, eyes gone misty. "But I saw it, all those years ago, when I went to visit. I saw something eating her up inside, threatening to pull her under."

My aunt turns to me. "I'm sorry, Dell. It can't have been easy for you growing up, carrying so much."

I stare straight ahead, swallowing down a ragged breath. *Don't you dare cry.*

"Does she know you're here?" June asks quietly.

I shake my head faintly, shame and emotion stretching across my insides, dragging me down like deadweight.

My aunt seems to understand, as if the hurt that mars my soul had made a home of hers too. She swallows. "I miss her, you know. I miss Lo so much."

The name pricks my ears like a dozen acupuncture needles. "*Lo?*"

A ghost of a smile dances across June's lips, her face steeped in far-gone memory. "Laurel hated her name when we were younger. She used to go by Lo back then. I'm sure she outgrew the nickname over the years, but I never did."

The floor beneath me tilts like I've missed a pivotal step in this maze I'm running. Lo was my *mother's* nickname?

Just when I thought I'd started scraping at the core of things—celebrating what I foolishly believed was a breakthrough—I'm wrenched right back to square one. If Lo had nothing to do with Willow, then did that mean the object of Mom's torment was…herself?

I clear my throat, struggling to keep my thoughts lucid and plain. "Earlier, you mentioned that Willow's death was an accident." From the way June's watery eyes glimmer at me through the shadows, I can tell she'd been waiting for this topic to resurface. "Do you really believe that?"

"The police ruled it an accident," June says gently.

Palmer squirms a little in place. Bear lifts his head, momentarily confused by her shifting weight beneath him. She seems pensive, like she hadn't given much thought to my story until this night—this conversation—and was being forced to second-guess everything she'd thought about me, every hateful word we'd exchanged without reason.

"But are you certain?" I ask again.

"I thought the circumstances were shady," my aunt admits. "I had a lot of questions back then. Doubts about the integrity of the investigation. Now I guess I've made my peace with the official record."

"What kind of questions did you have?"

June shakes her head, swinging solemnly.

"Questions about Abraham Urban?" I probe again.

The name had stuck with me ever since I'd read that article. The Klynes had issued a restraining order against a local man named Abraham Urban for loitering around Willow before her death. He'd stalked her at swimming competitions, even once attempted to kidnap her from a locker room. And he was the only person questioned in relation to her drowning.

"You've done your research." June closes her eyes and takes a sip of coffee. "He was one of many questions, yes."

She doesn't elaborate, her cryptic words hanging like thick fog between us.

"Do you mind telling me—"

"Dell…" June interrupts me, her whispered voice filled with deliberation. She runs a hand across her brow. "I'm sorry to let you down, honey. I know you must have so many questions. But I can't speak more on this tonight, it won't do either of us any good. Not with Mother's funeral this weekend, and emotions running high as they are."

Her words trail off into silence, and I can't help but feel ashamed for adding to her heartache. I'd been reckless to grill her about Willow's drowning, especially in light of the fact that she'd be scattering her mother's ashes in a few short hours.

My tunnel vision made me greedy, insensitive to grief. But if I want to get anywhere with these people, I'll have to be tactful, delicate. Prodding them like cattle won't amount to anything.

June sets a hand on my arm, warmth radiating from her skin to mine. She shoots me a knowing, motherly look. Empathetic but firm. "Don't burden yourself too much with this. Make your peace with it and let it go."

I understand well the intimation in her eyes, the cautionary words she doesn't dare vocalize.

Don't let this consume you the way it did your mother. That's what she means, what she truly fears. But I can't give up now, can't pack it in and spend the rest of my life wondering.

I've ventured too far down this rabbit hole not to keep digging.

CHAPTER SIXTEEN

Mojo and Palmer offer to drop me back at Cliffmoor House, a true kindness, considering my pathetic sense of direction and my soggy, illegible map. I sink into the backseat of the rusty Jeep Wrangler as we drive off, Virginia's bike clanging against the back rack. Palmer glances at me sideways from the passenger's seat, but I don't have it in me to dwell on why. My mind is still back at June's house, lingering on the endless questions she'd left unanswered, along with others I hadn't even thought to ask.

Mojo fiddles with the radio, tuning it to a song with electrifying guitar riffs and jarring cymbal crashes. He taps his fingertips on the steering wheel as he drives, breaking our otherwise pervading silence when he says with a teasing smile, "Your mom was rather on edge today."

Palmer rolls her eyes. "Just having us around puts Mom on edge."

I stare out the window, fully aware that this conversation isn't meant for my ears.

"It's okay, babe," Mojo assures her with a laugh. "I'm used to living at the top of June's shit list. It's kinda cozy up there."

"Not funny," Palmer complains. "The fighting is near constant now that Gram's…now that she's…"

I press my forehead to the cool glass, feeling like my presence is an intrusion on their privacy. But then the Jeep careens over a speed bump at full-throttle, and I instantly pull back. With Mojo at the wheel, a second head injury seems all too attainable.

Eventually, Palmer picks up where she left off. "I mean, I get it, to an extent. And I empathize with her, I really do. I can tell she's hurting. Planning the services and trying to keep it together for Leif…it's been hard. But at the same time, it's like she's bottling up all her anger and projecting it onto us. We're easy targets, the low-hanging fruit."

"It's all my fault, really," Mojo says. "I've terminally corrupted her daughter. She has to hate me on principle."

"Hey!" Palmer smacks his arm. "I was corrupted long before you came along. And if you don't want Mom to hate you, maybe you should try being a better conversationalist."

"I'm a great conversationalist!"

Palmer grunts in response, twisting her fingers through a lock of golden hair. "The least you could do is to stick to family-friendly topics at the dinner table, around Leif."

"What do you mean? I was *extra* family-friendly tonight!"

She glares at him. "On what planet are balls considered 'family-friendly?'"

Mojo opens his mouth to protest, then promptly shuts it and hangs his head dramatically, dark hair spilling over his face. "Alas," he laments, assuming a British accent. "How dare I be so brazen as to speaketh of human anatomy? Oh, for shame! Assemble the villagers with their pitchforks, my hour of reckoning approaches!"

Palmer rolls her eyes again, but I can see she's trying not to laugh. "You're. An. Idiot."

I snort my consensus, and she whips around to face me. I think for a moment that she might be annoyed at my disruption, but to my surprise, she just smiles.

"Mojo has a hard time understanding the complexities of our mother-daughter relationship," she explains.

A cell phone lights up the Jeep's center console, and Mojo lifts it to the steering wheel, scanning a text on his screen. "Leon's got a keg over on Sandspur." He tosses his eyes in Palmer's direction. "Interested?"

"Um…" She turns to me. "Do you need to get back right away, Dell?"

I shake my head no. I have nowhere to be, and nothing but time to kill.

"Cool if we make a little detour, then?"

"Fine by me." I can't believe she's inviting me along. What a whopping difference twenty-four hours makes.

Mojo swings an immediate right, and before I know it, we're parking curbside by a weathered sign reading *Public Access*. We hop out into the black night, and I yank off my boots, leaving them in the backseat. A winking of fire in the distance acts as our compass as we traipse across the sand. Mojo drapes an arm around Palmer's waist, kissing her shoulder, tucking her in close. She dips her head onto his chest, molding to him easily. For all their banter and bickering, they seem to care for each other deeply, solid and impenetrable, despite whatever outside pressures they're facing.

We approach the blaze and about thirty people come into view, congregated around a bonfire near the shoreline. Lira is among the party crowd, perched on a long piece of driftwood, chin resting in her palm as she nurses a cigarette. My heart skips a beat when I think I see Hatch laughing among the flickering, shadowed faces. It isn't him, though, just a trick of the shifting firelight, and I'm irritated with myself for wishing it was.

Palmer and Mojo approach two guys by the keg. One is pasty and freckled, with drugstore-enhanced red hair to match the Red Solo cup in his hand. He pours himself a beer, howling with laughter at something his friend said. The other guy is black with a muscular build and long dreadlocks pulled into a ponytail. His palmetto print shirt is unbuttoned, revealing a set of rock-hard abs underneath. He breaks into a bright, attractive smile when he spots us.

"Ey, ey, ey, party's here!" he whoops, pulling Palmer and Mojo into a strong bear hug.

I hang back to survey the others gathered around the fire, taking note of a group of guys fawning over a girl in a strapless black mini-dress. The girl's pin-straight hair falls down to her waist, her honey skin gleaming. She looks every bit like a supermodel—leggy and lithe and way too sophisticated for the slew of surf bums ogling her. Meanwhile, I'm serving just-rolled-out-of-bed chic, with a side of clumpy mascara eyes. I shake my wet hair from its bun and run my fingers through it so it looks like maybe I went for a swim.

"Dell!" Palmer waves me over. Tugging at the hem of my biker shorts, I join the group, my face blooming with heat.

"Boys, meet my brand new cousin, Meridel," she announces, using Leif's amusing descriptor from earlier today, and making me feel like a show-and-tell item. "Don't call her that, though—she'll bite your head off if you do. It's *Dell*." She drags out the sound of my name teasingly. "These are Mojo's bandmates, Finch and Leon." She waves a hand at Red Solo and Eight Pack, respectively.

"Brand new cousin?" Leon rubs his hands together, his eyes drinking in the sight of me like a refreshing summer cocktail. "Like, 'right out of the packaging' new? 'New car smell and shiny rims' new?"

Palmer rolls her eyes at his attempt at flirtation. "Please stop talking. I can't take the secondhand embarrassment."

"Lighten up, Palm. Dell doesn't mind." Leon flashes me another brilliant white smile. "Allow me to be the first to welcome you to paradise—"

"Dude, there's no way you're the first," Finch interjects.

Leon shoots him eyes like daggers. "I'm sorry, who's talking to *you?*"

"I'm just saying, man. She's got family here and stuff, so you're probably not the *first* person to welcome her to the island. Probably more like the *eleventh,* or something." Finch raises his dyed red eyebrows. "Kinda loses its impact after a while."

Leon groans, rubbing a hand across his brow. "Why do you always have to make shit so weird, bro? Is there literally no one else on this beach you can harass?"

"None half as entertaining as you."

Mojo's eyes flick between his squabbling friends, a smirk ghosting across his lips. "God, it's adorable when you two lovebirds fight."

In response, Finch makes a show of chugging back a freshly poured beer. It takes him all of three seconds to down it before crunching the cup in his hand, pounding his fists against his chest, and breaking out in a wild Tarzan yell.

Leon shakes his head disapprovingly.

"What do you all play in the band?" I ask them, stifling a laugh.

Leon answers, "Bass guitar. And occasional backup vocals. It's a tough job, but someone's gotta keep this jack-hole on key." He punches Mojo lightly in the ribs, causing him to wince, already sore from one too many elbows over dinner.

Finch is too distracted to answer, bouncing around like his feet have springs. He reaches for a fresh cup, spins on his heel, and lobs the tap over his head only to catch it in the cup. "Hole in one!" he cries triumphantly, rewarding himself with another generous pour.

"Yo, Bird Brain." Leon grips his fire-haired friend by the neck. "I believe the lady asked you a question."

Finch turns to me with a loopy smile. "Drums. I'm the heartbeat of this little operation. Whenever you feel the music hit you down deep in your soul"—he shoots me an exaggerated wink—"you know who to thank."

Before I can respond, he shimmies away to the fireside, where he starts flapping his arms like an electrocuted bird and making a series of raucous *cacaw* sounds.

"Attention whore," Leon mutters under his breath, while Lira and the others roar at Finch's theatrics.

"Didn't Bird say he was gonna be more diligent with his Adderall?" Mojo asks, eyebrows raised.

"You believed him?" Leon retorts. "The guy also says his hair turns red naturally in the sun. Can't trust him for shit."

Palmer and I exchange an amused look, a chuckle. Our tentative camaraderie, while still a bit strange, is a nice reprieve from the animosity that ping-ponged between us last night and this morning.

"Cool shirt, new girl," Leon purrs, leaning in to get a better look at my ratty tee. His eyes linger on my chest a second longer than necessary before flicking back up to my face.

"Oh. Thanks."

Leon's expression is balmy as the night, his smile broad. "Bet you look good in just about anything though…and *out* of anything too."

Mojo bursts out in a howling fit of laughter.

"Ew, Leon, what the hell! Creep, much?" Palmer grabs my hand and begins dragging me away.

"Aw, c'mon!" he calls after us, arms wide. "It was a compliment!"

"Keep it in your swim trunks next time, Romeo," she calls over her shoulder, flipping him the middle finger as she tugs me toward the bonfire. I can sense Leon's eyes on my back, my ass, as we walk.

"Ignore him, he's harmless," Palmer whispers in my ear. "Hits on anything with a pulse, but totally harmless."

"Palm!"

It's the tanned, modelesque girl in the skin-tight mini dress. She reaches out to Palmer with outstretched hands, wiggling her long, graceful fingers excitedly. "When did you get here? I thought you were tied up tonight." Her voice is a sultry coo that could seduce a priest.

"Just now," Palmer says, embracing her friend. "We came straight from dinner at Mom's house."

The girl flutters her voluminous eyelashes. "We?"

"Sash, this is my cousin, Dell." Palmer pulls me to the forefront. "Dell, this is Sasha, my best friend."

Sasha narrows her pretty eyes at me. "Dell."

It's not much of a hello, but I decide to be the bigger person.

"Hey." I offer her a smile, but Sasha doesn't catch it, already shifting her crackling chestnut eyes back to Palmer's face.

"Is this the one you met at your grandmother's will reading?" she asks flippantly, as if I'm utterly invisible and not standing *right here.*

"Well, technically, we met last night." Palmer giggles, like this is all so comical in hindsight. "I bumped into Dell at 'Cuda's, but I didn't know who she was. Isn't that weird?"

Sasha's eyes are contemplative, as if she's trying to decide how great a threat I am. "Small world."

"And getting smaller. Guess who spent the evening chatting up Dell at the bar?"

Crap, I think. *Please no. Don't drag him into this.*

"Who?" Sasha asks.

I silently beg Palmer not to say his name, not to open up this inevitable can of worms, but it's too late. The encounter is too freaking noteworthy not to share.

"Hatcher Seaborn."

Sasha's eyes drill into mine, glimmering with rage, like hot wax dripping onto my skin. "You know Hatcher?" Her tone is soft and deliberate, menacingly so.

"We just got to talking." I try to sound as indifferent as possible. "It was no big deal."

"Oh, yeah? Just two passing strangers in the night?" A furious little smile crawls across Sasha's lips while a vein throbs near her collarbone. The sickening, rapid pulse of it draws my eye. "How sweet."

"It wasn't all that—"

"You know how charming he can be, Sash," Palmer cuts in.

"Yes. I do." Sasha's eyes flash. "Look, Dell"—she says my name like it's something abhorrent—"take it from someone who knows Hatcher *very* well…steer clear of him. Don't waste your time."

"I wasn't planning on—"

"Who're we talking about?" Lira barges in on the conversation, materializing from the fiery shadows. She smirks wolfishly at me. "Thought that was you, Humpty! How's the head wound treating you today?"

"Swell, thanks."

"We were just warning Dell about the one-man-safety-hazard that is Hatcher Seaborn," Palmer says. I try my hardest to keep my face blank, but my insides feel like they've been hosed down with battery acid.

"What a coincidence," Lira says in that mocking manner of hers. "Seaborn came around earlier tonight, just before I got off my shift. He was asking for you, Humpty."

"He was?" This is the worst news I can possibly get right now, in front of this sorely hostile audience, but it doesn't stop my heart from leaping out of my chest.

"Mhm. He wanted to know if you'd been back to the bar. Even went so far as to ask if I knew where you might be staying."

Sasha snorts. "Well, that's rich."

Lira flicks her lip ring, giving me a conspiratorial wink. My popularity among the natives was already fast on the decline, but this revelation is the final nail on my coffin.

Mojo pokes his head over Palmer's shoulder, donning a pair of sunglasses in the near pitch-black darkness and making Shaka signs with both of his hands. He smells heavily of grass now. "'Sup, *muchachas.* Anyone craving a beverage?"

"Me!" I blurt, jumping at the chance for an escape.

Mojo points finger guns my way. "One lukewarm beer coming up for the new girl—"

"I'll go. You stay. I've got it." I stumble over my feet as I back off. The girl gang from hell watches on, shooting me varying expressions of disdain as I make my getaway.

Leon sits in a folding beach chair near the keg, holding a lighter to a small glass bowl, the night air around him stinking of musty earth. I silently grab a plastic cup from the stack and pour from the tap until a thick layer of foam rises, tossing it back while Leon takes a long hit.

The light pisswater taste of cheap beer fills my mouth, slides down my throat, and pools in my belly. I chug it down to the last drop in a matter of seconds.

"Like a champ, new girl!" Leon hoots when we both come up for air, pumping a lazy fist above his head. Dazed, he offers me the bowl.

"You want a hit?"

I lift my cup. "All good here. Thanks." I fill up for a second time.

Leon flicks the lighter again, puts the bowl to his lips, and pulls in another long, slow drag. When he's done—the air between us thick with a heavy, rolling haze—he lets out a weak cough. "You coming to our next show, new girl?" he asks, a sleepy expression in his eyes, already visibly stoned.

I detect some hopefulness in his question, but I'm quick to squash it. "Not too sure I'm welcome." In the distance, the girls are still clustered together, chatting and occasionally glancing in my direction.

Leon reclines in the sand, stretching out onto his side, washboard abs flexed. "Why not?" When he speaks, it sounds like his mouth is loaded with gum balls.

I take another sip. "Call it woman's intuition."

Whatever Leon says next is drowned out by Finch pouncing from the shadows, pinning him down, and dousing his head in beer. Leon's momentary shock dissipates as he scrambles to his knees, flipping Finch onto his back, sand spraying up around them. Some soft-core wrestling ensues with Finch cackling in either pain or amusement.

At some point, Mojo slips in beside me, reaching for the tap. "Having fun?"

"Like you wouldn't believe."

He chuckles, sunglasses dripping down the slope of his nose. "Did you try the hydroponic *hierba?* Homegrown by Leon's cousin's ex-wife's step uncle—"

"Not my thing," I cut him off, still watching his friends take turns pummeling each other.

"All right. Respect." Mojo pours himself another beer. "Palmer's not into the stuff much, either. Come to think of it, she's been cutting back on the drinking too. Probably some new health kick she's gonna try to rope me into."

I down another throatful of beer while Mojo rambles about my cousin's curtailed use of drugs and liquor. *This is Palmer's business, not mine,* I remind myself as I stare out at the endless stretch of black ocean.

"I heard the girls badgering you about Hatch," he says, swerving into a topic that *is* my business, or at least everyone wants to make it mine.

"Yeah. So?"

"Don't you want to know why they're all in such a tizzy?"

I shoot Mojo a look. "It's not rocket science."

Hatch had clearly made a bad name for himself around the island. Sowing his wild oats a bit too liberally, or something equally as contentious to get the girls all revved up and pissy. Funny to think that Hatch and I are both pariahs in our own right.

Mojo leans in close to my face, pushing his sunglasses up into his hair. His eyes are glassy and bloodshot. "Sasha is Hatch's ex-girlfriend," he whispers, as if it's some loaded secret.

"Thanks," I whisper back. "I got that much."

"No, no. Listen to me." He waves his hands emphatically, like I'm missing a pivotal part of this story. "She's got this demented vendetta against him now, see, and she's wrangled all the girls into drinking the Kool-Aid."

I sling back the rest of my beer and go in for round three. How I got caught up in the middle of this is well beyond my comprehension.

"Those shitty rumors going around about Hatch aren't true. Not even close," Mojo continues. "And it's messed up, 'cause he's one of the good guys, you know? Like...like a harmless little fly."

I take another slow sip, wondering where in the world he's going with this.

"Dude's all, like, buzzing around, doing his fly thing...when *bam!*" He slams his hands together and I jump, spilling beer foam all down my shirt front. "The man gets his ass caught in Sasha's web of chaos and hysteria."

Heart still pounding, I hold up my hand for Mojo to pause, and gratefully, he does, swaying a little in place. He blinks at me rapidly.

"Look, I recognize that you're trying to be nice here, trying to fill me in on context clues or whatever, but I *really* don't care what the deal is with Hatch."

Mojo makes a face like he doesn't believe me. "You don't?"

"I don't."

"But I thought you kind of…like him?"

"Like him?" I force a laugh. "I don't even know him. And I'm not about to insert myself into his stupid drama."

"But it's not his drama, it's Sasha's."

"His, hers—same difference."

"C'mon." Mojo smirks, his head dangling off to one side. "Methinks you protest just a touch too much, Dell."

I raise my eyebrows, partially impressed by the vague reference, but entirely annoyed by his insistence. "*Hamlet,* really?"

He shrugs coolly. "Yeah, I Shakespeare'd that shit. I'm pretty scholarly for a dude-bro. And I'm calling it right now—you're into him. You just don't know it yet."

"What are you, some kind of wannabe matchmaker?"

"Depends. Does that make better money than music?" He laughs, his gaze veering toward the bonfire. "Oh, man—incoming. You might want to duck and cover."

I follow Mojo's eyes to the flickering blaze, instantly spotting Hatch among the throng of partiers. This time it is him, not just my imagination wishing for it.

He weaves through the crowd with that lopsided smile, his eyes locking on mine from afar, magnetic and utterly captivating. Neither of us attempt to pull our gaze away, even as an obvious flush rises in my cheeks.

Mojo leans over and whispers, "What was that you were saying about how much you *don't* like the dude?"

I feel my jaw clench. "How old are you, five?"

I contemplate aiming a few more well-placed elbows at his ribcage, but that would draw way too much attention. What I need to do is make a clean exit, and fast. "Let Palmer know I took off, okay?"

Mojo's cheeky expression gives way to seriousness. "Wait, Dell, I was just messing around. You don't have to leave."

"It's not that. It's just getting pretty late. Way past my bedtime." I tap the watch on my wrist, daring another sidelong glance at Hatch. "If I don't leave right now, I'll turn into a moldy pumpkin."

"We can take you back—"

"I'd rather walk. It's not too far, right?"

"Not at all, just up the beach. But what about your bike?"

Shit. I shouldn't leave Virginia's bike behind, but the Jeep is a whole hike away, and in the opposite direction of Cliffmoor House. I can't afford to stick around any longer, not with the girls growing restless around me, Hatch's unexpected arrival, and my beer-fueled paranoia skyrocketing.

"Can you bring it by Cliffmoor House tomorrow?"

"Uh, sure." Mojo shrugs. "Your shoes too?"

Momentarily thrown by this, I glance down at my feet, my toes coated in damp sand. Mojo raises his eyebrows, surprisingly cognizant for being blitzed halfway to another galaxy. "Yeah, shoes too. Thanks."

He hiccups in response, shooting me a brisk salute before busying himself with the keg again.

I stumble down the dark stretch of beach, ignoring Leon when he yells, "Yo, new girl! Where're you off to?" at the back of my head.

The bloated moon sits at the tippy-top of a cloudless, black sky, bathing the shore in a dusty white sheen that helps me navigate across the beach despite the buzzing in my head and my clumsy feet. I know Cliffmoor House can't be too far up ahead.

Before long, I hear the thump of footsteps behind me. Then, a teasing voice.

"I thought you didn't drink?"

I whirl around to find Hatch wearing a playful expression and panting from the sprint. He shoves his hands into his jean pockets. "Or do you just not drink with eavesdropping swine like me?"

The cup of beer I'm still holding feels like it could burn clear through my fingers. "The second option. Definitely."

Hatch smiles, that gleam of vibrant green flashing in the moonlight. "Hi, Dell."

My head spins from chugging that last beer too quickly—and from seeing him again. "Hi back."

He looks like he's holding in a bout of laughter. "Leaving so soon?"

"Yeah, I should be getting back."

"Family stuff, right?" His sly, lopsided grin tells me he doesn't believe that lie for a second.

"Right. Yup. Family stuff."

"Well, where are you headed? It's dark out here. If you need help finding your way, I can—"

"No, I've got it. Thanks," I say in a rush, hastily whirling around to leave, nearly giving myself whiplash in the process. Before he can say anything else, I resume my lonely trek, resolving not to turn back no matter how tempting. I can't justify *any* distractions at this point, nor can I anticipate a scenario where spending time with Hatch works to my benefit, especially not when I'd just managed to scrape my way into Palmer's semi-good graces.

"See you around, Dell," he calls from behind, an indelible smile ringing in his voice.

I inhale a breath—*No you won't, Hatch*—and trudge off stubbornly down the shoreline.

Minutes later, a flicker of silver glints at me from the corner of my eye—something rippling across the waves, splashing and catching in the pale moonlight.

Probably a school of fish, I think, though I can't be certain now that the back-to-back-to-back beers I'd chugged in under fifteen minutes have taken effect. I don't bother investigating. It's been the kind of day that requires days to sleep off, and all I want to do is climb in bed and stay there.

Soon, the silhouette of an overbearing mansion rises in the distance, like a harsh beacon cutting through the fog in my mind. A wooden dock materializes from the shadows and I stagger toward it, following the path back to the dewy, salt-soaked grounds of Cliffmoor House.

CHAPTER SEVENTEEN

The next morning, no nightmares wake me. No alarms echo across the blind-drawn guest house. There are no overly perky knocks at the door. I wind up sleeping until well past noon, with nowhere to be until six o'clock, when the Klynes will assemble to dump Virginia's ashes over the bay.

I need to make the most of the solitary hours stretching before me, need to find something useful to help make sense of Mom's situation. To fill the muddled gaps remaining from yesterday's epiphanies…and to keep my mind from wandering to wherever Hatch may be.

I get up slowly, dragging my feet to the bathroom, the events of last night still a beer-tinged blur, but I'm in no hurry to bring them into focus. I relish my time under the steamy stream of shower, and once I've effectively boiled myself, washing off the last vestiges of sleep, I pull on a tank top, some worn jean shorts, and my old Chuck Taylors.

Stepping out the door, starving and crippled by an angry headache, I nearly trip over a large wicker basket resting on the stoop, with a handwritten note pinned to it that reads:

Miss Dell—an empty stomach is a miserable companion.

Bundled inside a checkered cloth is a mouthwatering assortment of muffins, pastries, and croissants. "Thank you, Briggs," I mutter under my breath, silently speculating as to whether the old butler might have some clairvoyant abilities he keeps under wraps.

I drop the basket inside the guest house, pop a piece of muffin into my mouth, and lock the front door behind me. Standing on the stoop once more, I'm momentarily baffled when I can't remember where I left Virginia's bike…until, all at once, I do.

I take quick stock of my options. The night I arrived, I hadn't thought to jot down the number on the side of the taxi that brought me to Cliffmoor House—strike one. I check my cell phone, still kicking from when I charged it over three days ago, but as anticipated, there's no internet connectivity and no way for me to run a quick web search— strike two. The map I'd been using is worthless now, thanks to yesterday's monsoonal bike ride to June's house—strike three. So I have no means of getting around town, no cell service to pull up directions, and no way of reaching the island taxi service.

Fan-freaking-tastic.

Running back inside the guest house, I try the landline as Briggs instructed in hopes that he'll pick up the phone. But the call keeps ringing in perpetuity, leaving me with one last feasible recourse, painful though it may be.

I jog up the path through the gardens of Cliffmoor House, praying that the back doors were left unlocked and that Briggs, by some fortuitous happenstance, is somewhere within earshot. When I tug on the handle of a curtained French door, it opens easily, and I slip inside.

The house is still as I tiptoe down the hall, peeking into several rooms in search of Briggs, but the butler is nowhere to be found. In fact, there's no one around at all, just the antlered animals gaping at me from the study, Virginia's bewitching portrait in the parlor, and the bronze statues littering the mansion like overpriced confetti.

"Briggs?"

I stop dead in my tracks at the sound of the voice calling from the foyer.

"Briggs? Back already?"

If I leave right now, he won't suspect a thing. I don't need a taxi all that bad. If I walk along the beach, I'm sure I'll bump into *someone* willing to give me directions.

"Meridel?" the voice calls uncertainly.

Shit, shit, shit.

Retreating back down the hall, I make for the back door, pausing when I hear the mouse-like squeaking of wheels.

"Meridel, darling, is that you?"

I hesitate a moment, peering into the shadowed corners where the walls meet the ceiling, searching for hidden devices or winking red lights. An estate of this size must have a massive security system, with cameras monitoring all who come and go. If I run off now, Briggs or some other underling would surely know it. They'd know that I ignored my grandfather when he called for me, snubbing a disabled, elderly man. My own blood and gracious host.

I take a breath, compelling my muscles to relax. "Yes. It's me."

The wheelchair comes into view as Ambrose enters the corridor. He smiles brightly, his hair neatly combed and his clothes pressed, looking very much at ease for someone about to scatter his dead wife's remains at sea.

"Good afternoon, granddaughter." His voice booms like the crackle of fireworks. I recoil from the sound of it, or maybe that nauseating word—*granddaughter.*

"Good afternoon," I respond politely. "Sorry to intrude. I was looking for Briggs."

"He stepped out to do some grocery shopping for Cook."

Wonderful. I should've taken my chances with the beach.

"Okay, um, I'm sorry. Again."

Before I can turn to go, Ambrose wheels himself forward, closing the gap of distance between us. "Something I can do for you, my dear?"

I don't understand why I'm so apprehensive around him. Is it those swirling gray eyes, or something more? The way he wears that ever-present smile like armor? Maybe I'd been too quick to judge him. Maybe I hadn't given him a fair enough shot. The man had lost his youngest daughter, and now his wife too. He deserved some sympathy, or at least my respect.

"I'd like to call a taxi."

"Ah!" Ambrose pokes one wrinkled finger in the air. "That I can help with. Right this way."

I follow him as he maneuvers through the foyer to the opposite wing of the house, down a busy corridor I've not yet explored. At the end of it awaits an antique elevator with tarnished brass accents and a stunning iron cage. Naturally, Ambrose would need some manner of getting upstairs in his chair. I just hadn't envisioned anything quite so elaborate.

And why the hell not? I silently berate myself. *Look at the rest of this place.*

Before reaching the elevator, we turn into a vast, cherry-wood kitchen, where a towering woman with curly white hair and a chef's uniform chops veggies at a cutting block. She works methodically, humming to herself, while an antique radio blares the latest weather forecast.

"—upward-moving Hurricane Ophelia, currently a category two storm, is forecasted to intensify before making landfall in Cuba this evening. While still a smaller system, Ophelia has dangerous flood potential, and may spell trouble for the Florida Keys and the Gulf Coast—"

When the woman spots us in the doorway, she starts and switches off the radio. "'Ello, Master Ambrose!"

"Good morning, Inga," my grandfather says with a well-mannered tilt of his head. "Do you remember my granddaughter, Meridel?" She nods warmly. I scan the woman's face, hoping to jog a memory loose, but I remember nothing, my mind like a blank slate. "Meridel, this is Inga," Ambrose continues. "Our loyal cook for over forty years."

Inga wipes her hands on her double-breasted coat. "Is great to see you, Miss Meridel." She speaks with a thick Scandinavian accent, her soft brown eyes wide with apology. "I would shake hand, but…" She shows me her fingertips, moist and coated in chopped bits of greenery.

"That's all right."

"We're looking for the phone book, Inga," Ambrose says. "Meridel would like to contact the taxi service."

"I'll get that for you, sir!" This chipper, youthful voice belongs to the maid who enters the kitchen from an alternate door, pushing along a bucket and mop.

"Ah, Emery. Have you met my granddaughter, Meridel?"

"Not yet, sir." Emery bows her head, stepping forward to shake my hand. "It's a pleasure, miss."

These formal introductions—all the bowing and capitulation—make me feel intolerably squirmy. I take a step away from Ambrose, trying to establish some separation between the ladies' aristocratic master and myself.

Emery sweeps through the kitchen, ducking beneath a tall cabinet and coming back with a hefty yellow book. She flips through it. "Let's see. U…V…W…*aha!* Here we are. Wave Taxi."

"Great, thank you." I reach for the book, but she's already punching in the number and holding the phone to her ear.

"Good afternoon. We need a taxi at Cliffmoor House, please. Five minutes? Perfect. Have a nice day." Emery hangs up and smiles at me. "Good to go, miss," she says, bowing again in that unduly servile manner. I want to take her by the shoulders and forcibly straighten her out.

"Thank you, ladies," Ambrose says, waving his fingers as he beckons me to follow him. The women watch curiously as we exit the kitchen.

My grandfather's awareness of the ginormous house is uncanny. He never clips a wall, nor so much as bumps a baseboard. His wheels never snag on the Oriental rugs. Ambrose knows precisely where he is and how to navigate without error. Moving gracefully, as if by second sight. This is a man whose mind is orderly and regimented. Not a single detail does he miss.

"Where are you off to today?" he asks, the question smooth and effortless.

I feel like I've been caught in a lie before I've even answered. "I thought I'd explore the shops around Main Street a bit before we head to the seaport."

It's a convincing enough excuse—nothing out of the ordinary—and Ambrose agrees, at least on the surface.

"Wonderful. We have some true treasures downtown. Make sure to visit Twenty Eight from the Main. They deal in unique knick-knacks and collectibles, and have a marvelous display room filled with rare nautical antiques and heirlooms."

"Thanks. I'll pass by."

We arrive at the front door and Ambrose unlocks it, nudging it ajar with one strong arm. "I'll open the gate for you, darling," he offers courteously.

When I glance down to meet his smile, I see that his eyes are wide and glaring—two cloudy, gray orbs penetrating my face. They probe at my insides, disrobing my buffer of careful civility, attempting to glimpse into the depths of my soul.

"Thank you," I whisper.

"It's my pleasure, my dear," Ambrose responds, studying me with a keener vision than the average human is capable of, seeing without sight. And without any sort of logical explanation, I'm certain that my instincts aren't wrong about him.

Some subtle yet undeniable thing about my grandfather is off, and not the negligible, kooky sort of off, like old Captain Patton with his rambling sailor's tales. No…Ambrose is off in the way that food spoils, an inside-out sort of rotten, like bad fish at the market. Everything about his exterior—his highly-curated, congenial façade—is a mask to shield whatever rancid truth lies beneath.

He smiles at me now, lips curling into that big, winsome grin I've come to expect, and I can't help but feel that he knows I've figured him out. He knows it like he knows the nooks and crannies of this house.

CHAPTER EIGHTEEN

"Can you wait up?" I ask the driver as I step out of the taxi, worried that my cell service will crap out on me again, leaving me stranded among thousands of corpses.

The chain-smoking cabbie squints at me, not bothering to reply.

I hand him a twenty dollar bill. "What'll that buy me?"

"Half hour, tops."

I nod and turn down the gravel path, trudging through the monstrous wrought-iron gates of Halcyon Bay Cemetery.

From the looks of it, the security post at the entrance is deserted, but there's a plastic receptacle attached to the door that's packed with shiny brochures. *Maps with Donation*, reads the small sign on the box. I drop a dollar in the slot and take one.

The cemetery grounds are arranged in a grid formation with clearly marked lanes and walking paths. Twelve call-out spots are featured across the map, highlighting various statues, gardens, and tombs of particular interest for visitors. I locate the one I've come to see—a towering mausoleum simply labeled *Klyne*.

I stick to the tree-lined trails meant for foot traffic as a quiet breeze wafts through the rows of the dead, palms swaying to the pulse of some soundless, otherworldly melody. The grave sites I pass are predominantly modest and plain, stippling the sunburnt grounds in respectful gray stones. After several minutes of strolling, scanning the epitaphs and flower-laden grounds, I spot my family's opulent mausoleum looming up ahead.

The marble structure is tall and imposing, with all the trappings of refined excess. It's surrounded by a short iron fence, though its shadow crawls well over those borders, cloaking its unlucky neighbors in near-constant darkness. A massive door at its center is coated in vines, flanked on either side by ivory Grecian columns. The slab over the door reads *Klyne,* and above this inscription, a sculpted coat of arms is nestled into a gabled roof. Elaborate carvings line the tomb's cornices— clustered faces peering out from the marble, beautiful and haunting, with identically vacant eyes.

Palmer was right; tradition be damned. This is the last place I'd *ever* want to end up.

I move off the walking path and tiptoe between the gravestones, ambling across clear patches of grass to get to the mausoleum. Once there, I step over the fence and run my hand along the nearest wall. Despite the summer heat, the marble under my fingers is cool, covered in moss and creepers.

A decaying bundle of flowers rest at the foot of the door, placed beneath a flat brown rock to keep them in place. The flowers are dry and wilted, but the faintest traces of purple still tinge their brittle petals. They can't have been here long, a couple weeks at most, left behind by some unknown visitor. The brown sprigs are droopy, with wispy leaves that cascade to the tip. I pull some from the bunch and hold them up to the breeze. They sway gently, lithe and graceful, like branches from a weeping willow tree.

An impressive lock is attached to the tomb's entrance. I try prying it open, even attempting a push on the door, but the marble doesn't give, firmly affixed in place. The inhabitants of the tomb—however many deceased Klynes, including my mother's youngest sister—are sealed inside their cave of stone, unreachable and totally separate from the realm of the living.

"You're not supposed to be in there."

I jump at the sight of a grizzled old woman wearing a broad straw hat and polka-dotted gardening gloves. She watches me with crossed arms, her stern face and shabby clothes covered in dirt and grass stains. "It's for family only," she adds.

Momentarily forgetting that I *am* family, I stammer, "I-I'm sorry. I was just—"

"You're one of those sea trumpet freaks, aren't you?" she spits, an irritated edge to her voice.

"No, ma'am, I'm not—"

"This is a holy place to honor our dead. Your sick rituals have no place here!"

She picks up the bucket of supplies at her feet and rushes toward me, obviously upset. I wouldn't be surprised if she tried to whack me with her rake.

"Hold on a second, hold on," I say quickly. "I'm not...what you think. I'm just visiting. I'm related to the Klynes."

"Related how?"

"I'm their"—my throat contracts grotesquely—"granddaughter." No matter how many times I think it or remind myself that it's true, it never gets easier to say. Much less now with this shriveled raisin of a woman wagging her gnarled finger at my face.

"No, you ain't. I know their granddaughter. Spunky little blonde with blue eyes." The old woman snarls. "I've worked at this cemetery for many years, and—"

"I'm their other granddaughter," I interject. "My name's Dell. I'm not from around here."

She pauses. "Laurel's daughter?"

I nod, relieved when she drops her bucket of spiky tools.

"Well, geez. I ain't seen Laurel in...must be something like—"

"Twenty years?"

The woman grunts begrudgingly. "You in town for Mrs. Klyne's services?"

Again, I nod.

"Did your mother come too?"

"No. Just me."

The gait of fast-approaching footsteps draws my attention to a tall young man headed our way, also uniformed in gardening attire. He brandishes a giant pair of shears in the air, his skin suntanned, flaxen hair shaved down close to the scalp, with a sweet, mild smile on his face.

"Found 'em!" he calls out jovially, waving the cutters. "They were hidden behind Beau's chair at the gatehouse."

"Hidden?" the woman sneers.

"Looks like it." He closes the stretch between us. "Wonder how they ended up there."

"I'll tell you how, Scotty. That buffoon stowed them in the damn gatehouse 'cause he's a big ol' chicken shit. I've seen him patrolling the grounds after dark…gets spooked by his own shadow! And he's supposed to come from some big-wig security company? I'd bet my ass that man ain't never secured nothing in his goddamn life."

"How about we give him the benefit of the doubt?" the young man suggests, handing the tool in question over to the bitter woman. "He's new to the job, and new to town—"

"No reason to act like a bumbling imbecile," she snaps, taking the shears from him. "If I'd have known the Claremonts were going to hire such a spineless pansy…" She continues to mutter nasty things about the security guard while the young man turns to me, his eyes apologetic.

"Hey! Nice to see an unfamiliar face around here." There's an oddly cheerful streak in his voice, considering we're surrounded by so much death. "I'm Prescott."

I shake his hand, which is warm and large enough to wholly encompass mine. "Dell. Nice to meet you."

"Says she's related to the Klynes," the old woman croaks, raising one thin eyebrow practically to her hairline, lips screwed up in a sour-candy pucker.

"Oh. Wow. I'm sorry for your loss," Prescott offers.

I shrug, not knowing what else to do or say. I don't feel right accepting Prescott's misplaced sympathies, but with this old woman glaring at me so contemptuously, I decide I'm better off keeping those thoughts to myself.

Prescott wraps a long arm over the woman's spindly shoulders. "This is my mom, Lettie. We're the groundskeepers here at HBC."

"And we've gotta get back to work." Lettie swats Prescott's arm away in a huff, lifts a hand to her eyes, and peers out at the beaming afternoon sun. "Time to pick up the pace. Enough chit chat."

With one last disparaging glance my way, she adds, "We'll be by Cliffmoor House tomorrow to pay our respects. I expect to see you there, missy."

I cringe, picturing hordes of islanders combing the Cliffmoor House grounds, crawling like crazed sugar ants. I can already hear them commiserating Virginia's passing, offering condolences to anyone that might listen. The thought of it is exhausting.

As Lettie tramps away with her bucket in tow, I'm left feeling empty. Coming here was a total waste of time. I don't know what I hoped to get out of my visit—what I expected to find at Willow's grave—but it turned out to be a fruitless mission. All I'd managed to do was make yet another enemy. How many was that now?

Prescott shoots me a rueful shrug. "Sorry about that. Mom doesn't have much of a filter. Self-awareness isn't her strong suit. Blatant hostility, on the other hand..."

I snort. "Don't worry about it."

"As you can probably tell, we're not big on strangers around here."

"That's cool. I'm not big on them either."

"Not big on 'sea trumpet freaks,' either. You're not one of those, are you?" He smiles sheepishly. "I could hear my mother screeching from half a mile away."

I furrow my brow. "I don't even know what *one of those* is."

Prescott laughs, wiping the beads of sweat from his forehead. "Phew. That's a relief."

There's an openness in his eyes and smile that makes him look quite young, his face hairless, smooth, and rounded out with baby fat.

"What's that about, anyway?" I ask. It's not the first I'd heard of these sea trumpet things…Captain Patton had mentioned them too.

"It's silly," Prescott says. "Whenever there's some kind of unusual tragedy on the island—like if someone dies unexpectedly, or, I don't know, plunges to their death of their own free will or something—people tend to wig out."

My ears perk up. "You mean Callie Oxton?"

Prescott looks surprised when I say her name.

"I, uh, saw something about her suicide on the news this morning," I say casually, trying to make my interest seem like nothing more than passing curiosity.

Prescott nods. "Yeah, her. The suicide's got everybody all worked up. They're even talking about *them* again, like maybe it's starting over."

"What's starting over?"

"You know…" Those sleepy, blue-gray eyes dance with curbed excitement. "The Brine."

The Brine. I'd heard of it from the captain, and again yesterday in that article I'd read. It was an island-grown cult that dissolved years ago, but what did that have to do with Callie's suicide? And what's the deal with these sea trumpet things? Why did Lettie assume I'd know anything about them? Because I'd been poking around the Klyne tomb? How and why is my family connected to any of this?

"I'd better get going." Prescott rolls his eyes. "Mom will have a coronary if she catches me slacking. But maybe we can catch up at the celebration of life tomorrow?"

"Sure," I say, flashing him a smile. Maybe if I play up the unsuspecting-tourist-bit, flirt with him a little, I can get some real answers. "It'll be nice to know someone there. Find me, okay?"

"Absolutely."

He shoots me a coy smile before bending down to collect his things, snatching up a flower that's floated away from one of the gravesites in the salty breeze. "For you, Dell."

I feel strange taking it from him—from whatever poor, deceased soul it's truly meant for—but I do anyway, planting a grin on my face.

Prescott waves as he turns to leave, glancing over his shoulder a couple of times as he goes, and I know I've hooked him. Now I just need to reel that fish in.

I spend another fifty bucks on taxi rides that afternoon, popping into the Main Street shops, driving past the defunct lighthouse, cutting across countless beachfront streets, and looping around the seaport.

I take in all the sights, every sand-swept neighborhood, until I feel like I've memorized the entire island, like I could sketch the whole thing out on paper. I think about Mom growing up here. I think about Mom losing her sister here.

The last stop of my tour is Sandspur Beach, where hundreds of people are strewn about the sand, speckling the sparkling water, basking in the UV rays. Floatie-clad toddlers run wild while their mothers chase them down with expensive camera equipment. Teenagers lay out to bake, savoring the unbridled freedoms of summertime with their waterproof speakers and vape pens in hand. Tourists with monogrammed hats and sunglasses snap selfies under their rainbow umbrellas. It's a languid, sun-soaked scene, one that makes me nostalgic for something I've missed, for childhood summers ripped out from under me.

I pick my way across striped towels to the shoreline, the same shore of last night's impromptu kegger. I hadn't made the connection before, but this is the beach where Willow was found, the beach behind Cliffmoor House where her body washed ashore.

A rush of cold hits me when my toes touch the water, rising up my feet to the ankles. I wonder where it happened, whatever it is that *really* happened.

To my right is a distinctive tree that sprouts up from the water. Its roots undulate in and out of sand and sea, inextricably marrying the two. I amble toward it, imagining what a terrible shock it would be to find a body tangled up in those roots. To discover a young girl, cold and blue, bloating beneath the eye of a cruel morning sun.

I bend down to touch those twisting roots, following their jagged path across land and water, when something silvery shimmers nearby, snagging my attention.

It's the same shining thing that splashed in the water yesterday, the memory pushing forth from the recesses of my mind—a shivering smear of silver, concealed in black surf and black night. And here it is again, winking at me now, sloshing in the shallows, blinding when it catches the light.

I squint at it, venturing to move a little closer, until I'm thigh-deep in the water, my jean shorts dampening.

"Watch out!"

A rogue football narrowly misses my head before landing in the water with a loud splash. I turn to find a group of guys with tattoos and too-tight swim trunks waving at me regretfully.

"Sorry about that," one of them calls as he darts to retrieve their ball.

By the time I catch my breath and look back to the shallows, the silver shining in the waves is gone, vanishing as mysteriously as it came.

CHAPTER NINETEEN

A stretch limousine glides up the driveway to Cliffmoor House—luxurious, sleek, and bullet-fast. It comes to a stop where the group of us stands, wrapped in reverential tones with a somber mood to match.

The onset of evening is cooler than the day, the palm trees shaken by the crisp breath of the wind. I somehow managed to pull together an outfit breezy enough for summer, warm enough for boating, but sober enough for the occasion—black linen pants paired with an ultramarine blouse, the color of storm-ridden ocean.

Before convening outside of Cliffmoor House, Mojo and Palmer deposited Virginia's bike and my forgotten boots on the guest house doorstep. They hadn't said much then, their eyes shielded in dark sunglasses, Palmer's cheeks splotched with agitated whorls of pink, and no one says much now as we take turns climbing into the backseat of the limo, pressed arm to arm.

Flip, Tristen, June, Leif, Palmer, Mojo, and I pack in, snug as cigarettes in a carton. Briggs maneuvers Ambrose into the passenger's seat while the driver stows his wheelchair in the trunk. Once the butler settles down beside me, we're off, winding across town toward the seaport, where a ship awaits to carry us to sea.

I avoid eye contact with everyone in the limo, slipping on my sunglasses and taking in the scenery. An unbearable silence hangs over us, each person occupied in private thought or emotion, making me all too aware of how numb I feel. I thought the occasion might've spurred something in me—unlocked some repressed sentimentality toward my grandmother, something besides this heavy sense of apathy and detachment—but it doesn't. So I decide it best to keep to myself, not wanting to smear my indifference over their pain.

The sun-bleached docks of the seaport are cloaked in golden afternoon light. It smells of fish and brackish water here, where a great many leather-backed fishermen work tirelessly to unload their catch before nightfall. The limousine driver parks and we disembark, scrambling out of the car to stand in a morbid cluster. Ambrose is situated onto his wheelchair, with Virginia's urn resting in his lap. His twisted, arthritic fingers clamp around the neck of it, a strange and strangulating gesture that causes my stomach muscles to contract.

Finley steps forward, helming our excursion. "This way, family." He points us toward a regal schooner with broad white sails a short distance away.

Onboard the ship, a towering woman dressed in orange silks peers out at the far horizon line. A mass of dark hair is collected in a bun at her crown. Her arms, ears, and neck are covered in chains of gold and glittering jewels, drenching her skin in amber sparkle as the sun begins its slow descent. She carries with her a small black book with a string of beads. Her bronze, molten-lava eyes land upon us as we approach the boarding ramp.

The ramp is manned by two sturdy-looking deckhands. They hop onto the docks, helping Briggs navigate Ambrose aboard first, with the rest of us following suit. June clutches Leif by the arm when he peeks curiously over the fenceless wooden path, drawn to the splashing water below.

"Mommy, there's tarpon down there," he whispers, eyes wide

behind his too-thick spectacles. "And they're hungry too. They keep going like this." Leif squishes his cheeks, cracking his mouth open and closed, making short popping sounds like bubbles bursting.

June presses her index finger to her lips, giving him a stern look.

The radiant woman on the ship does not introduce herself when we board. She stands at the bow, fingers interlaced, eyes dancing down the line of Klynes assembled before her.

"Family," Finley calls us to attention, coming to stand beside the graceful woman. "As many of you know, the late Mrs. Klyne was a woman with a great many interests. One of those interests was of a spiritual nature. This is Madame Freya Larisse"—he flourishes his hand before the woman—"Mrs. Klyne's former medium and spiritual healer. I have called Madame Larisse to lead us in some guided reflection this evening as we say goodbye to our dear friend, wife, mother, and grandmother."

Freya bows her head before spreading her arms to us. Ribbons of silk spill from her lean body, puddling at her feet. "Welcome, family." Her voice is deep and hypnotic, with a robust Caribbean accent. "Thank you for inviting me to join you this evening."

We murmur a communal greeting, robotic and enraptured.

"And, of course," Finley continues, "you all know our dear Captain Patton Fortuna." I'm stunned to see the big-bellied captain step out from the shadows, tipping his grimy bucket hat at each of us, fingering his messy beard. He winks at me with his one good eye—a flash of startling aquamarine. "The captain has graciously offered to escort us aboard this magnificent vessel to honor Mrs. Klyne's final request."

Captain Patton ducks behind the wheel while the deckhands go to work maneuvering out of the busy harbor—tugging ropes, lifting sails, snaking past scores of other schooners, yachts, and fishing boats, until we're slicing through open water and into the sun-drenched beyond.

Freya floats toward a lone bench, and this signals the rest of us to break away too, scattering across the deck to occupy our own quiet spaces. I claim a spot near the ropes, pressing my body against them, hair whipping in the wind, irrepressible and free. I relish in the spray of salt on my face and the playful tossing of the ocean, filling my body with a sense of weightlessness.

The same Halcyon Bay that welcomed me so angrily just two nights ago—with a fury that seemed to erupt from the deepest chambers of hell—is unrecognizably peaceful tonight, gentle and lulling. The water cradles our ship, wrapping us up in its cool embrace, ushering us toward the burning horizon.

The sky, however, is not to be outdone. The clouds burst with orange flame, coasting sleepily across a pink atmosphere as we forge farther and farther from land. Smears of sky-fire reflect across the surface of the water, turning it into a panoramic panel of stained glass. Shards of every brilliant color converge to mirror the heavens, glistening in the waning sunlight, each fresh wave consuming the last.

I watch the display with bated breath until Freya rises from her bench. She calls to us, tearing my eyes away from the sun melting like syrup into the ocean.

"Virginia's spirit is strong with us, family," Freya says with a knowing smile. "She looks upon all of you now, grateful that you have respected her wishes by bringing her to rest at the mouth of the sea. You lend her soul tranquility."

I watch the faces that surround me, each one treading through their own respective sea of emotions, swept below by grief.

"In our sessions together, Virginia learned that everything in this world, both living and dead, has a spiritual element working behind it, slowly revealing its purpose. The revelations are plenty, if we take a moment to look." Freya extends her palms to the metamorphic sky, her metallic eyes jumping across each of our faces. "This magnificent spectacle is not a coincidence, my friends. Nothing in this world is."

She flips open the black leather book to where her string of beads have marked a page. "I will recite a prayer for the dead, in honor of our dear sister Virginia. Whenever you are ready to proceed, Ambrose."

Briggs steers Ambrose up the bow beside Freya. He locks the wheelchair in place and helps Ambrose to his feet. My grandfather leans his body against the ropes as Freya begins to chant in a language I don't understand. She speaks in little more than a whisper, low and profound, sprinkling her spell amid the intersecting realm of sea and sky.

Ambrose pulls the pointed top from the urn with steady hands. He turns the vase over and a cloud of gray dust spills from it. The final beams of yellow haze fill the air as Virginia's ashes float down, down, down.

In a flash, the sun dips below the blue, the dust settling over the water. Freya announces, "Virginia has transitioned into the spirit world. This is a good thing. It means her soul is at rest. She is one of the lucky ones."

Night creeps in as we slip through the docks to the waiting car. The Klynes drag their feet and hearts while I trail a ways behind, unable to take another suffocating moment of this. What joys await upon our return to Cliffmoor House? Endless hours of insufferable small talk? Getting wasted to cope with Finley's horrible man-sobs? More of Ambrose's sightless scrutiny, his misty eyeballs always veering my way as if tugged by invisible thread? Only to get to do it all over again tomorrow, at this dreaded celebration of life.

I grab Palmer's arm to get her attention. She's pushed her sunglasses into her hair, and her blue eyes are swollen and tinged with red. "If anyone asks for me, tell them I went for a walk," I whisper. "I need to clear my head."

She frowns. "But the limo's leaving—"

"It's fine. I'll find my own way back."

Palmer pinches her lips together, not saying anything more. She nods once before turning to follow the others, while I take off in the opposite direction, ducking out of their line of sight.

Alone at last, I exhale the shaking breath I've been keeping in for what feels like hours, altogether exhausted by the day's events…only to gasp when I walk straight into Madame Freya Larisse.

She towers over me so much that I have to crane my neck to meet her eyes. "Yours was the one face I didn't recognize. But now I do."

She gives me a strange little smile, and the harbor around us begins to blur. I swallow hard as a veil of shadow envelops my surroundings, until all that's left in crystal-clear focus is Freya's dreamy face.

"*Meridel,*" she utters gently, and my name seems to reverberate for miles, rolling beyond the ships to open ocean and back.

I sway a little, but her hands are quick to find my arms, steadying me. "What's…happening…to me?" I'm certain this is her doing, but I can't find the words to say it, nor the strength to pull away.

"Come, come, Meridel. Let's sit, you and I."

She leads me to a bench backed up against a bait and tackle shop on the port, and we sit watching the boats rock at their moorings. The haze of shadows that clouded my vision begins to fall away, flitting from sight like light extinguishing from a streetlamp. I drink in the view of the moon rising like an egg in the sky.

"Better?" Freya asks soothingly.

I nod, my words catching in the back of my throat.

She speaks to me without looking at me, glimmering eyes trained on the scores of ships. "You've grown into quite the young woman over the past twenty years. Northern air has done you good, made you smart. Your mama did the best she could, taking you away."

She knows Mom?

"Of course, I know her." Freya makes a clucking sound with her tongue. "I know everybody from this town, Meridel. Every single person, living and dead, just as I know the wrinkles on my own skin."

I peer into Freya's oval-shaped face, the creamy mocha of her cheeks, her neck ageless and without blemish, not a single crease or wrinkle to be seen. Her lips are plump, a deep plum shade, her eyes glinting with embers and lined in stark black. Her hair is thick and inky without a hint of aging gray. She looks so young but speaks as if she's been around for centuries.

"You seek many answers, child," Freya says with a hearty laugh, weaseling into my head again, reading my thoughts like a transcript. "I feel you searching even now for clarity." She reaches into my mind, her observations sinking deeper, down to the heart of why I'm here…to

Mom, Willow, and whatever else I've yet to bring to light. "But I must warn you"—her tone turns cautionary, her eyes steady and sober—"this path is most unclear. The truths you seek about the past are not as straightforward as they'd have you believe."

Her face is inscrutable as she speaks. I want to ask who 'they' are, but I can't locate my voice.

"Be careful," Freya whispers, the warning like ice in my bloodstream. "Exhuming old skeletons is a dark business. And not everyone in Halcyon Bay is glad to have you back."

I don't know who she means or why, and I have no way to ask. One glimpse into Freya's hypnotic bronze eyes, and it's like someone poured cement into my mouth. I scan the murky contents of my brain, trying to recall if any one person had made me feel unwelcome or unwanted since my arrival, or if any encounters stand out as particularly unsettling, but it's a futile exercise. Two days on this island and I'd already come into contact with a gamut of characters, all of them weird and unusual in their own right.

She stands slowly, silk skirts ruffling in the breeze. "I expect we'll meet again, Meridel," she muses. "Sometime soon. When you are ready to talk."

Freya glides away, and I force out a hoarse "Hey!" at her back. I try to follow, try to stand, but something inexplicable holds me to the bench, a strange magnetism that I'm powerless to fight. "Hey!" I yell again. Freya doesn't turn. "Don't go. I'm ready to talk now!" I'm welded in place, helpless but to watch as her silhouette shrinks in the night.

An eerie mist pours in from the sea, almost as if from nowhere, and swallows Freya's body up with it. Only then am I released from my momentary paralysis.

I jump up, whipping around in search of whatever force ensnared me, but nothing and no one is anywhere near me. I'm alone on the docks, with only the tolling of ship bells to ground me, and the fat, rising moon for company, showering light from her distant hammock in the clouds.

CHAPTER TWENTY

Shaken to my core, I set off across the harbor, calming myself by counting back from one hundred while I try to extract myself from Freya's mystifying affect, the phantom touch of her fingertips still lingering on my arms.

When she smiled, everything seemed to slow to a stop, and a curtain of shadow fell over my eyes, blurring the world from focus. My words clung to my mouth. I'd been frozen in place, unable to stand or even move. And then that rolling mist had poured in, gobbling her whole, almost as if she'd never been there at all.

Distracted, I bump into an old sailor scuttling past on the docks. He's a scraggly creature with matted hair and a hole in his topsiders where the big toe juts out. "Sorry, lass," the man says, averting his eyes as he scampers off to a dilapidated shack nearby.

The shanty structure is thrown together with plywood, rain tarps, and torn fish netting. A tattered pirate flag flutters from the entrance, illuminated by a single strand of white string lights. The faded metal sign overhead, eaten up with rust, reads: *Come Wet Your Whistle at the*

World-Famous Sand Pit!

I trudge toward it, my nerves sharp and spastic inside my body, like some electric wire running from my head to my toes has split open. I'm sparking, malfunctioning, all my senses in disrepair. A stiff drink to still them might be just what I need.

The pub inside is a hazy crawl space. A shirtless man plays the banjo in an alcove by the door, his grimy fingers flying with remarkable acuity. Swarms of fishermen crowd the length of the bar, swapping beers and tales from their day at sea. Many of them puff from cigarettes and joints, the stench of marijuana mingling with tobacco, so thick that it seeps down my throat to my belly.

I tuck myself into an unoccupied corner table farthest from the rollicking group at the bar. There's a sort of makeshift porthole in the wall closest to me, a round glass window caked in a film of smoke. It faces the water, and as I stare out into the night, at the sleeping ships with their flickering lights, my mind wanders to a place two thousand miles away, to my father back in Woodbridge. Was he staring out some dingy window too, searching the gloomy forests of home for answers? Thinking of me, and why I hadn't answered any of his calls?

A laminated menu drops on the table before me and a tattooed woman with a terrible hunchback appears at my side, pulling a notepad from beneath the strap of her lime-green bra. "Something to drink?"

I order the first thing I see on the menu. "Uh, sure. Painkiller, please." I have no idea what it is, but it's got rum and I like the name.

"One, two, or three?" she asks, tapping the butt of her chewed-up ballpoint against the menu. The Painkillers (or PKs, as they call them) fall into three categories, each one corresponding to the number of shots you want—or how much pain you need to kill.

I order the strongest option. "Three."

The waitress tucks the notepad back into her shirt before disappearing into the throng of men.

In her absence, I hesitantly pick up my cell phone, resigned to do the one thing I've been avoiding since I got to the island. I dig my toe into the floor, take a deep breath, and slowly dial the number.

One ring in, he picks up.

"Dell," he says breathlessly, not bothering with paltry hellos.

"Hey, Dad." I lick my lips, nettled by the shame that's so evident in my voice.

"How are you? Is everything okay? You're all right?" Worry paints the edges of each of his questions.

"I'm good, I promise." I try to sound perky, but I know it comes across as forced. I've always been an awful liar, and perky is a stretch for me even on a good day.

"Please tell me you're on your way home?"

"Well...no. Not exactly."

"What were you thinking going back there?"

I sigh. "I'm thinking I want some answers, and no one's giving them to me in Maine."

"Listen to me, please." He sounds desperate. "Come home and we'll talk it all out, okay? Whatever you think you're doing in Halcyon Bay, whoever you think you're helping—"

"I'm helping Mom."

"But you don't understand how complicated that is."

"You're right, I don't understand. Whose fault is that?" There's bite in my tone, a simmering anger, and he seems to sense it.

"What about work?" he asks, grasping at straws.

"I took a few personal days."

"You're jeopardizing your career for—"

"Whoa, whoa. My career? I'm a temp, Dad. It's not that serious."

"What are you talking about?" he exclaims. "You ran that huge ad campaign on your own last year. The one with the, um...what was it? The animal snacks?"

"You mean Pawperinos, the gluten-free dog treats? Yes, that would be my greatest professional accomplishment to date. Couldn't forget if I tried, thanks."

"Please be reasonable. Come home. I know you're trying to help, but the best thing you can do for your mother is to get back to Woodbridge as soon as—"

"No," I say firmly. "I'm not going back until I know why—"

"She's worried, Dell."

I go silent for a moment, listening to his breathing at the other end of the line, my skin burning up. "You didn't," I say quietly.

He doesn't respond.

"Please tell me you didn't tell her where I am."

"I had to," he says. "What was I supposed to say? What excuse could I give for why you were missing all of a sudden, or for why I decided not to make the trip to Florida?"

My anger rises like lava, rushing from my stomach straight up to my head. "You say whatever you have to say!" I shout louder than I intend, but the wild bar patrons don't even turn their heads. "You lie, you change the subject, just like you did with me a billion times growing up!"

He tries to interject, but my temper is explosive. I don't let him get a word in edgewise. "All those times I asked about this place, you'd shut me down *hard*, but now you conveniently want to talk? Now you choose to be honest? Because honesty is so important to this family, right?"

"I know you're upset," he says, his level tone wavering, "but Mom's not doing well. And knowing you're there…she's…things are only getting worse."

"You have yourself to blame for that," I hiss, the words spilling like venom from my mouth. "It'll be a few more days before I make it back to Woodbridge. Take care of her until I do."

I end the call without a goodbye as the waitress hobbles over with my PK-3 in hand. She hasn't even set it down on the table before I'm already ordering a second.

CHAPTER TWENTY-ONE

A *No Trespassing* sign dangles from the roped-off stretch of dock before me. I glance around stealthily—there's no one around. No sound but the gentle lapping of water, rocking the boats to a quiet lullaby, and the men's distant laughter pouring out from the pub.

The lights flickering from the dockside posts are too dim to alert anyone to my presence, so I duck swiftly beneath the ropes and come to stand at the starboard side of a wooden fishing boat.

Before I can talk myself out of it, I jump over the edge, spilling clumsily across the boat's deck.

I had first noticed it from my corner table at the Sand Pit, winking at me through the grubby porthole window. The boat was big and proud-looking, with a certain lived-in character, and a name splashed across it in cursive script, faded from years of baking under the harsh Florida sun. I squinted at it from my table, trying to make out the letters in the dark, those looping w's and l's playing tricks on my eyes. Slowly, they came together, snapping into place like cryptic puzzle pieces.

Willow's Wind.

Of course, the vessel's name might've been a total coincidence—likely nothing to do with Willow Klyne at all—but my boozed-up brain would not be deterred. I sucked back my third consecutive PK-3, paid my bill, and charged the boat, bypassing all the clear signs that I shouldn't be there.

Onboard, the deck has recently been hosed down, still quite wet and slippery. I crouch for stability, trying to get a grip on my lazy, bumbling legs, and cross the slimy deck in a sort of crab walk, doing my best to avoid the scores of rusty hooks, poles, and spears glinting dangerously in the moonlight, like booby traps for the unaware. Buckets of tangled netting and rope jut into my walking path, as well as bins, cracked and brittle, exposing their insides. There are life rafts, rain jackets, a giant ice chest, weights, misshapen buoys, and other fishing supplies. Everything expected of a boat of this nature.

I'm not sure what I'm looking for, but this isn't it.

The boat deck encircles a central wheelhouse with a compact door and wraparound windows coated in salt. I approach it, pressing my face to a panel of glass to peek inside. There's a large steering wheel, a dashboard of switches and radar screens, a captain's swivel seat, and, against the back wall, a rectangular hatch leading to a cabin below deck.

I tug at the door, my heart racing as it gives, grinding open with minimal effort. Stepping inside, I notice a pair of wet flip-flops tucked under the captain's seat. There's a baseball cap crammed into the space above the dashboard, and a giant to-go cup rests in one of the cup holders, filled with amber liquid, unmelted ice floating at the top.

Someone was just here, I realize too late. Alarmed, I take a step backward, ducking out of the wheelhouse, when—

"Who the hell are you?"

I whip around to find a scruffy bear of a man standing on the dock. He wears a gray rash guard over a tanned body, crumpled beige cargos, and no shoes. An unruly mass of hair covers most of his face, falling into his eyes, cloaking them in shadow. They flash at me through the dark nonetheless, a menacing anger seething inside.

Before I can make a move, the bear man swings himself over the edge of the boat, landing a few feet away from me. "What are you doing on my boat?" he growls, enunciating each word, a scowl peeking through the beard that crawls up his cheeks like a rug.

The man reaches for something bulky at his waist, and I flinch, waiting for the pain of a knife or bullet to pierce my skin. I consider hurling myself over the side of the boat—taking my chances with whatever perils lurk beneath the black water—but the soles of my shoes must have melted into the floor. I'm paralyzed in place, utterly at the bear man's mercy.

Instead of a weapon, the man pulls a flashlight from his pocket, beaming it into my face. I shield my eyes against the burst of white light, backing up without thinking, and slipping into the captain's chair like a sitting duck. He takes another step forward, looming and fuming, as I scramble to my feet.

"You're not gonna talk?"

Words are slippery on my tongue, leadened by liquor and fear. I can't shape them into a coherent sentence. "I—I'm s-s-sorry—I was j-just…"

"Dell?"

I know that voice…

Past the bear man, standing on the docks, is Hatch, holding a box of leftovers from the Sand Pit. A concerned crease is drawn across his forehead, his sea green eyes sparkling in the night.

"Hatch!" I exclaim, swept up in the sheer luck of seeing a familiar face—of seeing *his* face.

"What're you doing here?" he asks, jumping aboard.

"That's what I'm trying to figure out," the bear man snaps. "You know her?"

"We're acquainted." Hatch chuckles, though the situation is anything but funny to me. "She's a mainlander."

"Can the mainlander read?" the man spits, eyeing me with contempt.

"As far as I know." Hatch's lips pull into a crooked smile and my heart sinks. This is what it must feel like to be hand fed to a shark.

"Well," the bear man booms again, blinding me with his light. "What the hell are you doing on my property?"

I take a deep, shaky breath, scanning my brain for a lie or explanation to help make sense of why I'm here. Unfortunately for me, nothing rational comes to mind. "I—I was j-just walking the docks, and I—I g-got turned around."

The man lowers the flashlight abruptly, releasing me from its piercing white stare. "Why do you look so familiar?" he asks, his voice lower now, more a rumble than a boom. "Who are you?"

He glares at me with a strange, mystified face, and when I don't answer his question, he turns expectantly to Hatch.

"Her name's Dell," Hatch answers easily. "Claims to be here for some family reunion."

I'm rooted in place, still as a statue, as the bear man squints at me, a medley of emotions coloring his face. He studies my eyes, my nose, my lips—all of my features working against me to reveal my identity. But how could he know who I am? And why does it scare me that he might?

After a long, scrutinizing moment, the man rubs a calloused hand over his brow, his eyes closing in resignation. The flashlight flicks off. "She ain't no damn mainlander," he mutters.

Hatch comes to stand over the man's shoulder, giving me a perplexed once-over. "Uh, yeah, Bram. I'm pretty sure she is."

The bear man, Bram, growls. "No, I *know* that face." His eyes cloud over like he's revisiting some old, upsetting memory. "Tell me who you are, and I won't call the cops."

I consider his offer in silence.

"You'll be in town a lot longer than you planned if I get the police involved," he threatens.

I'm sure he's right about that, and giving him my name can't be any worse than sitting in a prison cell overnight.

"Meridel Costa," I say, trying to keep from slurring.

"Costa." Bram's breath is shallow as he peers at me, like maybe I'm a ghost come back to life. "You're Laurel's daughter. Laurel Klyne."

Hatch looks at me, stunned. "Wait, rewind. You're a Klyne?"

I ignore him and ask Bram, "You knew my mother?"

"'Course I knew her," he mutters, more to himself than me. His dark eyes twitch, eyelids fluttering.

Hatch looks back and forth between the both of us.

"How?" I ask, a quiver jolting up the length of my body. "How did you know her?" Something is off here. Something feels wrong.

Bram doesn't answer my question. "Is she back in town?"

"No, she isn't. *How* did you know her?"

"We were friends," he says, "a long time ago."

"Friends?" A creeping sensation spreads over my skin. "Were you friends with Willow too?" Bram's eyes get wide at the mention of her. "Is that how you got the name for your boat?"

Hatch, likely sensing my growing distress, plants himself between Bram and I. The familiar scents of Coppertone and sunshine wash over me when he tries to reach out, but I take a concerted step back, avoiding his eyes.

"Whoa," Hatch says gently. "Let's back up a second. What's this all about?"

I notice his t-shirt, the same one he'd been wearing two nights ago. White with blue lettering across the chest. *Urban Fishing Company.*

Urban…

All at once, my head begins to spin. Only this time, it's not from the rum.

"Bram," I say, my voice shaking but certain. "Is that short for Abraham? Are you…Abraham Urban?"

Bram looks up at the swarming clouds overhead, tugging at his thick black beard, his face the epitome of guilt and regret—a man discovered.

White stars push into my vision, exploding behind my eyes. "I can't believe this," I breathe.

He doesn't speak right away, just shakes his head wearily, like it's taking every ounce of him to do it.

"You're Willow's stalker," I work out aloud, a horrified awe dawning over me. "You were the prime suspect when she died. The cops thought"—I choke up for fear of it being true—"they thought you murdered her."

"No," Bram says resolutely, the word bursting from his mouth like a gunshot.

"No, what?" I ask through clenched teeth, ready to tear into him. "They had to file a restraining order to keep you away from her. She was just a kid, you fucking pervert."

"You don't know what you're talking about," he snaps. "You don't even have a clue."

"Oh, I don't?" I'm so angry that I can't even find it in me to scream. With each panicked breath, a burst of rage glides over me. "Why don't you enlighten me, then? What the hell is this?" I hold my arms out, appalled. "Why is her name on your boat?"

"Don't believe everything you hear." Bram's eyes are firm against mine, but still empty, shaken, broken.

"It's not small town gossip, asshole. It's public record."

Heat stretches across my limbs, pulsing feverishly. I imagine Bram's face exploding into flame, reduced to ashes.

"I think it's best you leave," is his deliberate response. "Go. Now. Before I change my mind and call the cops."

A hatred I didn't know I was capable of pours out of me, vicious and immediate. "And if I don't, what will you do?" I ask, instigating. "Are you gonna try to kill me too?"

"That's *enough*, Dell," Hatch says edgily. "You don't know what you're talking about." His body is the only thing keeping me from clawing Bram's eyes from their sockets.

"Take your friend home, Hatcher," Bram says flatly, clenching those massive bear hands into fists. An inferno blazes in his eyes. "Take. Her. Home."

Hatch reaches for my hand, but I shake free, unable to stop myself. I spit at Bram over Hatch's shoulder, "You destroyed my family. You ruined my mother's life! You're the reason for all of it, the reason her sister is dead—"

My rant is cut short by the frightening way Bram's nostrils flare, the twisted shudder dancing over his face.

"Her sister?" His face convulses, transforming into that of a beast beneath the pregnant moon. "You think that poor little girl was Laurel's sister?"

A horrible, sickening laugh rips from his lips, a laugh I can't even begin to comprehend. It terrifies me, his wicked words reverberating in my ears, playing over and over with deafening intensity as the harbor lights revolve around me like a carousel.

"Let's go," Hatch says as he drags me from that place. Taking my arm, he pulls me onto the docks, leading me away.

I barely process any of it.

All I see is Bram's face as he watches on from that wooden boat, masked in shadow, eyes grim as the devil's.

All I hear are my mother's words ricocheting across my mind like a wayward bullet, leaving an unmendable trail of scars.

"Don't go back to Halcyon Bay."

CHAPTER TWENTY-TWO

Hatch pins me against a wall in an isolated, trash-filled alleyway, glaring at me like I've swallowed a bomb that will soon blow both of our bodies to slivers.

"Are you high?"

I thrash against him. "I'm fine."

"Fine?" he repeats. "Trespassing on private property and accusing people of murder is fine?"

I push against his chest, but he still doesn't budge. "Let me go."

"I'm not letting go until I know you're not gonna launch yourself in front of moving traffic. Whatever you've been drinking has clearly stripped away any sense of self-preservation you had left—"

"I said move!" I give him a hard, determined shove, and he finally concedes, lowering his hands from my shoulders while maintaining an active, ready stance, probably in case I try to bolt.

"You want to tell me what the hell that was about back there?" He watches me like one might watch a feral zoo animal—captivated yet uneasy. "Why were you on Bram's boat?"

"Because it has *her* name on it," I snap. "Willow's name, my mother's sister. After everything that pedophile's done to my family, he has the nerve to splash her name on his boat like some twisted memento—"

"And you didn't think to pause for a second and consider that you might be wrong about him?"

My cheeks redden as I'm struck with wave after wave of renewed anger, all while Bram's bear face ripples in the murky waters of my mind.

"I'm not wrong," I say through gritted teeth.

Hatch shakes his head, huffing like a parent scolding a defiant child. "What are even you doing at the seaport at this hour?"

"I could ask you the same question."

"I work here, Dell." Hatch tugs on his shirt, the *Urban Fishing Company* logo ruffling across his chest. "It's my job to be here."

"I didn't realize I needed a special invitation to—"

"To board someone's vessel in the middle of the night? News flash, you do!" Exasperation hones his words. "This part of the seaport can be dangerous at night for—"

"For who? Delicate, inebriated women like me?" My loose tongue lashes wildly. I'm in the mood to fight.

"For *tourists*," he answers coolly, not taking my bait. His green eyes are harsh—the flattest and darkest I've ever seen them. "In case you weren't aware, we've got our fair share of crackheads, muggers, and low-lifes in Halcyon Bay. It'd be great if you didn't go looking for trouble— or the goddamn undertaker."

"I don't have a death wish, Hatch!"

"You could've fooled me."

The storm inside my soul intensifies. My legs tremble and my stomach churns as everything rises to the surface, crashing over me and dragging me under. I slump against the wall, plotting my next move.

I can't return to Cliffmoor House tonight, to the guest house that faces that dark stretch of beach. The idea of it makes the acid swirl violently in my belly. June would take me in, but the thought of her nervous questioning—of her probing, watery eyes, so much like my mother's—makes me shudder. I could book myself a room at a hotel, but the idea of being alone in a strange, empty room is almost worse.

Come home, Dad's voice echoes in my head, the remnants of our disastrous phone conversation rising from the dust. I could leave right now—probably *should* leave, in fact—but doing so would mean abandoning my search for truth in my family's tragedy. It would mean accepting that I can't keep my mother from collapse, that I can't fix her. It would mean admitting defeat, so I know I won't be able to go through with it. I've come too far to turn back now.

Without another word, I skirt past Hatch and take off down the alley alone. I don't know where I'm going, but I need to get out of this wretched, stinking place.

Two seconds, and he's caught my elbow in his hand. "Where are you going?"

"Away from here." It's an honest answer, and the only thing I'm sure of.

"Then you're going the wrong way." He peers at me earnestly. "Look, my truck is parked over in the lot. Come with me. I'll take you wherever you want to go."

I eye him skeptically, scanning my mind for other viable options, debating the many ways this gesture of goodwill could go wrong. I'd already shown Hatch way too much of myself, given him an up-close look at the ugliest, most vulnerable parts of me. Do I want to set myself up for more of the same?

"It's a no-strings-attached offer," he says as if sensing my hesitation. "I only want to help you."

My knees buckle at the twinkling green of his eyes, beckoning and reassuring me. "Let me help you," he repeats solemnly.

Though I don't explicitly agree to anything, when Hatch moves toward the parking lot, I find myself trailing him in silence, all the way to a beat-up blue and white Ford Ranger. I climb stiffly into the truck's passenger's seat. Hatch slides in beside me and revs the engine, waiting for direction.

Pain bites my left hand as a stream of blood bubbles up from a cuticle. I've ripped a hangnail all the way down to my knuckle. I stare at it, unmoved. Numb.

"Where to?" he asks.

"I…don't know." It's nearly midnight, I'm utterly exhausted, and I can't get anything straight in my head.

"Okay," he says.

"Okay," I repeat, as if something's been decided.

Hatch goes back to waiting—adjusting the temperature in the truck, tuning the radio to an acoustic rock station, cleaning the windshield—while tears prick my eyes, about to overflow from a reserve that I'd been pushing down for months. Being back in Halcyon Bay has filled me up to the brim. Something, sometime, was bound to leak out.

All too soon, he notices. "Dell, no…please don't cry."

"Just drive," I mumble, staring out the window.

He does as I say, rolling out of the seaport and onto a backroad. The sleepy town slides past my vision, a muddle of darkness and shifting streetlights. At some point, the tears begin to pour in earnest, but I don't bother to dry or hide them.

"I know it's hard to talk about stuff like this," Hatch says, his voice a careful hum. I glimpse at him, taking in his face through the blur and sting of emotion. "But if you ever do want to talk, I'm willing to listen."

I shake my head, too drained to respond.

"I really am," he says. And when I meet his eyes again, he seems to mean it.

CHAPTER TWENTY-THREE

The residential marina is clear across the island, worlds apart from the bustling, commercialized seaport. It's populated by rows of brightly colored houseboats nestled at their moorings, comprising a tidy grid of quirky waterfront neighborhoods. Hatch parks the Ranger and we disembark, winding across a maze of docks until we stop at a sea-green houseboat bobbing gently in the water. He opens the door, flicks on a light switch, and we step inside.

There's an unmade bed and a small wooden nightstand. A pocket door in the corner leads to a bathroom the size of a broom closet. A sink is laid into a tiny square of counter space with a cooler tucked underneath. A box fan rests atop a compact chest of drawers, and on the wall nearby is the boat's steering wheel and accompanying control panels.

An assortment of photographs are tacked above the bed. Fishermen holding up an impressive catch. A beautiful young woman cradling a newborn. A young boy perched atop a man's broad shoulders. I scan the faces and scenes as Hatch cracks open the cooler. He grabs two frosted beers, pops both tops, and passes me one. Then, wordlessly, he tugs on the sliding glass door at the foot of the bed and disappears into the dark outside.

The patio deck overlooks still waters and the colorful houseboats that stipple the marina. Two plastic Adirondack chairs are set side-by-side beneath a worn sunshade. Hatch sinks into one and I the other, neither of us speaking at first, but I feel his ever-present eyes on me, drawing me in. The quiet swelter of them is almost too much to handle.

"Go ahead," I say after several minutes.

"What?"

"You've stared me into submission." I roll my eyes to mask that simmering inner rush, the warmth licking my face as he studies me. "Just ask already."

He puts the beer to his lips and I watch as he tips back the bottle. Catching myself, I avert my eyes, staring out at the drifting houseboats instead.

"Well, first off," he says, "are you really a Klyne?"

Of all things, this *is what he's itching to know?*

"Still waiting on the DNA results, but all signs point to yes. Unfortunately."

"Palmer's a Klyne," he points out. "I'm guessing you didn't recognize her the other night?"

"Last I saw Palmer, or any of the Klynes, I was four. It's been twenty years since I stepped foot on this island."

Hatch screws up his lips. "So why come back now?"

There's a flicker of red light in the distant water, constant and dependable. It winks on, then off, on, off—spurts of vivid color searing through the endless black. I squint at it, counting the seconds between each flash, racking my brain for the right words, the right explanation. None seem suitable or thorough enough.

"My mom's mom died," I say finally, sticking to the easiest, most surface-level excuse. "I came back for the services…for all the morbid pomp and circumstance."

"Oh, that's right. The big 'celebration of life' is tomorrow." He catches me staring and shrugs. "Everyone knows about it. Your family's like royalty around here."

"Phenomenal."

We drink our beers and settle into a comfortable silence. I find myself letting my guard down a bit, easing into the tranquility of this humble place, so far removed from everything I've come to know. I can almost forget all the bad now that I'm with Hatch, can almost let my troubles sink to the depths of my mind...but then my eyes catch on his t-shirt, on the sight of that hellish name splashed across his chest.

"Can I ask *you* something?"

He lolls his head in my direction, caramel waves falling over his forehead. I suppress the urge to reach out and brush them back. "Shoot."

"Why would you choose to be employed by that psychopath?"

Hatch gives me a serious look, his glimmering eyes sharp and discerning. "C'mon, Dell." The way he says my name is both cautious and cautionary, but he doesn't elaborate.

"I'm very interested, actually."

He shakes his head like I wouldn't understand, and he's probably right. "You don't know him, okay? Bram was my dad's best friend. He's like family to me, like an uncle."

I'm not sure whether this revelation lends credence to Bram's character or makes me question Hatch's. Maybe both and maybe neither, but I put this aside for the moment, clinging instead to the one word Hatch used that makes me lean in closer.

"*Was* his best friend?"

Hatch runs his tongue over his teeth, scrunching his nose like he's smelled something sickening. I sense the contents of his mind rolling over, thick with clouds of dark memory. "Yeah. My dad died. A few years back." He takes another swig of his beer.

"Oh. I'm so sor—"

"Stop. Don't," he says insistently. "Please don't apologize. There's nothing to forgive. Nothing that can fix it."

"Okay."

After another long silence, he adds, "I know you've got personal reasons for hating him, but I've known Bram my whole life. He's not the cold-blooded killer you think he is."

"Seemed about ready to kill me," I murmur.

"Any charges brought against him were dropped long ago, and all your family's allegations turned out to be bullshit. The Klynes were just looking for someone to blame. As unofficial overlords of Halcyon Bay, they've got a lot of sway around here, you know? But Bram was cleared. Police ruled your aunt's death an accident—"

"Doesn't mean they got it right."

"Maybe not," he concedes. "But I'm telling you, it wasn't him."

My thoughts toss back to Bram's most disturbing accusation, when he'd asked cruelly, indignantly, *You think that poor little girl was Laurel's sister?* It had sounded like the disgruntled ravings of a maniac, of someone predisposed to chaos and conspiracy.

"What did he mean when he said that Willow wasn't my mom's sister?"

"I don't know," Hatch says. "I thought that was weird too. And, look, I'll admit, Bram's not a perfect person. He drinks like a fish, detests pretty much everyone on this island, and talks to that boat as if it were his living, breathing companion, like it's the only thing in the world he can really trust. So, yeah, you could say he's not *all there* in the head. But that still doesn't make him a murderer."

If Bram isn't a murderer, then what is he? And what had he meant to insinuate about my family?

Did he think the Klynes had stolen Willow? Or bought her, like they did their mansions and jewels? Somewhere deep in his deviant mind, did Bram believe that he had some sort of depraved claim on her? That she belonged to him?

"I get it, you know," Hatch says quietly, bringing me back to the houseboat, his company, and the calm, dark night.

"Get what?"

"How hard it is to let things go, especially when it comes to family." He shakes his head, almost to himself.

I say nothing while I mull this over. All my life, I'd killed myself to hang on, to keep treading, keep everyone I love afloat, keep us all from sinking. How does one learn to 'let go' of that tendency, that need to be a safety net for others around you?

Hatch shifts his piercing gaze back to me. "This place has an uncanny way of dredging unpleasant things to the surface."

Warmth sweeps across my skin, and I'm forced to think up a quick distraction. "Those photos inside, are they of your family?"

He takes a slow sip, his eyes sliding back to the darkness. "Yup."

"Your dad?"

Hatch nods, the muscles tense along his jaw. I feel a gripping, compulsive desire to trace that rugged jawline with my fingertips, but I clamp my hands into fists before I do anything rash.

"You must miss him."

"Every day," he says. "Dad's the one who taught me to fish. That's what I remember most. Just being on the water together, sunrise to sunset, reeling them in, tossing them back. Things were easier then. Lighter."

"And your mom?" I ask, recalling the photo of the young woman with the newborn pressed to her cheek.

"What about her?"

"Are the two of you close?"

"We used to be," Hatch says carefully. "Ever since Dad died, not so much."

"Oh." I don't have the restraint to keep from asking, "Why not?"

He takes one last sip of his beer, tossing his head back lightly, and plunks the bottle at his feet. When he exhales, his chest and shoulders fall, strangely deflated.

"She sort of blames me for it, for what happened to my dad."

My mouth goes slack, dropping open. "Why would she blame you?"

Hatch bites his lip absently, his gaze shifting and blurring. I don't like the way the turn in conversation changes his face, bringing forth a heavy, latent grief buried within.

"We used to have this boat," he recounts. "A big sport fishing yacht with all the bells and whistles. My dad worked all his life to buy that thing. Named her the *Seaborn Lady*, after my mom. She was a real dream come true."

The sadness woven into his words is alarming. I can't keep myself from edging closer, pressing into that electric space between us, studying the gleaming, undeniable green of his eyes. They grow dimmer, glossier, as he unthreads the tapestry of his family history.

"One night, a few summers back, Dad stayed late at the seaport. He was down in the boat cabin, prepping supplies to head out the next morning—making lures, replacing lines, or what have you. Next thing we know, there's an explosion. The *Seaborn Lady* went up in flames with Dad trapped inside. She sank right there in the harbor, before anyone could get to him."

The gut-wrenching scene jolts to life in my mind, emotions swirling within me like the rollicking crash of waves, engulfing me in that old, familiar pain. Only this time, it's not for myself or my mother, but for *him*.

"Hatch," I say as gently as I can, "it was an accident. Not your fault—"

"But it was, actually." His expression is hollow and heartbreaking, rife with immeasurable guilt. "The explosion was caused by a trickle of fuel that had been leaking into the hull of the boat. Some corroded wires from the bilge pump sparked, and just like *that*"—he snaps his fingers, a piercing crack—"the place lit up like a tinderbox."

I shake my head a little, still not understanding.

"The wiring issue was part of a backlog of work I'd been putting off for a while," he explains. "If I'd done the work the way I was supposed to…if I'd taken the time one lousy afternoon and *just done it*, I might've prevented the fire. And besides, I should've been there that night. I should've stayed. Then maybe I could've stopped it…maybe I could've saved him."

"Or maybe you would've been trapped down there too."

He shrugs listlessly.

I don't know what more say, how to stem his pain, so we sit in thoughtful silence, things said and unsaid dangling between us, possibilities flashing before us, like the winking of silver stars in the sky.

He'd been so honest, I realize. I'd offered up simplistic half-truths, but Hatch…Hatch had bared his soul. He'd been vulnerable despite the wounds he'd have to rip open. Even in the thick of healing, he wasn't afraid to bleed. Even though it hurt, he still chose to let me in.

Maybe that's why I decide to admit, in a low and reticent whisper, "I didn't come back here for my grandmother's funeral. Not really."

He turns to me, eyes scintillating, but doesn't push for more. He simply waits for whenever I'm ready, whatever I'm willing to give.

"My mom's sick," I say, practically trembling. These aren't matters I know how to articulate, and sharing them with *him*—this beautiful, unexpected man that sets my skin aflame—is almost impossible. But, for whatever reason, I want to try. So I crack my heart open, reach out my hand, knowing how easy it would be to catch fire and burn. "Not physically sick, but…in her mind. And I think it all leads back to this place, to things that happened here before we moved. I'm still trying to figure it all out, I guess."

"You came back to save her," he says simply.

I shrug in response, pondering his words. *He understands that need more than most,* I think. The regret that would consume me if I didn't succeed.

But then I remember what I'd just told him—that in trying to save his father, Hatch could've easily doomed himself. He could've been trapped in that boat, while the fire raged and consumed them both. Would the same thing happen to me? Would I be able to pull Mom from her sinking ship in time, or would I lose myself in the effort and go down with it too?

Several minutes pass and Hatch grabs us another couple of beers, slipping a chilled bottle into my hands before dropping back into his chair. The calming toll of a ship's bell rings from somewhere in the marina while that red light in the distance continues its rhythmic flickering, a brilliant speck of calm amid a world of tumult.

Our fingertips brush from where they lay on the arms of our chairs, and for once, I don't give in to my hasty inclination to pull back, to shove down my feelings and seal them in frost and darkness.

So what if Palmer despises him, or that his father's best friend is a madman, or that he calls this treacherous island home? Why should we be enemies on account of factors we have no control over? I don't want Hatch to be my enemy.

Do I dare give in to the things I do want?

My fingers tingle with pulsing energy, longing to be touched, to be laced in his, but I keep still, letting myself enjoy the quiet pleasure of his company.

This is enough, I think firmly. As far as we can go. Far more than I could've imagined.

A yawn spills from my lips and I lean back, giving way to the heaviness pushing into my eyes, my heart, my mind.

"Do you want me to take you home?" Hatch asks tentatively.

"That place isn't my home," I answer without opening my eyes.

After a minute, he says, "You can stay here, if you want."

At this, I glance up at him, wondering if there's something more to his invitation, but Hatch's expression reveals nothing. No pushy grins or suggestive eyes, no sign of any clandestine motive.

"Take the bed," he offers.

"What about you?"

"I'm good right here." He burrows deeper in his chair. "Got my sippy cup and my nightlight." He lifts his beer to the swollen moon. "What more do I need?"

I nod, on the verge of standing to retreat to his bed, but I don't really want to leave him to go inside.

Despite all my usual impulses, I don't want to be alone tonight, in my self-inflicted house of stone. These hours spent by Hatch's side—the both of us exposed and susceptible, sad but thrillingly alive—are the greatest peace I've felt in months.

"I'm good here too, then." I sigh, allowing my eyes to close. *I'm good here with you.*

As I drift to sleep on that Adirondack chair, an easy weight comes over me. A blanket, soft and smelling of clean ocean breeze, coupled with Hatch's susurrant voice and his breath on my mist-dewed hair.

"Sleep tight, Dell."

I murmur a drowsy "Thank you" and surrender to the night.

CHAPTER TWENTY-FOUR

Sunlight spills down the length of the bed, cutting warmly across my face, waking me in a blinding yellow instant. I recognize the smell of him before anything else.

I sit up, the thin blue comforter sliding from my shoulders. Through the sun-drenched back door, turquoise waters glint in the morning light, swaddling rows of rainbow houseboats anchored to faded wooden docks.

I'd spent the night. And he'd carried me inside.

There's a note beside me on the small nightstand, scrawled out in messy handwriting.

Didn't want to wake you.
Hide out here as long as you need.
I'll find you this afternoon.

I try not to overthink those last words, try not to dwell on the perfect simplicity of that sentiment he'd scribbled in a haste, and on what it means to me.

I'll find you this afternoon.

A promise—one he doesn't owe me, a proper stranger, but for whatever reason, he chose to extend anyway.

I'll find you this afternoon.

I force myself to shake off those cobwebby implications—the thought and scent of him still assaulting my brain—and take in the houseboat space by daylight.

The bright glow of morning breathes new life across the wall of photographs. I inspect them more closely now, studying the many happy faces staring back at me, sepia smiles from golden eras long past. They're of a simpler time, back when fishing was a beloved Seaborn family tradition. Now, it's become something else entirely.

For Hatch, it's a steady line of work. A way of life and an income, rather than a place where joy can be found, ever since that fateful night in the harbor. For his mother, it's a nightmarish reminder of her loss, the floodgate for her pain, her ire, and disdain. And for both of them, it's a breaking point, an uncrossable line carved deep in the sand.

I understand why Hatch clings to his photos. The memories are what keep him moving forward, a daily reminder to put one foot in front of the other, and a vow that things can be good again. They're his hope in an often hopeless world.

I peer at the snapshot of the woman carrying the baby, her cheek pressed to the tufts of hair on the child's head, like fuzzy weeds poking up from cracks in the concrete. Their faces are squished together as if he were still part of her, a mere extension of her body. Hatch and his mother, bonded by love and blood.

My eyes skip several rows down, where three fishermen hold up a monstrous catch with a long, pointed snout—a swordfish, if I had to guess. An adolescent Hatch stands to one side, that lopsided smile present even as a lanky teenager, his eyes that same striking green that I might sink and drown in. At the center of the photo is a middle-aged man with dimpled cheeks and joyful eyes, that same uncanny, verdant shade—Hatch's father, brimming with life and vigor. The last man in the group is gruff-looking, hair disheveled and intensely bearded. No light reaches his dark eyes, like some mysterious thief stole his smile away. I know that I'm looking at a young Abraham Urban, and my head pangs at the sight of him as scenes from last night trickle into my mind.

I slip from the bed, retrieving my shoes from where they're placed by the door and my purse dangling lazily from the knob. I glimpse the contents of the room once more, trying to memorize every square inch of the small oceanfront sanctuary, taking a mental photograph of it. I fold it into the pocket of my heart and keep it like a treasure, a tiny escape I can return to anytime I need it.

Hundreds of islanders in their Sunday best pour in from every crack and crevice to graze upon the pastures of Cliffmoor House, paying tribute to my late grandmother. By three o'clock, I've received condolences from more people than I've spoken to in my entire life.

They swarm the family like bees to a honeycomb, humming their identical sympathies, a thousand impersonal "I'm sorry's" repeated over and over on a never-ending loop. I'm beginning to understand why Hatch hates hearing those damn words so much.

June, Palmer, Leif, and Mojo are posted up in the parlor like celebrities while crowds wait in line to fawn over them. They're far better equipped to handle occasions like this than I am. I keep to the background, trying to fade into the wallpaper or invoke some latent powers of invisibility. Every time a stranger approaches me, dabbing their eyes with handkerchiefs, reaching for my hands to hold, I get the urge to scream. But the Klynes are pros at dealing with an audience. They never even break a sweat.

Though I know practically no one here, every other person seems to recognize me. "You *must* be Meridel!" they shriek. "You look *just* like Laurel did at your age! I'm *so* sorry for your loss! This must be *such* a difficult time for you all!"

I nod through clenched teeth, skirting their questions as best I can before slipping back into the shadows, hoping to go unnoticed.

Virginia's portrait observes all the goings-on from her pedestal of marble. Below the mantel, someone has started a roaring fire—no matter that it's a sweltering ninety-eight degrees out. The flames crackle with restless energy, dancing feverishly in the hearth, as if my grandmother herself were animating them, making her presence known.

Ambrose, oppositely, is calm as a ripple-free sea. He sits near Virginia's portrait, his shining smile unflappable, reminiscing about his wife to a group of captive spectators. They pack in close, some even settling onto the floor at his feet so it looks like Ambrose is orating from a throne—a king holding court. He seems quite comfortable in that position.

Sasha arrives in a flurry of air kisses and jasmine-scented perfume, promptly linking her arm through Palmer's, affixing to her side like a parasite. I swear I see Mojo roll his eyes a time or two. Leon and Finch show up soon after, looking hungover and uneasy in their formalwear. Finch tugs at his shirt collar that's too tight around the neck. He's constantly fidgeting, scanning the room neurotically, as if waiting for someone to scold or spook him. Leon is more mellow as he locates the lunch table and bar, tossing me a sultry wink on his way there. Thanks to his antics, I actually smile for the first time all day—the one encounter I've had that hasn't tickled my gag reflex.

Tristen is tucked against the far end of the parlor, sullenness looming over him like a cloak. While his father chats with guests, my cousin remains withdrawn from the spotlight, rooted to one spot and stone-still. My eyes catch at his lips, which, to my surprise, are moving rapidly, low and discreet. I try to peer over the swarming heads, but I can't tell who he's speaking to.

His eyes connect with mine and his stare darkens, falling over me like a crippling, starless night. His lips stop moving, whispered curses frozen in time, sending a shiver racing down my spine. I've clearly interrupted something I'm not welcome to.

Freya Larisse enters the parlor in a dramatic swirl of silks, and I decide I need some fresh air *stat*. I squeeze quickly through the masses of mourners, zigzagging past with murmured "Excuse me's," my eyes dipped to the floor in hopes of avoiding an unpleasant face-to-face. I have no desire to be victimized by Freya's voodoo force field ever again.

Once in the hallway, I head for the French doors, only to wind up colliding into someone much taller and sturdier than me.

"Just the girl we were looking for," Prescott booms jovially, borderline inappropriate for an event of this nature.

His mother pops her head out from behind his shoulder, her frazzled gray hair sticking out at odd angles. "Not who I was looking for," Lettie grumbles, loud enough for me to hear.

"It's great to see you again," Prescott says, ignoring his mother. "Wish it were under better circumstances, but I'll take what I can get."

"Where're the rest of the Klynes, missy?" Lettie asks, not bothering to try recalling my name.

"In the parlor." I point in the direction I came from.

Lettie gestures for Prescott to follow her with one impatient, fluttering hand.

He sighs, eyes trailing his mother's back. "Catch you later?" he asks me hopefully. His gray-blue eyes are wide with anticipation. *Poor guy.*

"Sure," I respond with what I hope comes off as a mildly enthusiastic shrug.

When I make it outside, I see there are a handful of guests littering the grounds, taking a smoke break and scandalizing over their observations of Cliffmoor House and the grieving Klynes. Low whispers of gossip pass among them like rustling leaves, their fancy dress clothes dampening with sweat. I walk quickly past, crossing the lawn to the poolside gazebo, ducking beneath the curtain of cascading white lights, and sinking onto one of the stone benches. I take a deep breath of unencumbered air.

It feels like this 'celebration' has gone on interminably, but when I check my watch, it's only been three hours...three eternal, abysmal hours.

A text message jolts my phone to life in my pocket. I pull it out to find one signal bar lit up—an absolute miracle—and a string of backed-up calls, voicemails, and texts pour in. They're all from Dad, predictably.

More of the same, each one a repeat of last night's conversation. *Need you home, call me back, we have to talk,* and so on.

"Hi, stranger."

Hatch stands in the open archway of the gazebo, drawing the twinkling curtain aside as he peeks in on me. His emerald eyes are all the more vibrant in the haze of afternoon light. "Can I sit?"

I nod and scoot over to make some room.

He settles in beside me, thigh to thigh, and a wave of heat crawls over my skin. He looks sharp in his dark slacks and gray button-down, his hair sleek and wet-looking thanks to some manly-scented gel product. I breathe it in, trying to be inconspicuous. Whatever it is, I like it. A lot.

"Hiding?" He smiles at me surreptitiously.

I shrug, tucking my legs under the bench. "Let's just say I'm past my threshold for phony tears."

"Fair enough." He bows his head a little, hands restless in his lap, that lopsided smile painting his face bright. "How'd you sleep last night?"

A glowing ember of heat burns low in my stomach as I finish his question in my mind, putting words to what he must be thinking— *How'd you sleep last night…in my bed?*

"Better than I expected," I say honestly, biting my tongue to keep from revealing anything more. "Thank you for letting me crash at your place."

And for rescuing me when I didn't know I needed it, I think, though I wouldn't dare admit it out loud.

"Anytime."

His eyes smolder like small fires licking my skin, and I can't deny that something is building between us, growing stronger, more fervid, with every moment we spend together.

I turn to the guest house, the only safe place for my eyes to land.

"Sorry I ran off so early this morning," he says. "Bram had me scheduled for a sunrise trip, and—"

Bram.

The name hits me like the clashing of cymbals, ripping across the messy contents of my brain. The mere mention of *him* creates a dry lump in my throat, bringing the blood in my veins to a boil. Just when I'd almost managed to forget…

"Right. Of course," I say tightly. "Duty calls."

The contempt in my voice isn't lost on Hatch. He watches me with an earnest, pleading sort of look. Hoping, no doubt, that I'll let this slide, that I won't resurrect the testy conversation we shared last night.

I decide to spare him the grief and change the subject. I owe him one, I suppose. "So what brings you to the Cliffmoor House of Horrors?"

"I said I'd find you." He nudges me, our bodies swaying in unison. "Thought you might need someone today. A friend."

He's right, naturally, but I'm not about to concede to it. He'd already cashed in on his one free-pass for today, and I have to preserve at least a smidgen of my pride.

"Have you made your rounds yet?" I ask, my eyes catching on the guest house again. Something about it—so crisp and manicured—looks strangely off to me, though I can't decide why.

"Not yet." Hatch turns to glimpse the looming mansion behind us, brimming with black-clad guests. "I avoided the beehive and came in through the side-gate. Is it awful in there?"

"Yes." I think of Palmer and Sasha, arms looped together to create something of a wall…a wall wrapped in rusty barbed wire—bitter, sharp, and eager for blood. Or maybe just Hatch's head on a platter. "And you've got one hell of a welcoming committee to get past."

"Is that so?" Hatch's eyes are piercing even as his smile fades. "Does this welcoming committee have a name?"

"Two names, actually. My cousin and your ex make quite the formidable team."

Hatch leans back on his hands and inhales a long, protracted breath. I watch him do this, my eyes trained on the steady pulsing in his jaw, the winding and unwinding of muscle. It's unsettling how easy he is to look at.

"You've met Sasha," he says quietly.

I force my lips into a pinched smile, so tight that it feels like I'm sucking on a lemon wedge. "I had the"—a little cough escapes my lips—"*distinct pleasure* at the bonfire the other night."

I sneak another glance at the guest house. Some indiscernible thing about it gnaws at me like the incessant itch of a scab.

"She's fun, huh?"

"The funnest."

We're sitting so close, mere inches between us, and I feel the energy swirling, the underlying current drawing us nearer, to the brink of something wonderful and treacherous. No matter that we're discussing his ex-girlfriend, or that we're sitting on the fringes of my family's eerie estate. It saturates the atmosphere, demanding to be noticed, demanding to be acted on...but neither of us does.

Hatch stiffens slightly. "Well, I guess I'd better face the music." He stands.

Good, I assure myself. It's better this way. Maybe he knows enough to keep his distance from me too.

All at once, it dawns on me what's wrong with the guest house. The lights are on inside, every last one, and I don't recall having left them that way.

"Good luck," I say to Hatch as I stand too.

"See you in a few," he says, leaving me under the canopy of lights.

A shadow rolls behind the curtain in the bedroom—*my* bedroom. Someone is inside, gliding across the foot of the bed I sleep in.

The shadow slides past again, this time in the opposite direction, in a sort of pacing gesture. The back and forth motion sends my brain into a tailspin.

I sprint to the guest house, tugging at the door—it's locked. I pull out my key and turn the knob with shaking hands, that slow-creeping feeling tickling my skin again, peppering me in goosebumps.

The door creaks open.

The insides of the guest house are almost too quiet. Everything is as I left it, except, of course, the lights. The figure patrolling the bedroom is gone, vanished into the walls, far beyond my line of sight. But there's a subtle shift in the air, an obvious violation of space.

Who else has access to this place? Ambrose and Briggs, certainly, but both of them are back at Cliffmoor House right now, hosting the world's swankiest and most unbearable funeral ever. The maid? June? Flip? How could any of them have crossed the grounds without me seeing them? There are no open windows to climb through, no back door to slip past.

My mind veers back to that ghostly figure in the bathroom—the face reflected in the silver shower gel cap, so small and distorted, with the coal-black eyes.

The peach fuzz on my arms and the back of my neck rise.

Willow?

Part of me wants to whisper her name into the empty room, to exhale it like a breath, filling the space with the memory of her. What might come of it if I do?

I shake myself back to my senses. *You're losing it.*

Pivoting on my heel, I switch the lights off once more. I turn the lock and leave the guest house behind, stepping into the gardens and swallowing her name like air.

CHAPTER TWENTY-FIVE

I pause at the threshold of the bustling parlor, scanning the crowd that awaits me inside…scanning for Hatch.

"Looking for someone?" Mojo asks, sliding in beside me. He leans against the wall, offering me a massive goblet brimming with wine.

"Who would I be looking for?" I reply crossly. "I don't know anyone here."

"Which is why I figured you could use a social lubricant." He brandishes the goblet before me so the wine sloshes around, as if the splashing sound might make it all the more tempting.

"I'm managing all right on my own, thanks."

"*¡Por favor!*" He cocks his head to one side, brown eyes dancing with amusement. "Have you caught a glimpse of yourself today?"

I raise a defiant eyebrow. "Is there a problem?"

Mojo tucks some wayward strands of dark hair behind his ears. He's cleaned up for the occasion, donning a gray skinny tie—I'm surprised he even owns a tie—with a black button-down and some fitted pinstripe slacks. His attire gives me 'refined rockstar' vibes, and I wonder if that's what he was going for all along.

"No offense, Dell," Mojo says with a shrug, "but if blatant terror and constipation had a baby, it would be sporting your face right now."

I snort and he grins triumphantly, moving the goblet back and forth in a hypnotizing motion before my eyes. "Take the fermented grape juice. You know you want to."

"For goodness sake." I take it and tilt the glass to my mouth, letting the bitter taste of it race down my throat and settle on my lips. "There. Satisfied?"

He crosses his arms across his chest, exceptionally smug-looking. "Rule *numero uno* in the world of the Klynes: every event is a party, even when it's not. If you want to learn about these people, you've gotta work the crowd. This whole creeping around, acting invisible game you're currently playing at isn't gonna cut it."

"I'm not creeping," I protest. "And who says I want to learn about them?"

Mojo laughs. "You did! At June's house. You said you went to the library, did your little Google search thing—"

"Not seeing how that's any of your business."

"I'm just saying! If you're trying to figure out your family, stop searching for answers online and start where you are. Poke around. Be nosy. You have as much right to be here as any of them."

I don't know how to respond to this, but on some level, I suppose he's right. I hadn't thought to explore Cliffmoor House itself—partly due to my irrational terror anytime I come within five feet of Ambrose, and partly because I feel that I *don't* belong here. I never have and never will. The Klynes are like an elite club to which I've never felt worthy of membership. That feeling of disaffiliation—of estrangement—is tenaciously hardwired into my brain.

"This must be super weird for you, being back and all, but maybe it's just as weird for them to have you back," Mojo says. "If you get to know them, you'll see there's more there than what's on the surface. Take Palmer, for instance. She's a tough nut to crack, but she's all goo on the inside. You're growing on her."

"She actually said that?"

"Not in so many words, but I can tell. You're getting under her skin. She likes you, even if she doesn't want to."

Mojo waves at someone in the foyer, exchanging distanced greetings and pleasantries, while I take another sip of wine and absorb his words. I hadn't planned on liking Palmer, either. On liking *any* of the Klynes, in fact. But just because I like them—some of them, anyway—doesn't mean I know how to act, or who to be, around them.

I glance furtively into the hall, in need of a distraction from all this talk of family, and spot Hatch some distance away inside the bathroom. He leans back against the sink, arms crossed over his dark button-down, shoulders slumped in an unnerving manner that makes him look smaller than he is. His eyes are masked in shadow and lowered to his feet. The door is ajar, but I can't see the rest of the bathroom beyond him or discern why he looks so unhappy—so unlike himself.

I take a few steps closer, figuring something must be wrong, only to freeze at the seductive woman's voice wafting from that direction.

Sasha's voice.

From this angle, I can't see her, but I know she's in there, concealed behind the half-shut door. She's speaking in that gentle, sultry coo of hers, uttering private words meant for Hatch's ears alone.

My heart plunks like an anchor to my stomach, plunging into that shallow pool of red wine, all of my insides churning, rioting, screaming.

The bathroom door clicks shut, sealing both of them inside.

"Don't let her get to you," Mojo says and I jump, momentarily forgetting he was ever there. "Hatch is one of the good ones."

I can't pull my eyes away from the door, a sinking sensation building in my belly as I contemplate what the two of them could be discussing…or what they could be doing.

"Nice to know he gets the official dude bro stamp of approval." My voice is flat, my blood seething. "Seems you're not the only person that thinks so."

"They've got history." Mojo's face twists into a grimace, like he knows far more about Hatch and Sasha's storied past than he'd ever be comfortable sharing.

"History," I repeat on a low, exhaled breath.

"As far as I know, it's over between them," he says gently. "You should ask him yourself—"

"And why would I do that?" The question spills out with razor-sharp edges, far too revealing, much too jealous.

Mojo widens his eyes like a teacher explaining something to an obtuse student for the twenty-eighth time. "Because, Dell. You're into him." As if it's that plainly obvious.

"I'm not," I say, reiterating my sentiments from the bonfire. "Not in the slightest."

My feelings for Hatch, whatever they may be, are still too fresh—too alarming—for me to admit aloud. It's far easier, safer, for me to bury them, swallow them down swiftly like foul-tasting medicine.

"Right. Okay." Mojo squeezes my shoulder as he drifts away, slipping back into the parlor, chuckling under his breath. "You're a terrible liar. You might wanna work on that."

I take a long sip of wine, my eyes intent on the bathroom door, letting my emotions flood my tired mind, letting them get the better of me, coil me into something wicked and cruel. Everything feels like too much all at once, and part of me wishes I could snap my fingers and erase it.

Snap and watch the bathroom door combust before me. *Snap* and revel as it melts from its hinges, bursts into a hellish inferno.

Snap and let that fire swell. Let it rage and consume the entirety of Cliffmoor House, gobbling up every one of its filthy secrets.

Snap until all that remains is ash and ember, acre upon acre of absolute and utter nothingness.

Mojo's pep talk motivates me to venture into uncharted territory, a decision that aligns all too well with my recent streak of impulsive behavior and bad judgment.

Cliffmoor House's second floor is off-limits—not explicitly so, but more out of respect. None of the guests, intrusive as they may be, dare to climb the stairs into this part of the home. And while I'm technically as much a guest here as any of the others, I'm also *not* like them. For better or worse, I'm part of this family, a reluctant Klyne, but a Klyne nonetheless.

I loiter around the foyer, waiting for it to clear of prying eyes. Once the coast is clear, I steal up the staircase, minding my footsteps. At the landing, I swing a quick right into the east corridor. The walls are a shade of deep navy, like midnight sky, and covered in glinting picture frames, a treasure trove of old family photographs.

There's a young Ambrose and Virginia on their wedding day—a dazzling couple, plucked straight from the pages of some glossy *Vogue* editorial. There's Mom and June as sunshine-blond little girls, ambling through the gardens of Cliffmoor House, picking hibiscus flowers in their checkered sundresses and bobby-socks. There are several snapshots of Palmer and Leif through the years, a few professional portraits of the family at various social gatherings, a slew of glamour shots from Virginia's Hollywood heyday, Flip and Ambrose in their hunting gear…and there, dwarfed by all those cluttered, beaming faces, is a small square frame that seizes my attention completely.

The photograph is of a toddler in an olive-green onesie, her hair pulled into two fluffy brown pigtails. She looks squarely at the camera, not quite posing, but still keenly aware of the moment. A coy smirk brightens her round baby face, her hazel eyes discerning and luminous. I've never seen this image before, but I know in an instant that the child is me.

It's so bizarre and out-of-body to find my photograph hanging here among the others, as if this tiny part of me had always been locked up inside Cliffmoor House, trapped on this island without my knowledge or consent. This one photo—this small, incidental blip in time—represents a missing fragment of my life. Years that belong to *them*—to this strange, transfixing place—but not to me.

What other bits of my childhood are kept within these walls? What lingering pieces of my past might it still be concealing?

Willow, on the other hand, is notably missing from the rows of pictures. I search the photo-filled walls up and down, walking the length of the corridor and back, but there's no sign of her *anywhere*, as if the Klynes expunged her from their collective memory bank, erasing her tragedy from their idyllic existence. My throat goes dry, choked by an inextricable tangle of sadness and disgust.

A string of heated whispers spill from the opposite wing.

Curious, I follow the sounds, tiptoeing across the second-floor landing and pressing myself to the nearest wall. The door to my left is pulled forward, almost all the way shut but not quite latched, and though I can't see them, I hear two people having a hushed but lively exchange inside.

It's a man and a woman, that much I can tell, and they speak angrily—urgently—hissed murmurs passing between them. The male's voice is familiar, low and cutting…but then, so is the female's, cool and candid and perfectly articulate.

I take another step closer, trying to discern a snippet of conversation, when I hear the man say agitatedly, "—won't have another chance. If there's a right time, it's now." The voice belongs to Tristen.

I inch closer still, trying to make out the woman's response.

Someone moves inside the room. There's the squeaking of furniture springs, like one of them rose from their seated position on the bed. A shot of panic courses through me, but I don't turn away. Something keeps me there, some internal force of will that's more concerned with the nature of this clandestine interaction than it is with saving my own ass.

Maybe Hatch is right. Maybe I have lost all sense of self-preservation.

"Dell!"

I jump, terror-stricken at the sight of Prescott standing atop the stairs, wearing that stupid, smitten smile of his. The whispers in the bedroom cease abruptly—they must've heard him calling my name.

I move fast to meet him at the landing as the door shuts behind me, the latch engaged with a sharp *click!*

"What are you doing?" I hiss, grabbing Prescott by the arm and dragging him down the stairs, my heartbeat thrumming in my veins.

"I was looking for a bathroom," Prescott says. "What's the deal? All the ones downstairs are occupied."

My mind races back to Hatch and Sasha, still tucked away inside that damn bathroom. Are they reconnecting, making their peace? Making up, starting over? The train of thought is enough to make me physically ill.

"You can't be up here," I snap defensively, my fingers pressed to his arm as we descend to the foyer.

"Oh, shit. My bad. I just had to pee."

I let go of Prescott once our feet are planted on the first floor, the giant chandelier soaring high above our heads. I draw in a stabilizing breath, making a concerted effort to cool down. Going off on him, misdirecting my many frustrations, wouldn't get me anywhere.

"Sorry," I mutter, still a bit breathless. "It's been a long day."

He swats at the air. "Don't even worry about it. How are you handling things?"

"Okay, I guess." I paste an awkward smile on my lips. "Thank you, by the way, for stopping by. That was nice of you. And your mom."

Prescott shuts his eyes, letting out an aggrieved sigh. "That woman drives me insane."

"Don't all mothers?"

His eyebrows shoot up. "That's awfully forgiving of you, considering how rude she's been."

"She's not so bad."

"Yes, she is. She's snarky and crotchety and mistrusting. Like yesterday at the cemetery, how she treated you over *nothing*." He scoffs his annoyance. "She's got a serious people problem."

"She was just doing her job," I say, an idea spawning in my mind. I have to wind my way to it gracefully though, leading Prescott without him knowing it, like an unsuspecting horse to water. "I bet lots of weirdos come through the cemetery that need fending off...all those crazy 'sea trumpet freaks,' right?"

Prescott cracks a slow, sloping smile. "Yeah. That's right."

"So give the old lady a break"—I nudge his arm—"she's probably got a lot on her mind."

"I guess that's true." Prescott reclines against the banister, running a hand over his buzzed blond hair. "Halcyon Bay's got a pretty twisted history, and she's had a front-row seat for plenty of it."

"Twisted history?" I prompt.

Prescott nods. "This island's a magnet for all things weird and sinister."

My eyes widen suggestively. "How do you mean?"

"Well…I wouldn't want to scare you off or anything."

I scoff and smack Prescott's arm flirtatiously, ignoring how grimy I feel doing it, at the insincerity dripping off me. "For your information, I love a good scare."

"You?" he asks.

"Yes, me. Why's that so shocking?"

Prescott's smile deepens, an enthralled glaze in his sleepy-gray eyes. "You don't strike me as the 'weird and sinister' type."

"Oh, please. Try me." I say it like a dare. "Tell me a scary story. Tell me about *the Brine*." I wiggle my fingers for dramatic effect, pretending this is all one big joke, nothing of consequence whatsoever.

Prescott squints playfully, a twinkle of excitement in his expression. "I can show you better than I can tell you."

My smile is cautious. "Show me what?"

"The sea trumpet fields. *Their* place. I used to go all the time in high school, just fooling around, eating shit with my friends. It's a pretty cool spot if you're into that sort of thing."

"You mean the murder-cult thing?"

He flashes me an impish grin. "Exactly."

Admittedly, I'd wanted to pump Prescott for information. I'd hoped to get a local's take on the Brine, shed some light on Callie Oxton's suicide, and inform myself about whatever ties the cult may or may not have to my family. But a field trip is considerably more than I bargained for.

"Won't we get in trouble for being out there?"

He shrugs. "The fields are government property, so we could *technically* go to jail if we got caught trespassing, but no one ever patrols the place. I've never so much as seen a cop car on that side of the island."

"Are you sure you know your way around?"

Prescott shoots me a cool-guy smirk. "Piece of cake."

My time to get answers in Halcyon Bay is dwindling. Can I afford to turn this opportunity down? Will I be satisfied going home without exploring every connection, every avenue to the truth?

I think back to Hatch, still locked in that bathroom with Sasha, doing whatever they're doing behind that closed door. His calming voice and seagrass eyes swirl in my head like shattered snippets from a hazy dream—a dream I can't return to now that I'd been jolted awake.

All I want to do is run from this place, run as far as I can. Distance will help me see things clearly. Distance will put thoughts of *him* out of my mind, and replace each one with matters of import.

"Okay," I say, masking my uncertainty with resolve. "Take me to the sea trumpet fields."

CHAPTER TWENTY-SIX

It takes Prescott an hour to drop his mother off at home and return to Old Town, during which time I wait in the parlor, reverting back to my post as resident wallflower.

At some point or other, Finley makes an appearance, entering the house in an overwhelming fit of sobs and trapping me in his nauseating, gin-scented embrace.

By some miracle, I manage to avoid a run-in with Freya, though I speculate that the psychic knows I'm dodging her somehow. She smiles to herself as if amused by my concerted efforts to maintain distance between us.

Tristen doesn't resurface with his stealthy, second-floor companion, and to my greatest annoyance, I lose track of Hatch and Sasha too, and can only imagine what dark, clandestine corner they might've scampered off to.

Just before leaving, I spot Palmer breaking away from a hug with Sabine. My grandmother's personal assistant is on her way out of Cliffmoor House, arm linked with a tiny older woman wearing an eccentric maroon frock and cat-eye glasses. The woman's dwarfish build and hastened steps are easy to recognize.

"Hey," Palmer says as I approach.

"Hey." I watch as the pair of women retreat down the curving brick driveway. "Who's that lady with Sabine?"

"That's her mom, Greer, the island's head librarian." Palmer squints at me inquisitively. "You didn't meet her the other day, when you went to check out Gram's books?"

The pixie woman, Greer, turns back vaguely, though she can't have heard our exchange from this distance. She takes a long perusal at all of Cliffmoor House, from its towering peaks to its wraparound porch, with an expression on her lips that looks, weirdly, like amusement.

"Guess I must've missed her," I say, too preoccupied with the librarian's strange curiosity to recount the bizarre details of our last encounter.

Greer's sweeping gaze falls over me, and upon recognizing me, that enigmatic expression on her lips shifts into one of unadulterated delight. A knowing smile blooms across her pale, pretty face, but it may as well be a sneer for all that I can comprehend it.

"She's a bit of an odd bird," Palmer comments under her breath, breaking the tension with a haphazard wave.

The librarian tips her chin at us both—a final goodbye—before turning back to her daughter, nestling close to Sabine's shoulder. They shuffle through the gates as one, and turn left onto the tree-swaddled road, out of my line of sight.

"Odd," I agree, bringing myself back to the task at hand. "I'll be back in a bit, all right? I need some air."

"Okay."

A subtle hint of *something* rings in Palmer's voice, a quiet trouble brewing behind those sky-blue eyes, but she doesn't elaborate. She turns back to the house and straight into the arms of several weepy guests while I make my way down the driveway.

Prescott waits beneath an oak outside the Cliffmoor House grounds. He's perched on a fiery orange motorbike, his eyes shielded in

Terminator-style sunglasses.

"Your chariot, m'lady," he says with a smile, offering me a helmet covered in flashy bumper stickers.

I lower it over my head, breathing in the stench of man-sweat and fuel, and swing a leg over the bike, settling onto the narrow space of leather seat behind him.

"Hold on tight," he says, whipping his head around to shoot me a smile. I wrap my arms around his waist, and he punches the throttle, lurching us forward into the waning sun.

Zipping down the tree-lined road, I spot Hatch's Ranger nestled among the rows of streetside cars. He hadn't left yet, so where the heck was he? Why hadn't I seen him?

My stomach twists up, bile rising, but I push all thought of him away, leaving him amid the whirling clouds of dust kicked up by Prescott's wheels. I force myself to focus only on where I'm going, what's to come, and why.

Halcyon Bay's lively atmosphere and sandy terrain melt away as we drive into overgrown, isolated territory, deep into a part of the island long abandoned by civilization.

Asphalt turns to dirt road as I work myself into a minor panic, suddenly very aware of the fact that I'm in a secluded place, on the cusp of nightfall, with a guy I don't actually know—my finest hour in shitty decision-making to date.

We pull to a stop beside a stretch of dense brush and Prescott shuts off the engine. I launch myself off the bike, knees buckling as I disembark.

"Excited?" he asks with a chuckle, getting to his feet much more gracefully than I.

I yank off the helmet and toss it at him. I'd like to clobber him over the head with it. "Absolutely."

Prescott tucks the helmet into his back compartment and rolls the bike into the brush, concealing it from sight, which doesn't make me feel any better. No one will ever know we're here.

"Just in case," he says with a wink.

I bend down, pretending to adjust my boot while reaching for a jagged rock and slipping it into my pocket.

Just in case, I think.

"Ready?"

I shoot him a smile, more confident now with the stone pressed against my hip. Not the most sophisticated weapon, but with enough force and the element of surprise, it could do some damage. "You betcha."

"Follow me. The entrance is just up ahead."

The sun dips low in the sky, the onset of night less than an hour away, casting the treetops in darkness. I check my phone—one last-ditch hope—but as expected, there's no signal. I'm totally on my own.

Prescott leads me away from the dirt road into the massive, tangled brush through a well-trafficked hole. We move in a low crouch, hands raised against snagging twigs and blade-sharp leaves. A wayward branch nicks my cheek, and when I swipe at it, my thumb comes back bloody.

We reach a sign reading *U.S. Government Property, No Trespassing,* and Prescott teases, "We're heeere."

I have to suppress the urge to jab my rock through his jugular.

Behind the sign is a locked gate with a tall chain-link fence running along either side of it—a boundary line encompassing the sea trumpet fields, as far as the eye can see. Barbed wire tops the length of fence, rusted spikes stabbing the air, threatening all who dare to scale it.

Prescott leads me several yards down, to where a corner of chain-link has been ripped up from the ground. He pushes back the wild plants to clear our path. "This way."

I follow him through and into a vast clearing…into what can only be described as vacant, brutal wasteland. Everything here is singed to a crisp, the earth black and dead. There are no signs of budding life, no growth sprouting from the grounds. Just miles and miles of pure ruin, the land irreparably scarred.

Prescott looks delighted by the unease sparking in my face.

"Creepy, huh?"

It could just be my imagination, but I still smell the smoke and scorch of fire on the wind. "It's…something."

"Let's walk and talk."

He leads me along the perimeter of the fields, keeping to the shade of the underbrush rather than the exposed barrenness of the clearing.

"It seems so drastic," I say incredulously, taking in the rampant, all-encompassing destruction. "Wasn't it enough to just get rid of the Brine? Why burn all this land too?"

"The Brine and the sea trumpet fields were inseparable," Prescott explains. "So long as the fields were thriving, so would the Brine." His eyes slide past me to the shriveled expanse, my ears pricking with macabre fascination as his tale unfolds.

"Twenty-some years ago, this local guy named Kieran Blackbane ran in the Halcyon Bay mayoral election. He was a promising, up-and-coming politician. Well-respected, likable, a real stand-up guy, or so everyone believed. When Blackbane lost the race, he became a bit of a recluse, but his thirst for power and influence only grew. Over time, he drafted a small but loyal following to join him in the sea trumpet fields, where he'd built a covert encampment."

"Hold on. What are sea trumpets, exactly?" I ask.

Prescott smiles. "Sea trumpets are a type of flower, a very particular flower."

All this wreckage, all this devastation, over a field of *flowers?*

We push out farther toward the coastline, still keeping to the leafy, cool perimeter. "Initially, Blackbane's group wasn't viewed as a threat," Prescott continues. "The townsfolk assumed they were a bunch of tree-huggers and junkies looking for an off-grid, nonconformist lifestyle. But then, a few summers later, a string of suspicious drownings caught law enforcement's attention, and police were forced to take a closer look at Blackbane's supposed hippie camp."

"What'd they find?"

"Well, for one, they discovered that it was the practice of the Brine, as Blackbane's group had come to be known, to cultivate and harvest sea trumpet flowers for their hallucinogenic properties."

"Like a drug?"

Prescott nods. "It wasn't illegal at the time. They would eat the flowers during these communal rituals and have these really *intense* psychedelic trips."

"Intense how?"

"Ingesting the flowers put users in a state of lowered inhibition, reduced to their more primitive natures. In this state, they could submit to behaviors that would otherwise be considered improper, I guess. And the sea trumpets gave the Brine a certain susceptibility, an openness, making them receptive to the divine influence of Mother."

"Mother?" I repeat slowly.

"Mother was the Brine's deity," he says, a dark twinkle radiating from his sleepy eyes. "And Mother's prophet—Her chosen leader—was Kieran Blackbane."

"Convenient."

"Blackbane was Mother's messenger, the only one She spoke and worked through. He was dubbed the Death Harbinger"—Prescott makes air quotes at the moniker—"and they say he wore robes of scarlet, the same color of the sea trumpets he tended to and worshiped. Symbolic, too, for the blood that had to be spilled in sacrifice to Mother."

My mind unwittingly tosses back to Callie Oxton, and I have to swallow down a ragged breath.

"Mother offered the Brine protection, promising to shield the island from storm, disease, and famine. But in return, She required a series of offerings."

"The drowned girls," I say weakly.

Prescott nods. "Blackbane assembled a cabal of young men within the Brine to seduce and lure in local girls. They enticed them by telling them they were called to greatness, meant to serve Mother's higher purpose. These girls—the marks—weren't allowed to join the Brine, but instead were coerced to stage their own drownings. To die willingly, in service to Mother."

A shudder courses through me as I absorb his words. When I awoke this morning, I was sure that Virginia's celebration of life would be the most nauseating thing I'd have to face all day…but this story of children being brainwashed and led to an early martyrdom, manipulated with empty promises and flattery, is an entirely different kind of gut-wrenching.

"How many of them died?"

Prescott pouts in a show of uncertainty. "Hard to say. At least six that summer. Maybe more…" His voice trails off for a moment. "Have you heard anything about the sea spirits of Halcyon Bay? Some call them devilfish, or sea girls—"

"I've heard."

"Well, according to island folklore, they belong to Mother. The girls that drown become Her Watchers. An army of sorts, overseers of Halcyon Bay. Girls of the Salt."

Sea spirits. Devilfish. Girls of the Salt. I tread through his words like deep, churning water, barely keeping my head afloat, gasping for breath.

"Over the years, the stories took on a life of their own. You know how it goes—mermaid mythology intermingled with island history and superstition. Fishermen say that they're plagued by the devilfish to this day, making claims about the sea girls that spook their catch and disrupt their business. Some even think they're an omen for bad weather or death. People love to make up wild stories in an effort to explain away nature, or their own crappy luck with a fishing rod."

"What happened to the Brine," I ask, "once police caught on to their schemes?"

"After the investigation, the cult was formally disbanded. Their camp was destroyed, the fields decimated. Blackbane, along with several other leaders, were sent to the mainland to stand trial for their crimes."

"And the rest?"

"The others had to undergo extensive therapy before they could reintegrate into society. Most of them moved away from Halcyon Bay to big cities where they could blend and disappear. Only a handful of members stayed behind, the ones who showed a real disposition for change and fully committed to making amends." Prescott hesitates before adding, "Some locals believe there are remnant disciples of the Brine still practicing in Halcyon Bay, building their underground following. But, honestly"—he flashes me a small, sheepish smile—"that's a long shot."

If there are a select few Brine members left over, could they be responsible for Callie Oxton's drowning? Could the same pattern be unfolding again, right under everyone's noses? Were the rumors just that—petty fanfare and shock value—or were they something more, something sinister? It would explain why Officers Dash and Parris believed she might've been coerced onto that pier, like so many girls before her.

"Why did Blackbane wait to start these drownings?" I ask.

"What do you mean?"

"You said the Brine had been operating for several years before any girls showed up dead." The words flow out of me in a fevered rush. "What was it about that summer? What changed?"

Prescott bites his lip.

"Tell me," I insist, blood rushing to my cheeks.

"Now, I don't know this for certain," he prefaces, "but the idea is that Blackbane's bloodlust was inspired by the drowning of a certain girl, something of a local celebrity on the island."

I know who he means before he utters her name.

He winces. "Willow Klyne."

This revelation makes a disturbing amount of sense.

Blackbane was inspired by Willow's drowning. He'd discovered his ticket to greatness in the public's fanatic obsession with her, and so he'd done what any other narcissistic maniac would do—drive more innocent girls to the same fate, preying on their minds, fueled by a sadistic desire for fame and clout.

The man hadn't amounted to anything in government, so this would have to be his new crowning glory. Making himself a legend for the horrors he engendered.

My mind swirls with a thousand more questions, but quickly stills at the sound of approaching footsteps and chatter.

Prescott jolts to fast attention as I squint against the blanket of dusky blue darkness creeping across the fields.

Two silhouettes move in the distance, heading straight for us.

CHAPTER TWENTY-SEVEN

"Follow me," Prescott whispers urgently, wrapping a hand in mine and dragging me deeper into the brush, our bodies fading from view.

We drop to the ground, pressing against a wide trunk as the scuffle of footsteps grows closer, louder. I'm able to make out two distinct voices. Their words are muffled, largely inaudible, but a frustrated exchange passes between them.

Who else has reason to be out here? The police, certainly, or some dumb high school kids in want of a scare. Any other scenario would be…disastrous.

Logic tells me that whoever's coming must either frequent this place often or, even more terrifying, they'd followed us in. But why?

Needing a better vantage point to see what we're up against, I pull away from Prescott's grip and slide from the shelter of tree cover, careful to keep my footsteps light.

What are you doing? he mouths at me.

I put a finger to my lips in response. I'd humored Prescott before, but I wasn't about to blindly follow his directives at a time like this.

He remains flush against the giant tree trunk while I crouch low behind some shrubs by the clearing, listening as the two voices grow nearer and clearer. Snippets of conversation soon reach my ears.

"Over this way."

"Why are we even here?"

"I told you not to come."

"Our conversation isn't finished. Goodness, what is *wrong* with you?"

I stand slowly, my heart pounding in my ears like a bass drum. Prescott peeks his head from behind the tree, shooting wild eyes in my direction. *Get down,* he mouths.

"It's incredible that you'd drag me out here like this."

"No one dragged you anywhere."

"What is it about *her,* anyway? Why do you care about some nobody?"

I emerge from the brush to intercept their walk, rising up from the landscape like a resurrected corpse. Both of them jump back in unison, startled and afraid.

"What the hell!" Sasha shrieks when she realizes it's me. Her hand flies to her heart. "See, Hatch, I freaking told you. She's fine!"

Hatch's eyes glint at me in the semi-darkness, but he doesn't offer an explanation for why he's followed me here, or why he dragged his histrionic ex along.

"What are you doing here?" I ask.

He doesn't respond as his eyes glide over me, as if to make sure I'm in one solid piece.

Sasha speaks for the both of them, her raspy voice dripping with scorn. "Isn't it obvious? We followed you here to make sure you weren't off trying to kill yourself." She crosses her slender arms over her chest, lips pursed. "But you look plenty alive to me."

Prescott emerges from the brush now, coming to stand by my shoulder, close enough that our bodies touch. I shift my weight and take a pointed step away from him, his clinginess becoming more and more of a nuisance.

Sasha cackles at the sight of us together. "Cradle robbing, are we?"

Prescott stiffens beside me, his breath uneven, annoyed.

"If you wanted to go for a private romp with your boyfriend, there are *way* better places than this, I assure you." Sasha nudges Hatch, batting her lashes. "Isn't that right, Hatch?"

My skin catches fire at her words, bathing me in an angry red flush.

Hatch doesn't respond to Sasha's salacious intimations, his eyes trained on mine. "I saw you leaving Cliffmoor House." His words are careful. "You looked...upset. I thought you might need help."

"We were catching up in Hatch's truck when you two *lunatics* blew past us," Sasha cuts in, hissing like a split-tongued serpent. "And since Hatch has a massive hero complex, the thought of chasing you through the pitch-black murder-fields was too damn tempting to pass up."

Hatch grits his teeth. "I told you not to come, Sasha." Though his voice is measured, it conceals some quiet fury within, something writhing and raging, but deadly calm.

"And I told *you* we still had more to discuss," Sasha shoots back.

I wish so much that I could put her mouth on mute.

"You followed me all the way out here on the off-chance that I might need help?" I peer deep into Hatch's face. It's a rhetorical question, but some small, prideful part of me wants him to confirm it, to know that he cares that much.

"Oh, don't flatter yourself," Sasha barks, swatting a few strands of glossy black hair away from her face. "He would've done it for anyone. Any pathetic, broken thing in need of saving. You're just his latest project—"

"Enough," Hatch snaps.

Sasha's lips fall slack, absorbing the blow and the volume of his words. She screws her face into a tight pout, black eyes raised to the climbing silver moon.

Hatch takes a breath, a beat, before shifting his attention to Prescott. "You. You're Leticia Savage's son, aren't you?"

Prescott puffs up a little more next to me, tossing back his shoulders, shifting his posture so he reaches his full height. All for some imbecilic show of masculinity.

"You two run the old cemetery?" Hatch asks.

I can sense Prescott getting worked up, the testosterone surging in his veins. "That's right," he says. "Who wants to know?"

"Hatch," I interject quickly, wanting to squash the simmering tension, "I asked Prescott to bring me here. I'd heard about the sea trumpet fields and I wanted to see them for myself."

"Wow. Way to be a psycho," Sasha says. "I know you're new to town, but this isn't some offbeat tourist destination. Not for the mentally sound, anyway."

I've had about enough of Sasha's mouth. Everything she'd said in the last few minutes had stung, but I was fine with letting her insults run in streams down my back. But *this,* questioning my sanity, is a different story entirely.

"Did you hear about the little girl that drowned last Thursday night?" I ask. "The one that jumped from Prospero Pier?"

The others quiet as Sasha's pretty eyes go wide, the corners of her mouth bending into a frown. She doesn't answer me.

"I'm guessing that's a yes," I say, low and spine-chilling. "Well, I saw it happen. I saw her jump. And I think her death may be connected to this place, to these *Brine* people."

She shakes her head, gaping at me like I'm even more deranged than she could've imagined. "That's...impossible."

"Impossible or not, *psycho* or not, that's why I'm here. What the hell's your excuse? Why did you come if not to harass Hatch, who already made it perfectly clear he doesn't want you around?"

Sasha's cheeks burst into flaming red. My words bite into her like arrows, spearing through the fragile glass of her ego. They seem to reverberate, over and over, in the quiet night. *He doesn't want you around. He doesn't want...you.*

Sasha glares between Hatch and myself, hoping he'll come to her defense, but his silence is deafening, his expression damning.

Ultimately, it's Prescott who speaks up next. "Dell, you didn't tell me that you'd seen that girl before—"

I sigh. "Look, I know. And I'm sorry for not being more honest. But if this cult has legitimate ties to Callie's death—if there's really some kind of Brine 2.0 in the works—then I want to know about it."

"Brine 2.0," Hatch repeats slowly. "Like a copycat cult?"

"Could be. Maybe some of the original members are looking for a reboot or something."

"A reboot?" Sasha's voice feels like cat claws grinding down the insides of my skull. "This isn't some B-list horror movie, okay? Cults don't get reboots."

"Maybe there's a way to track down a list of past members," Hatch says, his gaze pensive. "The library might have something, some record or testimonial we could reference."

"Like I told you before, Dell," Prescott butts in, shooting me a meaningful glance, "most of the past Brine members are long gone by now."

"But what about the young people? The kids of the Brine?" I counter.

"Um, hi, I have a question." Sasha pokes one manicured finger in the air. My eyes roll so far into my cranium, I think they may actually get stuck there. "Assuming this theory isn't completely bonkers—which it is, but for argument's sake, let's assume it's not—this was *their place*. If the Brine were to make some big, momentous comeback, this is where it would happen. So shouldn't we be trying to get as far away as possible in case any of them happen to be, oh, I don't know, hanging around?"

"Whoa, hold the phone." Prescott waves his arms in frustration. "There is no *them* anymore. No one's out here! It's just us and this giant field of ash."

"I actually agree with Sasha," I say, garnering looks of surprise from all three of them. "Not that I think anyone's out here, but we should probably get going anyway. It's getting late. And it looks like bad weather coming in."

The blanket of muggy, misty night crawling over the fields holds the distant scent and crackle of storm. If the rain catches us out here, our path through the brush back to the road will be much more difficult to find, and harder to traverse without poking an eyeball out.

After a grumbled consensus, the four of us start the trek back in irritated silence. Sasha bolts up ahead with Prescott close behind. Hatch and myself bring up the rear, his steps trailing mine by a few deliberate paces, like he's purposely leaving some distance between us. I feel the intensity of his eyes on me even from behind, even without seeing them, but I don't—*won't*—give in to their soundless call.

Several minutes into walking, he sidles up beside me, speaking quietly so that only I can hear. "You shouldn't have come out here alone with that guy."

I snort. "He wasn't going to hurt me, Hatch."

My tone divulges a degree of confidence I didn't feel but an hour ago. The weight of the rock in my pocket is a private reminder of this.

"Do you know anything about him?" he asks, unconvinced.

"I know enough."

"How'd he get the gate unlocked?"

This brings me pause. "The gate?"

Hatch lifts his eyebrows. "Yes, the gate. The one by the big *No Trespassing* sign. You have a thing for those, don't you?"

A sinking realization washes over me, preventing me from taking another step forward. My feet are frozen blocks, rooted to the fields, as terror threatens to take me over. "Hatch…the gate was *open* when you got to it?"

"Yeah," he says slowly. "We found the chains on the ground. How'd the kid get it open without a key?"

"We didn't open the gate." My voice is grave, my mouth parched.

"What do you mean you didn't—"

"It was locked when we got here. We came in through a hole in the chain-link fence."

"Guys." Sasha's fearful voice is like a stake to my heart. "*Look.*"

In the distance, smoke snakes up into a towering pillar, rising from the endless, dusky fields to the infinite, gray-tinged sky. At the base of it, there's an orange light—the undeniable glimmer of fire.

Someone else is out here.

Without a word, we back into the brush, huddling together, holding our breaths.

"Prescott." I tug on his sleeve to get his attention, but his eyes are glazed over, enraptured by the flickering of flame between the trees. His face evokes total, utter shock. "Listen to me. The gate was unlocked when Hatch and Sasha got here. Whoever started that fire must've opened it *after* we came through."

Which means they must've seen us enter. They may even be watching us right now.

"It's gotta be police," Hatch whispers.

"Why would the police start a fire in the middle of the open like that?" Sasha hisses.

"Campers?" I ask, knowing how stupid it sounds, but also desperate for a simple, painless explanation.

Sasha glares at me. "Who in their right mind would think this is a good place to pitch a damn tent and cook freaking s'mores?"

"Whoever it is, we need to run, now." Hatch reaches for my hand, lacing his fingers in mine like it's second nature. I don't have time to fixate or overthink it.

"Run?" Sasha squeals.

"You have a better idea?"

"Prescott," I whisper again, shaking his shoulder, finally pulling him from his thrall with the fire. "Are you listening? We need to run, right now."

He nods, zombie-like. "Need to run," he repeats.

We break into a collective sprint, running for what feels like miles on end. Our thudding steps echo in my mind, so loud and clumsy that we may as well blare them on a loudspeaker, alerting the fire starters to our exact whereabouts.

No one is around us, but I swear I feel them at my back, pressing in closer, their breath hot, fear and panic stretching across my limbs. My legs ache terribly, begging me to pause for a rest, but the surge of adrenaline keeps my feet pounding against the ground.

Hatch never once lets go of my hand.

We reach the hole in the brush and scramble through to the other side, using the gate this time. It's just as Hatch described it—unchained and ajar, like a door cracked open between worlds.

"I'll take Dell home," Hatch says with authority, his fingers still woven in mine. "I've gotta go back that way, anyway, to drop off Sasha."

Sasha's eyes sear into the pair of us like glowing fire pokers, catching at our intertwined hands.

Prescott protests, "Wait, Dell, why can't I—"

"Where's your truck?" I ask Hatch. He points up the stretch of dark road. I squint, just making out the silhouette of a truck bed, two red tail lights flanking either side of it.

Prescott pipes up again, "I can take her. It's not that far a drive—"

"Look, don't worry about it," I say earnestly, reaching out to give him a quick hug. "Thanks for the tour, and the story. Get home safe, okay?"

"Uh…well, okay," he says hesitantly, his eyes jumping from me to Hatch. "I guess I'll check in on you tomorrow, then."

We scatter without another word, the three of us darting for the Ranger. Hatch slides into the driver's seat while Sasha makes a mad dash for the passenger's side. I jump in the back, much less concerned with where I'm sitting than I am with getting away. In the scramble, I lose sight of Prescott collecting his bike from its hiding place in the brush. Hatch peels onto the dirt road, filling the night with a massive flurry of dust, leaving the sea trumpet fields in his rearview.

CHAPTER TWENTY-EIGHT

Tristen leans against a vine-cloaked post at the mouth of Cliffmoor House. In his silky black suit and grease-slicked hair, he looks like the Angel of Death incarnate, like velvet night and darkness bend to his will. A lit cigarette dangles from his mouth, a smear of orange dancing across the bone-sharp angles of his face, battling the shadows that seem to exude from within. His shifty beetle eyes land upon the Ranger when we roll to a stop at the gate.

The atmosphere inside the truck is nearly as foul as Tristen's stare. Hatch, Sasha, and I sit in paralyzed silence, the truth of what we may or may not have seen brewing over us like a war-torn sky—an uncertain menace that chased us all the way from the fields, invisible fangs gnashing at our heels.

Sasha is the first to speak. She rotates around to face me, managing to shake off some of her terror long enough to replace it with a scathing accusation. *"You almost got us killed."*

I don't have the energy to rebut her statement, no matter how unfounded or melodramatic. Her words hang in the air like bad perfume while I silently contemplate an unnerving reality.

Who had lit that fire in the fields? That padlocked gate hadn't opened itself, meaning someone had to have access to the grounds—a key. Had they followed us in, or was I being paranoid?

"Give it a rest, Sasha," Hatch cuts in.

She zeroes in on him, betrayal swimming in her wide brown eyes. In a resentful flurry, she clamps her lips tight and yanks open her door, sliding from the passenger's seat to land upon the asphalt. Gripping the door again, she slams it shut with all her might, marching past my cousin and up to the house. Tristen's gloomy eyes trail after her, the end of his cigarette smoldering as he pulls in a drag, emitting a stream of smoke into the night.

After a long moment of silence—so long I could drown in that overwhelming stretch of quiet—I say softly, "I should go too."

Hatch peers around at me, his mesmerizing eyes like emerald pools that send shivers tingling down my spine. Last night he had offered me refuge, had let me inside of his innermost world, but now what am I to believe? All those hours he'd dedicated to Sasha, the secret conversations that seemed to go on and on between them, the way he'd brought her along with him to the fields…it all had to mean something.

"Are you sure you're going to be okay here tonight?" he asks.

I nod, cloaking my tenebrous thoughts with a tight-lipped smile. "I'll be fine. And…thank you. I don't think I said that before."

His mouth pulls into that signature lopsided smile, but it doesn't quite reach his eyes. "Are you always this impulsive?"

"Is that just a nice way of calling me reckless?"

Hatch doesn't clarify, but his eyebrows lift expectantly.

"No," I admit. "Believe it or not, back home, I'm never impulsive or reckless. Not even close. But ever since I got to Halcyon Bay, everything's different." I shrug at my own haphazard explanation. "Guess that goes for me too."

He nods thoughtfully, his next words uttered with a great deal of care. "I don't want to see anything happen…" He bites the inside of his cheek. A primal ache sings through me. "I *can't* see anything bad happen to you, Dell."

Waves of heat radiate down my body, filling me with a terrible urge to lean in closer, to pleat and hem that breath of space between us like fabric, when I know in my gut that I can't do it. I can't yield to the things I'm feeling, can't heed this intoxication.

I smile faintly before tugging on the back door, incapable of words, but deciding it best—urgent, in fact—to extract myself from his presence. I drop from the truck, wobbling on my aching feet when I land.

"Hey, Dell?"

I open the door a bit more to glimpse his handsome face again.

Hatch rubs his stubbled chin, a strange, conflicted haze in his eyes. "You don't need to jerk around some kid with a hard-on for you to get what you want," he says quietly. "All you have to do is ask. I would've helped, you know."

His statement plummets through me, sinking to my core like a fleet of ravaged, plundered ships. My rabbit-fast heartbeat slows as I realize what he must think of me, the person he must see reflected in my eyes.

User. Manipulator. Tease.

True, I'd been all those things, exposed even more of my ugliness. First, yesterday, in the hostility that oozed from me like lifeblood when I'd faced that monster, Abraham Urban. And now again, in toying with Prescott to pump him for answers, planting myself in harm's way.

I narrow my eyes to slits, embarrassed by my behavior, but even more aggravated by Hatch's judgment of it. Angry at him for calling out my idiocy, for casting stones with those glistering eyes.

Who the hell does he think he is to scold me on impropriety? As if Hatch's actions are so beyond reproach. As if his own reputation isn't splintered to absolute shit.

"Your hands were full." My words pour out in a beastly snarl—a sharp, hissing anger that scrapes out of me, all claws and teeth and venom. "With Sasha. For *hours.*"

"That's not…" The swirling sea of his eyes turns turbulent. "Look. She pulled me aside and asked to talk. One last conversation, that's all I was going to give her. And she promised she'd leave me alone…leave *us* alone."

I lift a hand, shaking with indignation, unable to process what he could possibly mean about him and her and *us*.

Us.

There's a freaking us *now?*

"You know what, Hatch?" I say, seething for reasons I can't articulate. "I don't care. Keep your girlfriend and your all-consuming drama away from me. Let me do what I came here to do."

"She's not my…" His steely voice falls away, the words squashed as his warm, golden face grows cold and acerbic. He inhales, jaw pulsing, trying to keep cool. Finally, he says, "I'm not trying to get in your way."

"Then stop swooping in whenever you determine I need saving. I'm not some damsel for you to coddle and chase. I'm not your pity project—"

"That's not what this is and you know it," he counters.

"What this is is nothing," I say, severing our conversation with my tone—fatal as the chop of an ax. "Thanks for the ride." I slam the truck door behind me.

I cross into the Cliffmoor House grounds, moving briskly under the whirling cloudscape, my feet pounding out their irritation as I go. Hatch doesn't follow, doesn't bother to fight. Instead, I hear the Ranger rumble to life as he peels off in a fume-filled tumult, burning rubber across the cul-de-sac and charging down the street. I can't decide whether I'm glad or hurt that he's gone.

I don't need his approval. I don't need anyone.

I repeat those words in my mind like a mantra, even though deep down, they pulse with insincerity.

When I pass Tristen at his post, he jeers at me. "Trouble in paradise?" He flicks his cigarette to the ground and crushes it with his toe. "So much like your mother," he murmurs with a slimy shake of his head. "Right down to your shared fondness for riffraff."

I don't know what he means by this, but it's clear he doesn't hold

Hatch in the highest regard. Nor my mother and I, for that matter.

I pause long enough to scowl at him. "Is there something you want?"

"How about some candor?" He approaches, pitch-black eyes glowering, narrowing in like two spotlights made of night, cornering me in their depthless darkness. "Tell me, cousin, what were you doing sneaking around upstairs this afternoon?"

Shit.

I should've seen this coming, should've kept walking up the drive and avoided him. But my time in the sea trumpet fields had half-devoured my brain, ripping my focus from anything that came before—like Tristen's whispers spilling from that second story bedroom, the tense scraps of conversation I'd overheard.

"I wasn't," I lie.

"Strange." His voice is smooth, treacherous, making the hair on my neck and arms stand on end. "I could've sworn I heard your name being called from the hall."

Prescott, I remember. *Dammit.*

"I was stuck in the parlor all day," I emphasize, keeping my voice steady as I counter his question with one of my own. "Why were *you* upstairs?"

Tristen smiles now, his teeth a twisted, crooked mess. "I needed a quiet place to make a phone call. Our business associates can be quite demanding."

Liar. There had been someone else in that room with him, a calculated woman's voice opposing his. I'm sure of it.

"And what business might that be?"

Tristen's jaw tightens. "Father and I are in the midst of brokering a considerable deal for the company. Something needed my prompt attention."

"Seems like odd timing for a work call. Right in the middle of a memorial service?"

"Yes, well, as devastating as Aunt Ginnie's passing is," he says callously and without emotion, "money never sleeps."

He lifts his face to the sky, where heavy storm clouds now swarm and billow, distant flashes of purple-white lightning crackling among them.

"Weather's worsening," he muses, his voice slippery-soft. "There's a hurricane headed our way. Could be devastating for the island."

The conversation hums with unspoken threats.

Tristen's sable eyes land on mine again, leadened down with emptiness and detestation—two cavernous pits. "Best get inside, Meridel. You wouldn't want to be caught unaware when it hits."

I don't budge or break eye contact with him, don't make a single effort to move, unwilling to convey even a speck of weakness. I stand perfectly still, watchful, the way one might confront a predator in the wild. Even as the blustery atmosphere stirs and swirls around us, I wait.

Eventually, Tristen tires of our standoff. He shoots me an unscrupulous smile and a derisive little chuckle before stalking toward the mansion, leaving me alone in the chaotic night.

The shuddering storm looms overhead, packing the air with the slow-burning promise of danger.

CHAPTER TWENTY-NINE

Once inside the warmth of the guest house and safe from the howling winds, I strip off my clothes in a hurry, as if undressing might reverse the last couple of hours, cleansing me of all that I'd learned and seen, erasing the poisonous words I'd snarled at Hatch—words I hadn't meant to say.

But now that they were out, now that I'd cast away his friendship and undone that thing that burned between us—that humming, magnetic stroke of magic—why would he ever want to see me again? I'd said goodbye without the words. Not *see you later* or *till next time,* but a slammed-door *goodbye,* plain and impossibly final.

A trail of garments mark my path into the bathroom, and standing before the claw foot tub, naked and shivering while the water warms, I observe Cliffmoor House through the half-moon window floating high above the bath.

There's something unnerving about the sight of it—all that clean, modern gray juxtaposed with haughty Victorian accents. Something unnerving in the slant of its walls, the keen slope of its roof, the turret rising like a watchdog in the night.

As I stare at the house, a face begins to form in it, eyes and a mouth built of windows and doors, each entry point emanating a sinister glow like the mark of some living, breathing pestilence. If homes have personalities, this one's isn't warm and fuzzy.

When the tub is full, I shut off the faucet and step in. Thunder echoes nearby as I sink down, down, down, plunging until the soapy water runs to my chin. I lean my head against the edge, imagining everything that's come to pass sliding off me, peeling back layers of my skin until I'm pink all over. Raw, new, and undamaged.

I try my hardest to unwind, to avoid thoughts of murderous cult leaders, menacing cousins, drowned sea girls, or sweet, green-eyed men that feel like sunshine on frozen skin. But that's all easier said than done.

An eerie darkness fills the bathroom and I start, glancing up as a shadow slips past the doorway.

It's here, I think, as every hair on my body stands erect. That creeping, spectral tenant of the guest house is *here,* right now. I can feel it—sense its presence—though I can't see or explain it. But I'm certain I'm not hallucinating.

I don't bother getting out of the bath to chase the shadow down. Maybe it's best to just let it come in its own time, whatever it is. Settling back into the water, I swallow hard and shut my eyes.

The storm outside rages on, and I shudder against it—against the unnatural *something* inhabiting this place. I let the water rise past my chin, tilting my neck so that my ears are inundated, so my face is all that's exposed and dry, and fade into a sleepless half-dream, a drifting state.

I'm not sure how long I stay there—maybe an hour or more, based on how the bathwater cools—but I spend the time thinking of my parents and of Woodbridge. Of soft, safe places nothing like this island.

How long has it been since I've known the comforts of home? Had I ever fully made a home in Woodbridge, or had parts of me always been left here, strewn across the shores of Halcyon Bay?

Perhaps I had left behind the darkest parts, the ones buried in the trenches of my past. The ones rising to the surface now, bathed in white sunlight, electrified by storm.

An angry banging sound rips across the guest house—someone pounding at the front door. In this weather? What time is it? Surely, there aren't still funeral guests roaming the grounds?

I try to lift up from the tub, but my body resists the effort. I can't pull myself out. There's a pressure lying over me, a weight that holds me down, submerged in water, all but my face. Panic climbs in me as I will myself to move, my neck muscles aching with exertion, but it's no use. I can't so much as wiggle my fingers or toes.

Another heavy darkness cloaks the bathroom in shadow, but I can't pivot my head to see why. I draw in a shivering breath, telling myself this is all in my head.

None of this is happening. None of it's real.

Halcyon Bay is like any other place in this world, a place where people live and die, where good and bad coexist. It's no better or worse than any other town, no more or less fraught with danger and darkness.

The banging continues at the front door, and I try to scream. *Help me, please!* But my words are smothered, crushed by some invisible and unyielding fist. No sound escapes my lips, not so much as a whimper…and then, another terrifying sound—

The squeaking of the faucet above the bath, the handle rotating slowly, slowly.

Water pours into the tub.

Within seconds, it seeps over my cheeks and up the edges of my eyes, tickling the corners of my mouth, grazing my nostrils. It glides across my face, teasing as it consumes me, while another set of powerful bangs tremble through the house.

The rushing water seals over the tip of my nose.

The night sky is as black as the sea I float in. There's no distinction between the two, and I am utterly alone among them.

I hold my arm at a distance and lose the shape of my fingertips in the blackness. My body is cold and heavy, but I sense my legs pumping beneath me, kicking at water, keeping me afloat.

A hand reaches up from the depths below, grasping me by the ankle and swiftly plunging me down.

I sink into the dark water, writhing, desperate to escape, but the hand has an iron grip on me. It drags me deeper and deeper as I gasp for air. Fighting its terrible power is futile.

I try to catch a glimpse of the creature that holds me, but there's not even a silhouette to make out in the abyss, just faceless darkness that drags me ever downward, to some hellish chasm where a blue orb glows. I squint against the flurry of bubbles and black water, trying to make sense of the radiating light.

We descend and the blue glow begins to take shape—arms, legs, a head with long, stringy hair. A human body, crumpled in the fetal position, cradled by darkness like it was born from it.

It's me, I realize as I take in that crushed, waterlogged body below. *Me,* curled and molded into myself. *Me,* asleep. Or dead.

Just as I'm about to make contact with her—with *me*—I open my mouth and push out a garbled scream.

The grip on my ankle releases, and rather than continuing to sink, I hang there in a suspended thrall. And the other me begins to transform.

Water ripples between us, wild with fury and force, and once it settles, my other body belongs to someone else. This girl is undeveloped. The face rounder, younger, the hair blonder. A birthmark like a cloud climbs across her neck and cheek.

She opens her eyes—an uncanny stormy blue—and again, I scream.

Willow.

The water shifts once more, bubbling and whirling, and when it stills, she's gone…but the blue light is not extinguished.

It belongs to a silver figure drifting in the distance. A face with wide, black rocks for eyes. A crown of silken hair. Thin arms undulating in the darkness. The bottom half of it tapers into a long, singular limb.

A tail, the tip of it forked in two.

CHAPTER THIRTY

Desperate hands wrench me upward, and a sickening, squelchy cough bursts from my lips.

Someone yells, "Throw me a robe!"

It sounds like Palmer.

"I don't see any—"

"For goodness sake, Mojo, a towel, then! Hurry."

A broad blanket of terry cloth drops over my shoulders, hands rubbing frantically down my arms through the towel.

"Snap out of it!" Palmer screeches, shaking my limp form like a rag doll. "Don't make me slap you, Dell. I swear I will. Open your eyes, dammit."

I do as she says, my eyes shuddering alive, and I'm stunned to find that I'm back in the bathroom, plucked from the consummate darkness, from the depths of the ocean.

But…it had all felt so real.

"Thank God." Palmer exhales. "What the hell were you doing?"

My cousin is perched on the edge of the tub, gaping at me in profound shock, while Mojo idles in the doorway, head turned away from me. I glance down and quickly realize why.

I'm propped up in the bath, my lower half still obscured by sudsy water, but my chest is exposed and peaked by the cool air, my shoulders wrapped in the towel Palmer aimlessly threw around me. I pull my legs up, drawing my knees to my boobs for coverage, and cross my arms around them securely. The towel gets soaked in the process.

"H-how did you get in here?" My voice is small and gurgly.

"Briggs asked us to find you. He gave us a key"—Mojo holds it up to the light, still not facing me directly—"in case you were sleeping or couldn't hear us over the storm."

"What on earth were you doing?" Palmer asks again. "What happened?"

How can I even begin to explain what happened? How can I describe what I saw, or thought I saw, in my dream—if that's even what it was?

"I was just taking a bath," I offer weakly, my mind racing. "I guess I must've fallen asleep at some point."

"And you just casually slipped underwater?" she huffs, breathless. "We were knocking for a long time."

"I'm sorry. I didn't hear—"

"And you're a crappy liar to boot."

"Uh, ladies," Mojo pipes up, waving his hands to get our attention. "How 'bout we shelf this argument for later? We gotta get going, like, yesterday."

"What's going on?" I ask.

"Hurricane Ophelia," he says, eyes hovering somewhere above the wooden doorframe. "Category three. She shifted course and is making a beeline for us. Power grids on the island will be down within the hour. The beaches are already flooded to shit."

"What time is it?"

"One in the morning."

I inspect my shriveled, raisin fingers. I'd been in the bath since a little before ten, meaning I'd been soaking for over three hours.

"Dell!" Palmer snaps her fingers in my face to pull me from my stupor. "Cliffmoor House has two backup generators, and it's on the highest ground of all the island. It's the safest place we can be tonight. So we need to go, right now, before this thing intensifies."

The safest place. That's laughable. Nothing about Cliffmoor House, or this godforsaken island, is safe.

Immediately, I shake my head no. "I'm not sleeping there, Palmer."

"The hell you're not," she retorts. "We have no idea how long the storm will sit over us. You could be trapped out here alone, without food, water, or electricity for days. So stop your whining, get your ass out of the water—"

"But I—"

"No buts! Grandfather had the staff prepare rooms for all of us. Briggs got you all set up in your mom's old room."

Mom's old room.

The thought of moving into Cliffmoor House is as unsettling as the hurricane about to plow over us, but if it means I'll get to scour the room Mom grew up in—probing into her past, and maybe her secrets— it's well worth it.

A brilliant flash of lightning emanates through the half-moon window, followed by a raucous, ear-splitting crack. The bathroom light flickers for a moment, then goes black.

"Great!" Palmer throws her hands up. "Now are you convinced?"

"Okay, okay. I'll go. But I need to grab my things first."

"Make it quick."

She scurries across the bathroom, shooing Mojo out the door, leaving me alone to get my bearings and get moving.

With the light of my cell phone, I scavenge through the guest house, stuffing my duffel with everything I've littered about in the last four days—dirty clothes, shoes, a half-eaten bag of chips—until a series of lifeless rooms stare vacantly back at me.

Each of us has an umbrella, and I tuck mine in close, the wind trying to pry it from my numb fingers. Mojo's the first one out the door, pulling his hoodie low over his head before stepping into the deluge, devoured by an onslaught of water. Palmer ducks out next and I follow suit, plunking ankle-deep into a puddle of mud. Together, we charge the manor in a sprint.

One of the back doors was left unlocked, and we scramble inside, out of the wet cold that has soaked us to our bones. I pull off my swampy shoes, my vision adjusting to the familiar corridor, a glowing table lamp the only source of light I see.

Cliffmoor House at night is infinitely worse than the day. Despite its overall immensity, the dark house seems to be caving inward—pressing, pushing down into my personal space. I shudder with pricklings of claustrophobia, my eyes crawling up the walls like a spider in desperate search of some small crack to creep through, to hide inside of until the sun comes up.

Briggs rushes forward from the tunnel of darkness, a stack of plush white towels and glinting candelabrum in hand. "Thank heavens you three are here. Take these." He passes a dryer-warm towel to each of us, snatching up our umbrellas and dropping them into a stand.

"Miss Palmer. Mister Moises." The butler's silver gaze falls over them in the hazy candlelight. "I left a flashlight in your bedroom. The generators should hold up, but better to be safe than sorry. Do try to get some sleep. We've got a rough night ahead of us."

"Thank you. Goodnight, Briggs." Palmer shoots me a cryptic look, one that says she hasn't forgotten about the incident in the bath. "'Night, Dell," she mutters, disappearing down the hall with Mojo at her heels. Within seconds, their bodies vanish into shadows, their whispered voices and quiet movements fading eerily fast.

"Miss Dell?" Briggs' old eyes find mine. The candelabrum in his gloved hand flickers, the flame and his fingers trembling in tandem. "Please, follow me."

He glides through to the foyer and up the stairs while I trail him silently, careful not to swipe anything with my duffel. We turn down the west corridor—the same one I crept across yesterday afternoon when I heard Tristen's mysterious, heated exchange.

Briggs reaches a lofty mahogany door that looks like all the others. "This was your mother's childhood bedroom."

He unlocks and yanks the door open, a light plume of dust trickling into our eyes. A spacious, pale blue room stretches out before us, with ornate furniture and a crystal chandelier dangling over a sumptuous bed. I enter slowly, almost reverently, assessing the bygone space. My fingers trace invisible lines across the dresser, desk, and armoire.

"Is this the way Mom kept it?"

"Just like this, miss," Briggs replies. "Master Ambrose hasn't had the heart to change it."

He pulls a lantern from the closet, setting it atop the desk and lighting it with a match. The space fills with a mild orange luster, faint as a watercolor painting. "We're out of flashlights, I'm afraid, so this will have to do."

Just my luck, I think.

"Only precautionary, of course," he adds. "We shouldn't lose power, but in the off-chance we do, you'll need to see your way around."

A giant thunderclap crashes in the distance. I squint at the curtained window, watching the flares of lightning move closer, like phantom limbs lashing across the sky.

"Is this the worst of it, Briggs?"

The look on his face is solemn. "Afraid not, miss. The storm's moving drearily slow. I'd say the worst is yet to come."

He bows his head a little, dutiful as ever. "Please make yourself comfortable. In the morning, breakfast will be served in the dining hall. We'll see how the forecast looks then, all right?"

I nod and the butler smiles thinly. He utters a brief "Goodnight," and retreats into the corridor. The door clicks shut behind him, and I'm alone in my mother's bedroom, engulfed by the private remnants of a life she fled in terror.

CHAPTER THIRTY-ONE

Cliffmoor House is unsettlingly quiet, like Captain Patton's description of the ocean when the devilfish come. *A terrible stillness,* he'd called it, when everything drops to a bitter calm. Cold and motionless. Petrified. Dead.

I remind myself that somewhere in this silent mansion, Ambrose and Briggs and all the Klynes lay sleeping. That I'm not alone here, stranded at the mercy of this brewing hurricane. But it's a difficult thing to believe in light of that deafening stillness.

My ears itch for some stirring of life, the creaking of a floor board, the settling of walls, even the rustling feathers of a garden owl outside. But all there is is the baying wind curling against the salted windowpanes, the spray of rain, the occasional shudder of thunder, and the consummate blackness of a night bereft of stars—a foreboding presence all its own.

Attempting to get any rest is impossible. I toss through the evening, trapped in a tangle of Mom's silky sheets, dripping in cold sweat. Eventually, I give up on sleep altogether, opting to investigate the crevices of the room, to find what, if anything, she might've left behind.

The drawers and shelves don't offer much. I find some handwoven blankets folded neatly in a stack. A delicate pewter hairbrush and comb set. Hardback books with dog-eared pages. A stained glass jar containing every kind of seashell, still gritty with sand. A hat box brimming with scarves in an array of splendid patterns. All of it so pretty…and pretty unhelpful.

I watch the clouds swirl and shift through the window as the sun finally makes its climb. One can barely even call this morning. The pale blue bedroom never brightens, the storm casting a near-constant aura of gloom, coating the Cliffmoor grounds in thick, dewy fog.

Had the brunt of it even hit yet? Surely, a category three hurricane would be more severe than this? The world had been quiet for so much of last night—contained and hushed and all too still—and now, this smoggy, ominous morning loomed, telling me to brace myself. This is the calm before the chaos.

A narrow beam of diffused sunlight sweeps in through the curtains, dust particles dancing up from the foot of Mom's bed. I run my hand over the comforter—milky-blue, with elegant ruching—stroke the carved wooden spiral tops of the bed posts, and trace my fingers over the glossy nightstand, taking in all the details of my mother's former life, hoping to glean something from their existence.

On some level, I hope that the room might divulge truths about her, that it might tell me things I so desperately want to know. But, to my dismay, I find nothing of consequence, nothing notable or distinctive at all.

I wait for hours for some grand epiphany, for the room to speak up and fill that indelible quiet, but it doesn't seem the least bit inclined to share its secrets. Around nine o'clock, I pad into the hall and tiptoe down the stairs, following the din of indistinct chatter spilling from one of the rooms near the parlor.

I peek through the doorway. Ambrose sits at the head of the vast redwood table, accompanied by June, Leif, Tristen, and Flip. They dip silver spoons into their porcelain coffee mugs, dab their mouths with linen napkins, and slather flower-molded butter over toast, making idle chatter over a decadent breakfast spread.

Something large and fuzzy rubs against my thigh, and I jolt in surprise. Bear looks up at me sweetly, his bushy tail swatting the air as a little tremor of excitement courses over his body.

I bend down to his level and stroke behind his ears. "I've missed you too, boy," I whisper. The dog's big, brown eyes roll back in his skull in response.

"Miss Dell," Briggs greets me with a warm smile as he comes around the corner, carrying with him a pot of steaming coffee.

I stand. "Good morning."

He appraises me over his spectacles, taking note of my tired eyes and my untamed bed head. "I do hope you slept well," he says doubtfully. "Come. Have a seat."

The others glance up as I step into the dining hall. Leif grins wide at the sight of me. "Dell! Dell! You'll never guess what happened to us!"

"Easy, Leif." Flip laughs from the opposite side of the table. "Let the poor girl sit and get some coffee before you bombard her." My uncle raises his mug to me in greeting.

I nod around the table politely, feeling my neck flush from the unwanted attention, and slide into the seat beside Leif. Bear plops onto the floor between us with an audible sigh. Leif takes this as his cue to proceed.

"Mommy and I went home last night to get Bear, and all the streets in our neighborhood were flooded," he says animatedly. "We could barely get up our stairs, it was so bad!"

"Leif," June cuts in with a warning tone. My aunt's hair is pulled into a messy ponytail this morning, her whirlpool eyes a tad sunken-in. "Please don't exaggerate."

"I'm not," he protests before turning back to me. "The water was so high, we could've gone swimming! I even asked Mommy to pack my swim trunks, but"—he leans in a little, raising a secretive hand to his mouth—"I don't think she liked the idea."

June rolls her eyes, sighing into her glass of orange juice.

"It's quite fine that you and Leif stay as long as you need to, Juniper." Ambrose's voice cuts clear across the table. He takes a sip from his mug, smiling. "Who knows how long it will take to make the necessary repairs to your *cottage*." He says it derisively, as if to suggest there's something inherently repugnant about June's house or the way she chooses to live. "Could be days, even weeks, until the neighborhood is habitable again."

"Oh, I don't think it will come to that," June says quickly, a visible tension rising in her face.

"If the flooding continues at this rate"—Ambrose lifts one shoulder into an austere shrug—"you and Leif will need a place to stay. And you know you're always welcome here. This is your home, after all."

"*Was* my home," June corrects with a shake of her head, hardened against her father's offering.

"Of course, you'll have to find some other arrangements for the dog," Ambrose continues, not bothering to call Bear by his name. "This isn't a suitable environment for an animal, much less one quite so mammoth."

"Well." June's voice is firm, the edges of it tingling with irritation. "Let's not make any plans prematurely, but I *truly* appreciate your concern."

"Of course, darling," Ambrose says. "Any word on when this blasted hurricane will make landfall?"

Flip makes some grotesque throat-clearing sound and wipes his mouth of bacon grease. "Forecasted for sometime this afternoon. Weather's supposed to worsen over the next twelve hours, effects even going into tomorrow, I believe. Terrible waste of time—"

"Tomorrow?" I pipe up, realizing that today is Monday, and I'd planned to be back in Maine by Wednesday afternoon at the latest. "I'm supposed to leave first thing in the morning."

Briggs, who glides around the table refilling coffee mugs, pauses. "I'm sorry, miss, but the weather won't be conducive for travel tomorrow. All the transport ferries are docked until further notice. You'll have to wait for safety clearance."

Crap. My parents will work themselves into a nuclear-level frenzy if I don't turn up soon.

Tristen, who hasn't so much as lifted his head from his cell phone, smiles to himself now. It's almost as if he enjoys other people's misfortune, gains some sick pleasure from their pain.

"How was your night, Meridel?" Ambrose asks, turning his head shrewdly in my direction, or at least in the direction of my voice. His mystifying gray eyes, thankfully, remain shut. "Did you sleep well?"

"I slept all right."

"We had a horrible night," Leif interrupts dramatically, bursting at the seams to tell me about it. "I hardly slept at all, and Bear wouldn't stop whimpering, and Mommy said I kept kicking her! But I didn't do it on purpose or anything—"

June makes a low grunting sound.

"—and since we couldn't sleep, we came down to the kitchen early and helped Inga and Emery make breakfast for everyone. And Palmer and Mojo had a big fight, and then he just left, right in the middle of the storm! Can you believe that?"

Tristen coughs out a laugh, pulling his face from the phone screen. I meet his beetle eyes across the table and he sneers, seemingly delighted by all of Leif's unwitting disclosures. *Sadistic piece of shit.*

"Where's Palmer now?" I ask.

Leif scrunches his nose, oblivious to the awkwardness blossoming around him. "I dunno. Sleeping, I guess." He pops a handful of blueberries into his mouth, his buck teeth stained a deep blue when he smiles.

I quietly excuse myself, grabbing two lemon-poppyseed muffins from a platter at the table's center, wrapping them in a napkin, and slipping from my chair.

"Upstairs, third door on the right," June says over her shoulder. She exhales heavily. "Maybe you'll have better luck than I did."

I duck out of the dining hall and shuffle up the stairs. As I'm about to knock on Palmer's door, it swings open.

She stands in the doorway, eyes raw and veiny. Her cheeks are streaked in tears, shiny streams that fall to her chin, and her lips are swollen. Briggs was right in what he'd said yesterday; it had been a rough night, for some more than others.

"Dell?"

"Hey, Palmer."

I stand there, stupidly, while she wipes her palms on her face, trying to hide the clear evidence that she'd been crying.

Maybe if things were different between us, if we were closer or knew each other better, I might reach out to her. But things between us are tentative, fresh, so I don't try.

"What are you doing here?" she asks.

"I came to see if you were okay."

"Well, here I am." She flourishes her hand up and down the length of her body. "A-okay."

"Okay. Um, cool." I nod absently and offer her a crumbling muffin. "Hungry?"

She stares vacantly at my hands, not fully present or even listening. Her posture embodies defeat and exhaustion.

After a second, I say, "I can leave you alone if you want, but I heard that you and Mojo had some kind of fight? I figured you might want—"

"You wanna help me sort through Gram's wardrobe?" she blurts, cutting me off mid-sentence.

"Uh. What?"

"Gram left me her all vintage couture in the will," Palmer explains, the words spilling out in haste. Her eyes get round and mirror-like, reflections of a perfect summer-blue sky. "Do you wanna, you know, help me sort through it all?"

I know she's just looking for some distraction from Mojo, from whatever caused their argument, whatever made him leave. I can't believe that it's the baby news that did it. Mojo isn't the type to abandon anyone, much less Palmer, much less at a time like this.

Some small diversion, that's all she wants. To play dress-up in our grandmother's closet, like we might've done together when we were little girls.

To dream a bit, adorn herself in fantasy…

And who am I to judge her for that?

CHAPTER THIRTY-TWO

Palmer and I spend much of the day tucked inside Virginia's dressing room, a massive jewel-toned chamber brimming with silk ribbons, chiffon poufs, and sweeping, pleated skirts. We sort the garments into three piles, keep, sell, and donate, of which the 'keep' pile is largest, rapidly mounting to Everestian proportions.

Palmer's back to her usual self, all glinting smiles and giggles, burying her troubles under luxurious mounds of cashmere. She bounces from one clothing rack to the next like a pinball on steroids. "Can you believe all this incredible stuff?"

"I didn't think one person could even own this much clothes."

Palmer laughs. "You didn't know Gram."

Her offhand statement is said in jest, but it strikes a chord with me anyway, emphasizing a certain undeniable truth. I hadn't known Virginia in life, but thanks to the items she'd left behind, I was getting to know her better in death. And one thing about Virginia had become abundantly obvious: she was a well-dressed woman.

Her style was chic and daring, streamlined with sophistication. The gowns she wore were magnificent, crafted by skilled hands, no expense spared—gowns destined for sparkling Hollywood starlets, charmed heiresses, and queens. I imagine the kind of elegant person that would wear these types of garments and wonder about the kind of glittering lifestyle she might lead.

Palmer dons dress after dress, admiring her ever-changing reflection in the gilded mirror propped against the far wall. "See anything you like?" she asks as she shimmies back into her joggers.

I peruse the room, layers of tulle and satin winking at me from all corners. Palmer looks like pure-bred royalty in Virginia's gowns, but I'd probably look like a three-armed baboon. I shake my head.

"A room full of couture and you can't point out a single thing you like?" she asks. "Are you sure you're even female?"

"Last I checked." I pluck a structured blazer from a hanger, holding it up to the light to inspect the material—an iridescent, lemon-yellow tweed. "They're lovely, just not for me."

"Humph!" Palmer scours through mounds of clothes, lips pursed. "I'm gonna find something in this room that suits you, Dell. Mark my words."

"Please don't bother." I can't help but laugh. "I have nowhere to go wearing anything like"—I brandish a flouncy, periwinkle skirt with a built-in petticoat peeking from the bottom—"*this.*"

Palmer drops her hands to her hips. "You don't go to parties back in Maine?"

"Yeah, sure, keggers and backyard barbecues galore. But black-tie soirées and charity galas? Not so much."

Palmer twirls away, pulling a gown I haven't seen from an intricate wooden chest. She lifts it high in the air and squeals triumphantly. "*Aha!*" She presses the floor-length dress to her figure, the bottom of it pooling all over the floor. "Can't you just hear this one calling your name?"

"No."

The slate-blue, backless gown has a plunging neckline and delicate straps at the shoulders. Its twinkling bodice is embellished with beads that glisten when they catch the light just right, like a million glittering stars—a shifting, wearable Milky Way. Rippling layers of tulle lie atop the full, flowing skirt, creating the illusion of movement, like waves undulating at sea.

"C'mon, Dell." Palmer swishes the dress in the air, the skirt fluttering around her prettily. "Wipe off your habitual scowl of disapproval for two seconds, and give me your honest opinion."

"My honest opinion? You're insufferable."

"I meant about the dress." She drapes the shimmery gown over her arms. It's positively stunning, something I could only ever dream of wearing—or affording, for that matter.

"Well?" she probes, wearing down my resistance.

"Fine. It's beautiful." Magical, if I'm totally sincere.

She throws me a smug told-you-so smile. "Then quit yapping," she instructs, "and try it on."

I give up the fight and do as I'm told. Surprisingly, the gown slips down my body like a glove, a far better fit than I could've imagined. The length is perfect and the bodice settles right at my waistline where it should.

Palmer claps her hands, overjoyed by her selection. "Oh, it's perfect!"

"Perfect for someone else," I murmur, pinching my lips together as I turn to examine the backside, the curve of my exposed back peeking out above the skirt.

"What are you talking about? That dress was made for you!"

No, it was made for Virginia, I think. And for that reason alone, I'm not comfortable wearing it.

"You're keeping it," Palmer says definitively. I mumble some lame protest, but she talks right over me. "Suck it up, buttercup. Decision made."

She drops to her knees to sift through more garments and winces, a hand flying to the base of her stomach like she's suffering a violent cramp.

I take a step toward her. "What's wrong?"

Palmer sinks to the ground, crossing her legs. She sighs deeply, the pain-induced grimace slipping from her face. "It's nothing." She waves me off, forcing her lips into a smile, but her eyes evoke something deeper, harsher. A quiet worry growing within her, one that can only go ignored for so long.

"I think we've gone through almost everything in here," she announces, surveying her multiple piles with pride, as though we'd made tremendous progress. To me, it looks like Virginia's dressing room threw up all over the floor. "Briggs mentioned there might be some more clothes in the attic. Shall we do some reconnaissance?"

Still wearing the dress Palmer handpicked for me, I realize I'm in no position to deny her. "You're the boss."

I shrug back into my sweats, and Palmer leads me down the east corridor to the last door. When she pulls it open, the space inside is not a room at all, but another stairwell, winding upward in a spiral formation like the innards of a nautilus shell. I follow her up, up, up to the rafters, to a level of Cliffmoor House that I haven't yet explored.

"It's too dark up here," she complains from somewhere nearby. "Help me find the light switch. It should be around here somewhere."

I run my hand against the rough wooden beams, tentative so as to avoid splinters, though perhaps I should be more concerned with spiders and rat feces. My fingers brush the switch. "Found it." I tap it and light floods the dank attic space.

Palmer lets out an ear-piercing scream.

"What?" I shout, panicked, my eyes struggling to adjust.

She stands near the center of the room, hugging a clear plastic garment bag to her chest, her blue eyes sparkling and dreamy. "Look what I found," she gushes.

An exquisite white dress glistens from within the bag, dipped in tiny, lustrous pearls like sprinkles on a decadent ice cream cone.

"A dress!" I yell at her, clutching my chest. "That's worth giving me a heart attack over?"

"Not just any dress," Palmer insists, ogling the beautiful gown. "This is Gram's wedding dress! I've gotta try it on!"

She unzips the bag and strips down to her undies while I desperately try to steady the erratic pumping of my heart. I pull open the curtain on a vast window, taking in the view of the bursting gardens below and the vibrant blue sea beyond.

"Don't just stand there," Palmer cries once she's pulled the gown over her head. "Come button me up."

She finds a small, dusty mirror tucked behind some sheeted furniture and holds it at arm's length. She looks drop-dead gorgeous— angelic, even—radiating the sort of discreet magic reserved for brides-to-be. She runs her fingers down the delicate, twinkling fabric, inspecting every detail of her reflection. I anticipate more squealing, or for a thousand-watt smile to burst from her face. But instead, Palmer begins to cry.

"Palmer?" I come up behind her, sharing a sliver of mirror space.

She doesn't respond, doesn't say a word.

I lift a hand to her wispy hair, petting it gently, like one might a stray dog. I'm not great at comforting people, or dealing with unexpected surges of emotion. Focusing on my mother for so many years meant that the pains of others were often lost on me, their tears foreign and strange. I wonder if I'm only making things worse. Maybe she'd rather I give her some space, but I resolve not to move, not to leave her alone. I wait in silence until she's ready to talk.

"I've ruined everything," she whispers, observing herself in that spotless white dress with a blatant look of disgust.

I know she's talking about Mojo. "What happened?"

"We've been arguing a lot," she says, her voice hoarse. "My fault. I've been picking fights on purpose."

"Why?"

She winces, struggling to mold her feelings into words. "I thought if I pushed him hard enough, maybe he'd leave."

"You don't want to be with him anymore?"

Palmer shakes her head vehemently. "No, that's not it. I love him, Dell."

"Then why would you—"

"Because of…this baby," she cries, crouching down to the floor. She settles onto her butt and stretches her legs, tossing the mirror away.

"Palmer." I drop down beside her. "It *is* Mojo's, right?"

"Of course," she says in a huff, her eyes earnest and pained by my question. "He's the only guy I've ever been with." Her voice trails off as a fresh wave of tears pour down her ruddy cheeks.

I tread carefully, trying to make sense of things. "You don't think he'll want to—"

"Oh, he will." She nods emphatically. "He'll want to be the best dad in the world to our baby."

"So why are you so against—"

"Because he'll give up everything," she says, throwing her hands in the air. "The music, the band, all of his plans. He'll pull the plug on all of it, no questions asked."

I frown. "It doesn't have to be that way. He doesn't have to quit music for you guys to have this baby."

"I can't do it to him." She shuts her eyes, blocking out whatever she saw in the mirror that filled her with such contempt. "I can't disrupt his life like this. It isn't fair."

"You're not doing anything *to* him, Palmer. You're both adults, in a consenting relationship. It's your life too. Fair or not, you did this together."

"No, no…you don't understand."

"Then help me to."

"Mojo asked me to marry him once before," she divulges after a breath. "Years ago, right after I graduated high school. He was so excited for us to buy a house and start a family. But I told him I didn't want to get married. That I didn't want kids, period. I was young and stupid, and I'd just seen my parents go through their divorce… I knew how deep it cut me, how it might affect Leif. I couldn't bear the thought that we could put another kid through the same thing."

Teary-eyed, she glances down at Virginia's gown, a painful reminder of the wedding she'd refused. "When Mojo asked me to marry him"—her voice cracks, like it's agonizing to dredge up the memory—

"I said that I didn't want him putting a *chokehold* on my future. What kind of sick, wretched person says something like that to the man she loves?"

"You were just a kid, Palmer. Give yourself a break. It's normal for you to have felt that way—"

"But it's not, Dell! It's not how I felt. It's just something that came out because I was scared and immature, and I regretted it the second I said it. And Mojo's so wonderful, he stayed with me anyway."

"Because he loves you," I say, confident in my words. "And you love him."

"But now I'm the one putting a chokehold on his future, and how unfair is that?" she cries. "How can I tell him? What would I even say?" She shakes her head, her mouth quivering. "Mojo deserves a girl who won't drive him crazy, a girl that won't make him do acrobatics to keep up with her mistakes."

"Mojo doesn't want that girl," I insist, my hands clamping down on my cousin's shoulders. "He wants *you,* and you're allowed to change your mind. You get to want something different now that you're older. I think Mojo would be thrilled. He'd never see you or the baby as a mistake."

"I asked him to leave this morning," she whispers, her eyes on her stomach, still so flat and unassuming, like nothing life-altering is happening inside. "I said I needed to think about things—about what I want, and whether we're on the right track. I've never said anything like that to him before."

However Palmer is feeling right now, Mojo's undoubtedly feeling the same way. Worse, even, since he'd been kept in the dark about so much.

"Where is he?" I ask.

She shrugs. "Back at the apartment, I guess. Or maybe his parents' place."

"You haven't called him to find out?"

She shakes her head. "I *can't.* I don't know what to say. I..." Tears well up in her eyes. "I think I really might lose him this time."

I'm sure that at the core of her heartache, my cousin fears more than simply losing Mojo. Her fears likely also lie in the unknown, in a future without a clear roadmap, and the incredible responsibility about to drop into her lap. She's scared of failing to step up, scared to make the hard choices and trip up along the way.

"I know it's scary," I say gently, "but you can't keep this a secret forever. Sooner or later, you're going to start showing. You need to see a doctor. Don't you want to make sure everything's good with the baby?"

She nods, rubbing her nose until the upturned tip turns cherry red. "There hasn't been a good time to tell him, you know? Everyone's been so focused on Gram's passing, and the band's gigs have been picking up recently—"

"Neither of which are more important than this."

"But my parents—"

"You're not your parents, Palmer. You won't make the same mistakes they did. You'll make your own. You and Mojo, together."

Her voice sinks even lower. "There's something else."

"What?"

Her lips tremble pitifully, cheeks splotched in pink, like she's embarrassed to say whatever comes next. "It's sort of unrelated, but...Sasha got pregnant last year."

The attic begins to spin round and round, my brain sloshing like putty in my skull. My fingers find the floorboards beneath me and I plant my palms, stirring up clouds of dust.

"It wasn't Hatch's," Palmer says quickly, and my breath hitches. "Though, Sasha tried to pass it off like it was."

I remember what Mojo said on the beach about Hatch, that there were rumors circulating around town about him, but that none of them were true. My skin pricks with heat.

"How could she lie about something like that?"

Palmer pauses, her face a twisted medley of sadness and regret. "She's not a very nice person sometimes."

"And that's who you deem to be your best friend?"

"Well…" Palmer shakes her head, her breath ragged. "Sometimes, I guess I'm not a very nice person either."

I keep my thoughts to myself, not wanting to rub salt in her wounds, but my expression likely says it all—I'm completely disgusted.

"She got knocked up by some spring breaker," Palmer explains, "and after the jerk had had his fun and went back to the mainland, she tried to patch things up with Hatch. It was too late, of course, he wanted nothing to do with her. For a long time, I was so mad at him for dismissing her, for not giving her a second chance—"

"That's not up to you," I spit, furious.

"I know that now…I do."

"Then why are you still so rude to him?"

"Old habits die hard, I guess." Palmer bunches her shoulders, squirming. "Maybe I still feel some weird allegiance to Sasha? I don't…I don't really know."

My eyes flash over my cousin. "So what, then? She just went around town, dragging Hatch's name through the mud?"

Palmer nods, head bowed low. "For a while, yes. She told anyone who'd listen that Hatch got her pregnant and didn't want to step up. The worst part is I'm not even sure she wanted to keep the baby. I think she just wanted to string him along, to force him to stay, by any means necessary."

"And you just watched her do it? You stood by her, through all that?"

I'm so appalled by this story—and Palmer's involvement in it— that even looking at her proves to be an onerous task. I wish I hadn't shown her such kindness today, wish I hadn't spent hours laughing at her side.

"I…" Palmer cringes before she says, "I didn't stand against her, and that's one hundred percent my bad."

There's so much I could say, so many seething, viperous things I could sling at her, but the words stifle in my throat, swept up in a jumble of emotion. I decide it best not to speak at all.

"You really like him, don't you?" Palmer probes gently.

I clamp my lips together, unwilling to broach the subject of my feelings for Hatch. Not when I'm pissed to high hell at her. Again, I choose silence, a noncommittal response all its own.

"I'm glad for you both, if you do like him," she concedes, her words uttered softly. "He deserves to be with someone good like you. Someone kind and—"

"What happened to Sasha's baby?" I ask, cutting her off fast, my voice sharp as a blade. I don't care to hear Palmer opine on the two of us, neither together nor apart.

She pauses. "A couple of months into the pregnancy, she got into a car accident. Some drunk asshole ran a stop sign and slammed into her driver's side. Sasha needed emergency surgery and…lost the baby."

I feel an unwitting pang of remorse. I wouldn't wish the pain of that loss on anyone, even someone as casually vicious as Sasha.

Palmer holds her head in her hands, eyes trained on her belly. "It's been hard, ever since, to talk to her straight. I don't know how she'll react about this…about my baby. And I don't want to hurt her."

I'm running out of advice and encouraging sentiments to offer. A weary sigh spills from my lips. "If she's really your friend, then I'm sure she'll support you. She won't drag her baggage into it, she'll just be there for you, like you deserve."

I stand and roll the tension from my neck, in need of something new to focus my mind on.

"Do you, um…" Palmer's voice is small and pitiful. "Do you hate me, Dell?"

I peer down at my cousin, at her lovely, tear-stained face, her lean body dwarfed in a puff of bridal-white. For all of Palmer's beauty, grace, and good fortune, deep down, she's just a sad girl drowning in a sea of fear and excuses. There would soon come a time where she'd have to pick herself up again—make for the shoreline, sink or swim. I couldn't do it for her.

"No," I say quietly. "But I do feel sorry for you."

She dabs the wetness from her eyes. "I hate me a little bit right now," she whispers.

I can't help but surrender to that twinge of compassion throbbing in my chest for my cousin. "Let's just find the rest of what we came for, okay?"

Palmer nods and we move in opposing directions, wary not to step into the other's space—an evasive little dance that keeps us both on the tips of our toes.

We sift through stacks of ancient-looking luggage trunks and towers of disintegrating cardboard boxes, until, finally, we locate the remainder of Virginia's wardrobe.

While Palmer pokes around the trove of garments, I continue my tour through the attic, taking particular note of the children's toys: wooden rocking horses, porcelain baby dolls, building blocks for learning the ABC's, an antique jack-in-the-box. They're all worn and shabby, marred in dents and dings and chipped paint.

"I think those belonged to our moms," Palmer says, breaking our unspoken pact of silence.

"Or Willow," I respond without thinking twice.

Palmer furrows her brow like she hadn't considered that. "Right. Willow."

I sense her hesitation. "What?"

She shrugs. "Horrible as it sounds, I forget that she existed sometimes…that Mom even had a second sister. It's weird how easy it is to forget."

I recall the family photo wall and Willow's pronounced absence from it. "There's not a single photo of her in this house," I say.

Palmer nods slowly. "It must've been tough on Ambrose all these years, living in this giant mansion, immersed in memories of his dead daughter. Maybe the photos made it harder on him. Maybe it's better to forget a little."

"Maybe."

"My mom never forgets," Palmer adds. "She takes flowers to the cemetery every year on Willow's birthday, just like clockwork. She always—Dell, watch out!"

I trip over a heavy wooden cane leaning against the back wall, slamming head first into an old metal coat rack and tumbling onto the floor in a heap. I narrowly miss a set of skinning knives displayed on a gleaming aluminum stand.

"Holy shit." Palmer runs over to me, shoving her hands under my arms and hoisting me to my feet—oddly reminiscent of our little bathroom adventure last night. "You were almost skewered. Are you okay?"

"Peachy," I grunt, rubbing my temple as I regain my footing. Just when that damn bruise was starting to fade…

Getting my bearings, I squint to inspect the artisanal walking cane, the handle in particular, which is chiseled into the shape of a wolf's face. An intricate pattern extends from the beast's fur, winding down the entire length of the staff, masterfully whittled.

"One of Ambrose's?" I ask.

"Yes. He used canes a while back. Now he sticks to his chair. I guess his mobility's gotten worse with age."

"What happened to him?"

"Hunting accident," Palmer says, flourishing a hand at the various silver blades. "Hence, the serial killer knife display."

I nod. "And his vision?"

"Just deteriorated with age, I think. He gets laser treatments now and then, but nothing seems to work—"

A swift, pained moan escapes her lips, cutting her words short. She doubles over, pressing a hand to her stomach, but before I can reach her, she exhales and smiles weakly.

"I'm fine," she assures me, looking like she doesn't believe it herself.

I pick up her cell phone from its resting place on the floor and dangle it in front of her. My cousin gapes back at me. "Please, no," she chokes out.

"Call Mojo," I say, my tone threatening. "Or else I will."

"But you promised," she whispers. "You swore you wouldn't tell anyone."

"That was before."

Despite everything I know about Palmer—every petty, nasty thing she'd done out of loyalty to Sasha—I care too much about her to let this linger on. Over the past several days, there'd been an unmistakable shift in our relationship, a softening, some gradual tugging of heartstrings. We'd slithered beneath one another's skin somehow. And if breaking my promise will ultimately help her, I'm more inclined than ever to go back on my word.

"Do the right thing," I say to my cousin. "Clear the air with Mojo, tell him the truth. Then, for my sake, go see a doctor."

CHAPTER THIRTY-THREE

The hurricane intensifies throughout the afternoon, planting itself over Halcyon Bay like an unwanted tenant refusing eviction.

"We should be in the clear by morning," Briggs says knowingly, but it's hard to believe that now with the walls rattling around us, the light fixtures flickering, and the trees violently whipping in the wind.

I wonder how Hatch is faring through the storm, whether he stayed in the houseboat or moved inland, someplace safe and far from the rising water. I shouldn't have left him so abruptly last night, shouldn't have let my pride get the better of me. But I'd been so swept up in my own righteous indignation, so angry over what he might think of me and whether he disapproved.

In my heart, I wish I'd kept his number, but the shrewder part of me is glad I didn't. Why would he want to hear from me, anyway? I'd been nothing but trouble since the moment I arrived.

Before night falls, Leif corners Palmer and I, utilizing every coercive power in his arsenal to persuade us into watching *Home Alone* with him in the theater room. It's a mental hurdle for me to accept that

Cliffmoor House has its own *theater*, but an easy yes to give my littlest cousin. The kid could ask me to go cliff-diving and I wouldn't have the heart to refuse him.

"Are you sure you want to watch a Christmas movie in the middle of summer?" I ask.

"It's my favorite!" he exclaims with his usual bright-eyed fervor.

Palmer leans into my ear while Leif fiddles with the remote, increasing the volume until the surround sound system reaches its max. "He's convinced he's the second coming of Kevin," she says. "He watches this shit at least three times a week, knows every freaking line by heart—"

"I can heeear you!" Leif yells over the blaring speaker.

The best part about our movie viewing plan is that Inga makes us individual homemade pizzas for dinner—at Leif's request, of course— and I'm spared another uncomfortable Klyne family dining experience. We're joined by Bear, who sets up camp in Leif's lap, popping his head up whenever Leif accidentally tugs on his fur, anytime a particularly funny scene captivates his attention.

Toward the end of the movie, Emery pokes her head in the door and Leif hits pause. "Miss Palmer? Mister Moises has returned. He says you're expecting him."

Palmer's eyes widen. "Where is he, Emery?"

"Waiting in your room, miss."

Palmer goes silent now, not saying another word.

My hand finds hers, squeezing. "Thank you, Emery. She'll be right there."

The young maid smiles before bowing out of the room.

"Awesome, Mojo's back! He loves this movie!" Leif exclaims. "I'll go get him."

He launches himself off the recliner, sending Bear flying through the air and sliding onto his belly. The dog frowns up at Leif, sneezing his frustration all over the floor.

"No, Shrimp," Palmer says quietly. "I, um…I need some private time with Mojo. I'll be back in a little while, okay?"

Leif shoots his sister a sagacious look, stern and adorable behind his giant glasses. "Fine. Just be nice to him, please? No more fights." He rolls his eyes and climbs back into his seat, hitting play on the movie again. Bear trudges over and sits timidly at his feet.

Palmer looks at me now, inhaling a deep breath. She squeezes my hand back. "No more fights."

Leif queues up another movie but falls asleep midway through, nuzzled up against Bear's fur, snoring over his long-forgotten pizza crusts and half-drunk glass of strawberry milk.

June swings by to collect him after ten o'clock, looking haggard and pale as she informs me of all the catering orders that had been affected by the hurricane—all the events that had been canceled, the food that she'd made that would surely spoil. She props Leif up by her side, his eyes fluttering and groggy, and with a sigh, bids me goodnight, retiring to their room with Bear plodding close behind.

Palmer never returns, which I choose to interpret as a good sign, probably because small doses of optimism are pretty much all I have anymore. But now that I'm alone with nothing else to fill my mind, I'm left with the undesirable prospect of sleep. Worse still, the prospect of lying in a strange bed, turning over every one of my tumultuous thoughts through a long and restless night.

The dull sting of a headache rolls behind my eyes, so I shut the movie off and make my way to the kitchen in the dark. I should've brought my lantern. The generators are going strong, but the majority of lights have been left off to conserve power, making my solo trek through the strange halls a bit of a struggle.

When I finally get there, I find Inga resting on a barstool, head in her hands, listening to the antique radio booming the weather report.

"—two experienced surfers who bypassed beach warnings to brave the fifteen-foot storm surge were rushed to Halcyon Bay General this afternoon, sustaining critical, and possibly fatal, injuries—"

Inga shakes her head, thin white curls brushing against her cheeks.

"—homes destroyed, entire neighborhoods flooded, downed trees and debris blocking the roads, making it increasingly difficult for emergency vehicles to pass through—"

She's probably thinking of her own family, concerned for their safety. The same must be the case for Briggs and Emery, working through this catastrophe despite having loved ones and homes of their own to care for.

"—houseboat and mobile home evacuees can take shelter at Halcyon Bay High School and the Calico Jack Community Center. Residents are encouraged to stay indoors as Ophelia's dangerous eye wall moves across the island, bearing wind speeds of up to one hundred twenty-eight miles per hour—"

Inga flicks the radio off, sighs spilling from her lips, but when she spots me in the doorway, her tired eyes brighten. "Miss Meridel," she says in her pronounced accent. "Something you need?"

"Hi, Inga. I'm looking for some aspirin."

She nods, waddling to the pantry. "I get for you."

"Thank you."

I swallow down two blue pills and a full glass of water while Inga watches, at the ready for any other requests I may have. I offer her a weak smile and she returns it warmly, but our smiles fade quickly when the house vibrates, the storm audibly ramping up around us.

Inga eyes the walls like one of them might split open, the rain and wind rushing in to devour us. "Time for bed now," she says, patting her chest. "Sleep through storm. Wake up with sun."

I nod. "Yes, sounds good. Goodnight, Inga."

The cook bows and skitters away while I grab a second glass of water, procrastinating the walk upstairs and the blustery night ahead. I stay there for some time, alone in the kitchen, silently watching the streams of rain pelt down the giant arched windows. I pour milk and cereal into a bowl and settle onto a stool, delaying the inevitable for a little while longer, contemplating the deluge and the dark night.

It's like the sky is crying, I think, mesmerized by those endless, angry rivers of tears, trying to cleanse us—trying to drown us.

Not until the distant clock chimes midnight do I finally abandon the kitchen and slip back down the dreary hallway. I'm met with no one as I navigate toward the staircase, the house unlit and still. But when I reach the foyer, I'm surprised to hear an agitated male voice spilling from the study—Flip's voice.

Usually so even-tempered and calm, his tone now seethes with deep-rooted fury, culminating in a vicious, unsettling growl. "I will not accept your vacuous excuses."

"I did explain the situation to them." That's Tristen, his voice tense.

"Evidently not well enough."

"There's still time to salvage the deal—"

"You can't manage to do a single thing right, can you?" Flip's voice is deadly cold.

I inch closer to the study, pressing myself into the ample shadows of the corridor, holding my breath as I peer into the room. Father and son stand beneath a large stag head, tucked against a towering bookshelf, illuminated by the murky light of a table lamp. Despite their obvious height difference, Tristen cowers before his father, shrinking into himself like an admonished child.

"An unequivocal failure," Flip sneers. "Profiting from my successes, riding my coattails, when you're not even capable enough to lick the lint off them."

Tristen winces visibly—a homeless dog being kicked in the street.

"You're a disgrace," his father hisses, voice loaded with contempt. "I thought I could groom you into a winner. That with some heavy-handed pruning, I could straighten that gnarled trunk of yours. But even I can't fight genetics! You were destined to be a scourge upon this family, just like your whore mother before you."

Tristen straightens a little at this. "Don't talk about my mother."

In a split-second, Flip raises an arm and strikes Tristen across the face. I cover my mouth to keep from screaming as my cousin staggers back into the wall, clutching his blood-stained cheek.

"Your mother," Flip enunciates slowly, running a hand down his sleek black hair, "was a two-bit drug addict who sold herself nightly to fuel her deplorable habit. You were born a sickly, scraggy thing. Not even the doctors believed you'd make it."

Tristen squeezes his eyes shut, wincing from the pain of his father's words and brutality. I consider stepping out of the shadows to do something, *anything*, but I'm petrified, Flip's outburst replaying in my mind.

"After your shameless, prostituting mother dumped you on my doorstep, she went down to the shipyards and offed herself." Flip snickers cruelly, tossing his head. "She chose to die rather than claim you for her own. The sight of you was too loathsome to bear."

"Enough." Tristen presses his hands to the sides of his face, covering his ears, sinking down the wall.

"I'll be the judge of that." Flip takes a predatory step toward him, cracking his fingers, preparing to unleash a second physical blow. When he lifts his arm, I gasp aloud.

My uncle pauses, his face angling toward the shadowed doorway.

"What was that?" he asks his son, eyes scanning for the source of the gasping—for me.

I run from the shadows, stealing across the foyer and up the stairs like my feet have wings, not bothering to silence my steps. All I can think about is putting as much distance between myself and my uncle as I possibly can.

I race to my mother's door and seal myself inside, haunted by Florian's devilish face and his terrible lust for violence.

CHAPTER THIRTY-FOUR

I slam my body against Mom's dresser, pushing it to one side so that it blocks the doorway. Stepping back into the room, heart walloping in my chest, I stare at the closed door, waiting for Flip's angry fists to come crashing.

Seconds of waiting stretch slowly into minutes, but no sound comes from outside the corridor.

Until now, I hadn't considered Flip the scarier Klyne brother. Despite his pompous, showy personality, he'd always seemed inoffensive to me. But once alone with his son, it's like he flipped some internal switch, shedding that garish but good-natured façade and slipping into a monstrous second skin.

Suddenly, his cheeky nickname exudes a much more sinister significance.

This can't be a one-off incident. Abuse like this doesn't materialize out of thin air. How long had it been going on? Tristen is a grown man, knocking on his forties. Had he never gone to the police about this before?

And what of the rest of the family? Had the Klynes never taken notice? I find this especially problematic, because in my mind, not seeing the signs of Flip's brutal nature was the result of not wanting to see them.

Which brings me to yet another gut-wrenching thought—what if they do know? What if Ambrose, June, and Briggs are all complicit in Flip's violence, keeping quiet over the years out of some warped allegiance to family, to preserve their reputation and protect themselves from scandal? Flip must think himself untouchable. No one would dare betray him, not without tainting the precious Klyne name. If he could batter his own son so viciously, without displaying a shred of remorse, he could easily do it to someone else. Maybe he already had.

What else are these people hiding?

I stumble backward without looking, reaching for the cell phone I abandoned hours ago on Mom's nightstand, summoning the nerve to call the police, but I don't make it two steps. My foot gets tangled up where a loose board rises from the floor space formerly occupied by the dresser, and I tumble down to my knees, squeezing my toes through my sock, barely containing the scream that's begging for release.

Upon inspection, a bloody tear now runs down the webbing of my pinky toe. I think it might be broken, already turning a nasty shade of blue. I grit my teeth against the throbbing pain and take a couple deep breaths before shifting my weight to examine the floor.

As suspected, I find a board warped out of shape, just enough to snag on an unsuspecting bare foot. And through the tiny crack between the loose board and its neighbors, I see something poking up from underneath. I run my fingers down the edge of the board, trying to pry it up, but after several minutes, I accomplish nothing but splintering my fingernail down to the nub. Frustrated, I search the room for something to help me jimmy the board from its crevice—something thin enough to fit through the gap, but long enough to draw the board upward and out. That's when I remember the pewter comb from Mom's hairbrush set.

I hobble over to the dresser, my bruised foot cracking under my weight. I pull the comb from the top drawer and jam it into the gap in the floor, using it like a lever. After some effort, the board bends up a little, enough where I'm able to shove my fingertips beneath it. I lift it carefully, slowly, and when it finally pops free, I find a small box nestled in the nook below.

I reach into the opening, holding my breath, and pull the box into the light. Blowing away a thick layer of dust, I squint at the intricate design embossed into the lid. It's a heart wrapped in thorns, coiled around the organ like a snake, choking it. The thorns pierce the heart all over, and a single drop of blood drips from one of its wounds.

I open the lid.

Inside the box are dozens of Polaroid pictures, all of a baby girl with hair as bright as unpolluted sunshine. I pick up a stack of them, inspecting each one, the brittle edges of them crumbling in my hands. I recognize Willow's ocean-blue eyes and the bruise-like cloud of purple across one cheek, the photographs chronicling her first few years of life—all the baths, the bottles, and the sun-soaked beach days. I find a glossy lock of hair tied with faded pink ribbon, and pinch the ringlet between my forefinger and thumb. It glints at me, yellow as freshly shucked corn. There are baby socks too—little powder puffs of pink with creamy lace along the ribbing—and a blanket, petal-soft and fraying, embroidered along one side with a sweet nursery rhyme.

Beneath it all, I find a tiny velvet box, square and delicate, like something meant for jewelry. I run my thumb across the peach-fuzz surface, gently turning it in the palm of my hand. The box is feather-light.

The contents of my mind stir in a wild frenzy, racing across everything I've come to know about this family—their willingness to lie, their multitude of secrets—and I'm filled with an inexplicable fear. The fear of truths I'm not ready to face.

I count to three, then lift the lid.

A small brown scab lies alone inside, a puny, crinkled thing, shriveled up and dry. It's repulsive to look at, repulsive to anyone but...a mother.

I recognize what it is immediately. Mom keeps mine in a similar box back home, surrounded by other sentimental childhood keepsakes.

It's an umbilical cord stump.

In a box of Willow's things.

Hidden beneath the floorboards of my mother's former bedroom.

A secret. A skeleton of her past…and mine.

A rush of bile climbs up my throat, nearly projecting all over the floor. Fingers pressed to my lips, I hurtle into the adjoining bathroom and violently throw up in the toilet.

Willow's umbilical cord stump.

I brace my hands on each side of the ceramic bowl while everything spins around me, the sweat thick on my neck, my forehead slick and icy.

Willow is…

Mom's her…

Oh, God.

I get sick three more times before I manage to scrape myself off the bathroom tile, crawling like a wounded animal into my mother's bed, dragging her box of private memories along with me.

Deep down, I knew this was coming. The plain, unequivocal truth of it was just too much to bear, too heavy to accept. So I'd denied it. Ignored every clue and every instinct in my gut. But now, like a hell-bent locomotive careening down a broken set of tracks, I know that I'm headed for disaster. For some tragic cliffside precipice, and the screeching crash of reality.

Willow…

Mom…

I never should've opened that box.

CHAPTER THIRTY-FIVE

The discovery of my sister hits me like the tight-knuckled punch of a fist, like the white-hot collision of lightning, the crackling splinter of bat against bone.

There's no gentle development, no time to brace for the grief. It's quicksand, an instant flood. I don't know what I am or what I've been without it. All I know is that this pain feels permanent, stitched to my being, encoded in my identity. Perhaps, without my knowledge, the grief has always been here, biding its time, waiting for me to uncover it…for my mind to awaken and finally see the light.

A knock at the door tugs at the edges of my consciousness.

My eyes flick to the doorway, still blocked by Mom's old dresser. I'd nearly forgotten what happened in the study, as well as my intentions to call the police. Had Flip realized it was me hiding in the shadows?

"Dell?"

The whispered voice doesn't belong to my uncle.

"Hey, Dell, you awake?"

I step off the bed, careful to avoid putting pressure on my swollen foot, and pad to the door. I press my back against the dresser and push, returning it to its usual resting place.

"What's that sound?" whispers the voice in the hallway, likely confused by the dull scraping noise of moving furniture.

Without responding, I unlock the door and peer through the crack, my eyes landing on a disheveled but smiling Mojo.

"Doing a little late night redecorating?" he asks.

I don't bother explaining. "What's up?" My gravelly voice sounds like the living dead, and I'm sure I've got the cadaverous breath to match.

Mojo's nice enough not to comment on it. "Sorry to bother you. Palmer told me this was your room. I was just headed down to the kitchen for a snack—can't sleep in this weather—and I saw your light was still on..."

Get to the point, I urge him with my eyes.

"She told me you talked her off a ledge today." He rubs the back of his neck. "Thank you for that."

"It was nothing." Everything feels so far away now, like I've become dislodged from the world and can't find it in me to care about things that felt so important hours ago.

Mojo looks down at his feet, smiling sheepishly. "So you knew about the baby before I did, huh?" He slaps a hand to his forehead. "How clueless am I?"

"You're not a mind reader, Mojo. It's not your fault."

He chuckles to himself. "You'd think the Big Man Upstairs would help a guy out. My emotional radar is shit. I was actually convinced Palmer was cheating on me, or—"

"Mojo," I cut him off. He shuts up and stares at me. "I'm thrilled for you guys, really. But this isn't a good time."

"Oh, totally. Yeah, no problem. It's late." Mojo nods vaguely. "Just wanted to say that I owe you one, okay? Anything you need, I'm your guy." He shoots me awkward finger guns before scooting down the corridor.

I open the door a crack more. "Anything?"

He glances back, nodding, though his brow is furrowed. "Sure. You name it."

I inhale deeply, the air tingling around me. "Can I borrow your car?"

Mojo doesn't press me to divulge where I'm going, though he makes me promise not to leave Cliffmoor House until morning—until after the brunt of the storm has passed, and some sunlight clears the cloud cover. But I can't wait that long.

I sneak out as soon as the heavy rains let up, around five thirty in the morning, while it's still pitch-dark and desolate. Swarming clouds consume much of the sky, but the rolling storm has quieted some, leaving behind a breadcrumb trail of eerie mist and drizzle.

Mojo's Jeep isn't difficult to maneuver, climbing over piles of debris and downed trees with ease, zipping down the empty, inundated roads. In no uncertain terms, the island is trashed—homes and businesses wrecked, walls and roofs collapsed like some nightmarish pop-up book. Like paper-thin cutouts meant for smashing and folding.

I follow a mental map back to Halcyon Seaport, taking only two wrong turns before getting to what looks like a ghost town of tattered ships. The parking lot is an extension of the sea, a dark and murky infinity pool. I park and jump out, trudging across docks half-submerged in water through a maze of battered boats and destruction.

When I see the Sand Pit leaning haphazardly over a private dock, I know I've made it to my destination.

Ducking under the rope to bypass the *No Trespassing* sign, I come to stand before the *Willow's Wind*. It looks to be in surprisingly good shape, no obvious storm damage to be seen. This time, I don't dare come aboard uninvited.

I call to Bram, seeing the light turned on below deck, glowing through the salt-drenched porthole. I pray he'll answer me even though I don't deserve it. My heart pounds in my ears, louder and faster by the second. He doesn't respond, but I can hear his movements downstairs;

heavy-footed steps, indistinct scraping and shuffling.

"Bram," I call again, my voice still weaker than I intend.

The cabin hatch slides open, bathing the boat in pale light. Bram's dark figure rises into the wheelhouse, grumbling and shirtless. His bloodshot eyes droop when they land on mine, his face hardening through the shadows.

He steps onto the deck carrying a bottle of scotch. "You're back," he grumbles before taking a hearty swig, likely bracing himself for another round of accusations and threats to spew from my lips.

I can't speak at all, neither to apologize nor explain myself, as I get a good look at him, take in his features. My voice crumbles before I can utter a single coherent sound.

I'd had a hunch before, but now…now I'm certain.

My mouth opens and closes like a fish gasping for breath. A physical ache that I can only describe as pure, unadulterated dread spreads across my chest.

The bottle of liquor sloshes in Bram's hand. "Well?"

Do I want him to deny this indisputable truth, buried deep within Cliffmoor House, ingrained within me? Do I just want to commiserate? For him to tell me that it's all going to be okay? Or, more accurately, that *nothing* will ever be okay again?

Bram runs a bear claw down his face, thick fingers tangling in a thicker beard, while I slouch over his dock, choking on my words. I wonder what pathetic thing he sees when he looks at me. Certainly, not the same girl that was here three nights ago. *She* was determined and fiery, armed with a sharp tongue, driven by purpose. What Bram must see now is a mere shadow of that girl, shaped by grief, inferior in every way.

I come to him with all of my weapons surrendered, white flag raised, a soldier with no fight and no country. Broken and unmendable.

"Figured some things out, have you?" he asks suspiciously.

I nod as tears steal down my cheeks.

Bram looks to the horizon where the rippling sea meets the sky. Flecks of morning light stipple the dark water in yellow, marking the birth of a brand new day.

"This hurricane churned up far more than the sea," he mumbles, taking another sloppy drink from his scotch.

I follow his gaze to the ocean's edge, and we remain that way for a while—engulfed in silence, watching the dawn paint the distant sky, a wordless understanding passing between us.

This man did not kill my sister. He never meant her any harm, never so much as touched her. He loved her only as a father loves a daughter, which is precisely what they were.

Shockingly, Bram doesn't ask me to leave. He holds out his bottle of liquor to share with me—breakfast of champions and the heartbroken alike, a kindness I neither expect nor deserve.

I climb aboard the *Willow's Wind* and, shaking, take it from him. I take a sip and sink down against the wheelhouse wall to settle upon the deck. The smoky-tart flavor of the scotch burns in my throat, but I appreciate the bitter tang of it, glad to feel something other than vacant numbness.

The sun pokes its head into the cloud-heavy sky, injecting some color over the ashen, post-storm island. Bram and I barely speak, our conversation strained and sparse, but we each seek comfort in the other's quiet presence. Two strangers bonded by one tragic, terrible secret:

A daughter—stolen.

A sister—concealed.

CHAPTER THIRTY-SIX

Hatch arrives at seven o'clock for a fishing excursion, looking surprised to find me perched beside Bram, passing the dwindling liquor bottle between us.

By now, the sun has risen, nestled high in a shifting sky that seems to want peace again, fending off storm clouds like demons. Hazy sunlight pours over the island, over the *Willow's Wind*, but its warmth hasn't so much as touched me all morning, the night sinking its teeth down deeper, into the lining of my flesh, my bones, my bloodstream.

Not until I lay eyes on Hatch does it finally, slowly, begin to recede.

The marina shakes awake around us. Fishermen crawl about the docks, assessing the damage to their property, phoning in their insurance claims, starting small repairs and early clean-up efforts. Some—the lucky few whose boats were spared, like Bram—ready to embark on what's sure to be a fruitful, albeit volatile, day at sea.

The rest of the crew shows up shortly after Hatch, and immediately go to work preparing the boat. I expect to be asked to leave, but in another surprising turn, Bram invites me to come along, though not in so many words. He tosses me a rash guard and asks if I'm prone to motion sickness. I shake my head no, assuming this means I'm allowed to stick around.

I pull the oversized shirt over my head, mulling over Bram's expression of sad resignation. He seems conflicted, keeping me at arm's length while simultaneously keeping me close, learning what he can from me, trying to connect, but never fully relinquishing his trust. I can relate.

Hatch doesn't ask for an explanation as to my unlikely truce with Bram, either connecting some vague dots or shelving his questions for later. He hands me a partially used tube of Coppertone lotion and folds a pair of sunglasses into my collar. His lips are unsmiling but his eyes are tender, as if to assure me that we're okay. I want to apologize for my part in our fight, things I'd said because I felt humiliated, but he slides quietly past to join his fellow sailors before I manage to dredge up the right words.

Bram takes the wheel, maneuvering easily through the cluster of ships and out into open waters, cracking open a fresh pack of cigarettes to kick off the morning's exploits. We anchor several miles offshore, where the waves are rough and the land too far for viewing, surrounded on all sides by a vibrant, cobalt expanse. Here, the men start chumming.

I cling to the ropes and observe their synchronized labor, filling the water with thick clouds of oats and fish guts, grinding away in methodical silence—a routine built from sharpened muscle memory. Before long, mobs of fish appear—lightning bolts that wriggle and flash their blue, silver, and yellow scales, glistening below the surface like fruit ripe for the picking.

The men swiftly get out their rods, wrap fighting belts around their waists, bait their hooks, and send lines plummeting. Almost instantly, someone's got a tug. I hear the rapid whirring of a reel, like a zipper being pulled fast along its track. In the blink of an eye, Bram's hooked one, then Hatch, then one of the others. Over the next couple of hours, the men bring aboard scores of large, colorful fish for eating. Snapper, dolphin, tuna, kingfish, Spanish mackerel, Hatch lists them all for me, one by one. The men throw them into a giant cooler chest brimming with ice while I watch on, mesmerized by the process.

When they pause for lunch, Hatch sidles up beside me. Wordlessly and without prompting, he hands me half of his homemade sandwich. We sit terribly close while we eat, sharing a bottle of Gatorade and trying not to be obvious about the way our eyes inevitably dart toward each other. I'm only half-listening to the crew's boisterous cackling, half-honed in on our calm, corresponding breaths, the instinctive way our bodies huddle close together, arms touching from shoulder to elbow.

"How'd your houseboat fare through the storm?" I ask, finally mustering the will to speak up.

"Haven't been back yet. I spent a couple nights at my mom's place."

"Oh." I'd wondered about this, hoped he hadn't been alone and imperiled. "Everything okay?"

"It is, actually," he says, somewhat reserved. "We talked. Made some things right."

"That's great," I say, offering him a weak smile. All I can think of is how to put words to my feelings, to that butterfly flutter deep in my chest. "Hatch, listen, about the other night…I was—"

"Right," he interrupts, catching me off guard.

"What?"

"You were right," he repeats. "And I was jealous."

Impossible.

"Jealous? Of who, *Prescott?*" I don't bother trying to contain my shock. Could Sasha's insinuations about me and Prescott having some secret rendezvous in the fields actually have gotten under his skin?

"Of anyone that might capture your attention," he says unflinchingly, "no matter how brief or inconsequential."

With that one statement, he's stolen all my words from me, a thief with dazzling, ever-amused eyes.

"Now." He nudges me playfully. "It's time for you to catch some dinner." His eyes weave past me to the monstrous fishing rods catching the sunlight, both an enticing and intimidating prospect.

The rod he sets me up with is heavy, working the flimsy muscles in my arms like dumbbells. I grasp it tightly with both hands while Hatch holds a live, silver fish up to my eye.

"Baitfish," he says, spearing through its scaly body with the hook at the end of my line. Hatch tosses the fish in the water, my line trailing swiftly behind it, and attaches a plastic fighting belt with a rotating rod holder to my waist.

His fingers move swiftly at first, then linger a bit, pressing gently against my hip. I turn to meet his eyes, relishing in that slight pressure, a flush rising in my neck. For one glorious, fleeting instant, it's like we're all alone out here.

"Hold tight," yells a crewman, and Hatch drops his hand. Where his fingertips dusted, my skin still tingles, and I'm amazed at the way he makes me feel things even when I think myself incapable of feeling.

At first, nothing happens. Bram takes a swig from a fresh bottle of scotch, stepping back to give me some breathing room, the others following suit. Hatch stays at my back, his breath in my ear, encouraging. "Steady," he whispers. "Wait for it. Wait for it…"

A vigorous tug nearly sends the rod flying from my hands, and I lurch forward, shrieking, "I've got something!"

The fish swims out like he knows his life depends on it, jerking my body hard against the boat's outermost wall. "Loosen the barrel and hold on," Bram commands, stepping up beside me to help.

Whatever I've hooked is a worthy adversary, but Bram instructs me every step of the way, and I follow along somewhat competently. My fingers cramp and spasm until they finally go numb, but not once do I ever let go.

After twenty minutes of fighting, I ask Hatch to take over and drag the fish in himself, but he shakes his head, chuckling. "No way. This one's yours."

"What if I lose him?" I shout back, my eyes on the line whirring farther out into the endless blue.

"Then"—he squeezes my shoulder—"you try again."

Nearly half an hour later, the fish tires of struggling and I'm slowly able to reel it in—a groaning, agonizing process. I'm utterly worn out by the effort, my arms, legs, and back trembling with fatigue. And when the creature finally breaches the surface, I'm stunned.

This is no fish of ordinary size, but an absolute behemoth.

One monstrous, bloated eye peers up at me from below, the skin of the creature a mottled pattern of browns and blacks. The giant folds of its lips droop into a permanent, corpulent frown. It's positively obese, if that's something a fish can be, all bulging and puffy like it might pop if punctured.

"Goliath Grouper," Bram says with an approving nod. "At least a sixty pounder, from the looks of it."

I pray that Bram cuts the line and returns the grouper to the sea. Something that massive shouldn't be caught.

Hatch comes forward, working quickly to de-hook the fish. "Keeping them is illegal," he explains over his shoulder. "Goliaths are protected in these waters. We'll release him here and send him back unharmed."

Within seconds, the grouper goes free, sinking back slowly to the cavernous depths. I breathe a sigh of relief, giving myself permission to relax. That is, until, out of the corner of my eye, I spot a familiar glint of silver in the distant waves…the same shimmery flash I'd noticed on the beach days ago, teasing me now from beneath the water's surface.

I press against the ship's outer wall, leaning as far as I can over the whirling eddies, tantalized by the rippling formation below—eager to see just what it might be.

The silvery mass draws nearer, pulled to me like a magnet by some strange, indefinable magic. But then the cloud-ridden skies above us yawn open, and a sudden rain shower begins to pour down, blanketing the boat, the ocean, the world around us in sheets of gray, and swallowing up the shiny silver thing with it.

As the rain courses over me, I find myself laughing—partly from the nerves and exhaustion, and partly from the thrill and sheer unpredictability of this day.

I exchange a look with Bram, and incredibly—miraculously—Bram smiles too.

He tilts his head back to face the rain full-on, teeth exposed in a wide and reckless grin, droplets mingling with tears on his cheeks. He laughs and I laugh and the watery world around us seems to roar and pulse with life and laughter too.

It's no more than a cursory flash of catharsis, a blip in our shared melancholia. And maybe it's all that either of us can manage, but maybe it's exactly what the both of us need.

After giving the *Willow's Wind* a hasty rinse-down, the men make quick work of unloading the cooler chest onto a trolley. They nod brief goodbyes at me and wind the trolley down the docks, stocking up the Urban Fishing Company delivery truck and swiftly zipping off to the fish market.

Once the others have gone—their loud voices and bustling hands no longer a buffer—Bram grows restless. He says goodbye to Hatch and I, ducking into his cabin with yet another bottle of scotch. The man must work exclusively to support that unbridled drinking habit.

I have so much I still want to ask him, but I can't blame him for his abrupt exit. It's five o'clock, meaning we'd spent nearly eleven hours together today. And, in all likelihood, having me around was tough on him, my presence an all-too-painful reminder of *her*. It's not Bram's job to explain things to me, anyhow. We're barely acquainted, more strangers than friends, and I'm not sure that either of us can handle much more than that.

The person I need to talk to—the one who owes me a real explanation—is my mother, but our looming conversation terrifies me to my core. It may be the hardest thing either of us have to do, to face one another with the ugly truth, no matter the fallout. What kind of relationship awaits us on the other side? Can I forgive her lifetime of lies? Can she forgive my betrayal—running to the one place she begged me never to go?

Hatch walks me to the seaport's parking lot. It's still flooded, though significantly less so, and mostly occupied by vehicles now—a small sign of the island returning to normalcy. He still hasn't asked any questions about me and Bram, a fact for which I'm deeply grateful. I couldn't deny him if he asked, but I also wouldn't know where to begin.

"You think the ferries are working again?" I ask, remembering that I was meant to be on one this morning. I'll need to secure passage on one tomorrow.

"Probably started up this afternoon once the weather cleared. Why, are you planning your getaway?"

"I was supposed to leave today," I admit, unhappy at the thought of sailing away from Halcyon Bay with so much left unsaid with Hatch…so much left undone.

"Oh." He steals a sidelong glance my way. Was he pondering all the unexplored things that might exist between us too? "So you're really shipping out, then?"

"Tomorrow morning." I sigh. "And I've got twenty-four hours of driving to do when I get back to the mainland." I can't imagine spending all that time by myself—anxiety skyrocketing with every passing mile, contemplating the innumerable ways things can go wrong once I reunite with my parents.

"What are you doing tonight, then?" His question and sparkling gaze are like a lifeline, salvaging me from my fathomless ocean of thoughts. "Do you have any plans? Family stuff?"

"Hell. No."

Hatch grins slowly. "Do you think, maybe, you'd want to—"

"Yes." My cheeks warm at my eagerness.

How many years have I wasted pretending to have my shit together, pretending I don't want someone to lean on? Wearing layers of armor over my skin, building walls between myself and the world? I don't want to repeat those same patterns now. Not anymore, and not with him.

"All right. Then it's settled." The glimmer in his eyes—a picture of triumph and delight—makes me go soft in the knees. "Where shall I pick you up?"

"Um…" A minor hiccup—I'm not sure where I'm headed. I'd brought all my belongings with me, never again planning to return to Cliffmoor House, but I do need to get Mojo's car to him somehow. And find a place to spend the night.

"48 Anchorage Lane," I finally say, hoping that the flooding receded enough to where June and Leif had returned home safely. "My Aunt June's place. I think I'm crashing there tonight."

Hatch tucks a strand of hair behind my ear. "Great," he says, still smiling. "Pick you up at eight."

All along that meandering drive to June's house, I find myself beaming like a damn idiot, my mind and my heart lighter than they've felt in days. I'm even breathing easier, having created some distance between myself and my twisted family, my lungs filled up with a day's worth of crisp, salty air.

Parking in June's driveway, I find the property surprisingly dry, save for several dark patches of swampy water inundating the tree roots, pooled at the first floor landing. The stilt house looks worse for wear after the storm—shingles lifted, the porch swing broken, bushes and debris littered across the lawn. But I'm thrilled that June's car is parked there and in good condition, and that the lamppost on the curb is lit— the electricity is back.

I skip over the puddles and take the steps two by two. The front door swings open before I can knock. I expect the usual furry assault from Bear, Leif's buck-toothed grin, maybe the aroma of whatever June's cooking…but strangely enough, none of these is the case.

The woman who opens the door is not my aunt. I take in the sight of her shoulder-length hair like faded straw, her fair skin stretched across a bony frame, her familiar and infinitely sad eyes.

The others crowd the doorway behind her, five sets of shifting eyes jumping from her to me.

"*Mom?*" I gasp as she steps onto the porch.

CHAPTER THIRTY-SEVEN

I gape at my mother as if she were a ghost summoned by my deepest fears and anxieties.

A pained combination of sadness, guilt, and betrayal washes over her hollowed face, and I can't help but feel that I'm to blame for it all, though my sins and my secrets pale in comparison to hers.

"Dell," she whispers.

"Mom," I repeat in disbelief. "What are you doing here?"

She doesn't respond, her watery eyes scanning my face.

I press my lips together, that familiar veil of darkness spreading, undoing every hopeful thought I'd had about my evening with Hatch. Pleasure isn't something I'm entitled to on this island.

Dad breaks from the cluster of concerned faces behind her, wrapping me up in a tight embrace. I pat his back stiffly, unable to set aside the fact that he'd been lying to me too. For decades, no less.

"Where have you been?" he asks frantically, gripping my shoulders. "We've been looking for you for hours. We thought you'd gotten hurt."

I stare past him to my mother. "I went fishing."

Mom's eyes go wide with understanding, her shoulders caving in slow defeat.

"We should talk, Mom."

"Yes, I suppose we should."

With a shaky breath, she extends her hand to me. I slip my fingers in hers, struck by how icy-cold they feel. "We'll be back soon," she says weakly to the others. "Dell and I are going for a walk."

I let her lead me back down the porch steps and into the hazy afternoon, shuffling in silence to the end of Anchorage Lane, where a small community park overlooks the ocean. Avoiding the mess of tree limbs strewn over the grass, we settle on a jetty wall where the bubbling water breaks.

Despite the visible hurricane damage, there's a sort of raw beauty in the park's wildness. Everything is misty, lush, and summer-rich, bursting with vibrant greens and blooms of all shades, come alive by the shared hand of sunshine and rain. Proof of some deep, inherent magic in nature, shining through all of this temporary devastation.

Where we sit atop the jetties, a stream of golden light filters through the clouds, dancing beautifully upon the waves and my mother's pallid face. In this yellow twilight atmosphere, with her flaxen hair, dripping blue eyes, and near-pearlescent complexion, Mom resembles a woodland fairy. Will she flit away if frightened, leaving nothing but a trail of tears and stardust in her wake? Leaving me with more questions than answers, more lore than truth?

I squeeze her hand three times, praying on my life that she won't leave, won't run. It's our old, familiar ritual. *I love you*, it says, with each consecutive squeeze. *I'll always love you, no matter what.* It's strange to do it here, in this setting, this place, with so many unspoken secrets hanging between us, but that doesn't make it any less true. And it's important she knows it, now more than ever.

"Dell…"

"Why aren't you back in Woodbridge, Mom?"

"When I figured out where you were, I checked myself out of Hopewell and had your dad book our flights."

"But your treatment—"

"Is entirely voluntary," she interrupts, her expression darkening. "I had to be here with you, making sure you were all right. And now that I know that you are, the three of us are leaving for good in the morning."

Her eyes are firm and motherly, her words deliberate, as if to emphasize that, come hell or high water, we're getting off this rock at first light. It strikes me how lucid she sounds, jolted awake from her former delirium, driven to clear action…all to ensure my safety.

"We would have been here sooner if not for the hurricane," she continues. "Our flight was diverted to Cyprus. We were stuck there for nearly two days before—"

"Why, Mom?" I ask, unable to contain it. I can't endure another second of trivial conversation.

"We had to wait out the storm before—"

"No." I shut her down, my voice cracking. "*No.* That's not what I'm asking."

She falls instantly quiet, her lips blanching with fear.

I inhale. "What I mean is…why didn't you tell me? Why did you keep Willow a secret all these years?"

My question looms large as the ocean before us. I've never uttered words more painful. The stifled truth of them digs into me—into her—like a set of jagged teeth, ripping flesh and piercing bone.

The tip of Mom's nose burns crimson. "How did you find out?"

My eyes glaze over. Her question is confirmation enough to know that it's true, unequivocally.

Willow is my sister.

"No one came out and told me, if that's what you're wondering. I had to figure it out for myself."

Mom's lip trembles, her cheeks dampening to match my own. "What could I ever say to make this make sense?" she whispers. "I had a chance, Dell, a chance to spare you from this heartache. So I thought, why not try?"

I shake my head in silent refusal. I don't understand. I will *never* understand.

"I believed I was doing the best thing for you," she insists. "The truth would have hurt you terribly, and that's not something I ever wanted."

"Did it occur to you that maybe it would hurt me *not* to know?" She reaches out to me, but I quickly jerk away. "I was so confused about why you were sick. About how you got that way, and if it was my fault. If I'd done something to mess you up somehow." I put a hand to my chest, my heart racing so fast that it actually hurts to breathe. I inhale shallow gulps, gasping and unsteady. "You should've told me, Mom. I *deserved* to know."

"It was wrong to keep it from you," she says, the words coming fast between sobs, "but I only ever wanted to protect you. I didn't want this burden on your shoulders. You were entitled to a happy life, free from emotional trauma."

Her expression turns fierce now, as if the apex of her whole existence hinges on this next point. "And, to be clear, my sickness is *not* your fault. Being your mom is the single greatest joy of my life. You are a wonderful daughter, and *I love you*. Do you hear me?"

I swipe rough fingers down my salt-streaked face, rubbing my cheeks until they're sore. Processing. Grieving. Feeling it all. My ears ring with soundless torment, as if the sea breeze plays some ancient instrument upon the waves—a lament I hadn't been tuned into before, but now it's all I can hear.

"I've seen pictures of her," I whisper after a long minute. "I read things about how it happened online. I even found your memory box hidden up in your bedroom."

"You found it?" Mom chokes out, looking like she might burst at the news.

"I can't believe you left it behind."

Her lips pull down as if tugged by invisible string. "We took off so quickly...I couldn't bring myself to go back to that house...but, Dell, why do you think I asked your father to return for the will reading? You really think I care about anything we might inherit from my parents?"

She grinds her teeth, the gesture more desperate than angry. "All I care about is getting that box back. It's everything...everything I have left of her."

I'm heartbroken, and breaking even more as we speak. For my mother, myself, and the incalculable pain we'll share forever.

"Why did you lie about being her sister?"

Mom diverts her gaze to the rocks at our feet—to the place where the fitful waves roll, hiss, and crash. Her eyes travel along that breakwater, frenzied, distressed. I can only imagine she's scouring the limpets, barnacles, and sea foam for the proper words.

"It was my mother's idea," she recalls quietly. "I was only fifteen when I found out I was pregnant—a child bearing a child—and I was so terrified. I went to my mother immediately with the news, and she told me..." Mom shakes her head, taking a heaping breath. "She said that being an unwed teenage mother would ruin my opportunities in life. That I'd be a disgrace to the family, that *she* was better suited to raise Willow as her own.

"I didn't know what else to do but to go along with Mother's plan, and I've regretted the decision every day, every minute, since. But how could I ever go back and undo it? Coming clean would've destroyed Willow's entire belief system, shot her whole sense of self to hell. I didn't want to cause any more damage than had already been done."

"But after she died, you went on pretending." There's an accusation in my voice that I don't bother to conceal. "You and Dad withheld everything from me, everything about Halcyon Bay and the Klynes, even when I asked."

She swallows. "I know."

"Did you ever consider that I might find out the truth someday? Or wonder what damage your lies would do to *me?*"

"I'm so sorry, Dell."

"And what about Bram?" I snap, a fresh surge of anger rising in me. Mom's eyes go glassy, her mouth slack.

"He *is* Willow's father, isn't he, Mom?"

She nods almost imperceptibly, her fluttering lashes lined with tears.

"And you forced him to stay away?"

"No...not exactly. I never told Bram about Willow being our daughter. He grew to suspect it on his own. That's why he kept coming around, trying to talk to her when she was alone. He wanted to see for himself...to see if she was his."

A sickening cramp knots up my stomach. "How could you let your parents go through with that restraining order?"

"Believe me, I felt awful about that," she says. "But by that point, I was too far swept into the lie. There's no excuse for my part in it"—she rubs her forehead with a quivering hand—"but I swear I didn't want to hurt him. He's a good man. We'd been friends for years. I was just scared—so, so scared." She closes her eyes as silence drops over us.

"Who else knows the truth?" I ask, my voice jarring against the quiet.

"Mother didn't want me confiding in anyone," she responds. "June was the only other family member who knew."

"Not even Ambrose?"

"Not even him."

"How could Virginia keep that from him? Wouldn't he *know* if she was pregnant with his child?"

"My mother was smart, and equally as conniving. She convinced my father that Cliffmoor House desperately needed a renovation, then left the task in his hands and transplanted the rest of us to New Orleans. There, she faked the entire pregnancy."

Low, scathing contempt fills up Mom's voice now. "It's like my mother was right back in show business, waddling around with this giant, silicone belly, buying herself a fancy maternity wardrobe. It was an Oscar-worthy performance." She grimaces. "Ginnie Gold's greatest act."

Despite every lie and fear-driven misstep, I wonder whether Mom is as much a victim in this as Bram—forever kept at the fringes, deposed from her rightful role, her child wrenched away by more powerful forces.

"June and I were homeschooled to minimize fanfare," Mom adds with a tired shrug. "Mother made me wear oversized clothes to hide my stomach. My medical team—the doctors and midwives—signed airtight NDAs. She took every precaution to be certain that no one saw or spoke of me."

"And Ambrose never realized?"

"He was too busy building his empire to pay any mind to my sudden weight gain. And as far as being intimate with my mother when he visited, she made it clear that she didn't want him touching her until after the baby was born. She concocted some lie about it being a high-risk pregnancy—that she couldn't overexert herself and needed plenty of bed rest. It wasn't rare for them to sleep apart, anyway. Their marriage was usually rocky at best."

"And you're sure he still doesn't know?"

Mom shakes her head. "I doubt Mother ever told him."

The dysfunction in this family is palpable. Gross. Damn near barf-inducing.

"What about Dad?"

"I told your dad the truth after Willow, um…" Her voice trails off, unable to complete the thought as streams of tears moisten her cheeks again. "He was upset that I'd kept it from him—rightfully so—but he also knew that we couldn't stay here anymore. He wanted the best for you, for our future as a family, and when I told him the whole story—when I showed him the threatening messages I'd been getting—well, that was the last straw."

"What messages?"

"I'd been receiving anonymous letters, like those ransom notes you see on the news made from cut-out magazine text. Someone had worked out the truth about Willow, and they were trying to extort money from me in exchange for their silence."

Blackmail, I realize. *My mother was blackmailed.*

"Did you pay them off?"

"No…it didn't come to that." She hesitates. "I knew the person sending the letters. Or, at least, I think I did." A contorted expression comes over her face. "I believe it was my cousin, Tristen."

"Why on earth would he need your money?"

"It was more about retribution for the ways our family had wronged him. Tristen always had a volatile relationship with the Klynes. He was treated like an outcast by his father, and his mother, sadly, died when—"

I raise a hand for her to pause. I can't stomach this story again. "Spare me, please. I already know what happened to her."

Mom nods slowly, and I can practically see her piecing together all that I'd gathered in my brief time on the island. "Tristen used his perceived illegitimacy as a fountain for his hate. He never felt included in the family. I can't count the number of times I heard Florian yell vicious obscenities at him—"

"He beats him," I say flatly. "I saw it happen just last night."

"Last night? And you…saw?" Mom's face screws up in disgust. "Do you understand now? Do you see what I'm talking about? About this place, these people? It's not safe for any of us here—"

I cut quickly to my next question, not wanting to veer off track. "How did Tristen find out the truth about Willow?"

"I can't know for sure. He always watched us a little too closely, and he was mistrusting, eager to push his own misery on everyone else. One day, out of the blue, he confronted me with all these crazy conspiracy theories. He didn't believe that we three were sisters, for one. He claimed that Willow was"—she winces—"a bastard child, just like him."

A shiver snakes down my back. "What else did he say?"

"Tons of awful things. He implied that my mother had multiple ongoing affairs, including a fling with our family butler."

My eyes widen at this. Briggs was certainly fond of my grandmother, but I figured it stemmed from years of loyal servitude. Was there something more going on between them? Some clandestine romance, right under Ambrose's nose?

"He said that my father's money came from corrupt business dealings abroad. That the Klynes' wholesome, all-American success story was one giant farce." Mom runs a weary hand across her temple. "The slanders went on and on. And when letters started appearing, I assumed it was Tristen stirring up trouble again, trying to intimidate me."

"So what did you do?"

"Nothing," she says. "I ignored them, hoping he'd go away. I didn't care to feed into his empty threats. And nothing ever came of it."

"Until Willow drowned," I retort, my tone unforgiving.

Mom shakes her head. "That was months later. And it had nothing to do with this."

"Isn't it possible that Tristen was involved somehow?"

"No, it's not. I kept a close eye on him all through the summer solstice party. He didn't have an opportunity to go off alone, much less with Willow."

A horrible suspicion dawns over me. "What if he got someone *else* to do it for him?"

"No," Mom emphasizes, shutting her eyes against my morbid claim. "Willow's death was a terrible accident—"

"Oh, come on, Mom," I interject. "You all grew up on that beach, right? Willow would've known to avoid the reef. Wasn't she a competitive swimmer?"

"It doesn't matter how good a swimmer you are if you get caught in an undertow."

Even as she says it, I know that part of her doesn't believe it. It's just a story she's told herself for years, slipping easily from her lips like a long-rehearsed script. And though it pains me *deeply* to bite my tongue on the matter—I'm practically coming out of my skin with outrage—I decide it best to do so, for both of our sakes.

"Who's Lo?" I ask abruptly, remembering the phantom figure from Mom's dreams. "June told me that was your childhood nickname, but I thought it might have something to do with Willow."

"Lo was my nickname growing up," Mom admits, "but after I gave birth to Willow, I used to call her Lo in secret, when my mother wasn't around to stop me. It felt good to share something private between us, something uniquely ours. It was one small thing that connected us, a piece of her that was all mine, that no one could ever take from me."

So Mom's visions of Lo—a ghostly composite of her traumatized younger self and the daughter she gave up—were symptoms of her unresolved past, lingering resurrections of a truth she'd entombed on this island, just as the Klynes entombed Willow's corpse.

"I'm sorry you had to find out this way. That you had to see me so…broken." Mom's mouth settles into that familiar frown. "When we got word about your grandmother, everything just came rushing back, and I couldn't stop it. I felt I was drowning in that pain all over again. How I failed to protect her. How I'd spent a lifetime lying to you. I got lost in it, and I couldn't find my way out."

"It's not the first time, Mom. I'm used to it."

She steels herself, nodding a little, her lip twitching at the swift sting of my words, and the knowledge that she'd let me down.

"Is it really better?" she asks. "Knowing the truth?"

I narrow my eyes. "Knowing is painful, but not knowing? That's worse. That's…that's *killer*." My voice shakes, but I don't allow myself to cry again. I'm not done being angry, despite the way my heart twists in agony for my mother.

Eventually, she nods again. Reluctant acceptance. "I understand what you mean."

"Why didn't you stick around after she died?"

"Because I needed to get you away from this place," she says, as if it were the plainest answer in the world. "Away from the Klynes, and all their lies and deceit. I owed you a better life than the one she had."

"And who kept pressure on the HBPD in your absence? Who made sure they carried out a thorough investigation? That they got to the bottom of what really happened that night?"

"I know what happened." Her voice simmers with tearful frustration. "Willow snuck away to the beach during the party. The tide was rough. It dragged her under and onto the reef. End of story."

My jaw tightens. "You don't believe that."

"Yes," Mom asserts. "I do."

Her tone gets quiet and charged with muted reproach, like part of this mess is mine now, simply for poking my nose in it. "I warned you, Dell. I warned you never to come back to Halcyon Bay."

CHAPTER THIRTY-EIGHT

June sets my parents up in Palmer's former bedroom, flitting around like some punch-drunk butterfly, arms loaded with pillows, linens, and towels. She offers me the living room couch, but Palmer insists that I spend the night at her and Mojo's apartment instead.

"You can be our first official house guest," she says with a wink. "As long as you don't mind sleeping on a mattress on the floor, or having a cardboard box for a nightstand."

I can tell that my parents aren't happy with this arrangement—that they'd hoped to keep me suffocatingly close tonight—but that's all the more reason to go. They remain silent when I accept Palmer's invitation, but upon declining June's dinner offer, the protests inevitably arise.

"What do you mean you're going out?" Dad asks, apprehension crawling across his face. "With whom, exactly?"

"A friend." I shrug, adding, "Palmer knows him." Like that's a selling point. My parents know as much about Palmer as they do Hatch, which is absolutely nothing.

"A friend?" Dad gives me a pointed look. "Wouldn't your friend understand if you canceled?"

Normally, a line of questioning like this would result in me caving in, not wanting to ruffle feathers or unduly aggravate my mother, but I'm feeling decidedly less acquiescent tonight.

"I'm sure he would," I say simply, "but seeing as how I don't have a valid reason *to* cancel, it's sort of a moot point."

"Do you at least know where you're going?" Mom's question is tentative, wary.

"No, I don't."

"Isn't this a little unreasonable?" Dad's face bursts with agitated pink splotches. "You don't have a clue where you're going, or even how long you'll be."

The unwarranted third-degree is getting on my nerves. I don't appreciate them micromanaging me like some leashed and curfewed teenager. Especially not after I'd spent five days navigating this island on my own, uncovering the unthinkable depths of their lies. I'm sure they assumed that once they swooped in to collect me, I'd go swiftly, quietly, without an ounce of resistance. That's what they're accustomed to. But not tonight.

"I didn't think to ask him for a detailed schedule of events," I say sharply, "but since it's dinner time, I can assume our plans will involve food. Maybe drinks too, but only if we're feeling really wild and crazy."

Before I leave, Mojo gives me the address to the apartment, dropping a spare key into my hand.

"We're telling June and Leif the news tonight," he whispers when the coast is clear, his voice at once anxious and excited. "Sometime soon…once the vibes perk up."

"Wow, that's amazing. And I'm sorry for the weird vibes."

My eyes dart in my parents' direction. They'd blown through the Marin house like a second storm, upending what was surely meant to be a happy moment for Palmer and Mojo.

"Oh, it's *more* than okay," Mojo insists, breaking into a sheepish grin. "Can't bring me down off this baby high. Once everyone mellows out a bit, some good news will be just what the doctor ordered."

He glances at Palmer giggling intimately with Leif while they set the table. "We can't change the past or fix what's happened, but maybe this baby will help bring everyone together."

"How?"

"With hope, Dell." Mojo smiles, ever the optimist, exuding that goofball brand of positivity that makes him so exasperatingly endearing.

I nod in return. Hope is something we can all use more of, but I'm still not holding my breath. "Good luck tonight."

"Thanks. *Buena suerte* to you too." He wiggles his eyebrows. "Don't stay out too late, all right? Save a li'l something-something for date two."

I cringe. "When did you become such a dad?"

"Dad?" Mojo repeats the word, a dreamy glaze in his eyes. "Whoa. That's actually got a pretty nice ring to it."

Standing alone on June's dark curb, waiting for Hatch's headlights to cut down the foggy road, I jump when a shadow-cloaked figure steps out from behind a large oak tree.

As the tall silhouette approaches, I stumble backward, my feet confused and molasses slow. I almost let out a scream, but then I recognize the young man's lanky build, his short, fuzzy haircut, and sleepy gaze.

"Hey, Dell," Prescott says in a timid voice very much unlike his own. He closes the gap between us, looking somber and frazzled. Violet circles have puddled beneath his gray-blue eyes, and his rumpled t-shirt reeks of stale sweat.

"Prescott!" I put a hand to my thrashing heart. "You scared the crap out of me! What are you doing here?"

"Sorry to scare you," he whispers. "Can you talk for a minute, please? It's important."

Grappling with all this family drama has left me with little brain space to dwell on much else, but some small part of me feels guilty for not checking in on Prescott sooner. The last I'd seen of him was through Hatch's rear-view mirror, fading into a cloud of dust and darkness outside the sea trumpet fields. I'd never even bothered to wonder whether he'd made it home safely that night.

"Sure. What's up?"

He takes a step closer, wringing his shaking hands and scanning the quiet neighborhood around us. "After you left on Sunday…I, uh…I saw something."

The hair on the back of my neck prickles.

"I was getting on my bike," he explains, "about to peel out after you and the others, when I realized I'd dropped my wallet, so I had to double back."

"Back to the fields?"

Prescott nods grimly. "I saw *them*," he breathes. "A whole group of them out there, circling the fire in the distance. They were…chanting something."

"W-what? What were they saying?"

"I didn't stick around long enough to find out. I just ran like hell as soon as I saw them. But now…I think I'm in trouble." Dark desperation crawls across his face. "Someone knows I was out there. They must've seen me, or maybe found my wallet, I don't know. But someone tried to break into our house last night, right in the middle of the hurricane, while Mom and I were sleeping." He grinds his teeth anxiously. "Someone was trying to get to me."

"Are you sure it wasn't just the wind?"

"Wind doesn't rattle a door handle like that, or bang and scrape across windows." Prescott frowns miserably. "We figured it was some dumb neighborhood kids looking for easy loot, but then this morning I stopped by the cemetery to check the storm damage, and I got this eerie feeling that someone had been inside Mom's office too. Things were out of place, disorderly, like someone had been rifling through her stuff."

"Did you go to the police?"

"Yes, but they couldn't be bothered to look into it," Prescott says. "They said they were too busy dealing with hurricane emergencies to go around chasing phantoms." He runs trembling fingers through his already mussed hair, becoming increasingly agitated with every turn of his story. "They told me to go home and sleep it off, as if I'm some kind of strung-out nutcase. Can you believe that?"

"That's awful."

Prescott reaches for my hands, his fingers clammy against mine. "Come back with me. Help me find some evidence in the fields to prove that I'm not crazy. You saw the fire, and the unchained gate! Brine or not, something weird is happening out there, and whoever's involved doesn't want me knowing about it."

I can't help but feel that I'm partially to blame for this. If not for my interest in the Brine—and Prescott's irritating need to impress—we wouldn't have been anywhere near the sea trumpet fields that night. And he wouldn't be coming apart at the seams now.

"Whoever's after me isn't going to stop at break-ins and stupid scare tactics. I could wind up dead. Or worse, they could hurt my mom. But"—he squeezes my hands—"if you corroborate my story and help me get to the bottom of this, the cops won't have a choice but to listen. They can't tune us both out."

Despite how badly I feel for him, something about Prescott's urgency to return to the fields doesn't sit right.

Gently, I slide my hands from his. "I'm sorry the police aren't taking this more seriously." I try to deliver my words as diplomatically as possible. "But I don't think going back there is the answer. You could be walking into a trap for all you know."

"There's safety in numbers," he insists. "That's why I need *you*. You're the only person that believes me."

"I know," I say. "But things imploded with my family today, and I'm leaving town first thing in the morning. There's just not much that I can do at this point."

"Well, what am I supposed to do?" he snaps, his tone growing more forceful. "I can't go back there alone. Who knows what they'll do to me? To my mom?"

Bright headlights abruptly swoop onto the street. Prescott's words falter as the Ranger pulls to a stop before us. His wide-eyed gaze and shocked expression tell me he was unprepared for company.

I step away from him, moving toward Hatch and the truck, but Prescott's fingers find their way around my wrist. He flares his nostrils, the vein in his temple throbbing.

"Dell, *please*, I really need your help."

"Let go of me." I clench my teeth, tearing my arm away. He hadn't hurt me, or even grabbed me particularly hard, but still. The sheer physicality of it feels unnerving. Wrong.

Hatch jumps down from the driver's side and is at my side in a blazing instant. I can sense the quiet vigilance ticking under his skin, his posture stiffer than usual, muscles taut and at the ready. Every inch of him screams danger as he confronts Prescott with a deadly calm voice.

"If you value your hands, I suggest you keep them off her."

Prescott scoffs. "Is that some kind of threat?"

"Let's call it a promise." Hatch's jaw pulses. "If you put your hands on her again, I'll rip them clean off. Cross my fucking heart."

"Hatch—" My voice is caught somewhere between a gasp and a whisper.

Prescott doesn't respond to Hatch, but wildness flashes in his eyes, like something you'd expect from a cornered alley cat.

Hatch glowers at him, shifting his weight to land solidly between us—my buffer and shield. "Ready to go?" he asks me.

Something about this moment—this standoff between the men, the tension thick, Hatch's eyes so penetrating and grave—forces a series of haunting realizations to push forth from my mind.

How did Prescott know I was here?

I'd never told him where June lived, and we're nowhere near Cliffmoor House. This meeting hadn't occurred by accident, nor by some cosmic twist of fate. Prescott had tracked me down.

If he had a good reason for it, if he had nothing to hide and truly needed my help, then why loiter outside of my aunt's house in the dark instead of ringing the doorbell like a normal person?

And if his intentions are pure, his words true, then why not invite Hatch along with us to the fields? He'd been there that night, he'd seen the smoke too. Wouldn't more witnesses lend credence to Prescott's story? Hadn't he just talked about 'safety in numbers'?

His words don't add up.

And what if this isn't about validating his story to the police? What if it's not about protecting his mother? What if Prescott's desperation hinges on getting *me* back to those fields? On getting me out there *alone*...

"Sorry," I say, clinging firm to my suspicions. None of this will matter once I board that ferry tomorrow, leaving Halcyon Bay and all its mysteries to fade like memories behind me. "I'm not going back there, Prescott. And you'd be smart not to either."

I leave him looking dumbstruck and defeated on the curb as I turn around and climb up into the Ranger. Hatch shoots him one last menacing scowl before sliding into the driver's seat and slamming the door shut. The engine quivers to life.

"Are you okay?" Hatch asks when our eyes connect in the dark.

"Drive," is the only response I can muster.

CHAPTER THIRTY-NINE

The lighthouse looms over a sea of fog, swaddling the beach in a dreamy haze that separates the two of us walking along the lapping shoreline from what feels like a world falling into disrepair.

Hatch laces his fingers in mine, leading me up the dunes and onto a path delineated by a rickety fence. It snakes all the way to the mouth of the lighthouse, to a dilapidated metal door covered in grime and graffiti. Passing me his overstuffed backpack, Hatch begins to fiddle with the lock, using what looks like a bent wire hanger to jimmy the mechanism open.

Neither of us had attempted to broach the subject of Prescott again, not wanting to taint the evening—our first and last date—with matters so sour and strange. I force all thoughts of Prescott's panicked face and cold fingers curling around my wrist like a shackle from my mind, wanting to focus solely on this moment—on these precious few hours alone with Hatch.

I tilt my neck to get a better view of the spiraling tower that stretches endlessly to a sky glinting with stars.

"Are you sure no one's up there?"

The lock snaps and Hatch presses his shoulder to the door. With one good push, it grates ajar, welcoming us inside with little complaint. I take a tentative step into a space darker than the night, saturated in the scents of salt and must.

"Idyll Point has been non-operational for years." Hatch slings the backpack over his shoulder again. "They built a newer lighthouse six miles out, the Halcyon Reef Light. See it there?"

He gestures toward the ocean to a distant point where a white light flashes in regular intervals. "There's been talk of turning Idyll Point and the former keeper's quarters into a museum. Till then, it's just another piece of defunct island history."

"Is it safe?"

Hatch shoots me a mischievous smile. "So far."

He takes my hand and we begin to climb the exposed spiral staircase, weaving tightly up and through the overwhelming darkness. I stall a moment when we reach a cracked window at a landing, peering through to get a sense of how high up we are. From the far off, blurry glow of the city, I'd say about four stories.

Another steady beam rolls in from the Halcyon Reef Light, like a swift, bright kiss in the dark. When it's gone again, Hatch whispers, "Just a few more steps."

We reach the top of the lighthouse and step onto a cozy half-moon platform surrounded in salt-speckled glass. A panoramic view of Halcyon Bay stretches out below us, the inky city flickering with glowing amber light. Encircling the island is a world painted black, with nothing to differentiate sea from sky besides the big yellow moon and a drizzling of stars.

It's undeniably romantic, once you get used to the smell.

Hatch unzips his backpack of goodies. He spreads an oversized sheet across the floor, strikes a match to light a small bronze lantern, and begins to unpack a picnic for two.

"Since I know you're a burger-and-fries kinda gal..." He pulls two delicious-smelling, foil-wrapped sandwiches from a paper bag, followed by two greasy cartons of fries. "I picked these up from my favorite food truck. I was surprised that they were open so soon after the storm, but"—he shrugs, eyes twinkling brighter than that distant starlight—"I guess tonight's my lucky night."

He tunes a handheld radio to a local station and pours out two generous glasses of red wine.

"You came awfully prepared," I note. He raises an eyebrow. "Do you go through this much trouble for all your dates?"

"All my dates?" he repeats slowly, tossing me a look of confusion tempered with humor. Clearly, he wants me to spell it out for him.

"You can't expect me to believe that I'm the first girl you've brought up here." The intimate space, the winking of city lights, the pre-chilled wine, the moody music…it's all too perfectly plotted for me to be the first.

Hatch hands me a glass. "What exactly do you take me for, Dell?" He doesn't bother hiding his amusement. "Do you think I whisk hordes of women up here at random, like some Casanova douchebag?"

My eyes widen. "I never said that."

He laughs. "Did you think it?"

I take a small sip of wine, fighting back a playful smile. "C'mon, seriously. How many girls?"

"*Ouch*. That hurts." He whistles his disappointment, though I can tell by the glint in his eye that he's not offended. "To tell you the truth, this place has always been a bit of a girl-free zone. I used to come here as a kid before they shut it down. My dad was old friends with the light keeper, MacGleeson. He'd invite us over every New Year's Eve and Fourth of July to see the fireworks. We'd climb up and camp out here for hours, watching the sky light up."

Hatch hesitates, his happy recollections dimming to something solemn and quiet. "Even after MacGleeson retired—after the lighthouse went dark—we'd still come back sometimes, Dad and me. He called it his thinking spot. It's a good place for that sort of thing."

His voice catches, but he's quick to clear his throat. "Not long after Dad died, the place was locked up, deemed a public safety hazard.

But I got pretty good at breaking in."

He turns the deadbolt on a narrow side door and tugs it open. Fretful winds whoosh hurriedly into the space, whipping my hair, the lantern shooting feverish shadows across the walls. He steps out onto the exposed upper deck, leaning against the old iron railing with ease, face pressed to the blustery atmosphere, like it's something he's done a million times before. Like his presence here is as natural as the wind or the sea or the stars.

I approach the opening with trepidation, clinging to the sturdy safety of the walls, peering over the edge from a cautious distance. I take another sip of wine for courage.

"I still come back sometimes, late at night." He looks out at the sleeping city below, the crashing waves echoing their haunting refrain into the night. "Dad was right. It's a great thinking spot for whenever the island gets too loud or life gets too messy."

This place means a lot to him, I realize. A bright spot from his childhood that had eroded over time. And even though the man he once shared it with is gone—and the building irreparably neglected—Hatch comes back to preserve it somehow. To give it new purpose. To keep it alive.

"No girls allowed, huh?" I hold his gaze. "So why bring me?"

"I wanted you to see someplace special," Hatch says. "Someplace you'd remember. Someplace good." The ghost of a smile flickers across his lips. "I don't think you've had much good to hold onto lately, not since you've been here. I was hoping to change that, tip the scales a bit."

His sweet sentiments knock down every last one of my walls. *Closer,* I think. *I want him so much closer.*

"Thank you," I whisper, too intimidated to move.

He lifts his wine glass, moonlight dancing over his face. "To you, Dell, and every good thing you deserve. May you find as many reasons to smile as there are stars in this sky."

Those words crack something wide open inside of me.

Without thinking, I release my hold on the wall, stepping into the wind. It feels for a moment like I'm airborne, swept up in a flurry of salty air, utterly weightless and free.

My free hand finds his arm, our faces inches apart. "To the good, Hatch," I say, clinking my glass against his.

We stare at each other for a long moment as we sip, one heartbeat shared between us—nothing more than a flutter, nothing short of an earthquake.

When I lower my glass, a trickle of wine lingers on the edge of my mouth. His thumb delicately soaks it up.

"You're really leaving tomorrow?" he asks, his voice husky with restraint.

The atmosphere between us tingles, humming with sensual energy. I don't dare make a single move, uttering a simple and deafening, "Yes."

Hatch turns his face to the slumbering city again. All I can see is the angular cutout of his features against darkness, the silence and space between us agonizing. The muscle in his jaw throbs unevenly, like he's keeping a world of words inside. Bottled up emotions beat at his throat—emotions that would be useless to express the night before we separate.

I lower my eyes to my glass of wine, my thoughts slipping out in a whispered pool. "I really wish I wasn't."

All I'd wanted since arriving on this island was to leave it, but now, leaving feels like the hardest thing I'll ever have to do. Now that this tentative, burning thing between us is crumbling, coming to an apocalyptic end before it's begun.

Hatch tucks a finger under my chin, pulling my face up to meet his, bathed in a streaky blur of distant city lights. I swallow, breathless—a glowing ember in the shadows, set alight by his oxygen.

His emerald eyes rake over my body like hot coals sizzling across bare skin. "What do you wish for?"

Indecision and promise thicken the space between us.

"You first," I whisper.

He raises an eyebrow. "I wish…you'd quit being so evasive."

I shoot him a scowl, and the corner of his lip inches up.

"Fine." He shakes his head and takes my face in both his hands—

his rugged sailor's hands. His thumbs stroke down my cheeks, so gently I could cry. "I wish you knew how much it's meant to me to get to know you."

"That's kind of a tongue twister."

"If twisting tongues is what you want, love, then I'm more than happy to oblige."

The offer is so enticing, I can't be bothered to roll my eyes. I can't ignore the unadulterated pleasure I derive from his words, the quiet blaze he'd set in motion with his touch.

"I wish," Hatch continues, his smile growing like he knows the intoxicating effect he has on me, "that you could stay a while longer so I could show you what you mean to me, rather than tell you. I wish I had more time to bask in your company. And I wish—I *hope*—that you choose to come back someday. That this isn't where our story ends. That it's only the beginning."

I take a shallow breath, dizzy with longing. Aching, craving, *burning* for him.

"Now you," he says in a low command.

Summoning every nerve and scrap of bravery from my head down to my toes, I say in all sincerity, "I wish…that I could stop thinking about you long enough to catch my breath. That I hadn't been so quick to judge you. That I'd been more open from the start."

Hatch waits, but I see the effort it takes him to keep still, to keep his breathing steady. He knows that I'm not finished, that I've only scratched the surface of what I feel in my heart and soul, but it's no secret anymore that he yearns for me, dreams of me, wants me too.

"I wish that I were better at fighting it," I say, looking up at him through my lashes, "this thing between us…you…but I can't. You consume me with every passing glance you throw my way."

A slow, dreamy smile breaks across his face, a smile that feels like sultry nights, safe arms, and coming home.

"And, for the record? I wish this wasn't the end either," I whisper in a small appeal to the heavens. For the intercession of the stars, the moon, and all things divine.

"Dell…" Hatch says my name like it's a sacred word, like his universe revolves around the very sound and shape of it.

His lips touch mine, achingly gentle, like the cool caress of water on a sun-drenched shore, and I melt against his body, the thread of desire unspooling within me. All there is in all the world is *him*. His fingertips grazing the skin under my blouse, his wavy hair slipping through my hands like silk, his muscles tensing and softening under my touch, his torso crushed against mine, pressing me to the damp lighthouse wall. It's too much and not enough all at once. I feel we might erupt into flame where we stand.

We pull away long enough to catch our breaths, and I'm filled with clashing feelings of thrill and dread. Being with Hatch for this fleeting, brilliant speck of a moment inevitably means missing him later. Long after I've gone home, on a night as dark as this one, with a sky as brimming with stars, I'll find myself alone and heartbroken, pining for this memory, when all I'll have left are my own imperfect recollections.

I'll never find anyone quite like him again—never fall for someone this deep, this quickly—and for that alone, I almost draw back in fear.

But then Hatch's mouth is on my lips, my neck, my collarbone, leaving a trail of wildfire in his wake. His hands are on either side of my shoulders, caging me to the lighthouse, and I come alive under his touch, under that silver-pale moonlight, and the salty spell wafting in from the beach.

We reach a boiling point and he pulls back slightly, hesitant. His forehead dips to mine, breath hitching, and his lips graze my nose, as if to say he's fine with stopping. That he's okay with slowing down, cooling off, if that's what I need. But I'm not ready to be done.

Hatcher Seaborn is exactly the kind of good I need tonight.

My fingers feel their way to the belt loops in his jeans. *Closer, closer,* I think hungrily.

With a shudder, he gives in to me, just like I knew he would.

CHAPTER FORTY

Perched on the lighthouse deck, back to the wall and knees up by my chin, I watch as the dewy morning slow-crawls over the island. Something on the beach below catches my eye—a rippling of silver cutting sharply through the surf.

The lingering shroud of night is still too dense to see it clearly, but it moves steadily back and forth, up and down the length of the shore. The thing seems to have tentacles, or maybe seagrass trailing its body. It undulates, pale and strange, in the short waves. I swallow hard when I realize what it looks like from afar.

A mass of human hair.

Within seconds, I'm on my feet and making for the stairs, but I pause for a long moment to look back at Hatch—his sleeping face so sweet and undisturbed, his chest rising and falling.

I fight a stubborn tug in my heart to go to him, to lie close beside him and prolong this fantasy of ours a bit longer. It had been a remarkable evening in so many ways, one that would trail me for countless years. We'd spent it here, in the ruinous lighthouse, wrapped in Hatch's sheet beneath a milky puddle of moonlight. He'd listened to me brood over the Klynes, my mother, Willow, and Bram. He'd dragged me to my feet for a dance when a soulful tune shot through the radio. He'd twirled me round and round in the lantern's orange glow, pressing kisses to my knuckles. He'd worshiped me, made himself unforgettable. Legendary.

But with the sunrise comes a harsh reality, and I force myself to leave in silence, without waking him to say goodbye. I convince myself it will be better this way. I've never been any good at goodbyes.

I steal down the steps, latching the main door behind me. Light trickles in through the low-lying clouds, guiding my trek to the beach, and soon I'm standing on that same stretch of shoreline I watched from above, eyes peeled on that glittering of silver in the waves.

Why do I keep seeing this thing? What the hell is it? Some weird algae bloom or luminescent jellyfish, skimming the water's surface like a deflated balloon? Why does it call to some buried part of me, at my most basic, atomic level?

Before I can stop myself, I'm kicking off my sandals and unzipping my pants. I leave them in a messy heap and bound headlong into the sea, determined to find out once and for all.

The bay is cool, not yet warmed by the fiery morning sun, as I cut across the waves and into shoulder-deep water, the spray of salt tickling my cheeks. Every hair on my body stands on end as I watch the luminous silver creature drifting some thirty feet away. I take another step toward it, and the water laps against my chin. Any closer than this and I won't be able to touch the bottom.

I take a breath and push off from the sand, swimming into vast, open water. Soon, I'm twenty feet away from it…fifteen…ten. I'm so, so close, and feeling prematurely triumphant, when, without so much as a splash, the creature stops moving. It goes eerily still—unnaturally, deadly still.

I do my best to freeze in place too, treading ever so lightly. We remain locked in this bizarre stalemate for a long stretch of time, while the sun climbs higher in the sky. Did it stop moving because it sensed my approach? Is this some weird territorial response? Maybe it's playing dead, trying to lull me into a false sense of security, all the while calculating how big a threat I am or how easy I'd be to attack.

Regardless of the reason for the creature's odd behavior, I'm obviously dealing with an intelligent being. Its mesmerizing façade could just be a lure to draw in unsuspecting prey. And along I came like a tasty morning snack.

Hoping to avoid a gruesome gutting, I quickly reverse track, deciding it best to slowly back out of the creature's line of sight. I draw in a short breath and gently kick away. But the instant I move, the creature melts into the blue, vanishing beneath the ocean's surface.

The atmosphere on the beach begins to shift.

The cool, salty breeze falls away in an instant, the water going glassy and smooth as a sheet of ice. A pod of pelicans that had drifted by in a lazy V-formation has disappeared, leaving behind a shore that seems like a barren desert, devoid of any signs of life. The clouds don't glide across the sky anymore, but hang down from it like petrified ornaments from a tree. I can't hear a thing but my own ragged breathing and the erratic hammering of my heart inside my own eardrums.

The world as I know it shudders around me. Everything goes still—terribly still—as something unnatural unwinds in the air.

It's a song, I think, a breathy chorus of distant voices, only I can't so much hear it as I can *feel* it. A mystifying string of whispered wails and gospel-weeping, soaring like a funeral hymn across the ocean and back. The song is ancient and miserable, seeping into me like a fast-spreading poison. Precisely as awful as Captain Patton described it.

I scan my surroundings, floundering like shark bait. If I scream, will Hatch hear me from the top of the lighthouse? Will it be enough to wake him, to feel this terrible stillness too, or is it all happening somewhere inside my head? Have the stories and secrets embedded on this island finally worn down my sanity for good?

The ocean flexes around my body and a current knocks me over, feet over head. I'm dragged underwater, breathless and flailing as I try to regain my balance, kicking up to the surface for air. But it's no use. The tide is too mighty, and rapidly pulling me out, out, out.

I'm so disoriented that I can't tell up from down, powerless but to let myself be carried away, losing oxygen and all control of my senses. A murky film of blue-green obscures my vision as I tumble through the water. My eyes sting but I keep them open anyway, searching for whatever awaits me there in the darkness.

They land on a slender, silver body. *The creature,* I realize. It watches me curiously.

I blink once, twice, desperate to capture its features in my memory. Those cavernous eyes carved deep into a colorless face. Long, gossamer hair forming a silver halo around its head. That translucent skin gleaming like fine porcelain.

Skin or scales? It's impossible to tell.

It's the most human-looking sea creature I've ever laid eyes on, but decidedly *inhuman* at the same time. More spirit than substance, wondrous and brutal, much like the ocean itself.

We're face to face now, and I burst out in a scream, tiny bubbles streaming from my mouth as more water—ceaseless water—rushes into my lungs. My heartbeat slows to a faint thrum as the creature leans in close. I wince, expecting its jaws to snap my neck. But instead, I feel the searing burn of ice when it presses its mouth to the edge of mine, giving me a bitter kiss.

The piercing, shocking pain of it makes my vision cloud over. Gushing saltwater overwhelms me. My eyelids flutter, the light inside of me fading. Everything goes bone-chillingly cold.

The creature's face is the last thing I see before my eyes clasp shut for good.

CHAPTER FORTY-ONE

Unfamiliar memories flash in the darkness. They play out like a muddled film reel, strange scenes materializing as if from nowhere. I see them, relive them, though the memories aren't mine. It's like I've landed in the mind of another, returned to some distant place and time, on a black, black night, to a house I faintly recognize, perched on a quiet, lonesome beach…

I sneak across the wooden footbridge at midnight, leaving the summer solstice party behind, as well as those awful, diamond-encrusted sandals Mom bullied me into wearing tonight.

Daddy just made his toast, meaning that everyone's probably tossing back flute after flute of champagne, laughing fake laughs, spilling their drinks, and generally acting like overdressed buffoons. There's the distant splashing of someone winding up in the pool, then a torrent of splashing as others join in. Poor Briggs really has his work cut out for him with that crowd.

The walkway from the house curves over a long stretch of grass and sea oats, landing on the quiet side of Sandspur Beach. It's kind of stupid that a place called Cliffmoor House isn't actually surrounded by cliffs, but my parents like the name anyway. They say it's 'historically significant,' but I think it just makes them feel important.

As I approach the beach, my body thrums with excitement, like a well-tuned instrument ready to be played. The sky is filled with stars, cradling the moon like a baby, and it casts a bright spotlight over the water—a beacon calling my name.

Night swimming is my favorite.

Laurel has begged me a gazillion times not to do it. Big surprise there, she's a hopeless worry-wart. And now that she's a mother, the worrying has only gotten worse, like some catastrophic disease of the mind. Thank God Meridel occupies so much of Laurel's attention these days. I'm perfectly capable of taking care of myself.

I've almost hit the sand when a rustling noise startles me. I squint back into the shadows, Cliffmoor's lights twinkling in the distance, worried that it's my mother coming to scold me for not sucking up to her face-lifted, medicated group of girlfriends. Maybe it's someone else, like my ball-of-nerves sister coming to shoo me from the beach, or that loser Herby Wyatt from two blocks down, who I caught rifling through my underwear drawer at last year's Christmas Eve party. I gave Herb the Perv a black eye that night, and the creep's looked at me sideways ever since.

When the culprit for the rustling—an icky-looking iguana—finally emerges from a cluster of palm leaves, I giggle stupidly. Everyone at the party is way too preoccupied with being seen at the 'most glamorous social event of the season' to follow me to the beach. I actually read that headline in the paper this morning, and my eyes rolled back so far in my skull, I thought they might get stuck that way permanently. Mom would absolutely love that.

Once at the beach, I strip off my sundress and dump it near the shoreline, not caring that the salt might ruin the fabric. I wore a bathing suit underneath, like I do on most days. I'm always prepared for an impromptu swim.

Dipping quickly into the shallow water, I run through my normal routine, swimming several laps in freestyle before moving onto butterfly, backstroke, and breaststroke, completing every move in perfect sequence, pushing my limits, bettering my times. There's nowhere I feel more at home than the water. It's my constant, the one place I can totally be myself. I mentioned this to June once, and she teased that I must've been a fish in another life. June likes to joke around a lot, but I'll be laughing last when I'm an Olympic gold medalist someday.

After twenty minutes or so of concentrated practice, I surface to find the silhouette of a man standing alone on the beach. I can't see his face, but I can only assume that the dope had wandered away from the party, looking for some dark, secluded place to take a pee. I've come to realize most guys are gross like that, especially the ones my age.

I wave at the man, wondering who he might be. I know mostly everyone at the party. He lifts an arm and waves back slowly, and next thing I know, he's venturing out to meet me in the water. I'm a little confused, but I don't freak out. Nothing bad ever happens in Old Town. It's basically Snoozeville, U.S.A.

Maybe it's Abraham, this local bum who shows up at my swim meets now and then. Despite the scotch smell that comes off him like cologne, Abraham doesn't bother me any. Sure, he's a little weird and maybe not all-there in the head, but I think he's sweet and misunderstood. He asks about my grades and my swimming like he actually cares, and he's never once given me weird, rapey vibes.

June told me that Abraham used to be friends with Laurel, but that they'd drifted apart after high school. Whatever happened to him then must've been crappy as hell, because the poor guy's a straight-up hobo now. He lives out of his boat and doesn't shave, and I've never seen him wear anything that isn't stained, frayed, or holey. I think my parents jumped the gun with that dumb restraining order, but what do I know, right? I'm only thirteen. And everyone loves to remind me of it.

As the man draws nearer, I try to get a clearer look at him, but then, without warning, he pummels right into me. A fist connects hard with the side of my head, and I slam beneath the waves, gurgling, struggling. The blow disorients me, but it doesn't knock me out. The muscle I've gained in training helps as I kick, punch, and scream—anything and everything to keep him from pinning my head underwater.

I can hold my breath for up to two minutes and forty-eight seconds on a good day. But today is not a good day.

I scramble toward the shoreline, exhausted and sluggish after taking such a hard hit to the head. A warm substance seeps from my skull, and when I put my hand to it, I realize it's blood. Lots of blood.

The silhouette of a second man is on the beach now, and when I scream for him to help me, the man doesn't even move. He simply watches on as my attacker continues his chase, a silent spectator to this sick cat-and-mouse game.

I feel his hot, rasping breath on my neck when he catches up. He swings a heavy object in the air, striking my head with a piercing crack. The pain is sharp and instant, and I cripple beneath it, falling to my knees, sputtering water and blood. The man strikes me several more times before everything goes numb, my body lying still in less than two feet of water. I'd gotten so close to land.

My attacker wipes the blood from his weapon and tosses the object onto the beach at the silent man's feet. He thrusts his hands under my armpits, wading us into deeper water, dumping me out there like old garbage before slinking back to shore.

Beneath the cold spotlight of the moon, I slip quietly underwater. Eventually, gratefully, all the world goes dead.

"Stay with me, Dell," cries a desperate male voice.

There's a repeating pressure on my chest, strong hands working to resuscitate me.

"C'mon, breathe." He puts his lips to mine, blows hard, and drops an ear to my heart. Then, more chest compressions. "Stay with me…breathe…breathe!"

I gasp, choking on a surge of saltwater rising into my mouth. I cough it out and draw in a sharp breath while the man cradles me in his arms, swiping soggy hair from my cheeks and forehead.

It's Hatch…and he's crying.

We're huddled together in the wet sand, soaked and shivering on the desolate beach at sunrise. He tucks my head into his shoulder, rocking me like a child.

"H-hatch," I manage after a few minutes, my voice a suppressed and gravelly croak.

His green eyes swirl with shifting fear and anger, his hands desperate on my hair and face. I cough again, my throat raw, lungs fighting to recover.

"We need to get you to the hospital," he says urgently.

"No." I shoot up too fast, a crushing headache unwinding in my brain.

"Easy…" He guides me into a seated position, his hand strong against my back.

"D-did you see her?"

"That *thing* out there?" Hatch's eyes jerk back to the ocean, fixed on a distant point. He shakes his head gruffly. "I don't know what that was. Didn't look like any fish I'd ever seen."

"Hatch, listen to me." I inhale as deeply as I can, trembling as I fill my chest with glorious oxygen. "What you saw in the water…it wasn't a fish."

"What was it?"

"I think…" This makes no sense. He'll never believe me. *I* barely believe me. "I think it was my sister."

Worry washes over his face, settling deep into the furrows of his brow. "Let's get you to a doctor. You'll feel much better once—"

"It was *her*," I insist, trying my best to seem lucid. "I know how it sounds, I know it's insane, but she was there. And she showed me what happened on the night she died."

"Dell, you almost just drowned, okay?" The words spill out of him hot and fast. "That thing attacked you out there, nearly killed you. You're not thinking clearly. We need to get you checked out—"

"No, Hatch, listen to me! That thing *was* Willow, I swear it! She kissed me and"—I touch the edge of my lips, still able to feel that bitter, icy-cold brush—"it's like her memories flooded my mind or something. I can't explain how, but I *saw* what happened. I saw everything. *I watched her die.*"

Hatch gently rubs his thumb across my mouth. "Your lips," he whispers, as if noticing for the first time. "They're…blue."

I take his hands in mine. They're fire-warm despite still being wet. "I know how this must sound, but it really did happen. Like I was inside her body, reliving her final moments. Willow didn't drown that night. It wasn't some random freak accident. She was murdered."

And she'd been here ever since, tethered to this hellish place, unable or unwilling to move on to the next.

"I need to find her," I say.

"Whoa, hold on." His hands cup my shoulders, keeping me from bounding to my feet. "There's no way you're going back in that water. Whatever that thing was, it's gone now, all right? I scared it off when I swam out after you."

Hatch is right. The effort alone of trying to swim could kill me—my body already worn down with fatigue, my breathing terribly belabored—but somehow, some way, I need to make sense of this. To untangle the knotted threads of what I'd seen…of that faceless, rippling sea creature.

I need the help of someone who understands the underlying currents of this island, and the spirits that occupy its waterlogged depths.

Someone like Freya, I think. She would know what all this means and what I'm meant to do about it.

I expect we'll meet again, she'd said with premonitory knowledge days ago. *Sometime soon. When you are ready to talk.*

I'm incontrovertibly ready now.

"Do you know Freya Larisse?"

"The psychic?" Hatch is visibly caught off guard, eyes narrowing. "Yes. She's got a little storefront downtown."

"Can you take me to her?"

"What, now?"

"Yes. Right now."

"It's six in the morning, Dell. You need to go to the hospital, you almost drowned—"

"But I didn't drown," I insist, holding his gaze. "And I wouldn't ask if it wasn't important."

Hatch shakes his head, equal parts amazed and baffled by my request. "More important than seeing a doctor?"

"I don't need a doctor, Hatch. What I need is to know what the hell happened out there. Whether you believe me or not, I know *in my bones* that Willow is trying to communicate with me. And Freya Larisse might be the only person who can help."

His piercing eyes dim when he realizes I'm not letting this go.

"Please," I repeat, imploring him to have sympathy. To not look at me like I'm some certifiable madwoman, even if he thinks it. Even if I think it. "Am I going to have to do this alone, or are you coming with me?"

CHAPTER FORTY-TWO

Freya's brick-faced storefront is tucked inconspicuously into an unlit corner street. The sun-faded plaque that sits atop the mail slot in the door reads:

Madame Freya Larisse, Spiritual Consultant
Specializes in psychic readings, channeling, palmistry, & tarot
For private appointments & séances, inquire within!

Hatch immediately shoots me a look that says, *You've got to be kidding me.*

Before I can try the handle, the door swings open, but the person standing on the other side isn't Freya.

"Delly!" comes the familiar boom of Captain Patton's voice.

My mouth falls a bit at the sight of him standing there. He looks like he just rolled out of bed, haphazardly wrapped in a dingy blue robe, barefoot and bare-chested, his silver hair sticking up at odd angles.

"Cap'n?" Hatch asks, confused for the both of us.

"Morning, Seaborn." The captain tips his head, sneaking a teasing glance between us. "Looks like you managed to hook your girl after all!"

Hatch stiffens, glancing at me warily. I jump in. "Um, we're looking for—"

"Freya, of course," he finishes my sentence, nodding with certainty. "Yes, yes, she's been waiting for you. Come in, I'll get you some towels. You look like a pair of soggy sewer rats."

He steps aside and we slip into Freya's itty-bitty lobby, with strips of ornate purple wallpaper peeling from the walls, cheap ambient light flickering overhead, and a mass of glass bottles wrapped in old twine dangling precariously above the entryway.

The captain spots me staring at the cluster of hanging vessels. He chuckles and says, "For trapping unruly spirits."

My eyes quickly adjust to the dark interior of the space. Two rickety chairs are shoved in a corner beside a coffee table, loaded with pamphlets and brochures on various occult topics. *What's in the Cards for You?* one of them asks, while another discusses *Psychic Phenomena for the Average Jane.* The captain hobbles past the seating area to a utility closet, pulling out a pair of towels and tossing one to each of us. I wrap mine snugly around my shoulders, and he proceeds to lead us down an uneven, narrow hallway.

"Is this a conversation for tea or whiskey?" he asks when we reach a rounded alcove. Dusty decanters, jars, and jugs of all shapes and sizes line the wooden shelves in the nook from floor to ceiling.

"It's about my sister," I say, then realize that doesn't answer his question. "The, um…the sea spirits, I guess. The devilfish."

Captain Patton strokes his birds-nest beard. "Well then. In that case, better stick with the whiskey."

Hatch grimaces. "Uh, Cap'n, isn't it a bit early for—"

"Leave your sanctimony at the door, son," the captain snaps as he plucks a curvaceous amber bottle from his soot-covered collection. He pulls the stopper and sniffs the liquor inside, gesturing us toward a rich crimson curtain. "Head on in. I'll be along in a minute."

I take an obedient step forward, but pause before crossing a thick line of red powder spread across the threshold. Warily, I glance back, but the captain nods reassuringly, winking with his aquamarine eye.

"For trapping unruly humans," he says, before turning back to his bartending work.

I slip through the curtain with Hatch close behind, careful not to disturb the rust-colored dust. Freya is seated at the center of a ruby-red room, arms folded over a round table. Her eyes are closed, there's a little twitch in her lips, and her hair is wrapped up in an assortment of silk scarves. She looks to be in some sort of trance.

I gulp down a mouthful of air and wait, taking in the contents of the room from corner to corner, all of it crammed with the strange and macabre. There are jars of a white talcum-like substance, misshapen artifacts, and carved wooden masks. Rows of soft-hued crystals line the shelves along the walls—some of them chalky and bulbous, others polished and sleek—nestled beside heavily weathered books with broken seams, spitting loose pages from their tops. An ornate iron birdcage dangles from the far right, stacked high with glossy blue-black feathers, but oddly, no bird. Perched atop a gilded side table is a rope-wrapped bundle of yellowed bones. I swallow hard, praying they belong to some poor, woebegone animal, but they look an awful lot like human fingers.

"Meridel," Freya greets me after a lengthy moment of silence, her accented voice as hypnotic as I remember it. The edges of her lips curve into a distant, dreamy smile—a smile not of this world. "I've been expecting you, child."

She weaves a twirling pattern on the tablecloth, her bejeweled fingers scintillating in the low light. "Sit, please. Tell me why you've come."

I sink into the velvet seat across from her, with Hatch hovering at my back. The smell of rotting flowers saturates the room, catching in my throat.

"I'm here to talk about...to ask you about...my sister."

Freya doesn't probe as to who this elusive sister might be, and I have to assume that, somehow, she already knows the truth about

Willow. That she knows the truth about most things, no matter how deeply buried or closeted. It would seem that some people, like myself, are doomed to endless questions—always asking, never knowing—while others are doomed to answers. Which of these fates is worse?

"Go on." Her striking face is mild and encouraging.

"Well…" I take a breath, wondering how to put the unthinkable into words. "I experienced something strange in the ocean this morning. A creature of some kind, only it was so much more than that."

"Yes."

"I just learned that I had a sister…that she died, twenty years ago. And, um…it's crazy to consider, but…I feel that it was *her* in the water with me…that she's been there all along, trying to reach me, ever since the first day I came back."

The curtains swish as the captain hobbles inside. "Here you go, Delly, my girl."

He passes me a glass brimming with honey-colored liquor. Flecks of gold float delicately on its surface, a circling of flaxen dust that give the drink a tempting, magical flair.

"What is it?"

"Special brew of mine." Cap'n cracks his ancient, gold-toothed smile. "Drink up. It'll warm you to your core. Help you think straight."

I tilt my head back and let it glide down my throat, coating my insides with the sweet, fiery taste of smoke and wood and nutmeg.

"Good?" he asks.

It is good, like someone is holding a hot torch to my belly. I nod gratefully.

"So you believe you met your sister in the sea, and now you want to know why that is, I'm sure?" Freya asks, acting like this situation is totally normal.

I have no idea how things work in the world of psychics, telepaths, and spiritualists, but in the lowly, mundane realm of the ungifted, things like this don't just happen.

"Yes, I want to know why…and how. *How* is this not completely impossible?"

What could Freya possibly tell me to make this all real? To make what happened even marginally plausible? *Stuff like this doesn't exist.*

Freya laughs heartily. "Why should it be impossible?"

"Because Willow is dead," Hatch says abruptly. I narrow my eyes at him, bristling against the coldness of his statement. "She's dead, Dell," he repeats, his voice softer, gentler. "And there's no coming back from that."

Captain Patton scoffs. "That's the problem with you young people today," he grumbles. "With all your technology 'n' your science, there's no room left to just *believe* anymore. You lose so much, whittling the world down to numbers 'n' data."

Freya, however, doesn't seem at all fazed. "Meridel, all things considered, where did you expect Willow to go?"

Where all dead people go, I think, unsure of what she's getting at.

Freya chuckles in response, though I'm certain I didn't speak aloud. "When someone dies so suddenly, especially a youth with so much life ahead of them—such unfulfilled potential—leaving our world can often be problematic."

"But how can I know for certain it was her?" I ask, pleading for some proof of what can never be proven, some evidence that I'd been spirited away on that beach, touched by something truly unimaginable.

Freya turns to Captain Patton, a private language passing between them. "Patty, my sweet. Would you bring me my suitcase, please?"

Hatch and I exchange a meaningful glance at her words.

Patty, my sweet?

The affection between Freya and the old captain is palpable, easy as a tender breeze carried in from the ocean, as if the two have coexisted—maybe even cohabited—for years. The thought of them together is unexpected, but having seen them up-close, having felt the echoes of their strangeness, I can *almost* see how they might work, disparities in age and appearance aside. And I've learned nothing of Halcyon Bay if not to expect, and even embrace, the unexpected.

The captain hobbles over to a wide credenza, dragging a massive leather suitcase from behind it. Hatch helps him lift the worn piece of luggage onto the table, and Freya flips open its heavy bronze latches, tossing the lid open. I watch on quietly, perplexed and steadily growing woozy from my drink.

Inside the case is an assortment of random items—scraps and hunks of junk gently pressed into foam for safekeeping. There's a dry piece of twig, a bobbin of pale yarn, a shard of broken mirror, a chipped marble ball, one lone puzzle piece. It all looks like garbage to me, a collection of objects destined to be dumpster fodder. But, for whatever reason, Freya's taken great care in preserving each and every one.

"What's this?" Hatch asks.

Freya smiles vaguely, her eyes warm on mine. "Meridel, would you please run your hand over each of these items and select the one that speaks to you?"

I catch Hatch's eye. He shrugs.

"Take your time. There is no rush," Freya assures me.

"But how will I know—"

"Choose whichever one you gravitate to the most."

This seems like a silly, frivolous exercise, but I'm compelled to go through with it anyway. I came to Freya for help, after all. To some degree, I have to trust her methods. And I've got nothing to lose.

I lift my hand over the case, fingers hovering a few inches from it. Nothing happens as I pass my hand over an old copper penny, a broken chain, and a pink-hued cockle shell. Each item is the same as the last, producing in me no reaction at all. Next is a rusty pair of pliers, a dry ivy leaf, one tarnished sapphire earring…still nothing. A swatch of dark leather, some shattered reading glasses, a plastic yo-yo, and—

"This one!" I blurt before my mind can register it.

My hand floats over a hunk of pale blue sea glass with a luminous aura around it—a tiny glow I can feel more than see, humming with a secret power that sings to my heart.

Freya carefully lifts the bit of sea glass from its tiny burrow in the foam. "Do you know what these items are, Meridel?" She gestures at the case of arbitrary odds and ends.

"Not a clue."

"They are tokens left to me by the undeparted souls of this island. They belong to the spirits of Halcyon Bay, the ones unable to procure eternal rest."

Undeparted souls. That's exactly what I'd wondered, if Willow had ever truly departed after death.

"How do you find them?" I ask.

"The spirits lead me to them after they pass," Freya says simply, as if that explains everything. "They trust me to protect them, to act as their guardian."

She lifts the sea glass to one glittering bronze eye, inspecting its smooth ridges and curves, turning it over in hand. "Sadly, I am only able to listen to their whispers. I find and shelter their tokens, preserve their stories. But try as I may, I cannot free them."

"Is that what they want, to be free?"

"Usually, yes. But the means for obtaining that freedom vary greatly. Some spirits are vengeful, seeking harsh retribution for some unresolved matter. Others seek justice, a rightful conclusion to a wrongful grievance. A great many souls are simply lost. They believe themselves still alive after death but forgotten by the world, and thus unable to forge a path out of it. Most spirits, however, simply aim to relay a message, often to a person they once loved."

"A message?"

The psychic nods. "A message of great importance. Something they were unable to share before they met their end. Something worth crossing realms for."

During our encounter, the creature had conveyed a specific memory. It had let me know that her death—my sister's death—was far from an accident.

Freya hands me the glowing sea glass fragment. "I've not held that token since the day I procured it. I was led to it twenty years ago, washed up on the shores of our beaches. That's Willow Klyne's token."

I swallow hard as Freya purses her lip in thought. "Your elder sister is a reclusive soul, one I've not seen about the island since her passing. I suspected long ago that she'd made a home of the sea, like so many unlucky Halcyon Bay girls, but there was no way to know that for certain. The spirits have to seek *you* out, you see, and Willow is a quiet one, unwilling to share her secrets with just anyone, including me. The fact that you reacted so strongly to her token tells me that you must've encountered her spirit directly, just as you say you did. And I would agree with your assessment—she's likely been trying to get you in the water for much longer."

"She showed me what happened on the night she died," I say. "I don't know how it happened, exactly. She kissed me, and her memories flashed behind my eyes as if they were my own."

"A devilfish kiss?" This question comes from the captain.

I nod. "I saw her death play out in my mind, scene by scene, like a movie."

"Assuming that's what this is," Hatch asks, "is it dangerous, this kiss? I mean, Dell would've drowned out there if I hadn't gotten to her in time. Is she going to be all right?"

"There're plenty of sailors' myths about what the mermaid's kiss means," the old captain says. "Some say a kiss from a sea girl holds the power to heal you of any ailment, a kiss so powerful it can save you from imminent death. Others believe that a sea girl's kiss will drive you mad—drive you to suicide. I've also heard that a devilfish kiss can show you the deepest truths you seek. Who can say which one of them is right, in the end? Perhaps they all are, a little bit, in some way."

His words reverberate in my skull like rolling waves crashing against rock.

"What exactly did you see when your sister kissed you, Meridel?" Freya asks.

"I saw a man beat her in the water," I say solemnly. "He approached from the darkness. She couldn't see his face. And there was another man, standing on the sand at a distance, watching…just watching." I shake my head. "Do you know anything about this? Any idea who might've wanted to hurt her?"

Freya shakes hers too, sadness brimming in her iridescent eyes. "My knowledge is limited, child. I can sense traces left behind if the soul is open to my intervention, but Willow is not such a soul. Already, you know so much more than I."

"So what do I do now?"

"Only time will tell what this means. You experienced a miracle, without question, but it is not something to dwell on forever. Life must continue to be lived."

How can I not dwell on this? I wonder. How will my every waking breath, my every thought, not be totally centered on this one inexplicable moment?

Freya smiles. "Your grandmother also found it difficult to separate herself once she was touched by the spirits."

Of course. Freya was Virginia's spiritualist. Maybe she'd been searching for answers about my sister's drowning too. Maybe she'd even had a ghostly experience of her own, something similar to what I was facing now.

"Did Virginia ever tell you whether she encountered Willow's spirit, back when she was alive?" I ask the keen-eyed psychic.

"Virginia first came to me when she was met by another spirit of Cliffmoor House. Your grandmother believed it might have been Willow trying to make contact, but we came to find that it wasn't. I'm afraid there are a great many spirits at Cliffmoor House, child, all of their stories intertwined, all of them tragic. It's just a matter of whom they choose to reveal themselves to."

I think back to the deformed shape of the girl in the shampoo bottle, dwelling in that guest house like it belongs only to her. The shadows flickering through the curtained windows, the lights turned on when I'd left them off, the strong force manipulating the bathtub faucet while I laid there helpless, on the verge of drowning…I'd chalked each of these moments up to brief stints of insanity, the product of an overactive imagination or sheer mental exhaustion. But that isn't the case. I also thought that maybe it was Willow's spirit that haunted those rooms, but it doesn't feel like Willow, doesn't carry the same energy or tug at our sisterly bond.

Without a doubt, *something* inhabits that guest house, an entity that had tried multiple times to make contact, but I elect not to bring this up to Freya. Time is running out for questions, though I still have many more to ask. Mojo and Palmer are supposed to drop me off at June's house—and into the arms of my panicking parents—in less than an hour.

At least I'd managed to confirm one pivotal thing—the creature I'd faced this morning was, in fact, my sister. But I have no idea what I'm supposed to do with this information.

Beyond a shadow of a doubt, her death had been cold and calculated murder, but the police would laugh in my face if I went to them with ghost stories. They wouldn't so much as peek into Willow's case files without concrete evidence of foul play, much less reopen any kind of investigation.

Suddenly, I can empathize with Prescott. Being dismissed by the HBPD had pushed him into a dark corner, desperate for someone to believe him. My tales tower over his in comparison. And I'd been so quick to turn him away too…to leave him alone and frightened on that curb, without anyone else to turn to for help.

Freya places her hands over mine, muting my chaotic thoughts. "It is not your duty to free your sister, Meridel. Sometimes these matters are beyond our control. Take comfort in knowing that she sought you out. She *chose* you. But heed my words: you must move along."

She wraps my fingers snugly around the bit of sea glass, inextricably fusing it and me together as one. "This belongs with you now. I suppose it always has."

Hatch pulls up to Palmer and Mojo's apartment complex with a tight expression on his face. They wait for me at the gate—Palmer with raised eyebrows, furiously tapping an invisible watch on her wrist, with Mojo's hand at her elbow, trying to curtail her obvious fury.

In hindsight, going totally off the grid last night without so much as a courtesy text was not my finest moment. I can only pray that they hadn't told my parents anything. Palmer's wrath I deserve, but Mom's drippy-eyed stare and Dad's endless interrogations I could do without.

I squirm around in Hatch's passenger seat, fully understanding that this is the prime time for me to say something thoughtful, something *thankful,* anything of substance to encapsulate what we'd been through.

"Thank you, Hatch…for everything."

The rest of my words are stifled deep in my throat, crushed by the heel of my own ineptitude and my clumsy handling of critical moments.

No amount of gratitude could ever encompass all that he'd done for me, just like no words could scratch the surface of what I felt for him. But this? This is all I'm capable of? This worthless, pathetic excuse for a thank you?

Hatch stares at me in silence, his gaze penetrating, searching for something that isn't there.

My fingers graze the door handle. I can't think anymore, can't speak, can't take the fixating heat of his eyes. All I want to do is sleep— sleep myself sick, sleep myself to death.

"You left without saying goodbye." His low voice rips through my paper-thin heart.

"What do you mean?"

I know what he means.

"When you took off this morning down the beach," he elucidates sharply, "you left for good, without saying goodbye. Right or wrong?"

I don't need to respond for him to know that he's right. I'd left this morning with no intention of ever seeing him again. Goodbyes were too raw, too real.

"Hatch, I'm sorry. I didn't know how to—"

"Right." He raises a hand to stop me, those emerald eyes sweeping over me one last time. "Good luck, Dell."

"Hatch—"

He turns his head from me, inviting me to leave without words. It's an irrefutable dismissal, one I've merited by my own thoughtless actions.

Shaken, I slide out of the Ranger and shut the door behind me. Without hesitation, Hatch slams on the gas pedal, steel in his expression, and blasts down the street.

I watch him drive away, tears pricking my eyes as numbness claws across my tired bones.

There would be no goodbyes for us, no closure at all.

Just the way I wanted.

CHAPTER FORTY-THREE

Three Months Later

It's been eighty-four days of ruthless night.

Eighty-four days since I've been touched by island sun, smelled island air.

Eighty-four days since my parents whisked me back to safe, secluded, stagnant, suppressed Woodbridge.

Eighty-four days since Hatch turned his eyes from me, thundered away in a plume of black smoke, and washed his hands of my excuses, never to look back.

Eighty-four days since I found my sister, and lost her for a second time…lost myself too.

Eighty-four days of walking in a haze, barely scraping through my own bleak existence, aching from a depth I never knew I possessed.

I know that it takes time, this process of healing wounds. It takes time to scar broken skin, time to repair broken things. But there's another side to time as well, like a coin flipping in air. For me, time only seems to deepen the hurt, causing it to fester into a full-on infection. Pain, like a seed, drops into some gaping crevice within me. It stubbornly takes root there, and then it grows and grows.

My feelings associated with my week on Halcyon Bay, and my abrupt departure from it, are difficult to reconcile. It's still a place of darkness, secrets, and unspoken dangers, but to my own bewilderment, it's also a place that holds people I care deeply about, and a handful of memories I can't help but cling to, carving space in my mind like a beloved scrapbook.

Hatch's voice is the hardest to quiet, his entrancing eyes impossible to forget. My thoughts and dreams linger with him steadily through the weeks, while I try and fail to sink back into normalcy. But I miss the warmth of him, and that salty, Coppertone, sunshine-heavy scent. I miss how he'd catch me in his arms whenever I stumbled, the roughness and softness of his hands on my skin. I miss the way my heart felt lighter, more alive, in his presence.

I see his face everywhere and nowhere—brief glimpses across a dingy grocery store aisle, through the frost-slicked windows of a coffee shop, in the smudged mirrors that line the elevators of my office building. But every time I turn around, elated that he's there, breath suspended in my throat, it's never really him.

The others won't leave me alone either: June, Leif, Bear, Mojo, Bram, and Briggs. They had only ever shown me kindness, even when I didn't always deserve it. Though my relationship with Palmer is a bit more complicated—cousins but not friends exactly, yet still somehow more?—we'd forged a surprising bond practically out of thin air. Every text we exchange makes me sick for a home that isn't mine. I miss her…I miss them all.

It's easier to pretend that these things don't bother me, that I'm not struggling with being back after leaving so much unresolved. Life in Maine is changing too, and I'm trying desperately to adjust.

Mom has moved out of Hopewell and back into the cabin. She's still going to therapy three times a week, still medicating, but the rosy flush is slowly returning to her cheeks. Her appetite has greatly improved, as has her general mental condition, and without the invisible weight of shame bearing down on her, the night terrors have all but disappeared. Willow—*Lo*—isn't a secret she has to keep anymore, and with that comes a sort of freedom. An unburdening.

I can't relate. Willow occupies my thoughts almost constantly, as does the knowledge that I abandoned her by leaving. That I gave up, like so many before me, and I don't feel good about it. This, too, I keep under wraps, deciding it best to carry the emotional load in silence, for fear of derailing Mom's progress. The littlest setback in her recovery would feel like defeat, and I'd shouldered more than enough losses lately.

I don't share with Mom the truth of my encounter with Willow that fateful morning. I don't divulge the dark memory that my sister had shared with me. I don't tell her about Freya's confusing words, or show her the bit of sea glass I wear on a chain around my neck, tucked into my shirt by my heart. Why speak on matters I don't understand? Why risk dragging her down with me?

I rent myself a studio apartment. Now more than ever, I need my own space to make sense of things and process all that had been upended. Space to accept this permanently altered version of myself, a version I'm still getting used to. Space to grieve and space to forgive, to stitch every fraying thread back together. But despite my best efforts, I wear the marks of Halcyon Bay like sleeves of fresh ink, an intricate web of tattoos etched far beneath the skin.

Without Mom to worry over or some semblance of purpose, everything begins slipping from my fingers. Work is miserable, as is scrounging for rent money. My handful of old acquaintances—I wouldn't venture to call them friends—are all but absent, turned off by my constant flaking and ever-present air of melancholy. My dating life is nonexistent, quite literally laughable. Painful as it is to be alone, the thought of being with someone else, someone that isn't *him*, is far worse.

I bury myself in a solitary hole and pretend I'm fine with it.

CHAPTER FORTY-FOUR

I swing by my parents' house to collect a few moving boxes and some mail that's been piling up. Dad meets me in the driveway and helps me load my trunk with crap, trying to make vague small talk. Considering how close we've always been, the situation is…uncomfortable.

I haven't spent too much time with my parents since our return to Woodbridge, but whenever I do visit, our meetings are strained and short. I haven't grown to trust them fully again, and our family dinners often drive us into difficult terrain, so I choose to opt out pretty often these days. Not because I'm angry. I just need a break.

Dad hands me my stack of mail, including a thick, pearlescent envelope peeking out from under a pile of bills. It's a formal invitation, the name and address penned in lovely, swirling calligraphy.

We both know what it is before I even break the seal.

Palmer and Mojo are getting married next month, in the Cliffmoor House gardens no less, and I'd already been threatened upon pain of death that *my ass had better be in attendance.* Those were Palmer's words, verbatim.

Dad tries to press me as to whether I'm going, but I shrug him off, ignoring the worry setting up camp in his eyes. I haven't made up my mind either way, and I'm confident about where my parents stand on the matter. There's no need to rehash the same tense discussion, no need to tell them I've been considering going back since the day—the hour—I left.

Back in the utter isolation of my apartment, I check the webpage for *The Halcyon Bay Beacon*.

I've made a habit of keeping tabs on the island, scanning news articles for impending disasters or names I might recognize. Thankfully, in the months I've been gone, the island has been nothing but tranquil and calm, free from strange weather and stranger occurrences. But tonight, a tragic headline rocks me to my core.

Year of Terror: Second Local Girl Commits Suicide by Drowning

Her name's Viola Green and she was only sixteen, on the cusp of her junior year of high school. Employed by a local sailing company, Viola wound up in the water during a routine excursion. Attempts to rescue her were futile. The Coast Guard later found weights in her clothes meant to keep her submerged and seal her fate.

There are no records to show that Viola had any history of depression or self-harming behavior, no explanation for why she might've wanted to end her life.

The article doesn't report on any possible links to the Brine, but I take this with a mighty grain of salt. After all I'd learned about my sister's alleged drowning, I know better than to take anything at face value anymore.

Callie and Viola had drowned within months of each other, a coincidence far too great to ignore. There's something larger at play here, of that I'm certain. But if law enforcement can't string these cases together and won't even bother considering ties to the island's cult history, what hope is there for the citizens—for the girls—who call Halcyon Bay home?

Why the hell would I ever want to return to a place like that?

It's minutes shy of daybreak, and despite the fact that I'd downed an entire bottle of cheap Merlot and called it dinner, I haven't slept a wink all evening. I laid in the dark through the perpetual night, twisting and restless to the point of frustration, as the clock crawled its way toward morning, giving me far too much time to think.

The sun rises, winking through my bedroom window at last, and I resolve to finally make the phone call I've been dreading.

I search for the number to the Halcyon Bay Police Department, and promptly dial in before I can stop myself.

"HBPD, what's your emergency?" asks the woman who picks up on the other end of the line.

"No emergency, ma'am, um…I was hoping you could transfer me to Officer Dash?"

"Marcus Dash?" the woman asks.

"Um…I don't know. His partner is Officer Parris?"

The woman huffs out an irritated, "Hold on," while my heart beats like a bass drum in my chest.

This is a stupid, stupid idea.

After a long moment, a male voice hops on the line. "Hello. Marcus Dash here."

"Officer Dash, hi. I'm Meridel Costa."

"What can I do for you, Ms. Costa?"

"We met earlier this summer. I was one of the passengers on Cyprus Ferry Four the night that Callie Oxton, um…committed suicide." My sentences all sound like they're punctuated with question marks.

"Okay."

"You came to speak to me at Cliffmoor House. I don't know if you remember…"

"Cliffmoor House, Cliffmoor House…" Dash murmurs under his breath. "Ah, yes. Ambrose Klyne's granddaughter. Out-of-towner."

"Yes. That's me."

"How can I help you?"

"I was wondering if there'd been any developments in Callie's case. If you'd determined the circumstances for why she did it."

"The investigation is ongoing," Dash says. "At this time, we're unable to provide any more detail than what's already been stated publicly."

The officer's voice is not unkind, but firm nonetheless. Just because I'd witnessed something on accident didn't mean I was privy to special information.

"Yes, of course. I understand, but…I heard the news about the latest drowning victim, Viola Green, and I wondered if there might be some—"

"You're wondering if the drownings are connected," he finishes my sentence.

"Yes."

"Ms. Costa, the circumstances of the two suicide-drownings are vastly dissimilar. As such, we're currently treating them as unrelated. Unless valid information arises to establish ties between the two, we have no reason to assume that they're linked."

"Have you considered the Brine at all?" I hold my breath.

Dash exhales a deep sigh. "Not at this time, no. The Brine was disbanded long ago, Ms. Costa."

"What about the tip you received last summer? From Prescott…um…"

"I'm sorry, who?"

"Prescott…um…" *Shit.* I can't remember his last name. Had he never mentioned it before?

"Sorry, I think you're cutting out," Dash says. "Repeat that for me?"

"I…I'm sorry. I don't recall his last name. He works at the cemetery with his mother, Lettie…Lettie and Prescott…something."

How am I supposed to seem remotely credible when I don't even know their name? I take a breath, silently scolding myself. This conversation is swiftly going off the rails.

"I know Prescott reported an incident back in early summer. He'd been in the sea trumpet fields and thought he was being stalked. He had concerns about possible Brine activity—"

"Hold on one second," Dash interjects, not waiting for me to respond before muting our call.

I wait out the next eight and a half minutes by tearing back each of my bloody cuticles and wishing I had another bottle of wine to uncork. Had anything come of Prescott's initial report? Had anyone taken him seriously after all? Did he ever go back to those fields on his own? Were he and his mother doing okay?

"Ms. Costa," Dash rejoins the call.

"Yes. I'm here."

"We have no record of any such report."

"W-what?"

"There's nothing like that on record," Dash repeats. "Perhaps your friend only thought he filed a report. Or maybe the in-house officer he spoke to wasn't convinced that the tip was credible."

Whoever Prescott had spoken to at the HBPD had not only dismissed his story, but they'd deigned it unworthy to even write up. No file had been created. There'd been no follow-up.

"Ms. Costa," Dash says gently. "I know we discussed this previously, but I'd still like to encourage you to take advantage of our PTSD program for witness survivors. It wouldn't cost you anything, and the benefits to your mental health are considerable. Do you still have the card I gave you last summer?"

In Dash's eyes, I'm just a traumatized girl concocting stories, just like the cops had thought of Prescott. It's an easier route to take than actually doing their job.

"Yup, I've still got it," I say quickly, reaching for the business card where I'd tucked it in my wallet ages ago. Dash wouldn't help me. He'd only made me realize that the HBPD was doing absolutely nothing to safeguard the island's youngest and most vulnerable citizens. "Thanks for the tip, officer. Talking to you has been…enlightening."

I toss the card in the trash bin and hang up the phone.

Atop the kitchen countertop rests Palmer's wedding invitation, still unopened, the envelope pristine and glinting—a treacherous gift awaiting its unwrapping. I pick it up and sink to my cold linoleum floor, confronting that impossible question mark hanging over my head like a noose primed for my undoing.

I rip open the envelope, an ugly tear slicing across the elegant lettering, my name fractured in two. I slide the invitation out with trembling hands, the RSVP card falling lightly into my lap.

I dig out a red pen from a junk drawer, contemplatively rolling it between my fingers. Then, slowly, deliberately, I mark the RSVP checkbox that reads *Accepts with Pleasure*.

The island isn't done with me yet.

CHAPTER FORTY-FIVE

Upon disembarking from the plane, I flag a cab to the Halcyon Bay Waterside Inn, and am met by the same sour-faced taxi driver who first unloaded me at Cliffmoor House last summer.

I was ignorant then of all I'd come to discover about my family, and this full-circle moment makes me yearn for the innocence I've lost. But innocence is something you can never get back, yet another piece of me that would be forever embedded on this rock. A lasting imprint—a fossil—of the girl I once was.

The driver eyes me skeptically as I sink into his backseat. This time around, I'm gloriously puke free. I lean back, breathing in the island's salt-pregnant air drifting in and out of the open car windows. It's just the way I remember it, and strangely comforting, like some part of me actually missed this tiny, near imperceptible detail. Can the smell of salt and the sea really leave such a profound impression on a person?

The driver gets me to the inn in record time, and within twenty minutes, I'm checked in, unpacked, and debating what to do next. The day stretches ahead like an unpaved road, rife with potholes, hairpin turns, and obstacles I can't see clearly through the gravel-haze of my mind.

The wedding isn't until four o'clock tomorrow afternoon, which means I have twenty-nine long hours to fill before the ceremony. I'd arrived on the island far too early, but the next flight in would've landed right as Palmer and Mojo exchanged their I do's. And since I have no interest in pissing off the pregnant and fiercely hormonal bride, arriving early was my best bet.

I hadn't told anyone I'd be attending the wedding, had given no notice besides the RSVP card I mailed weeks before. I'd fabricated a story for my parents, telling them I'd be vacationing with friends at some luxury spa in Montréal. Lying came easier to me now that I knew I'd been lied to for so long. I didn't even care whether they believed it or not.

The concierge directs me to a bicycle rental shop down the block, where I rent a shiny, periwinkle cruiser and ride out under the late morning sun. My first thought is to stop at June's house—to reunite with the family I'd been missing so dearly—but without meaning to, I turn off in the opposite direction. I'll only get in the way if I show up now. Amid the bustle of last-minute wedding prep, my presence will only be a distraction. And I'm not in the right headspace to help decorate, cook, or whatever else needs doing on the day before 'the big day.'

I let my pedaling feet lead me through the serpentine streets of Halcyon Bay, taking a vaguely familiar route until I wind up at the seaport. I secure my bike to a lamppost and pick my way across the docks, the complex maze of boats slowly coming back to me, unfolding in my brain like a time-weathered map.

I'm not optimistic that I'll find the *Willow's Wind* at her mooring. It's the middle of the day, the sun perched at the apex of a breezy autumn sky, and I imagine the men are likely out fishing. But I figure I can grab a Painkiller at the Sand Pit to calm the nerves barreling over me and wait. Wait to see Bram, and to see Hatch, who's pretty much all I can think about anymore.

I know I need to apologize for how I acted last summer, to ask if there's any way to salvage what I'd wrecked between us. I'd dreamt of his green eyes every single night for months, and I need to reassure myself that they're real, that I didn't imagine them into being. I need to be sure that he's not a delusion, something I'd created to keep me tied to this place.

When I get to the boat slip, the *Willow's Wind* is not there, and I'm surprised to find another vessel in its place—a glossy white sport-fishing boat with a tuna tower and three massive Yamahas. Onboard, a brawny man in a muscle tank adjusts the blaring stereo system, while two topless girls with string bikini bottoms sunbathe at the bow. Inching closer, I see that the boat is named *Fish 'n' Chicks*—a far cry from the *Willow's Wind* in basically every way.

"Something you need, sweetheart?" the beefy guy calls, raising his reflective sunglasses to get a better view of me. The tanning girls lift their heads absently, one of them reaching for a nearby glass of rosé.

"I'm looking for a friend of mine," I call back over the music. "Name's Abraham Urban. Have you seen him around?"

The man drinks me in carnivorously, eyes traveling up and down the length of my body. He lowers his sunglasses once more in an unimpressed and dismissive gesture, as if there's something inherently repulsive about a woman clothed.

"Don't know him," he responds. "You've got the wrong slip, sweetheart."

Bram had relocated the *Willow's Wind,* and I had no way of finding either of them now. This is not a scenario I'd prepared for.

"Thanks a lot, sweetheart," I shoot back, turning on my heel and navigating back through the seaport to my bike.

I can't fathom going an entire weekend on this island without touching base with Hatch, but showing up at his houseboat, unannounced and unwelcome, is by no means ideal. I'd wanted the buffer of Bram and his crew when we met again, hoped a public setting might soften Hatch's temperament, making him more inclined to react gently at the sight of me. But I'm short on options now.

Driven by my own ballooning sense of desperation, I pick my way toward the resident's marina, praying that I'll find him there—and that he'll be receptive.

Once I arrive, I weave through the labyrinth of houseboats, on a mission to find Hatch's place. Everything looks so different now. The rainbow-colored houseboats that once seemed vibrant and lively had turned dull and dreary, dampened by grime and washed-out shades of gray. Or maybe that's just me.

When I finally locate Hatch's houseboat, I'm met with yet another unhappy surprise.

The front door is wide open, exposing the uninhabited shell of all that used to be his. I step inside the space, astounded by what I see. The mattress is stripped bare, the former wall of photographs now blank and expressionless. The cooler and the patterned curtains and the worn blue sheets are all missing—every bit of his personality is gone. It's just a dark and empty box perched on the edge of an even darker ocean, and my stomach heaves at his vacancy—the lifeless space matching the hole he'd carved into my chest.

"Can I help you?"

A nasally man loiters in the doorway, wearing a rumpled, mustard button-down, with a business portfolio in his arms. He sniffs the air as if I'd dragged in some horrible stench with me.

"Who are you?" I ask.

The man raises a bushy, caterpillar eyebrow. "I'm the property owner, wondering who *you* are and why you've illegally entered this residence."

"I'm looking for Hatcher Seaborn. He lives here…or used to live here."

"Moved out about a month ago," the man says curtly, glancing at the silver Rolex on his wrist. He sniffs again, gulping down whatever gunk he's managed to dredge up from his throat in the process. It takes everything in me not to gag in his face.

"Do you know where he went?"

"It's not in my job description to keep tabs on former renters," the sickly man responds. "It is, however, my job to meet with new tenants, which is precisely what I'm scheduled to do in"—he checks his watch again to drive home the point—"less than five minutes. So either you skedaddle on your own, or I'll have security escort you out."

I barely make it through the door before he slams it shut.

"Prick." I say it loud enough for him to hear through the thin wall.

"*Psst.*"

I glance around the docks for the distant whisperer.

"*Psssssst.*"

My eyes settle on a wrinkly woman with curly hair dyed a wild blueish-purple shade. From the cotton-candy pink houseboat across the lane, the woman sits in her cramped patio, reclining on a rusty lounger with a cracked coffee mug in hand. She waves me over enthusiastically.

"Looking for Seaborn?" she croaks.

"I am."

"Moved back home last month," she says. "Poor, sweet boy. Wanted to help out his momma with mortgage payments so they wouldn't lose that old house of theirs."

"Oh, I see."

Before I can ask my next question, she says, "Corner of Bleaker and Camellia Street, pumpkin. The house is bold green, just like them Seaborn eyes. You can't miss it."

I nod my thanks, and she waves me off again, sipping lazily from her mug.

Headed back to my bike with renewed determination, I slow to a stop when an ice-cold dose of reality sinks over me.

What right do I have to barge in on Hatch at his *mother's* house? The idea speeds past intrusive and into borderline aggressive territory. How can I show up on his family's doorstep—in some unassuming, quiet island neighborhood, no doubt—and broadcast my crazy for all to witness, after nearly four months of hardcore radio silence?

I amble through the tree-shaded streets, unsure of my next move, until I happen upon a divey-looking coffeehouse called The Crow's Nest and decide it best to get some caffeine in me. Hopefully, it'll subdue the headache ramping up behind my eyes, and offer me some much-needed clarity.

The Crow's Nest is not a place I recognize, but it feels familiar somehow as I walk through those heavy wooden doors. I'm instantly swaddled by the homey space and the scents of ground coffee beans and pastries. Velvet armchairs and tufted settees break up the wide room, where a smattering of locals are dispersed, reclining and chatting as they sip and graze, utterly at ease. Oversized shabby rugs blanket the floors, and the walls are decoupaged in newspaper clippings and ripped pages from books. It's the sort of place that serves beverages in eclectic teacups and sweets on assorted plates—where nothing's part of a set, nothing matches, but it's all undeniably charming and quaint.

To the twang and strum of a folk singer's banjo, I place my coffee order with the barista before plopping down in an unoccupied section, burying myself in a plushy armchair and my own bleak thoughts.

Nothing on the island is as I'd left it last summer. The *Willow's Wind* is gone, the two people I most want to see are all but missing in action, and I have no safe place to run to. Zero sense of comfort. And here I'd been hoping to finally have a good day.

A good day.

That's when it hits me, all at once—I know *precisely* where I am. This is the same coffeehouse that Mom, June, and Willow had been interviewed in for that article I'd read online, "The Girls of Summer." Willow had been wearing that witty t-shirt, the one that said, *Have a Good Duh!*

The journalist's description of the coffeehouse is exact, right down to the musty atmosphere and bad lighting. It seems that nothing had changed about the place over the course of two decades. For all I know, I may be sitting in the same armchair my sister did way back when.

"Dell?"

A stunned male voice plucks me back from my thoughts.

Looking up, I find Prescott standing before me, looking tall and strong and seemingly back to his usual perky self. He wears a wide smile, nothing like the dismal face he had when I last saw him outside of

June's house. Beside him is a petite girl, strawberry-blonde with poppy-red lips, peeking around his shoulder to catch a glimpse of me.

"I thought that was you." Prescott beams at me like I've got sun-rays shining from my face. "You're back!"

"For a few days, yeah." I stand hesitantly to greet him. "My cousin's getting married—"

"Oh, that's right! I heard about some big shindig going down at Cliffmoor House this weekend."

His smile suddenly fades, as if he'd remembered the specifics of our last conversation. How scary he'd been, and how aggressively he'd acted.

Sucking his teeth in contemplation, Prescott turns to his female companion, slinging an arm around her shoulders. "This is Riley, by the way."

The girl smiles demurely. She's pretty, but reserved, particularly in comparison with Prescott. "Hi," she says in a soft, baby doll voice.

I'm glad that Prescott has a girl in his life. The guy spends the majority of his time in a cemetery. It's good for him to be surrounded by some youthful energy. Someone other than his hard ass mother.

"Nice to meet you," I reply.

"We were just on our way out," Prescott says. "Mom's expecting me back at work in twenty, but it'd be nice to catch up, if you're free at all. I have, um…a lot I'd like to say."

His gray-blue eyes are wide and earnest, charged with ample apologies and regret. *I'm sorry, for everything,* he seems to say. *Give me one chance. Let me explain.*

"Sure." I'd like to let him explain himself, and I have nothing but free time between now and four o'clock tomorrow. I also have plenty of questions to ask regarding what had happened since our last bizarre conversation.

"How about later tonight? We can meet you out for a drink or something. Name the place."

There are so many places I want to return to, things I want to relive while I'm here. In truth, the only person I want to do those things with is Hatch. But with every passing second, our prospects of reconnecting feel like a swiftly dwindling pipe dream.

"Do you know Barracuda's Teeth?" It's the first place that comes to my mind, familiar and well-trafficked.

"Of course." Prescott nods eagerly, squeezing Riley's shoulder. "Eight o'clock?"

"Sounds good."

The pair retreats as the barista calls my name. I collect my to-go order and step out onto the sidewalk, undoing my bike lock, and lifting my face to the cloudless sky.

I take a breath and speed off toward the corner of Bleaker and Camellia, heart on my sleeve, searching for a house that same brilliant shade of green that pervades and haunts my dreams.

CHAPTER FORTY-SIX

His old Ford Ranger's parked out front, so I know for certain he's here.

I knock, expecting him to open the door, or maybe the woman with the tawny hair and the heart-shaped face from that picture I'd seen once. Instead, the man that opens the door looks just like Hatch's father, only younger, with the same thick mustache and beard. And, of course, those vibrant Seaborn eyes.

"Hey." His expression is friendly. "Can I help you?"

I dry-gulp some air. "Hi. I'm an old friend of Hatch's. Is he home?"

The man nods before calling over his shoulder. "Yo, Hatch!" From somewhere in the house comes a muffled response. "You've got company, bro," the man calls again, a cheeky smile shining through all that facial hair.

Hatch pads barefoot down the hallway, grumbling something at the man's back. He's just as I remember him—better, actually. The scruff along his jawline. Sandy-brown waves curling over his forehead. That piercing gaze, at once intense and electrifying. I warm at the sight of him.

He approaches the doorway—approaches me—without a word.

"Hatch," I breathe, wishing I could run to him and throw my arms around his neck. But I stay painfully still.

"Dell," he responds, an unyielding wall.

The man who first answered the door—who I can only guess is Hatch's older brother—bows out quickly, likely detecting the tension that mars the space between us. "I'll give you two some privacy."

Hatch steps onto the stoop as his brother shuts the door behind him. Before I can speak, he says, "You cut your hair."

My hand flies to my newly chopped locks, dusting my shoulders. It's a big change from the mess of tangled waves that used to fall to my waistline, but one I hadn't expected him to notice. "Yeah, a couple weeks ago."

He nods. "What are you doing here?" he asks, dropping the pleasantries in exchange for blunt candor. The tone of his question feels like an accusation—like a pointed finger in a courtroom—and I know that this is what I deserve. Not niceties, not polite observations about my appearance, just dry, unfeeling honesty.

"I, uh…" How had I not come up with one coherent thing to say to him *all day,* or in the nearly six hours I'd spent flying to get here, or in the months I'd pathetically wasted since we last talked?

"Are you in town for Palmer's wedding?"

I nod, my cheeks instantly flushing. How do I tell him that the wedding is just a surface-level excuse for my return? How do I say that *he* tops the laundry list of reasons I really came back?

"Figured," he says. "I'm going too."

This is the last thing I expect to hear. "You are?"

I'd be lying if I said the possibility of him reconnecting with Sasha hadn't crossed my mind about a million times. Maybe they're dating again. Maybe Hatch is her plus one.

He shrugs vaguely in response, refusing to give me an inkling one way or the other. "How'd you know where to find me?"

"I went out to your houseboat. Your neighbor told me you were living here now, so I figured I'd come by and…say hi." This all sounds so ridiculously lame. "Your old landlord's a prick, by the way," I add. My bad attempt at lightening the mood.

Hatch lets out a half-snort. "Yes, he is. And hi."

"Hi back." My heart swells just a little.

We'd had a similar exchange of hellos when we first met, but the mood behind these moments is vastly different. One lent itself to beginnings—to flirty one-liners, dreamy eyes, and stolen glimpses—while this one sounds like a slamming door and feels like a punch to the gut. We're only a few feet away from each other, but it's like we're still miles apart. I wish I knew how to bridge that gap, wish I knew the right thing to say.

"I went to see Bram," I say feebly.

"Bram's gone," Hatch says. "Sold the boat and took off a while ago."

Impossible. That boat was Bram's whole world, the one thing that tied him to his daughter's memory, and the sea where he made his living.

"He sold it?"

Hatch nods.

"Why? Where'd he go?"

"Haven't spoken to him in a couple of months, but last I heard, he was headed to New York. Manhattan, I think. Must've gotten sick of this dump after so many years."

"I can't believe he's gone." Nor can I believe that he'd given up his most valued possession for some random trip to New York. "What about the fishing business?"

"Closed up shop. Most of the crew found other work on the seaport—"

"And you?"

His jaw goes hard at my question, like the memory of how I left came flooding back to him. Like he remembers that I'm not privy to the details of his life anymore. I'd made that choice myself.

"What are you doing here, Dell?" he asks stonily. "For real."

Why am I here? What do I want?

"I wanted to apologize for the way I left last summer…the way I left things with you."

He hates apologies, yet here I am, disappointing him again, regrets spilling from my lips like dripping water from a faucet.

"I couldn't say goodbye because the prospect was…daunting." I hold his gaze, reaching out to him without touch, begging him to throw me a sign or a smile—some small life raft to cling to on this dark, catastrophic sea. "I still don't know how to say goodbye to you, Hatch."

The front door swings open again, and Hatch's brother pokes his neck out, eyes hovering just beyond the door frame.

"Sorry to interrupt"—he glances warily between us—"but Mom wants to know if your friend is staying for dinner."

"No," Hatch pipes up quickly, and just as quickly, my heart plummets. "She can't. She's got other plans…family stuff."

Admittedly, I deserve that. I deserve that and more.

His brother's eyes widen as he ducks back inside the house, looking like he wished he hadn't asked at all.

"Hatch, please," I say again as soon as the door closes. "I know I did everything imaginable to push you away. I'm sorry for all of it, and I'm trying to make it right. Trying to—"

He raises a hand, offering me a crushing little smile that feels like a fatal blow. All tight-lipped detachment, nothing like the real, warm, sunshiny thing I know so well and miss so dearly.

"It's all good," he mutters. "Thank you for stopping by. And for the apology. I appreciate it."

The fire that once burned in his eyes for me is dim, like only a few embers remain in that hearth, growing ever fainter. I feel myself breaking more and more by the second as a sinking truth dawns over me…

Hatch can't look at me the way he used to.

CHAPTER FORTY-SEVEN

"Thanks so much for meeting me!" Prescott's smile is bright as he slides into my booth, tucked against a wood-paneled, neon-lit corner of 'Cuda's.

Despite the heavy desolation that's taken root inside of me since seeing Hatch, Prescott's fresh-faced enthusiasm is infectious. I sit up a little straighter, shaking awake from my corpse-like daze.

"Where's Riley?" I ask, recalling the young redhead.

"Oh, she got roped into some dumb family thing." He shakes his head like he'd like to elaborate, but I don't probe him. His relationship drama is the least of my concerns.

"She seems nice," I offer, hoping to keep things light. "Sweet."

"Yeah. It's still a bit new, but we make a good team."

Lira stands behind the bar, cloaked in boredom and pouring out a foamy draft into a glass, while Salty Masterson—of banyan tree infamy—slumps over his corner hightop, nursing his beer can and his private world of misfortunes. A ragtag band of shirtless youngsters croons from the corner stage to the applause of the local crowd. Stale cooking grease and tobacco saturate the hazy atmosphere, just as I remember it.

At least this place hasn't changed much since last summer.

Lira catches me looking at her, recognition twinkling in her sharp little smirk, and she lifts the beer to me in greeting, mouthing the words *Hey, Humpty* from a distance.

I muster a feeble wave in return, noting how perfectly her nickname fits me these days. Like the fabled Humpty Dumpty, I too had irreparably fallen, become a broken shell of my former self. Lira had pegged me right from the start.

"I'm so glad I bumped into you today," Prescott says. He wrings his hands, his ears and cheeks bursting a wild pink, like a guilty culprit at his hour of confession. "I'm actually kind of relieved Riley couldn't make it. If she were here, it might be awkward, considering everything I need to say."

"Okay."

"I owe you a massive apology. Last I saw you, I was incredibly hostile—acting like a raging lunatic, actually. I'd been freaking out over what we saw in the fields, and then the hurricane hit, and my paranoia got the better of me. I think, in part, I also wanted your attention, or maybe to garner your sympathy, I don't know. But it was wrong of me to scare you like that, and I'm so, so sorry."

"So all that stuff about the people in the fields, the attempted break-in at your house, and at your mom's office..." His stories come back to me easily. The unsolved riddles I'd abandoned on Halcyon Bay hadn't abandoned me for a second. "You're saying you made all that up?"

"I'd convinced myself it was true, at the time. Convinced myself that I was embroiled in some wild conspiracy. Something exciting to make up for my pathetic, boring ass existence. So I stretched the truth, concocted a story. I've always had a knack for shit like that."

"Shit like what?"

He shrugs, head low and repentant. "Embellishing. Exaggerating. Blowing things out of proportion."

"*Lying?*" I clarify.

"Lying," he agrees. "To make myself seem more interesting, more…important. Stupid, I know. It's supposed to be some sort of coping mechanism."

"For what?"

"Lots of things, apparently. I started seeing a therapist to help me work through some of my"—he makes air quotes—"deeper issues."

I squint at him quizzically.

He obliges, seeming eager to confirm his own transparency, to prove that he's an open book. "Oh, nothing all that shocking. Just the regular litany of crappy circumstances: absent father, economically challenged household, recreational substance abuse, et cetera." He ticks them off one by one on his fingers, then shrugs in resignation. "Therapy is finally forcing me to address all that and more. It's been a long time coming."

"Oh. Well, that's good. I'm glad you're getting help."

Even if Prescott had made up everything else he'd said—chalk it up to his imagination, some penchant for deception, or a psychotic, drug-induced episode—the pillar of smoke we saw in those fields wasn't something he could easily explain away. Hatch, Sasha, and I had all witnessed it.

"What about the smoke we saw before we ran? Did you ever figure out what that was?"

"Apparently, the island's forest service organizes these prescribed burnings on the fields every few months, to make sure nothing's growing out there," he explains. "The smoke was from one of those controlled burns. Nothing cult-related, just standard environmental procedure."

"That's why the gate was unlocked," I work out.

If what Prescott says is true—and I'll admit, his explanation does make the most logical sense—then maybe my theory about Callie and Viola's deaths being connected to the Brine is just that, a *theory*.

Maybe the suspicion percolating in my mind—that an extinct cult had been revived, and was picking off island girls one by one, with chilling echoes to my own sister's drowning—is all overblown fantasy.

And maybe I like the chaos of it.

Maybe I get a morbid thrill from having some circuitous, dead-end trail to follow, a mystery to solve, and someone to save. Isn't that what I did for my mother, why I went against her wishes and traveled to Halcyon Bay in the first place?

Maybe my altruistic efforts are selfishly motivated at their core. If I can prevent other girls from meeting a tragic fate, then maybe I can finally learn to cope with Willow's. Maybe, after everything I've been through, my mind is that convoluted.

In light of my own defects and missteps, Prescott's suddenly don't seem all that vile.

"The point is," he says, his face strained with remorse, "I was out of line that night, and I'm truly sorry, Dell. I hope you can forgive me for lying, and I hope we can be cool again. Maybe even friends?"

It would be unfair of me to hold him to a golden standard I'd fallen short of myself, unfair of me to cling to the wrongdoings of his past. Not when he hadn't done anything to hurt me, and was taking obvious steps to better himself. Not when I had so few friends.

"It's okay," I say, worn down by the inner swirling of my own self-loathing. "We're cool."

The light and levity quickly returns to his eyes. "That's awesome, thank you. Thank you so much. Friends again?"

"Sure. Friends."

His grin stretches so wide—cheeks pulled tight as a bubble, exposing a straight, pearly smile—I think his whole face might pop. "This calls for a drink! My treat."

We glimpse around for a waitress, but no one appears to be manning the tables. There's only Lira, leaning against the bar top, half-assedly wiping down counters with a filthy rag.

"I'll grab us something from the bar," Prescott offers, reaching into his jean pocket as he stands. "What'll you have?"

We don't have a menu, but in all honesty, I don't care what I'm drinking, so long as it's got alcohol.

"Something citrusy?"

I try to seem casual, easygoing, *normal,* when inside, I feel anything but. I can't help but think of Hatch and the bottomless vacancy in his eyes, weighing him down like an anchor. That one look had confirmed the absolute worst—he'd never let me in again. I'm too late.

After a few minutes, Prescott returns with two monster-sized beers, setting one down in front of me. Without asking questions, I knock back a heaping swig of something distinctly Floridian, orange-flavored and tangy. It's good, *really good,* and all I want is to drown in it.

"Wait for me," Prescott protests, chugging fast to catch up.

We chat and drink for a long while, and I find myself having an unexpectedly pleasant time with him. For one thing, Prescott's eyes don't go dead when he looks at me—they're not charged with disappointment or broken expectations, like Hatch's. Nor does his laughter hide an inner heaviness, his thoughts unoccupied by bitterness—again, unlike Hatch, who'd struggled to spit a few measly words my way. Talking to Prescott feels like talking to an old friend, and I lose myself in our easy conversation, time slipping like sand through an hourglass.

I accept his offer to grab us a second round of beers, and then a third sometime thereafter. Before long, the bubbles start floating up to my head, but I can't deny that I feel so much better now—lighter, weightless, like I'm coasting high above the ocean I'd been drowning in before. I can hardly even remember why I was so sad in the first place.

Prescott gets up to grab us round four, pulling out his wallet again with a loopy, drunken smile. That's when I remember it—*his wallet.*

He'd dropped it in the sea trumpet fields last summer.

"Is that n-new?" I point at the worn leather wallet in his palm. It doesn't look particularly new to me, but my vision's gone pretty fuzzy.

"This? Nah, I've had this thing forever."

"Oh. S-so you g-got it b-back?"

"Got what back?"

"Your w-wallet." I try to enunciate, but my words slide tipsily into one another nonetheless. "You s-said you lost it in the f-fields?"

"Oh, right. Yeah." Prescott nods vehemently, as if trying to imbue his words with greater conviction and sincerity. "Yup, I found it. Thank goodness."

"Okay…" There's a throbbing pulse in my head that makes it difficult for me to concentrate. The bar lights are blinding all of a sudden. "I think I g-gotta g-go to the b-bathroom, or s-something."

I shield my eyes as I try to stand, crippling under what feels like a searing white-hot sun. My feet are strangely unsteady beneath me, my knees buckling of their own accord. I stumble, but Prescott is right there to catch me, his reflexes lightning fast. Hadn't he drank as much as me?

His lips twist into a wry smile. "You good?"

I lean into his arms, grateful for his sturdiness as the dive bar revolves endlessly around me. "I'm j-just f-feeling a little…"

My limbs go utterly numb, my legs bending inward, shuddering under my weight like snapping twigs in a forest.

Prescott supports me, cradling me by the waist with one arm. I never realized how strong he is.

"*Hey.*"

I swing my head around, fighting the haze pushing stars into my vision, coming to focus on Lira. She stands before us wearing an edgy expression, eyes shifting between Prescott's face to mine. "Is everything okay here?"

Before I can slur out an answer, Prescott jumps in. "We're all good. I think she just needs some fresh air." There's a strange storm in those sleepy eyes of his. "Let's step outside, Dell."

Lira seems uneasy with this arrangement. "Or you can chill here for a bit," she offers only to me. "I can call you a cab."

"We're fine," Prescott insists, wrapping his arm tighter around me, possessively. "Just need some air."

I try to protest, but he quickly shuffles us toward the door, half-carrying, half-dragging me, my head lolling about aimlessly. On our way out, I catch a glimpse of Lira lifting a cell phone to her ear. The glow of fluorescent blue illuminates her worried face.

We slip into the cool night and Prescott turns us down an alleyway, where a run-down orange car awaits near a dumpster. The car is running, smoke and fumes shaking loose from the exhaust.

Prescott opens the door and eases me into the backseat, promptly shimmying in beside me.

"Bar Bitch might be a problem," he says, his tone hard and flat.

"Too public," warns the driver—the voice of a young woman.

"I had to improvise," he growls.

I try to move, clawing for the door, but my fatigued arms fall limp by my sides. I have no control of my body, my exhaustion far surpassing that of any drunken stupor. How many beers had I even had? Three, maybe four?

Food or no food, a few beers would not have had this effect on me—unless it's not only beer in my bloodstream. Unless it's something more potent, something dangerous.

Unless…he'd drugged me.

Prescott notices my futile squirming. "Shh, come here," he breathes against my forehead, tucking me snugly against his shoulder blade. He strokes my hair gently. Cool fingers graze my face. "We're going for a little ride."

We speed away from the blur of downtown lights, the screeching of brakes ripping through the night like a wolf's howl. After a few long moments of immobilized panic—of wondering what terrors they might have in store for me—I shut my eyes, unable to stop myself.

I succumb to an irrepressible, medicated slumber as Prescott whispers hauntingly through the darkness, "Nighty night, Dell."

CHAPTER FORTY-EIGHT

I wake to a foggy, anesthetized consciousness, my numb body lying on a slender metal cot.

What the hell happened?

The last thing I remember is drinking with Prescott. He'd swept me out of the bar and into the back of a strange car—I hadn't been able to move so much as an inch on my own—and a young woman had driven us away.

Where am I now? How long had I been asleep?

Three distinct voices argue nearby. I keep my eyes closed and my breathing steady, afraid to draw the attention of my captors. My mind races to distinguish the cadences and lilts of their voices.

"…becoming a pattern. Are you going soft?" asks a female—the driver.

"No." That's Prescott.

"It's like you've got a crush on her or something."

"I don't."

"Leave him. He's done his job."

This comes from a second female, the sound of her voice vaguely familiar.

"And what will Mother say about the mess he's made in the process?"

"I don't know, Riley," sighs the second female again, an audible twinge of irritation in her voice. "Feel free to ask her when she arrives."

Riley? As in Prescott's girlfriend, Riley?

"I won't have to ask her," Riley retorts haughtily. "She'll have Prescott's head on a platter faster than I can say—"

"Shut up," growls a fuming Prescott. By the brutality of his tone, I can only assume the two of them aren't actually dating as I'd been led to believe. "You've only just been brought into the fold. Don't think for one second that you're irreplaceable, all because you claim to be one of Bla—"

"Keep your voices down," urges the other female.

"What good is it to keep this one like some sort of pet?" Riley asks. "She's not of this island, like the other girls."

"You idiot," Prescott spits. "Do you have any idea who she is?"

"Should I?"

"Meridel Costa," the unidentified female utters. "Goes by the name Dell. She's Willow Klyne's younger sister. Is that a name you recognize?"

How do they know Willow and I are sisters?

"Of course," Riley replies indignantly.

"Then take my word for it," the other woman snaps. "She *is* of this island, and her blood is sacrosanct to us. Far more important than any of the others."

My blood is sacrosanct.

"What now?" Prescott asks.

"Based on the dose you gave her, she should be awake within the hour," the woman says. "She'll have to be restrained before seeing Mother. Get the rope."

The sound of footsteps and bickering grows fainter as two of my captors leave the room in search of rope. If they bind my hands and feet, I'll be completely at their mercy, so I need to move quickly if I'm going to attempt an escape. Only one of them is left behind to watch over me. One to one—I like those odds.

I crack my eyes open and the room where I'm being held comes into harsh focus. It looks like a laboratory, sterile and white, with buzzing fluorescent lights and wall-to-wall silver cabinets. Inside one of the open cabinets is a trove of medical supplies—clear bottles filled with rust-colored pills, syringes loaded with a thick, reddish liquid, and jars of what look like crushed herbs and flower petals.

There's a metal door on the wall farthest from the table where I'm lying. It's the only door in the room, my ticket to freedom. It gapes into a shadowed corridor, where a petite woman stands in the doorway. She wears an all-black outfit, hair pulled into a sleek bun at the nape of her neck, and in her hand is a flash of dark metal—a gun.

When the woman glances back in my direction, I slam my eyes shut, biting the inside of my cheek to keep from screaming. I recognize that pale face and those crimson lips. *Sabine,* my grandmother's former assistant. Her voice was the one I couldn't place earlier.

I wiggle my fingers and toes, glad to find that I can move of my own accord again. I'm not sure how competently I'll be able to launch myself from this bed, catapult across the room, and knock Sabine's gun from her hand—all without tripping, falling, or shooting myself in the process—but I have to try.

She's distracted, exchanging hushed words with someone in the corridor, their face out of my line of sight. If it's Prescott or Riley returning with the rope, I'll be bound within minutes, ensnared like prey.

Time to go.

I jerk upward, propelling myself into a standing position despite the crippling sense of dizziness dragging me down. The springs of the cot groan beneath me, betraying me like a motion-sensor alarm. Sabine turns fast, her scrupulous eyes locking on mine. She makes a move toward me, gun at the ready, but I fling myself at the medicine cabinet, reaching for anything I might defend myself with. I grab a syringe in one hand and a glass jar in the other, hurling the jar at Sabine's head. She avoids the projectile easily, and when it smashes against the far wall, a fragrant red powder bursts through the air.

I begin to cough.

"Calm down, Dell." She aims the barrel of her gun at my chest. "Don't do anything rash."

In the space between us rests a wide aluminum table with rolling legs. With a feral scream I didn't know I had in me, I slam myself onto the table top and crash into her, knocking both us and the table to the ground.

My shoulder hits the metal doorframe and an electric jolt of pain courses down the length of my body. I groan, pushing myself up to my hands and knees. Sabine's hand is pressed to her wounded ribcage as she scours the ground for her gun.

There. I spot it, lying in the beam of fluorescent light spilling from the room into the dank corridor.

Crawling on all fours, I creep through the doorway, reaching for the gun, my fingertips barely grazing the handle.

A chunky black boot comes down on the weapon, catching two of my fingers along with it.

I shriek, recoiling from the instant pain flaring up my hand. I lift my head, still coughing thanks to the floral-scented clouds of red dust dancing in the air, and barely make out the shape of a looming figure.

He leans in close, rage and gloom warring across his ashen face. His eyes are black and bleak as night, and they hone in on me fully, sucking me in.

"*Tristen,*" I choke out, gaping up at him in terror.

"Fancy seeing you here, cousin." He kicks the gun out of my reach.

I remember the syringe still tightly molded to my palm, and in a fierce panic, I swing my arm, aiming to pierce his neck with the needle. Tristen deftly catches my wrist, knocking the syringe loose. It drops to the ground, the glass shattering, red liquid spraying onto my clothes. He clicks his tongue in disapproval.

Sabine has made it to her feet again. She swoops to my side, gripping me by the hair and tugging until my neck dips back at an unnatural angle, exposed and vulnerable.

"Why are you doing this?" I scream, pulling away with all of my might, but her grip on me is iron-clad. "What do you want?"

Tristen reaches into his pocket, his fingertips stained crimson, and blows a handful of powder into my eyes. It coats my face, dripping from my lashes, the syrupy-sweet aroma singeing my nose and throat until all I see is red, all I breathe is red.

Reality begins to slip away from me. I imagine myself falling like Alice in Wonderland, tumbling down hills of vibrant crimson flowers. The perfume of them is like poison to my lungs, the alien color polluting my vision, injecting my world with floral venom. The flowers are *everywhere*—pushing into my brain, stretching it like modeling clay, the snow-globe world of my thoughts flipped upside down and inside out.

My cousin's harsh voice blares down from the red-tinged sky swirling far beyond my eyes. "Mother will see you now."

I sputter back to life with a pronounced aching in my jaw.

"Is that necessary?" Tristen asks from somewhere off to my right. Dry boredom oozes from his tone.

"No," replies Riley, standing closer to me, panting a bit. "But it's *fun*."

A hand connects hard with my cheek, the blow sending my body careening to one side.

"*Aha!* She lives!" Riley jeers cruelly when I stir.

"Stand back," Sabine orders from my left. "Let Mother get a look at her."

My eyes flutter open, crusty with the remnants of that sickening powder, my vision blurred and stinging. I'm no longer inside the white-walled laboratory. Now I'm in a room teeming with plants—blood-red, drooping, bell-shaped flowers, popping up in droves from the dampened soil. There's no floor in this place, only rich earth, with broad glass panels making up the ceiling, showcasing the starry night sky above.

It looks like a greenhouse, but unlike any greenhouse I've ever seen before.

"Welcome, Meridel."

The cool voice instantly transports me back.

A woman comes into slow focus, the fog of the drugs receding as I take in her elfin stature and sharp eyes, her wild style of dress and smart manner of speaking.

The cryptic librarian, *Greer*.

She peers down at me while I struggle and squirm against the ropes tightly securing my wrists and ankles. My aching body is curled around a system of intricate knots, completely disabled and utterly in their control.

"Where am I?" I croak.

"You're in the sea trumpet fields, dear girl." Greer smiles wickedly, contempt swirling in her gaze. "Well, below them, technically. We've been rebuilding under our former territory, tending to our seedlings, nurturing them to life. And here they are once again, blossoming, magnificent as ever."

Vivid greens and bursts of red glint at me from all angles of the greenhouse—a crop of fresh sea trumpets growing undetected, right under everyone's nose. How had they managed to keep this place a secret?

"But…why? How did you—"

"Build it?" Greer's eyes dance around the space, brimming with admiration. "We're quite well-connected, dearie. Our tentacles spread far and wide across this island. Still, it's been no small feat to keep our efforts concealed. Dodging suspicion from police and the forest service wasn't easy. However, we do have our methods."

She pulls a tiny silver remote from her pocket and aims it at the glass-paneled ceiling. A solid metal sheet begins to slide atop the glass, disguising the underground room from the outside world. All that's left is to cover the metal panel with some charred turf, and it would look no different than the rest of the fields.

"The sea trumpets are pivotal to our existence, you see," Greer says. "They're the channel through which we commune with Mother. Making certain that they not only survive, but thrive, is of tantamount importance to our cause."

The hazy, creeping pull of the drugs still tug at the fringes of my mind, making Greer's words choppy and hard to process.

"You're…trying to…bring back the Brine," I say slowly.

"We are the Brine. We're the revival, the second wave." A crinkle forms atop Greer's button nose. "After my husband was detained years ago and the fields reduced to ash, I struggled with how to carry on with our mission. How could I renew our movement in the face of such terrible adversity? How could I persist without my beloved Kieran's instruction?"

I'm floored by this, my mind reeling. Greer's husband is Kieran Blackbane? As in, *the* Kieran Blackbane, the crazed cult leader and founder of the Brine? A man currently rotting in jail for countless, unspeakable crimes?

"Of course, I had to amass the right disciples," she continues. "So many of our former members defected, crumbling under the pressures of public scrutiny and tensions with law enforcement. They spurned our lifestyle and desecrated our traditions. I knew that I needed fresh blood, a new generation of believers." She flourishes a hand at the group of young people surrounding her. "And who better than Kieran's own children to groom in his image?"

I stare at the group assembled before me as the awful truth of Greer's words sinks in. "You're…Blackbane's children?" My eyes jump between them, utterly horror-stricken.

"My husband has a great many descendants, dearie," Greer says, a warped sense of pride laced into her words. "I believe you already know *my* daughter, Sabine. And there's Prescott and Riley, whose mothers were former members of the Brine." She smiles fondly. "With Kieran's children leading the charge, we finally have the numbers we need to carry on his legacy and begin recruiting again in earnest."

The bile rises in my throat as I hone in on Tristen. How did he fit into this twisted dynamic?

"And you?" I ask.

Deep-rooted darkness swirls in his stare. "Not a Blackbane. I'm as much a Klyne as you are, unfortunately."

"Tristen is like family to us," Greer interjects, placing a hand on his arm. "Though not of Kieran's direct lineage, Tristen's father—your uncle, Florian—was Kieran's dear, dear friend. In so many ways, we wouldn't be here without him."

I knew that my uncle was an abusive scumbag, but I never could have predicted this. Flip and Blackbane were *friends?*

"Florian served as Kieran's greatest inspiration." Greer glides to the nearest cluster of sea trumpets, running a slender finger down one fiery petal. "Without your uncle's guidance, I'm not sure Kieran would've ever found his true calling."

Her statement sets the sweat-doused hairs on the back of my neck on end. "What do you mean?"

"Well, apart from being our chief monetary backer, Florian also made the first kill," she explains calmly. "His actions were our inspiration. His kill was the one that started it all."

My muddled mind chugs through this surge of information, processing what feels truly unimaginable. I try to remember what Prescott had explained while we'd walked these fields last summer.

He'd said that Girls of the Salt were sacrifices, created as a sort of army to protect against that which brought the island danger or misfortune. The girls' deaths were modeled after one particular incident, a drowning that served as the catalyst for everything.

The one that started it all.

"My sister," I mutter, head spinning. I feel the weight of the sea glass shard tucked against my chest—an ever-present anchor and reminder.

Greer's vicious eyes flash in acknowledgment.

Based on Willow's memories, two men were on that beach the night she was murdered—the killer and the watcher—both working in lethal conjunction to bury their secrets and evade justice. They must have shared a great deal of trust between them. If one went down for the crime, then, like domino pieces, they'd both go down. So the men relied on each other, confident in their alliance. But maybe it was *more* than an alliance. Maybe it was a bond one might expect from a pair of lifelong friends.

Friends like Kieran Blackbane and Florian Klyne.

I turn again to Tristen—my cousin, my blood—and ask a question I never imagined I'd need to ask.

"Your father killed my sister?"

The words scrape down the length of my throat like I've been fed a thousand microscopic blades, slitting me open from the inside out.

Tristen's face is stony, revealing nothing, but the muscle in his jaw works agitatedly, telling me that he understands the gravity of my question.

I scream at him, ropes digging into my skin, "Answer me!"

"Yes," Greer says, filling the quiet. "Florian made the first kill and inspired our movement. It was your sister's destiny, Meridel—the price she had to pay. Because of her sacrifice, and that of all the chosen girls thereafter, every citizen on this island was afforded life, safety, and abundance."

The tears spilling down my cheeks run hot and thick—a product of fury rather than sadness. I'd depleted myself of my grief long ago. All that was left now was blind, encompassing rage.

"You're sick," I spit, writhing erratically, as if my useless struggling might magically loosen my bonds and set me free.

Greer sighs as though I'm being terribly unreasonable. "We all have our roles, Meridel. We all must pay a price. Willow's demise set off a sort of frenzy in Kieran, and our great movement was born. That was her price—death to bring forth a new era—and soon, you will pay yours, reigniting the flame your sister first lit. The Brine will be reborn, all thanks to your sacrifice." She smiles at this.

I howl in response, feral and wild. "*Why?*"

"Because it's Mother's direction, dear girl. And I, as Her

surrogate—as the Brine's Second Mother—must tend to Her divine interests. I intercede on Her behalf. And I decide what's best." Greer's eyes blaze with a deep thirst for power and blood. "And *you* have been chosen, Meridel."

"Chosen," I snarl. "Chosen to be your next victim? Marked for death? For murder?"

"Murder is not our usual practice," she responds unfeelingly. "The spilling of island-born blood is a sacrifice Mother requires in exchange for our safety. Once the girls understand this—once we *make them see*— they often go along with our plans willingly."

"You mean after you drug and brainwash them? After you terrorize them and threaten their families?"

Greer glares at me as one might a squirming cockroach, dripping with repulsion, her boot poised for my squashing. "I do hope you grow to see things my way, dearie. It's a true honor to join Mother's ranks and serve our great purpose." She smiles again, her crooked, graying teeth like a row of gravestones. "But rest assured, whether you cooperate or not, you will die. Best get used to the thought."

She turns from me to address the others. "At nightfall, we begin. Assemble at the pyre for the hour of *Salemorte*. Riley, you stand guard with Blake and Maven. Cover each entry point along the fence-line. Go armed. Sabine, you inform the others. I want them robed at dusk, no delays. Prescott, you watch the girl—"

"Someone will come looking for me," I spit. "My cousin's getting married today. They're expecting me to be there."

"A minor snag," Tristen interjects. "I'll handle it." He nods at Greer confidently, as if my whole existence is nothing more than an inconvenient wrinkle to be swiftly ironed out.

"See to it that you do."

Without another glance my way, the librarian exits the greenhouse and stalks down the dark, snaking corridor, her wildly patterned skirts undulating in her wake.

"You won't get away with it," I snap at Tristen. His face is an expressionless, pale canvas. "June and Palmer will know something's wrong. They'll figure out—"

"No, they won't, Meridel," he counters flatly. "No one will care whether or not you're at the wedding. If you don't attend, they'll assume you flaked. And on the off-chance someone does show a shred of interest about your whereabouts, I'll cook up a convincing story."

My eyes well up with scalding tears of hate. "They won't believe you," I grind out through my teeth.

"You'd be surprised. I'm a supremely talented liar."

His words terrify me to my core, my heart plummeting when I realize that not even my parents know the truth of where I am. By the time they realize I've gone missing—that I'm not actually in Montréal, the way I'd said—I'll likely already be dead, thousands of miles away, drifting on the shores of Halcyon Bay. Just like my older sister before me.

Who else knows I'm here? Lira? The concierge at the inn? They won't be much help to me now.

Hatch.

Hatch knows I'm here. He said he'd be at the wedding, and he'd certainly notice my absence if I don't show. Then again, he might pass it off as another one of my disappearing acts. I'd left without a proper goodbye once before, why wouldn't he think I'd do it again?

"Take her," Sabine says, prompting Prescott and Riley to lift me by the arms and drag me, kicking and screaming, from the humid greenhouse.

They lug me through a dark tunnel system, and ever closer to my death.

CHAPTER FORTY-NINE

When morning comes, Prescott leads me from the underground facility up a narrow stairwell and through a manhole-like opening in the ground. We spill onto a vast, uninhabited wasteland coated in gloomy, early-morning mist—the sea trumpet fields.

The navy sky peels itself back in streaks of dusty pink, but my eyes don't need to adjust to the darkness. I'd been confined to it for hours below ground, chained inside a supply closet, with no company but my own racing thoughts and the knowledge that I'd soon be dead.

My wrists are bound with rope as we walk, and I have a sea-trumpet-soaked rag shoved in my mouth to prevent my screaming. It keeps me manageably sedated, breathing in a constant, steady stream of intoxicated air.

"Just a little farther," Prescott coos. His deceptively sweet voice doesn't dull the sensation of the gun he has pressed against my spine.

We walk in unison toward a giant pit in the earth piled high with logs and kindling, surrounded by various sacks, barrels, and other supplies—the pyre. We're way out in the fields here, practically bordering the coastline, far from civilization and anyone that might hear or help me.

Prescott sets me down on the burnt ground and takes a seat on a log across from me. His sleepy eyes study my face pensively, and after a long moment of pin-drop silence, he asks, "Do you remember the day we met, Dell?"

I couldn't respond even if I wanted to, but Prescott doesn't expect a response. He just wants to be heard.

He cocks his head to one side, the gun dangling loosely from his fingertips. "It was at the cemetery. You'd gone looking for your sister's grave, and my paranoid mother mistook you for…well, for someone like me." He snickers with sick amusement. "Lettie always was a crappy judge of character."

I wonder how much Prescott's mother knows of her son's dalliances with the Brine. Greer had said that Lettie was a former member, and from the sound of it, she'd ventured pretty deep into its trenches. Deep enough to become pregnant with a child of Kieran Blackbane, though that clearly wasn't uncommon among the women in his group.

Lettie seems to have genuinely switched sides since, leaving any ties to the cult far behind her, and acting somewhat panicky and traumatized by it now. She nearly ran me out of the cemetery over mere suspicion of my involvement with sea trumpets. So I have to believe that she doesn't have a clue about Prescott, and would likely keel over if she ever found out.

"I look back on that day fondly," Prescott recalls, his gaze dreamy. "Greer had already decided that you were our next mark. Sabine was the one to inform her of your return, and when she met you at the library, that sealed the deal. The question was, how to lure you in? That's usually my job, to draw in the girls…guess I've taken after my father in that way. The second Death Harbinger, new and improved."

He smiles. "Still, the others were concerned about you and me. You were only in town for one weekend, meaning I'd have to work quickly to get in your good graces. And they didn't much like the age difference." He rolls his eyes, as if this is a major sticking point. "It's true that the younger girls are easier to control, less hardened by life, more open to suggestion. They thought you were out of my depths, too smart to be enamored. But that was easy enough to get around."

Every nerve in my body pulses frenetically, shooting bolts of electricity across my veins, setting me on edge despite the sea trumpet fumes pouring into me. I feel like a live wire dipped in water.

"What we needed was an organic way for me to insert myself in your path without tipping you off. And, as Mother would have it, that moment arrived sooner than we imagined, almost fatefully." His coy flash of teeth is terrifying. "You came to me, Dell, without prompting, without chase. You showed up at my cemetery, asking all the right questions, and everything unfolded so perfectly from there."

All this time, I thought I'd been the one using Prescott—flirting with him to get my way, twisting his arm for glimpses of the truth—but I'd been so fatally wrong. He'd been playing me since day one.

"It didn't take much coaxing for you to trust me," he continues. "Remember your grandmother's service? All you could talk about was the *elusive* Brine, and you practically jumped at the chance to see the sea trumpet fields when I offered to bring you."

Memories of that day flash behind my eyes. I'd stolen away from the celebration of life up to the second floor of Cliffmoor House, eavesdropping on Tristen whispering with someone in a bedroom. I can only assume now that it was Sabine or Greer. I remember Prescott sneaking up on me at the landing, shouting my name loud enough for all to hear. I'd practically dragged him down the staircase, pissed that he'd blown my cover, annoyed by what I'd perceived as his juvenile infatuation with me. But it wasn't nearly as innocent as that.

Thinking back now, Prescott hadn't been looking for an unoccupied bathroom, though that was the bullshit excuse he fed me. He'd been on his way upstairs to *meet* Tristen and the others, to discuss the plans they were putting into motion—plans that revolved around drugging, abducting, and ultimately killing me. When he'd seen me standing there, listening outside the door, he'd blurted my name to alert them to my presence. And once we'd gotten to talking one-on-one, he'd steered the conversation toward his desired outcome, which was getting me alone and onto the fields.

"Unfortunately, that night didn't go quite as planned." Prescott sighs. "That oafish boyfriend of yours showed up and foiled everything."

What would've happened if Hatch hadn't spotted me riding off on the back of Prescott's motorbike? What if he and Sasha hadn't followed me here? The small, jagged rock I'd hidden in my pocket wouldn't have been worth a damn against a cult armed to the teeth with guns and narcotics. The Brine would have killed me months ago, just like they intended to now.

"And then that ridiculous hurricane blew in, and you were holed up in that giant house for days"—Prescott shakes his head—"and when the storm finally cleared, you went and decided to spend the whole day fishing! I nearly went out of my mind trying to keep tabs on you."

His confession makes my skin crawl. My every move last summer—all of my whereabouts—had been monitored, surveilled, violated. I suspected that Prescott had been following me that night at June's house, but I couldn't grasp the reasons why, nor the gravity of what it all meant.

"You were always with someone," he complains, as if I were a toy he coveted above all others. "Always slipping out of my reach. When I confronted you the night before you left, I invented some cockamamie story hoping to play upon your emotions, hoping you'd be worried enough over my well-being that you'd abandon all logic and follow me here."

Which is why Officer Dash had found no trace of a report regarding Prescott's claims. Prescott never actually went to the police. He and his mother were never in any danger. It was all an elaborate scheme to entrap me.

I'm the one in danger. It's always been me.

He shrugs. "When you left town, I thought we'd lost our chance. But then, a few months later, you came back to us, like a precious gift delivered right into my hands. It was almost poetic, getting to see you again."

Hearing Prescott speak this way—romanticizing the two of us like star-crossed lovers destined for tragedy—feels like a fate somehow worse than death. I'd convinced myself that Prescott was some dumb, smitten kid. I'd given him the benefit of the doubt, despite an overwhelming feeling in my gut to the contrary. I'd been so hell-bent on getting my answers that I was blind to the fact that his every move was calculated. I'd allowed myself to be manipulated, over and over again.

"I know what you must think," Prescott continues, his voice low and sober. "But I'm not the heartless monster you take me for. Look!"

He points to the distant horizon, vividly painted in smears and strokes of every color imaginable, where a glowing orb would soon rise from its watery grave to signal the start of a brand new day. In my case, the last day.

"I brought you to see one final sunrise," he says jovially. "I wanted to give you something nice to think about when…you know…"

Prescott's voice trails off, and I can't help but think that, to some degree, Riley's right. He *had* developed a weird crush on me, like some kind of pet he wished he could keep for himself. He didn't necessarily want me to die, but he was bound to his duties to the Brine, bound to follow Greer's orders. Meaning he might be persuaded to unfollow them, given the right push.

I either give it a shot or resign myself to the prospect of my imminent death.

Squirming around to get his attention, I force garbled sounds from my mouth and shoot him my widest eyes.

"What is it?" he asks.

I talk through my gag, trying to communicate with muddled noises rather than words. *Come.* I beckon him with my eyes. *Come closer, you twisted son of a bitch.*

Prescott stands, gun in hand. "What are you trying to say?"

There's a twinge of genuine hopefulness in his tone, as if he thinks this is the moment where I profess my undying love for him. I hold my breath, my windpipe filled with the raging scent of sea trumpets.

He squats down low until we're face-to-face, his long fingers tracing the line of my jaw up to that throbbing spot on my cheek, evidence of Riley's violent assault. He caresses it, brutally gentle, getting off on the feel of my skin in his hands. I remain perfectly still, forcing myself not to recoil from his touch as a volcanic river of fury rises within me.

He may not be persuadable, but I will certainly make him pay.

Prescott's thumb dances on the edge of my mouth, grazing my lips. He pinches the corner of the rag. "Can I trust you to be a good girl?" he asks, a flickering thrill in the sleepy blue mist of his eyes.

I nod, slow and deliberate, the drugs still making a scrambled mess of my thoughts. *Of course you can trust me, you psychotic fuck. Come on, ungag me. Watch me rip that narcissistic face of yours from the bone.*

He hesitates, still tenderly stroking my lips, outlining my cupid's bow. "They won't be happy with me, you know."

Bile roils deep in my core. *Ungag. Me.*

He slips the gun into his waistband, obeying my silent command. *Yes. That's it.*

"I want to believe you won't scream, but..." The flare of excitement in Prescott's gaze dims, turning soft and wistful. After a moment, he sighs, cupping my face in both hands. His lips hover inches from mine, as if he might try to kiss me. "How do I know you won't betray my trust?"

He's worried that *I* might betray *him?*

My brain nearly explodes.

A surge of adrenaline like a lightning bolt shoots past the poison fogging up my mind. I jerk my head forward with all my might and— *crack!*—slam into Prescott's nose.

He falls back with a pained yelp, blood spurting down his face, and I scramble to widen the space between us. My temple throbs, wrists stinging from the ropes tearing into them, but I don't care. All I can think of is distance. Getting far away from him, to someplace safe.

Prescott roars, fingers probing his swelling nose, and lunges for me. Like some starved, feral creature, he catapults through the air. I tuck myself low into the charred ground, narrowly avoiding the impact of his body. He rolls away from me, groaning with pain and humiliation.

I writhe and squirm back into a seated position. If I manage to get to my feet, I can run for the forest's edge.

But Prescott is on me in seconds, one unyielding hand gripping my arms, keeping me in place. My heart sinks as the window of opportunity slams shut in my face, my chance for escape escaping me.

"I didn't want to have to hurt you," he hisses.

The lower half of his face is doused in blood, ruby-bright streams undulating down his neck. A nasty bump blooms on the bridge of his nose, the bone beneath it terribly deformed. Broken.

Prescott wrenches the gun from his jeans and shoves the barrel into my ribcage. I shut my eyes as he lowers his face to mine, his lips pressed against my forehead. His other hand slides around my back, affixing me to him.

"Wrong move," he pants, his hot breath prickling my skin. "And here I thought we were having such a pleasant morning."

I swallow down my whimpers, withhold my tears. He won't coax them from me, not a single one. If this is the end, at least I know I went down fighting. That's far better than waiting for nightfall, like some lamb being led to the slaughter.

"What are you doing out here?"

Prescott separates from me abruptly as Tristen's razor-edged voice slices across the fields. My cousin storms toward us, his expression furious.

"I was checking on the pyre," Prescott lies as he stands, leaving me in a heap on the ground.

"I mean"—Tristen enunciates each word sharply—"what are you doing here with *her*? She could've gotten away from you, or someone could've heard her scream."

"I gagged her," Prescott protests. "And she wasn't going anywhere. Not when I've got this." He waves his gun in the air, emphasizing his willingness to shoot me if needed.

"Do you even know how to use that thing?"

"Ha. Hilarious." Prescott's eyes taper to slits as he assumes his seat on the log across from me. "Why are you back so soon?" he asks, the question tinctured with bitterness.

"I came to prepare for *Salemorte*." Tristen grabs a metal shovel lying near the pit. "I'll be preoccupied most of the day at this asinine wedding, so I wanted to make sure everything was in order for tonight's ceremony. Not that it's any of your business."

My death ceremony, he means. *Salemorte,* a strange and terrifying word. I don't need to be a skilled linguist to derive its meaning.

Salt and death.

Prescott cocks his chin. "I could've taken care of that."

"Please. You couldn't even adequately take care of *her.*" Tristen's face twists into a sneer, his eyes lingering over Prescott's bloody nose. "I reckon you'll need to have that bone reset. Pity."

Prescott falls silent now, turning the gun over in his hands, his ears bursting red. The mistrust and in-fighting among this group is palpable. They all seem to be loyal prisoners to their cause, but they also appear to despise each other in spite of it. Prescott in particular, who's glaring at Tristen like he might unload that entire magazine of bullets on him.

Seemingly impervious to Prescott's intensifying rage, my cousin begins shoveling a light grainy substance from a barrel, sprinkling it all around the circular pit.

Salt.

With each fresh shovel, the falling salt cascades like water around the pit's perimeter. Once that ring is complete, Tristen moves on to a sack brimming with fragrant red powder.

Crushed sea trumpets.

He repeats the process in alternating, concentric circles, inching ever closer to the wood-laden center.

"What's with your eye?" Prescott asks him after a while.

I squint at Tristen's face, masked behind those greasy strands of ink-black hair. Sure enough, a bluish-purple lesion discolors the skin below his left eye. The bruise is fresh and unsightly. I'm sure he didn't have it last night.

Tristen doesn't acknowledge Prescott's question, totally engrossed in his meticulous work. But Prescott isn't ready to let this one go.

"Did Daddy Picasso your face again?" Prescott chuckles to himself. "What was the reason this time? Too much starch in his boxers? Not enough cream in his coffee?"

Out of nowhere, Tristen lifts the metal shovel into the air and swings it wide. It connects with the side of Prescott's head, the unmistakable crack of bone tearing through the atmosphere, a sound that reverberates all the way down my body.

Prescott collapses face-first onto the ground.

I scream through my gag and Tristen, panting heavily, turns to me next, his fingers still gripping the shovel, a wild streak running through his eyes.

He hoists the shovel up a second time. I brace for impact, for life-ending pain…

Shockingly, the blade digs into the ground instead, the shovel standing rigid as a corpse by my side.

I meet Tristen's eyes, stunned to find that as quickly as my cousin's anger had materialized, it's gone again. His labored breathing grows calm, his crazed gaze steadies. The rage-filled whirlwind drains completely from his face—a moments-long tempest swallowed in a tranquil sea.

"Listen carefully," he says to me, his voice smooth and unwavering. "I'm going to untie you, but you cannot scream. You cannot run. You must stay perfectly still and do exactly as I say."

It's impossible to process what Tristen's saying with Prescott's unconscious body bleeding out right next to me.

"If you do as I say, I promise to get you out of here and back to safety," he asserts. "But if you scream, if you try to run, you will be found and killed, and there will be nothing I can do to stop it. Do you understand?"

I understand none of Tristen's words, nor can I believe that he truly intends to help me. After everything he'd done—everything I know—I can't let my guard down for a second.

"Dell." He squats down before me, meeting my eyes. "If you stay perfectly still and perfectly quiet, I will set you free and get you to safety. I promise I'll explain everything, but you need to trust me. No screaming, no running. That's the deal. Nod if you understand."

Trust him? How can I trust him?

"We don't have time to waste," Tristen warns, black eyes scanning the withered expanse past my head. His teeth clench. "Nod. Your. Head."

Then again, do I have any other choice?

I find the wherewithal to nod once, and Tristen goes to work untying the knotted ropes that bind my wrists. When my hands are free, he plucks the rag from my mouth, tossing it into the pit.

I spit out a mouthful of pink, sea-trumpet-tinged saliva. He takes a step back.

"Can you stand on your own?" he asks.

Though my skin is burnt from tugging against rope, my mind still steeped in a thick drug-fog, I pull myself up to my feet without aid. I remain in place and quiet, as agreed, though all my instincts are screaming for me to bolt. I keep one eye on my cousin, the other on Prescott's body, lying nightmarishly still and much too close for my liking.

"Good. Okay. Follow me."

Without further explanation, Tristen takes off toward the coastline rather than back inland. If the goal is to get me to safety, why is he leading me to the water?

I pull my bleary eyes away, looking back the way I came. I know there's a path to freedom that way—a human-sized hole I once crawled through, and a gravel road beyond it, leading into town.

"You won't make it two steps over the fence-line," he urges. "Didn't you hear Greer? It's being guarded. If they find you out there, you're dead. The only way you're making it out of here alive is by sea."

I sway a little, feeling dizzy and jelly-soft to my core. I look from the dense brush on my left to the coastline on my right, weighing two options that seem equally treacherous.

Eventually, my eyes settle on Prescott's limp, hemorrhaging body. I'm not sure he's breathing.

"What about him?" I rasp.

"Don't worry about him," Tristen snaps sternly. "Worry about what's going to happen to *you* if you don't do as I say."

My insides burn at his haughty demeanor. I don't want Tristen's help, if that's really what he's offering.

"I had it covered."

My cousin's black eyes narrow to slivers. Did he expect my gratitude, my unending thanks? How do I know I'm not worse off with him than I ever was with Prescott?

"I was doing just fine before you showed up," I add sharply, in case he has any doubts about what I mean.

Tristen yields, his tight expression giving way to exasperation. "All right, Dell, yes. You mutilated his face, congratulations. Can we get moving now? We don't have time for this."

He trudges toward the coastline again while I seethe in my ire, forced into making a split-second decision.

I don't want to test Tristen's claims about the fence, but I also can't blindly follow him to the ocean without some manner of protection.

I reach down to grab Prescott's gun where it fell, tuck it carefully into the backside of my jeans, and trail after my cousin across the blackened fields to the sea.

CHAPTER FIFTY

Tristen guides me in silence toward the jetties that border this side of the island. We reach them as the sun breaches the ocean surface, casting the fields and the waves alike in radiant amber light.

Standing upon the rocks, the surf lapping at our feet, Tristen gestures vaguely into the far distance. "You're going to walk along the breakwater for about two miles and change. Eventually, you'll reach Prospero Pier. Do you know it?"

How could I forget it?

I nod, still suspicious of Tristen's true intentions, only slightly more secure now that I possess a weapon of my own. I'd shot a gun once before, years ago when a friend offered to set me up with her huntsman brother. He'd taken me skeet-shooting in the woods on our one and only date, and though we hadn't left with a romantic connection, I'd managed to get some solid target practice in. So if this all comes down to defending myself, I know I have a chance of at least scraping by.

"There will be a ship waiting for you by the pier," Tristen continues. "Go to it. You'll be safe there."

A ship? Whose ship? And how exactly did he expect me to get to it? By swimming through the same churning waters that drowned Callie Oxton?

"Do you really expect me to believe anything you say?" I ask him bitterly. "How do I know this isn't another trap?"

Tristen had been a willing participant in my capture last night. He'd apprehended me when I tried to escape, crushed my fingers under his boot, and blown powder in my face before hauling me off to the greenhouse. He'd vowed to lie to Palmer and June to divert suspicion at the wedding. He'd just prepared a sacrificial pyre for my murder.

"It's not a trap," he says emphatically. "And I'm not one of them. I'm only pretending to be."

"Pretending?"

He nods. "I'm working to take down the Brine from the inside. I'm...undercover."

"Like a cop?" I ask in disbelief.

"An informant," he corrects. "The HBPD and I have been working together for months, building a case against Greer and the others. And we're about to crack this thing wide open."

So the police *are* aware of the Brine's developments. They just don't want to admit it publicly, for fear of wrecking their sting operation, for fear of creating panic.

"Why now?"

"Because of you," he says adamantly, as if the stars had aligned thanks to my unwitting participation. "You're the first real abduction, and I finally have evidence of the Brine's intent to carry out premeditated murder. Before this, I could only nail them for smaller crimes—trespassing, unlawful assembly, drug possession and manufacturing. That's *nothing* compared to what they're actually capable of. Those charges wouldn't have kept them locked up for long."

"What about the other girls?" I ask. If what Tristen says is true—if he really is law enforcement's eyes and ears within the Brine—then why hadn't he managed to save Callie and Viola?

His hands ball into rigid fists, his Adam's apple bobbing agitatedly.

"Nothing linked the Brine directly to their deaths—nothing that could be substantiated in a court of law, anyway. Greer's smart, and she doesn't like getting her hands dirty. Her expertise lies in manipulation, and there's nothing intrinsically illegal about suggestion. Pushing bleak thoughts into a weakened mind, encouraging someone to end their lives for a larger purpose, is a nearly impossible thing to prove."

I shake my head, unwilling to believe there wasn't something he could've done to stop all this sooner, anything that might've prevented tragedy from striking twice in a matter of months.

"Why didn't you warn them?" I ask.

"I didn't have access to the other girls," he insists, "and I couldn't risk Greer catching wind of my subterfuge. I reported back to the police every detail I could, but I didn't know when or even how the girls were being groomed to die. My hands were tied."

Even if I could acknowledge some of Tristen's efforts, his excuses still fall far too short. "As Blackbane's wife, shouldn't she have been monitored all these years?"

"Wife is a very loose term. The marriage wasn't legal. Most people don't even know—"

"But isn't the fact that she was *in* the Brine reason enough to keep her on some kind of watch list?"

"Cops can't surveil citizens without cause. Greer's made herself a pillar in this community, the picture of a reformed woman. She's not an easy nail to hammer."

All this may be true, but I can't help but cling to my hatred for him. For all he'd done and failed to do. "Why should I trust you? You tried to blackmail my mother," I say quietly, resurrecting Mom's old stories. "You tried to use Willow against her, to hurt her."

"That was a long time ago," he replies darkly.

"And that makes it all right? Just water under the bridge?"

"Look." He grits his crooked teeth. "I'm far from perfect, okay? My life's been…tumultuous, and I haven't made it any easier for myself. I'm not asking you to forgive the things I've done. In fact, you don't have to like me at all. But I am doing what I can to make amends here.

And I'm going to get those girls the justice they deserve."

Tristen's words are a solemn promise breathed over the rolling sea. His face is partly cast in shadow, partly aglow in sunlight, like two warring camps—one light and one dark, mirroring the conflict within. Echoes of a mind pervaded in chaos.

"How valiant," I sneer at him. "Your crusade to save the girls, to make your little amends. You must think yourself so heroic."

Tristen looks away from me, a pulsing in his jaw. He doesn't jump to his own defense.

"You really expect me to believe that this has nothing to do with your father? That you're not motivated by your own desire to put him in prison? Be honest, Tristen. You want him to pay for how he's mistreated you. That's what this is about—revenge."

This is about more than justice for my sister, or for any of the other Girls of the Salt. This is Tristen seeking retribution.

His black eyes flick back to me. "Of course this has *everything* to do with my father," he snaps. "Greer's testimony is enough to put Florian behind bars. The HBPD will be forced to reopen Willow's case, with him as their prime suspect. He'd finally be held accountable for his crimes, for *all* the innocent people he's hurt. Yes, even me. Is that so bad? That I might want him gone? That I might actually want to secure some peace for myself?"

I remember seeing my cousin cower to his father's abuse. How much of that fear was real and how much of it was an act? Was it some meticulously crafted charade, or does he genuinely live in a constant state of terror—a boy who never outgrew his bully?

I cock my chin at his freshly bruised eye. "Did he do that to you?"

"Not this time," he says before quickly moving on. "Think whatever you like about me, cousin, but you need to get going, for both of our sakes."

I stare at him flatly, begrudgingly, with no choice but to put aside my feelings and do what ultimately needs doing. "Fine."

He nods. "Now, I do have one favor to ask of you, and I need you to do it, Dell. No questions asked."

"What?"

"I need you to promise that you will go about your day as if everything is normal," he insists. "Do not rush off to the police department. Do not run your mouth around town. Do not cause a flurry of any kind. Get yourself cleaned up and get to Palmer's wedding. Can you do that?"

How Tristen expects me to attend Palmer's wedding as normal—to eat, drink, dance, and be merry—after all I'd endured over the last eight hours is ludicrous.

"Tonight, the Brine will assemble at dusk for *Salemorte*," he explains. "They expect to bear witness to your sacrifice, but what they don't know is that the fields will be surrounded, swarming with police ready to arrest anyone that shows their face."

"And where will you be?"

"At the wedding, with you," he says matter-of-factly. "I have bigger fish to fry than Greer and her zombified minions."

It dawns on me what my cousin plans to do. My mind coils as tight as a corkscrew at the prospect.

"You're going after your father tonight."

Tristen nods, his mouth slipping ever downward. "The timing isn't ideal, but I'll have to make do. I'll wait until the wedding proceedings are over. After the party winds down, I'll pull him away from Cliffmoor House somehow. Once we're alone, the police will intervene. No one has to know a thing."

Except for me, I think. I'll know. And I'll be losing my mind with worry over every little thing that could possibly go wrong.

"Promise me you can do that," he implores. "Everything has to go off without a hitch tonight. Promise me you'll keep it together at the wedding. I'm counting on you."

His dark eyes latch onto mine. All his plans hinge on my total cooperation. All I have to do is enjoy the party and not act like an utter nutcase.

I owe my unsavory cousin at least that much.

CHAPTER FIFTY-ONE

Trekking alone down the ragged coastline, my mind is burdened by one all-consuming thought: I have no idea what to expect when I reach my destination.

Tristen hadn't given me the chance to ask many questions. Once I swore to keep my mouth shut at the wedding, agreeing to the somewhat obscure terms of our alliance, my cousin hurried off to take care of Prescott. What was left of Prescott, anyway.

Now, trudging across miles of uneven rock, I find myself second-guessing this harebrained arrangement. Tristen wouldn't want to draw attention to my escape, so I don't think I'll find a police escort waiting for me at Prospero Pier. Which begs the next question—if not the cops, then who?

Surely, he wouldn't want to involve any of the Klynes in his plan. The potential for someone to tip off Florian is too risky, and Tristen doesn't strike me as the gambling type. Who else would he trust?

Why did I ever agree to this?

Confidence waning, I scan my vicinity for other viable options. To my left is all dense, heavily-wooded forest. Attempting to enter and tramp through it blindly would get me nowhere but lost. To my right is endless ocean, drizzled in flecks of sunlight, with absolutely no rescue boats in sight. Turning back to the fields isn't an option either, unless I want to take my chances with the trigger-happy spawn of Blackbane. As daunting as it seems, the only sensible recourse is to continue onward, just as my cousin instructed. But I don't feel any better about it.

After an exhausting hour of walking, I turn a corner and finally get my first look at Prospero Pier by daylight. It's exactly as I remember it, jutting from the island like splintered bone from a body. Rickety, crumbling, and overwrought with decay, I can still envision little Callie Oxton hopping across those rotten beams like a bird, her nightgown chasing each careful step, her white figure perforating the total darkness.

As Tristen had described, an elegant wooden ship idles less than a hundred yards away from the pier. But I never imagined it would be this particular ship.

The schooner we'd taken to spread Virginia's ashes glints at me like a precious pearl of the sea, captained by none other than Patton Fortuna. As I plod closer to the pier, I spot the bearded captain himself planted at the ship's bow, face hidden behind a spyglass pointed toward land—toward me.

"Dell!"

My eyes snap to the sandy banks beneath the pier, my heart soaring at the sound of that voice.

Hatch is perched on the rocks below, and beside him, angled haphazardly into a crevice between the boulders, is a sun-worn tender boat big enough for two.

Seeing him here is too good to be true, like a lovely, flickering mirage.

He sprints up the jagged embankment to meet me, and I drag myself forward, practically tripping over my feet to bridge the gap between us. Once he's arm's length away, I pause, afraid that if I reach out he'll vanish—turned to dust or ocean spray in my fingers.

But then his hands are on my tired arms, his emerald eyes intently searching mine, and I know that this is no illusion. He's real, and he's here.

"Dell…" He says my name breathlessly, still panting from the uphill climb. "You're okay."

I nod, still a little dazed at the sight of him.

"I've been looking for you all night," he says.

"You have?"

He looks me over with a wild fury, eyes catching on every bruise, bump, and tear in my skin. "Lira called me. She said she saw you leave 'Cuda's with some guy she didn't recognize. Based on her description of the bastard, I guessed it was Prescott."

I don't react, solemn and unmoved, but it's enough to confirm Hatch's worst suspicions.

His nostrils flare. "Lira didn't like how intoxicated you seemed. She was under the impression that he might've drugged you, that you were in trouble."

I'm caught off guard by Lira's willingness to help me. I wouldn't have considered her a friend, exactly—more like a reluctant, derisive acquaintance—but Hatch's revelation makes me see her in a new light.

He reaches up, his thumb gently tracing the tender spot on my cheek the same way Prescott did earlier this morning. Except his touch has the polar opposite effect. All I want is *more*.

"Did he…" His green eyes flash, a far more dangerous gleam than that of the sparkling waves I attribute to them. "Did he do this to you?" His voice lowers, quiet and deadly. "Did he touch you at all?"

I shake my head, knowing full well that Hatch would willingly murder Prescott with his bare hands if he ever got him alone. If Tristen hadn't already, that is—and that's a big *if*.

"Who?" he asks, jaw clenched. "Who did it?"

"Some girl, Riley." I shiver in spite of the sweat I'd worked up. "It doesn't matter now. I'm okay. What happened after Lira called you?"

"I drove around for hours looking for you. I had no clue where you were staying, so I circled back to Cliffmoor House. That's where I ran into your cousin—"

"Palmer?" My stomach plummets at the thought of my pregnant cousin, on the eve of her nuptials, getting dragged into this chaos.

Gratefully, Hatch shakes his head no. "Tristen. I told him you were missing, that I was worried about you, but he insisted everything was fine."

Fine. What a gross understatement. I bite my tongue hard, cursing Tristen in silence.

"He was being super vague about where you were," Hatch goes on, "refusing to give me a straight answer. I got pissed and...things got physical."

I recall Tristen's swollen eye, the fresh bruise that he'd unexpectedly donned this morning. My gaze lowers to Hatch's hands, catching at the knuckles. The skin is cracked and caked in dry blood.

"You punched him?"

Hatch raises his eyebrows in silent confirmation, as if to suggest he'd gladly do it again. "The guy wouldn't tell me where you were. What'd you expect me to do, take him at his word and call it a night?"

"No...no, of course not." Giving up is the last thing I'd ever expect of Hatch. It isn't in him to abandon someone in need. He'd never once abandoned me. "What happened then?"

"I threatened him. Said I'd go to the police if he didn't come clean. That I'd cause a massive blow-out at the wedding in front of your entire family. Oddly enough, that seemed to do the trick. Tristen said he'd tell me everything, so long as I kept quiet and agreed to do exactly as he said. He came up with this plan—he'd return to the fields to release you, while I'd work on getting a boat out to Prospero Pier by sunrise. I knew I had to go to someone trustworthy, someone that wouldn't ask too many questions. Ergo, good old Cap'n Pat."

I squint out at the regal ship, from where the captain watches us through his spyglass. "How'd you convince him to come all the way out here?"

"Oh, easy." A hint of a smile plays upon Hatch's lips. "In exchange for a ride to the pier and back, I promised I'd pitch in with whatever labor or maintenance the ship needed, totally free of charge."

"You're working for him without compensation?"

"Something like that." Hatch shrugs, downplaying the lengths he'd gone to to ensure my safety. "It'll be fun, I think. What's a lifetime of indentured servitude anyway?"

It still amazes me that even when I don't deserve it, even when I have nothing to offer in return, Hatch is there for me, resolute and unwavering.

"Thank you," I say earnestly. "For coming for me."

"Of course." He shakes his head, his gaze on me soft. "It's the least I could do."

I'm not sure what he means by this, but he seems to be contemplating saying something more, putting words to some unspoken thought or long-buried emotion.

Please say something, I silently wish.

He gestures toward the captain's ship, tossing through the distant waves against a luminescent backdrop. "We'd better get going…"

Gingerly, he takes my hand and directs me to the tender. We walk without exchanging words, our footsteps wary, as though both of us are fearful of scaring the other away. All I can focus on is the sensation of his touch on me, and how right that feels after feeling wrong for so long. How vacant the world seems when his hand isn't wrapped in mine, when his arm isn't curled around my shoulders, when he's not leading me from darkness into the sun.

"Dell, you should know"—there's a dim ferocity in Hatch's tone now—"I asked your cousin to pulverize Prescott as a personal favor to me. I would've loved a shot at the bastard myself, but…logistics."

The image of Prescott's misshapen, lifeless body is still too fresh in my memory to offer any objective detail. I honestly may throw up if I give it too much thought. "Well. Consider him pulverized."

Hatch's jaw ticks. "Good."

He eases me into the tender, where I sit and watch like a lame duck while he works. I'm desperate to talk things out, to make amends and make us okay again, but Hatch is all business. He unties the ropes fastened to one of the pier's gnarled beams, cranks the engine until it purrs awake, and pushes off into open water, jumping into the boat in one swift, fluid movement.

We traverse the short waves to the captain's ship, making the trip almost entirely in silence. The closer we get, the more I lose my chance to reach him, as if bridging the ocean's distance only drives us farther apart. The morning sun glares down at us, incessantly bright and demanding, and Hatch gives it his full attention, eyes squinting against the rays of light, avoiding mine when I try to make contact.

Too late, I remind myself soberly. *I'm too late to fix this.*

Moments before we arrive at the ship, the tender lurching steadily forward, Hatch pauses and abruptly shuts off the motor. Our vessel sways uncertainly, moved by the gentle whims of the water, while Hatch straightens his back and inhales a salty breath.

When his eyes find mine, my heart stirs in my chest, rising up from the place where it fell last night, fluttering faintly with something like hope. Hatch's eyes are alive and burning, radiant as the sea that rocks us. And there—*right there*—is the look that I'd been missing, the look that brings me back to the heat of last summer. To us.

I don't know where or how to begin, but I know in my soul that I have to try.

"Hatch, listen, I—"

"I'm sorry," he blurts, his voice tight as a fist.

I shake my head, overwhelmed by what I haven't yet said, and astonished by what he had. "What in the world do you have to be sorry for?"

"For being such a jackass when you tried to apologize yesterday." He screws up his face. "I shouldn't have treated you like that. I can't help but feel like this is all my fault."

Leave it to Hatch to blame himself for my stupidity, to think that he'd failed me for being rightfully angry. For letting his momentary humanness get in the way of his habitual superhumanness.

"No, Hatch—"

"If I hadn't been so quick to turn you away…" His voice trails off for a few long seconds, rife with remorse, thick with emotion. "None of this would've happened. You wouldn't have been alone—"

"None of this is your fault."

"I don't know why I acted like that," he rambles, barely listening to my sporadic interjections. "I guess, because you showed up out of the blue, after months of not hearing anything, and…I don't know…I was pissed. And I just…lost it."

There's no way I'm letting him assume the burden of my choices. I'd arrived at this place by my own hand, no one else's, least of all his.

"Hatch, I'm the one who should be apologizing to—"

"Don't," he says sternly. "Don't try to make what I've done okay. Even last summer, when you were dealing with everything, I was so intense with you…I get that now. Between the news about your sister and your mom showing up, I shouldn't have expected so much. I shouldn't have pressured you."

Pressured me? My mind reels at him dumbing down everything between us, everything we'd shared, to physical nonsense. There'd been no pressure, nothing for me to resent. We were as natural as the current or the breeze, as infinite as the salt and the sea.

"But, Hatch, that's not the case at all—"

"I want you to know that you don't owe me anything," he insists without pausing for breath. "It's enough for me to know that you're okay, that you're safe. That's all I'm trying to do here, just make sure you're okay."

"Hatch, will you shut up?" I snap abruptly, taking his face in my hands, his stubble tickling the insides of my palms.

His lips part a little, shocked by my outburst.

"I'm sorry for the way I left things with you last summer." My words are a flood rushing straight from the heart. "You have every right to be pissed. You were so good to me, and I just made a horrible mess of everything. None of this is your fault, okay? It isn't."

Tears sting at my eyes. "I wouldn't take back anything that happened between us, not one second of it. So stop talking about me like I'm something you regret, like it was all a mistake. Because…because I don't feel that way at all, and I couldn't handle it if

I thought you did…"

I let my hands fall back to my lap, immediately missing the heat of his skin.

He's perfectly still, his eyes keen, waiting for me to finish my speech or give in to that crackle of electricity between us.

Or to let it fizzle out, once and for all.

Raw emotion tugs at the back my throat, the urge to kiss him overwhelming. Rallying my every last nerve, I lean in to his space—

"Delly!" Captain Patton calls from above.

—and stop short. Pull back.

The ancient captain waves at us, his singular crystalline eye glinting. "Seaborn didn't tell me we'd be scooping you up! What the devil are you doing out here?"

A rope ladder unfurls down the side of the elegant schooner, but neither Hatch nor I make a move toward it.

No, I think, my heart sinking, making a home of that depthless blue instead of with him where it truly belongs. *We're not ready to go.*

"What're you waiting for, an invitation? A carrier pigeon?" the captain howls, his every word ripping the moment farther from my grasp. "Get on up outta that damn dinghy!"

Like a bubble bursting, Hatch snaps out of his transfixed state. Silently, he starts up the tender's motor again.

No, no, no.

Within seconds, we cross the span of ocean to the captain's ship, and Hatch promptly reaches for the ladder, hands working tirelessly to keep his mind occupied.

Please, not yet.

"You first," he says quietly, eyes trained on the rope ladder.

I almost start to cry.

CHAPTER FIFTY-TWO

When Captain Patton again questions why I'd been traipsing down the north side of the island alone, I concoct a weak excuse about a solo camping trip gone awry, beefing up the part where Hatch indelibly comes to my rescue. But he doesn't so much as glance my way as we navigate to the seaport, as if he regrets our conversation and wishes he could take it all back. Like he'd unwittingly cracked open Pandora's box, let the feelings we'd shared clumsily slip out, and now couldn't fit them back neatly in place.

We disembark and say goodbye to the old captain, and Hatch wordlessly delivers me to the inn. He walks me to my door like I'm an obligatory job that needs completing, a task to be checked off a list.

At the door, he pauses, his expression distant—a language I can't decode scrawled across his face. It pains me to be so disconnected from him, like I'm hopelessly illiterate when all I want is to read him, cover to cover. I want to devour the chapters of his mind, savor every complexity, cling to the shape of every beautiful phrase, and write myself solidly into that story.

"Are you sure you're okay?" he asks. "You don't need to go to the hospital? Have someone take a look at your face?"

My hand flies to my cheek, probing the damage wreaked upon my flesh. The spot is hot to the touch and tender, but I'm pleased to find the skin unbroken. Still, I must look awful, like a waking nightmare. Like I'd been drugged, kidnapped, terrorized, and beaten.

Hatch's eyes trail the movements of my tentative fingers. "Your hand might need attention too."

The memory of Tristen's boot biting down on two of my fingers comes flooding back. I give them a hasty inspection, wincing at the sight of the swollen tips dipped in unsightly black bruises. Under other circumstances, I might entertain a visit to the hospital, but I can't elicit any unnecessary scrutiny today.

I shake my head. "I shouldn't. Tristen made me promise to lie low—"

"I don't give a crap about Tristen's mandates right now." His words are harsh, honed with frustration, and something else too…concern, maybe? Reticent affection? He sighs. "I only care about making sure you're all right."

"I am all right, Hatch," I respond gently. "Really, I'm fine. Promise."

He shrugs—not a gesture of dismissal, but of disagreement. "If you say so."

He glances down the hall, fidgeting in the silence caving in on us, insinuating that it might be time for him to go, time to leave the mess of this morning behind him—to leave me behind him.

And why shouldn't he want to? He'd gone well above the call of duty for some girl he barely knows. A transient romance from last summer, with no claim on his heart, hardly a blip in his memory. Plus, he had his own set of plans for today—plans to attend Palmer and Mojo's wedding.

Still, I can't help but ask him, "Do you…want to stay a while?"

Hatch hesitates, a quiet conflict swirling in his eyes, those shades of green twisting like the blocks of a Rubik's Cube, an ever-shifting puzzle

I can never seem to solve.

"I figured you might want some time to yourself," he says.

"I don't want that," I blurt, unable to keep it inside any longer, ignoring how pathetic and useless I sound. This is my last-ditch effort, my Hail Mary plea. "Don't leave, Hatch. Just stay, please? Stay and talk to me."

He inhales deeply, uncertainty radiating from his stance. I'm sure that he's going to say no—bracing myself for that heel turn, his retreating figure, and my own inevitable misery—but instead he says, "Okay. Let's do this inside."

I unlock the door with trembling fingers, and Hatch swiftly walks past me through the threshold. Hanging my head, I trail after him, baffled by his abrupt demeanor, the sharpness with which he moves.

I shut the door and turn to face the dark, curtained room.

Without warning, Hatch swoops on me, pinning my body to the door. His lips crash into mine, desperate and hungry, and I gasp into his mouth, surprised at first, then ignited by his passion. The depth of his kiss, his touch, brings me to life. Awakens me, as if I'd been unknowingly dormant for months. Asleep. Bereft. But now...

"Don't *ever* say that I think you're a mistake," he says fiercely when he pulls back, his eyes and hands traveling every inch of me. "The problem is not that I regret you, Dell. The problem is that I can't forget you."

Every muscle in his body is tight with longing, the room around us fading into colorless static. "And if I don't make myself leave now," he adds, "I won't be able to at all. I won't be okay if you up and vanish again."

I pause, my panting breath uneven. There lies the truth, the reason why he'd been so dizzyingly distant. Guarding himself from me and whatever harm I might inflict.

Every second we spend together makes Hatch all the more vulnerable, more susceptible to pain if I disappear a second time. In all honesty, the time away—the distance I'd forced on us both—should've dissolved whatever hold I had on Hatch's heart. But somehow, some way, that hold remained, like the bond we'd forged was shatterproof, wrought of sea and stars. Like we were anchored by unshakeable forces, far greater and more resilient than time or distance or dumb human weakness could ever destroy.

For some reason, Hatch still wants this, still wants *me*, despite knowing my tendency to run from any joy that drifts my way. But his desire doesn't make him a fool. He isn't blind to the truth of who I am—what I've done and what I'm capable of doing to us again. I'd put us both through a silent hell for months. So I can't blame him for denying me, for rejecting my apology, even if it did feel like a punch through my chest.

I need him to know I'm not the same girl from last summer. I know better now than to let him slip from my grasp.

I grip Hatch's neck and press my mouth to his again. His hands crawl around my back, caressing me, molding me to his body, until there's no space left between us, like an invisible seam runs from our heads to our toes, irrevocably joining the fabrics of us, blurring the lines of where he ends and I begin.

He moans my name against my lips, blazing a trail down my jaw and into the hollows of my neck. I'm drunk on him, consumed by his smell and taste, the sensation of being alive in his arms, and the knowledge that something had *finally* gone right.

Hatch presses his forehead to mine when we separate. He's steady as a rock—a fixed point for me to cling to—while the world spins madly around us. "Now I'm definitely not leaving," he murmurs, the tip of his nose brushing mine ever so softly.

"Good. Don't, ever."

A crooked smile spreads across his face. "For a minute there, I was sure you were going to kiss me in that tender boat. And when you didn't, I thought—"

"Shh. You thought wrong," I murmur, holding him close, relishing in this tiny, unbreakable moment. I don't know what the next moment, the next hour, or the next day will bring. But right now, this is everything. Everything and more.

Hatch shakes his head, fire dancing in his dusky green eyes. "I was waiting for you, Dell, hoping you'd come back…"

I can't help but laugh ruefully. "I'm sorry I made you wait." I mean it too, and not just for the last hour. I'm sorry I made him wait far longer than that. Not knowing whether I'd ever come back, whether I ever wanted to see him again. When, all along, I did… *I do*. Always.

"I'm not." His thumbs stroke down my cheeks, sending little tingles all across my skin. He bends down and kisses me, over and over, until my lips are raw and aching, until I'm dizzy with joy.

"You're worth every second," Hatch breathes, looking at me like I hold the key to his personal heaven. Like I'm the only thing that might quench some bottomless thirst in him—life-giving water, all he'll ever need. "I'm not a damn bit sorry."

When he smiles again, it fills me up with an inexplicable feeling. Solid yet intangible. Gentle but strong. Magic and real.

It dawns on me that I could look at his face—in his eyes—forever.

"What is it?" he asks.

I smile back, and for the first time in a long time, I'm not faking it. Not even close. "Need a wedding date?"

The slow, breathy kiss he plants on my lips is answer enough.

CHAPTER FIFTY-THREE

The Cliffmoor House gardens are shrouded in a camera-worthy haze of sparkling silver and gold. Crystal ornaments hang like water droplets from the canopy of oaks overhead. Chiavari chairs are arranged around an aisle dusted in snow-white rose petals. A crisp tent stands at a distance, boasting candlelit tables and lush flower arrangements, with a polished dance floor at its center. Wedding guests are scattered about the lawn, sipping their flutes of bubbly, abuzz in gossip and feverish chatter. Every one of them is oblivious to the dark threads pulsing behind the estate's shiny façade.

Walking in with Hatch on my arm is a welcome comfort amid a deeply uncomfortable setting. For one thing, the dress I'm wearing—the slate-blue, backless gown that Palmer gifted me months ago—hugs my body in all the right places, but still doesn't seem to fit me quite right. Maybe because it once belonged to my grandmother, and wearing it now makes me feel like a ghost myself.

For another, Sasha's eyes are red-hot laser beams on us the moment we cross the garden gate. She's draped against the cocktail bar looking stunning in a midnight-blue sheath, her glossy hair parted down the middle. No amount of professional makeup can mask her frown at seeing us enter hand in hand, scrutinizing us for a quick moment before turning back to her conversation, camouflaging any signs of jealousy behind a pretty smile.

I can't find it in me to be bothered by her today. Sasha is child's play compared to the real devil at this party.

I spot Florian rubbing elbows with a crowd of sharply dressed guests around a cocktail table. His hair, smile, and tuxedo sparkle as he lands some velvet-edged joke. He raises his martini glass in a toast, captivating his audience with that slithery, snake-like charm. Laughter erupts from the group with a vengeance, the roaring sound like an ax embedding deeper and deeper into my chest.

The weight of Prescott's gun tucked safely inside of my shimmery clutch purse is my most reassuring accessory tonight. I'd brought it as a last resort, in case something went off the rails with Tristen's plan, never imagining that I'd actually need, much less want, to use it. But now that I've seen Florian in person again—that bullish form and predatory flash of teeth—the thought of aiming the gun at his chest and pulling the trigger doesn't scare me. It *empowers* me.

Ridding this island of the monster in plain sight—watching the light drain from his eyes like he'd watched it drain from my sister's— would be worth every single year I'd spend in prison for the crime. But I know that killing Florian won't put a stop to the Brine's reign of terror. It won't vindicate Willow's murder or erase the lingering stain over Bram's name. Killing my uncle won't bring me closer to closure, so I have to do as Tristen instructed. I have to see this through.

Worry courses in my bloodstream, filling me with dread at the thought of who might get caught in the crossfire if bullets really did start flying. Hatch, probably sensing the war inside of me, laces his fingers in mine. Reminding me without words that he's got my back, guiding me away from a plunging cliff's edge. I hadn't told him about the gun in my possession, not wanting to trouble him unnecessarily, but he knows enough to direct me far from Florian anyway.

We settle into a couple of vacant chairs to await the start of the procession, and Hatch makes every effort to lighten my mood. He rolls his eyes each time an outlandishly-dressed invitee passes by, mocking the exotic frocks and jewels they'd dusted off for the occasion. I humor him, smiling along as best I can, but never losing sight of my uncle in the throng.

Eventually, the other party guests begin meandering through the rows to their seats. Leon and Finch plop down next to us, bickering quietly among themselves.

"Why would you show up at this swanky event looking like that?" Leon snaps at his friend.

Finch runs his hands down his sprayed-on, heather gray ensemble. He pouts. "What's wrong with the way I look?"

Leon's expression is deadpan. "That suit's suffocating you, bro."

"*Nuh-uh.*"

"*Yuh-huh.* You look like a castrated leprechaun."

He's right. Between the flaming red hair and the ill-fitting getup, Finch's leprechaun likeness is truly undeniable.

"This is Tanner's suit," Finch shoots back, his blanched lips pulling into a deep frown. "And it's the best I could do on short notice, so lay off, will you?"

Leon grimaces. "Your brother's half a foot shorter than you, Bird Brain. And about fifty pounds lighter too."

"Well, *excuse me* for not having any spare cash to buy a suit of my own. I blew all my savings helping you pay for repairs on that shitbox you call a car."

Leon gasps. "Too far. Completely uncalled for."

Finch folds his arms over his chest, the moody gesture causing his cramped jacket to stretch, tugging precariously at the seams.

"You've got a lot of nerve, insulting Mustang Sally like that," Leon says. "Especially since all she ever does is lug your pasty ass around town."

"The least you could've done is let me borrow one of your suits," Finch grumbles.

"The hell I could." Leon dusts the shoulders of his tailored maroon jacket. "I'm not about to let you ram your nasty, unwashed junk into my clothes. I invest a lot of money into looking this good—"

"My money!" Finch howls. "You invest *my money* into looking good."

Leon waves him off. "A minor technicality."

In spite of myself, I choke out a small laugh. Their banter is a welcome diversion from the mayhem of my thoughts, a lighthearted distraction I desperately need. But it's gone as swiftly as it came the moment I spot Briggs situating Ambrose at the front of the assembly.

My grandfather looks great, per usual. As charming as an old film star in his dapper tuxedo, he accepts handshakes and kisses from his many doting admirers. I don't see a reason to go out of my way to greet him. Since fleeing Cliffmoor House last summer without so much as a goodbye, I'm sure Ambrose knows there's no love lost between us. Plus, his uncanny resemblance to Florian is enough to launch my stomach into cartwheels. I decide to try to avoid him—and his eerie, unseeing eyes—altogether.

My attention soon turns to Tristen, who trails behind his father like a towering shadow. The two men join Ambrose at the front of the congregation, my cousin cloaked in an all-black tuxedo with a scowl drawn across his face, his hair gelled back neatly to the nape of his neck. He avoids my eyes as he slumps in his chair, settling into his dark and brooding persona.

I'd been wondering where he was for the last half hour, among a million other pressing questions battling for space in my mind. Is everything on track for Florian's arrest? Is Prescott alive? Has anyone else in the Brine gotten wise to my absence?

In an effort to preserve what remains of my sanity, I decide to take Tristen's routine surliness as a sign that everything is under control. That his plan—sketchy and obscure though it may be—is still on course.

When the musical duo, a talented harpist and violinist team, breaks into the initial refrain of some sweet and delicate melody, the wave of animated chatter among guests patters away. Heads turn and eyes fall upon the center aisle, everyone awaiting their first glimpses of the forthcoming wedding party.

A surprisingly well-groomed Mojo leads the procession in a bold, olive-green suit. He's accompanied by a middle-aged woman who shares his kind eyes and dark waves. They walk together, arm in arm, with wide smiles and bated breath, separating at the top of the aisle after an emotional embrace. *"Te quiero, mijo,"* the woman says sweetly, adjusting her son's boutonnière one last time.

Mojo takes his place beside the officiant, tapping some inaudible tune against his leg, beaming at the crowd, eagerly anticipating the arrival of his bride.

Leif walks down next, looking every bit like a pint-sized intellectual in his thick-rimmed glasses and adorable groomsman suit. His toothy smile has a few more holes in it since I last saw him, and he appears taller too—a realization that brings with it a twinge of remorse. I'd missed his seventh birthday. How had he changed so much in just a handful of months?

Bear plods beside Leif like a show dog, with a big, satin ribbon wrapped around his neck. The pair reaches the top of the aisle and files in beside Mojo, to the absolute delight of the guests. A collective laugh sweeps through the assembly when Bear settles back on his haunches and glances up expectantly. Leif offers him a bone-shaped treat from his jacket pocket.

Next is Sasha, model-strutting down the aisle with a small bouquet of white roses and eucalyptus, dazzling the crowd with her effortless beauty. Leon lets out a suggestive whistle when she passes, prompting Finch to burst into a fit of snickers, and pretty soon, they're both aggressively shoving each other back into silence.

The music morphs into a soft, lilting melody when the time comes for Palmer's big entrance. There's the rustle of skirts and creaking of chairs as everyone turns and stands to get a better view. And when she finally does emerge, everything else falls away.

Palmer is a walking dream.

Our grandmother's wedding dress drips from her body like it was made only for her. Tiers of white lace stippled in pearls cling gracefully to her figure, cascading down to an ethereal puddle at her feet. She'd had the gown's antiquated long sleeves modified to a gentler, off-the-shoulder style, giving the dress a certain fairytale quality. Her wispy yellow tresses are pulled back into a romantic bun, pieced together with a twisting vine of pearls and diamonds. Her freckled face is fresh and glowing as a summertime burst of sunshine, and a fluffy veil surrounds her like a ring of divine light. A bouquet of lilies spills from one arm, and the other is linked with June's, who looks flushed and teary-eyed, like she's spent the last hour battling a stream of waterworks.

Everything about this is achingly beautiful, a picture-perfect fantasy, and that makes me all the more uneasy. For Palmer and Mojo, today is a fresh start, a turning page in their love story. But beneath that idyllic, gleaming surface, it's also a day of reckoning, of closing the book on our family's history of horror, violence, and deceit. It's an intersection of beginnings and endings, innocence and justice, good and evil. When all is said and done, and the sun slips beneath the sea again, which side will prevail?

As she walks, Palmer's bright blue eyes connect with mine and widen with excitement or maybe relief, like she'd been worried that I wouldn't make it. Knowing full well how close that came to happening, I smile back at her reassuringly, unwilling to reveal the restless demons scraping at my mind.

There's no reason for alarm, I think. Tristen's handling everything. I'm safe—*we're safe*—and I refuse to put a damper on this magical moment.

Palmer passes my row and I'm able to make out the faint traces of a growing belly through her white gown. When she reaches her groom, slipping her fingers in his, it's heartwarming to realize that it's not just two of them up there, vowing to take on the world together.

It's three.

A new family growing from the ashes of another. And for the briefest of moments, this makes things immeasurably better.

CHAPTER FIFTY-FOUR

Mojo taps the silver microphone head. "Mic check. One, two. One, two." His voice rings through the tent, snapping the chatty, boozed-up crowd to fast attention.

Dinner service had already sped by—without incident, to my relief—and Mojo and Palmer have just cut into their decadent lemon meringue cake. As the wait staff distributes dessert plates to each table, Mojo stands to one side of the dance floor with the mic in hand, a mischievous smile on his lips.

He looks more like himself now, having loosened his bow tie, untucked his button-down, and shaken his hair back to its unkempt form. Behind him, Leon and Finch are chaotically scrambling to finish assembling their instruments, wrestling with a mess of electric cables, while predictably arguing about one thing or another.

"Evening, everybody!" Mojo nods around the space, acknowledging the hundreds of eager eyes on him. "I wanted to take a moment to say, on behalf of the new Mrs. Jordana and myself, thank you all for coming to celebrate with us today!"

Cheers and applause burst from every table. Champagne flutes are raised in the air, forks clinking discordantly against glass, and Palmer, sitting nearby at the sweetheart table, lifts a coy hand to her lips to shield her smile.

"And," Mojo adds teasingly, "as a special thank you, we have a surprise we'd like to share with all of you."

The guests instantly launch into whispers, humming their speculation, tantalized by the promise of fresh gossip.

"Palmer and I are excited to be welcoming a new addition to our *familia*. Come March of next year, we will be joined by—drum roll please…" Finch beats his drum set in rapid succession, ramping up to the moment of truth, marked by a crashing of cymbals. "A beautiful baby girl!"

Cries and squeals of congratulations spark up from the crowd like the boom and peal of fireworks.

"Thank you, thank you!" Mojo waves in Palmer's direction as if to yield all the credit to her. "Palmer's doing most of the work, but as you probably can tell, I'm responsible for the cringey dad jokes."

Rumblings of laughter again sweep across the assembly.

"We're thrilled to be embarking on this journey together, and to mark the occasion, I wrote a little something for the love of my life, my gorgeous bride…" There's more boisterous applause as Mojo picks up his acoustic guitar and climbs onto a wooden stool. He winks meaningfully at Palmer. "Here's my promise to you, sweet cheeks. Hope you like it."

The band breaks into the opening notes of a soft ballad, a tune that's as warm and honeyed as the feeling of first love. Amid his nimble picking and strumming, Mojo gently begins to sing.

The path ahead has long been tread by lovers and hopeful hearts like them.
You ask me, can we make it? How ever will we do?
What some might see as normalcy brings seas of new uncertainty.
You ask me, can we do it? Are you and I enough?

Oh angel, please, don't you ever forget…

That if our sleepless nights steal from the stars their light,
I'll find your diamond eyes—the dearest thing to my heart.
And if our days turn gray, clouds eclipsing the sun away,
I'll reach for your hand and stay—the nearest thing to my heart.

Miracle or coincidence? Perhaps a perfect accident?
However you'd like to call it, I'm shining by your side.
Drown out the fears and naysayers, your goldness blinds the haters.
My love they'll never shake, no matter how they try.

And Palmer, please, don't you ever forget…

That if our sleepless nights steal from the stars their light,
I'll find your diamond eyes—the dearest thing to my heart.
And if our days turn gray, clouds eclipsing the sun away,
I'll reach for your hand and stay—the nearest thing to my heart.

It's been this way since the ancient times,
Two lost souls walk the tightrope of life.
Can't help but think we'll be just fine…
I know we've been wrong before, but three feels right.

By the time the song ends, everyone is on their feet, gushing with praise and begging for an encore. Palmer flies from her seat into Mojo's arms, their embrace garnering a massive second wave of applause.

Taking advantage of the crowd's heightened energy, Leon sidesteps the couple and approaches the mic.

"All right, all right, party people!" He dons his best disc-jockey voice. "Grab a drink and get your fine selves out on the dance floor, because this night is just getting starrr-ted!"

Enthusiastic cheers pour from the crowd as the lights dim, and right on cue, Leon and Finch break into their next track—a trippy, guitar-heavy number that gets the entire party on their feet.

Within minutes, the elegant wedding morphs into a euphoric club scene. The dance floor is swarmed with women kicking off their heels and men slipping off their jackets, gyrating deliriously to the pulse of the music. Mojo and Palmer share the mic, half-singing, half-screaming the lyrics to one of the band's songs.

I crane my neck to peer through the tent opening, squinting into the night in search of Hatch. He'd stepped out a while ago to grab us some drinks, missing Mojo's announcement and subsequent performance, and he still hadn't made it back yet. I grapple with a sense of dread at not knowing what might be keeping him, especially considering that it's well past dusk. If all had gone according to plan, the HBPD had carried out their raid on the sea trumpet fields, and every last member of the Brine was in custody…or so I can only hope.

Tristen disappeared sometime during dinner, vacating his obligatory seat beside Florian to venture up the grounds to Cliffmoor House with a cell phone pressed urgently to his ear. Was he getting updates or giving them? My mind spins with questions like a game show wheel of unknowns and what-ifs. My fingers keep reaching for my clutch, for the security of the weapon hidden inside. Being relegated to the fringes of this plan—knowing both too much and painfully little—is driving me insane.

I have to find Hatch.

"Hey, Humpty."

Lira intercepts me as I squeeze through the undulating droves of dancers. She's dressed in a fiery red gown with a risky slit cutting up the length of her thigh. Her short hair is slicked back and wet-looking, and her dark gaze is accentuated by a metallic cat eye.

"How are you?" she asks tentatively, loud enough for me to hear over the booming music. It's a loaded question, fraught with unspoken worry, but she's treading carefully.

"I'm good," I reply earnestly. "Thank you for calling Hatch last night. I was out of it, and…you totally saved my ass."

It's impossible to verbalize how much she'd helped me without giving too much away, but I hope that on some implicit level, she understands what I mean.

Lira smirks. "It's girl code," she says candidly. "Us ladies need to stick together. Too many little boys with overactive imaginations out there."

I nod in agreement as she squints into my face, pointing bluntly at my cheek—a clear sign that she'd seen my bruised skin through the layers of makeup I'd applied. Concealer had softened the discoloration, but the stuff isn't magic. You can still tell something's wrong if you know to look close enough.

"Had another fall, Humpty?"

I shrug. "It's a disease."

"Tragic." She rolls her eyes. "But I'm glad you're okay, anyhow."

With a wink, she skitters away to the dance floor, leaving me wondering whether I might have more friends on this island than I'd originally thought.

I step out of the tent in search of Hatch, and before long, I see him, emerging from the inky swaddle of trees behind the guest house.

What's he doing out there?

He makes a bee-line in my direction, and the deep concern in his eyes hits me like a semi-truck.

"What's wrong?" I ask, instantly on high alert.

"Dance with me," he says as his hand scoops around me, fingers slipping beneath the fabric of my backless gown. A shiver of warmth ripples from that spot.

"Now? But—"

"Indulge me."

Hatch ushers me onto the dance floor, sliding a hand down to my waist. I wrap an arm over his broad shoulders. He tucks me in close, and we begin to move.

Dancing with him is everything I'd hoped it would be—our fancy dress clothes crushed between us as we sway and grind under the neon lights, his forehead dipped to mine, our eyes at once dusky and blazing-bright. If not for that lingering worry tugging at the edge of my consciousness, I'd be utterly captivated by him, the music, and the way our bodies fit like two halves of a whole. Everyone and everything else vanishes into the salty night air when we're together this way…but still, I know something isn't right.

"Hey." I lift my bruised hand to his cheek after a few minutes, cursing myself for waking us from this dream. "Tell me what's going on."

He sighs. "Can't we share one dance together before this night inevitably implodes? We're supposed to be enjoying ourselves, remember?"

My eyebrows shoot up. "Hatch."

He curls a finger around a lock of my hair, brushing my collarbone gently. We fall suddenly still. "Bram's back," he says quietly. "He's here. Now."

I'm stunned, my muscles tensing as I untangle myself from him. "You mean, *here* here?"

I scan the crowded party tent from left to right, a lump forming in my throat. Bram isn't permitted anywhere near the Cliffmoor House grounds. Why would he show up here during Palmer's wedding, where he could easily be seen by any number of people?

"He's out back. Says he needs to talk to you. Tonight." Hatch shakes his head like he can't understand it either. "And he says it's important."

CHAPTER FIFTY-FIVE

Even through the ebony darkness of night, it's plain to see that Bram is more distraught and disheveled than usual. His messy hair and beard are wilder than I remember. Stains mar his moth-eaten clothing. And while he still has a relatively brawny physique, he seems smaller and thinner now, as though he hadn't eaten much in the past few months.

There's an exhausted curve to his posture, a sunkenness in his eyes, and I have to refrain from throwing my arms around his shoulders, wishing I could keep him together when he's so obviously coming undone.

Bram nods at me in greeting, an unreadable expression in his eyes.

"Where have you been?" I ask breathlessly.

"Acquiring this."

He holds out an official-looking document, and I take it with shaking fingers, using my cell phone to shed some light on the page. Hatch leans in to read over my shoulder.

The document is titled *Halcyon Bay Medical Examiner's Report.*

"What is this?"

The question flops out of my mouth before my eyes can process what I'm seeing.

"Read it," Bram implores gruffly.

The Halcyon Bay Medical Examiner's Office has completed its death investigation of Willow Jane Klyne, a 13-year-old female born in New Orleans, Louisiana and resident of Halcyon Bay, Florida, and hereby releases all public data pertaining to this case, as defined by Florida law. This report summarizes all findings related to the post mortem examination of the deceased, including the conclusive manner and cause of death.

My eyes fly down the page to the section detailing these circumstances.

The deceased was found on Sandspur Beach the morning of June 28th, and was later identified by parents Ambrose and Virginia Klyne at Halcyon Bay General Hospital.

Evidence implies that the deceased was beaten prior to submersion. Autopsy of the body indicates that drowning was not the primary cause of death, but rather a secondary event. The overwhelming cause of death were injuries sustained to the cranial and spinal regions due to multiple blunt force traumas.

As such, the manner of death is reported as HOMICIDE, per the brutality of the deceased's injuries, which defy the justifiable parameters of any 'accident.'

I glance up from the page to meet Bram's dark gaze. "If the coroner's report classified Willow's death as a homicide," I say slowly, "then why did the HBPD close the case so quickly? Why call it an accident?"

"Because that's not the official report," Bram replies. "Not the one filed by the police department, anyway."

The hair on the back of my neck rises. "What is it?"

"This is Willow's *original* autopsy report, but not the one legally recorded by the state. This report was altered to describe a different set of circumstances, and the altered report—the fake—was sent to the State Attorney's office."

An instant head rush overtakes me, and I feel myself wobble in place. My every thought twists, writhes, and bends, making a pretzel of my brain.

"But why—"

"Somewhere along the line, the report was revised to state that Willow's cause of death was drowning," Bram says brusquely. "That her manner of death was accidental. They chalked up her injuries and blood loss to her body being slammed against the reef, and any record that she'd been savagely beaten was conveniently deleted from the record. Just like that—*poof*—no blunt force traumas, no homicide."

"Someone doctored it to cover up the truth," Hatch says, filling in the blanks.

"I'd always suspected this was the case," Bram growls, "but there was no way of knowing. The coroner, a man named Alan Katz, resigned in the weeks following Willow's death and moved his family up north. That in itself set off my alarm bells. I tried finding him through the years, but my efforts never went anywhere…at least, not until I met *you* last summer"—he squints at me with a tilt of his head—"when I decided to buckle down and track him, no matter the cost."

That's why Bram needed quick money, I realize. That's why he sold the *Willow's Wind,* and closed down the fishery. That's why he took this secretive trip to New York City, of all places.

"I spent every last cent I had hiring a private investigator to hunt Katz down. Selling the *Willow* was hard…but she paid off big. I had an address in my hands in weeks. And a couple of days later, I was on a plane bound for Manhattan."

He doesn't elaborate about what exactly went on during this visit or what methods he'd used to squeeze Katz for the truth, but the way Bram inhales sharply and the unsettling spasm in his lip tell me everything I need to know. It wasn't pretty.

"I got him to give me this," he says, taking the report from my trembling hands. His fingers cling to it for dear life, as if this singular document is his one shot at deliverance. "Katz confessed that in the days following Willow's death, he'd been paid handsomely to alter the report. He was bribed, and thanks to his greed, he let my kid's murderer go free."

Between this unnerving development, the distant throbbing of music, and the black night colliding with fluorescent party lights, the world around me seems to be slipping into pandemonium, blurring and distorting like a carnival funhouse.

It's not hard to imagine who had coerced Katz to falsify that report, or to deduce who had a bottomless reserve of money to pay him off.

Telling Bram about Florian will undoubtedly throw a wrench into Tristen's plans—it could even send Bram on the warpath, catapulting the evening into irreversible mayhem—but I can't bear to keep what I know from him. After everything he'd suffered at the hands of the Klynes—losing his daughter, his livelihood, everything he'd ever loved—I can't lie to him too.

I can't be like them.

"It was my uncle," I say, looking him straight in the eye.

Bram pauses at this, his breath quiet.

"Florian Klyne." I hold his darkened gaze even though it hurts. "He killed Willow, along with his best friend Kieran Blackbane, former leader of the Brine—"

"Dell…" I'm surprised at Bram's calmness as he interrupts me, pulling another sheet of paper from the stack in his hands. "I want you to read this next part too."

He hands me an addendum to the autopsy report with further detail regarding the supposed murder weapon.

The weapon in question is a long, heavy object like a walking stick or cane, bearing notable, carved features. In particular, the cane might have a hook-like handle or protrusion, which would

inflict a distinctive kind of wound consistent with the impressions noted in the injuries sustained by the deceased.

The horrible tightness in my chest worsens. "A cane?"

"Do you know who might've owned something like that?" Bram's words are slippery and far away.

Last summer, I'd seen a cane that fits the coroner's description, up in the rafters of Cliffmoor House, hidden in the attic like a devastating secret. Or, more likely, a damning piece of evidence.

My grandfather's wooden cane, with the fanged wolf face whittled into the handle.

"Dell?" Hatch nudges me, scanning my terror-struck face. "What is it?"

Had Florian used Ambrose's cane to kill my sister? Why would Florian even *have* his brother's cane if not because Ambrose gave it to him? Walking canes aren't something you pass around—they're a necessity, and Ambrose certainly needed his at the time. So why give it to his brother unless he had a good reason to?

Willow's shadowy memory of the two men on the beach floods my mind. The watcher stood there, paralyzed and unmoving, as his accomplice beat my sister to a pulp before dragging her into the deep.

Based on Greer's claims, I had assumed that Blackbane was the other man involved, the silent one watching from the shoreline.

But now, I can't be sure.

CHAPTER FIFTY-SIX

Tristen catches me by the arm as I sneak through the back doors of Cliffmoor House. He presses a finger to his lips and swiftly leads me down the hall and into the dining room, away from any prying eyes.

"What are you doing here?" he hisses.

"What are *you?*"

"Checking in with my team." He waves the burner phone in his hand. "The raid went smoothly. Everyone's in custody."

"Prescott?" I ask, my chest tight as a balloon.

"They found him tied up in the closet, right where I left him."

Recalling the closet where I spent the better part of the evening chained to a wall like a howling animal, my fingers ball into fists.

"He's still alive?"

"Still breathing," Tristen replies vaguely. "They're moving him to the hospital now."

"Are you in trouble for what you did?"

I can't imagine that bashing someone's skull in with a shovel is acceptable practice, even in the course of a covert operation.

Tristen shrugs like he couldn't care less. "Prescott had to be subdued so that you could escape, simple as that."

Of course, he's right, and I'm in no position to dispute his methods.

"Now, tell me the truth," he says. "Why are you poking around the house?"

"There's something I need to find," I divulge quietly. "Something that might be useful in reopening Willow's case. Abraham Urban came to see me tonight—"

"Urban," Tristen repeats the name as if to jog a memory loose in his head. "You mean your—"

"My sister's father," I finish his sentence, surprised at the ease with which I utter those words. It had been a secret buried for so long, encapsulated by so much mystery and speculation, the truth was practically begging to be said.

"Apparently, he's been doing some investigative work of his own. He managed to track down the coroner who performed Willow's autopsy, and, get this, her death was originally classified a *homicide*, only someone paid the guy to forge the report and skip town."

"Surprise, surprise," Tristen murmurs, likely working out in his mind who that someone might've been.

"Her real cause of death was multiple blunt force injuries. And the description of the murder weapon reminds me of something I saw last summer."

This piques Tristen's interest. "What?"

"Based on the shape of Willow's wounds, the coroner determined that the weapon was some kind of walking stick with a carved, hook-like protrusion. It sounds an awful lot like one I found in the attic."

"This attic?"

I nod solemnly. "It belongs to Ambrose."

Tristen's coal-dark eyes narrow as he grasps the unavoidable implications of my words.

"What if it *wasn't* Florian and Blackbane who killed Willow?" I ask, desperate for an opinion I can trust—some levelheaded clarity to bring me closer to the surface, up and away from the murky depths of my thoughts. "What if it was *Ambrose* pulling the strings all along? What if your father was just…his lackey?"

"We need to find that cane," Tristen affirms.

Anticipation surges in me as we rush down the hall and up the stairs in tandem.

"You don't have to babysit me, you know," I say. "You should be back at the party, keeping an eye on things. I've got this."

"I'm not babysitting," he replies cuttingly, keeping pace with my hurried steps. "If there's a development in your sister's case, then I need to be involved. I can't have anything going awry when my father is apprehended. Once he's in custody, I need him to stay that way. And now we're looking at *two* possible arrests. Identifying a murder weapon and turning it over to police would be major. Who knows, maybe it still has some usable DNA on it that can be tested."

We slip through the door at the foot of the attic and ascend the familiar spiral stairwell. Stepping through the threshold at the top of the landing, I make sure to drag the curtains all the way across the window, effectively blocking us from view.

"Don't hit the light," I warn my cousin, "or else they'll see us from the gardens."

I pull out my cell phone, using the white glow to search the attic space. As far as I can tell, nothing had been touched since last summer, and it's not long before I locate Ambrose's collection of knives. Perched right next to them is a cane, the one I tripped over months ago. The one with the carved wolf's face.

I sink to my knees to get a closer look. The wolf's jaws are open, its fang-like canines bared, poking from the cane in a bizarre hook shape just as Katz's report detailed. I hadn't noticed before that the wood is marred by dark, rust-toned stains.

A shudder runs from my shoulders to my toes. This could very well be Willow's blood, infused deep into those layers, her source of life bonded to the instrument of her destruction.

"Is that it?" Tristen winds through the dusty clutter to reach me.

I nod, handing him the cane, careful not to touch *that* section. He takes it from me gingerly, using my cell phone light to scan the length of it, examining the series of striations and smears sunk deep into the wood.

I slide to the floor while he does his preliminary inspection, letting myself be swallowed up in a cloud of grime and grief. The sounds of the party below glide up the walls like some nightmarish soundtrack.

"I've got to call this in," Tristen says finally, returning the cane to my hands. He begins dialing a number on his burner phone.

The overhead bulb in the room flicks on, and the space bursts with brilliant light, momentarily blinding us both.

"Well, well, well. This is a strange sight."

I jump at the creeping voice coming from the top of the stairwell.

Florian leans casually against the iron banister with an inscrutable curve on his lips. How long had he been lurking there? How much had he heard?

I scramble to my feet while Tristen takes a hesitant step in front of me. I can practically see his gears already grinding out some explanation for why we're here.

My heart beats wildly as I scan the room for my purse, for the *gun*. I'd put it down atop the windowsill when I drew the curtains…and there it sits, right next to Florian's hand.

Shit.

"I've been looking for you everywhere, Meridel," Florian says with a cryptic smile. "Your grandfather heard you'd returned home, and he's quite eager to speak with you. But why the pale face? You look like you've seen a ghost!"

"Meridel was looking for an old trinket," Tristen jumps in, the lie rolling from his lips as easily as dice. "A necklace that used to belong to Aunt Ginnie. She wanted to give it to Palmer as a wedding gift."

"Oh?" Florian runs his tongue across his teeth. "And did you find what you were looking for?"

I shake my head, reluctant to speak for fear of saying the wrong thing.

"Seems that Briggs tidied up a bit since last summer," Tristen chimes in. "I was about to escort Meridel back down to the party."

"Yes, that'd be best," Florian agrees slowly before his eyes land on the object in my hand—the wolf cane.

My grip on it tightens as Tristen tenses beside me, his stony façade quietly crumbling.

Florian breaks into a devilish smirk, as if he's figured something out in his mind. "Why do I get the feeling I'm being lied to?"

"What would we have to lie about?" Tristen counters.

"I haven't the foggiest, son." Florian cocks his eyebrow. "Perhaps Meridel can elucidate for us." His vacuous eyes land squarely on mine. "What's that you're clutching so intently?"

"This? I fell over it. Clumsy feet." My words squeeze out from behind clenched teeth.

"Oh, well then, it's a wonder you're all right." Florian's eyes flash at me. They're black as coal, like his son's, only emptier and more desolate. Cold and severe as a Siberian winter. "A cane like that could do some terrible damage, you know."

I could gouge his eyes out with my fingernails. Is he actually taunting me? Mocking my sister?

I loathe him.

Tristen nudges my back like he can sense the rage threatening to sweep over me. I feel him willing me to calm down, leveling me out, unruffling my feathers.

Act normal. His urgent words echo in the quivering chambers of my brain, both a warning and a lifeline meant to keep me in check.

"Before you manage to maim or mangle yourself, cousin"—Tristen snatches the cane from my hands, his words laced with snark and superiority—"I'll just put that back."

I subtly meet my cousin's eyes. I can practically hear him breathing stern commands my way. *Cool it, Dell. Don't blow this now.*

Tristen returns the wolf cane to its resting place while I watch on tensely, wishing I could stop him somehow. Ambrose's cane is a pivotal piece of evidence for us—our only piece of evidence—and now it's caught in the crosshairs of this stalemate with Florian. He'll make that cane disappear at the first opportunity. How the hell are we going to retrieve it without him noticing?

My uncle flourishes a hand toward the stairwell, tilting his head in that slimy manner of his. "After you."

I slide quickly past him, grabbing my purse in a haste. A small wave of relief washes over me at having the gun back in my possession. I'm itching to shove the barrel into Florian's smug mouth, but I quickly descend the stairs instead, remembering Tristen's instruction, expecting the men to follow suit.

When I don't hear footsteps behind me, I turn to find Florian pressing an arm against Tristen's chest, restraining him from leaving the room.

My uncle glances down at me and cracks a terrible smile. A smile like an omen. "We'll be another minute, dear."

The sweet tone of his voice doesn't match the red rage in his eyes. Something terrible brews in the air—the unmistakable tingle of danger, and the scorching threat of abuse.

"Go on ahead. Find your grandfather."

Florian moves to shut the attic door at the top of the stairs, one I never even noticed was there. The last thing I see before the light is extinguished and the stairwell consumed in darkness is Tristen's face: eyes wide, jaw clenched, bracing himself for a vicious confrontation.

My fingers fly to the clasp of my clutch, twisting it open, my swollen fingers pulsing. Two seconds and I can have the gun out and at the ready, muzzle trained at Florian's chest. Two seconds.

But Tristen mouths at me sternly, *Go.* He's trying to save me, to shield me from becoming the object of his father's violence, and keep me from shattering his fragile plan like glass.

I'm rooted to those spiraling iron steps for a long moment, paralyzed as the attic door clicks shut above me, closing in terrible slow motion, until I'm alone in the blackness.

Eventually, I have no option but to slip back downstairs, wondering what Florian is doing to his son, what cruelty Tristen is having to endure, and if this is the moment he'll deliver his father to the police. Wondering if he'll be able to keep his emotions in check, or if he'll shed all control and retaliate with brute force, the way he had with Prescott in the fields. Wondering, wondering about all of this, until it nearly drives me mad.

The grounds are chaotic now that the party has spilled into the gardens, everyone chirping excitedly as they assemble to send off the bride and groom. Guests cluster into two long lines, all of them grasping lit sparkler sticks, most of them belly-laughing and out-of-their-minds wasted. Truly, deeply, enviably happy. Blissfully unaware of the hidden menaces around them.

Palmer and Mojo weave through the guests, pausing for photographs amid the lively crowd. It's hard for me to focus on them when I'm searching for Hatch among the blur of faces. I'd asked him to help Bram sneak away from Cliffmoor House unseen, but that feels like eons ago. What if something had happened to them? What if someone had spotted Bram on the grounds? What if the cops surrounding Old Town, armed and ready for Florian's capture, had intercepted *him* instead?

"He's not here."

I turn to find Sasha glaring at me with her pouty face and crossed arms.

"Hatch," she clarifies, the downward slant on her crimson lips deepening. "I'm assuming he's who you're looking for?"

Apart from the fact that I'm wholly uninterested in anything Sasha has to say, the last thing I need right now is to get swept up in some jealousy-fueled pissing match. I ignore her and continue scanning faces, praying for Hatch to materialize among the raucous crowd and electric whirl of sparklers.

"If I happen to see him, I'll let him know you're looking for him," she offers, completely catching me off guard.

"What?"

Her lips twitch a little, like she's made herself uncomfortable by extending this small and unexpected kindness. "You *are* looking for Hatcher, aren't you?"

"Yes."

"So I'll just, you know, give him a heads up if I see him."

I narrow my eyes at her. "Why would you help me?"

Sasha lifts one perfectly bronzed shoulder, avoiding my narrowed gaze. "I'm trying this new thing where I don't act like a heinous bitch all the time. Maybe earn some points in the 'good karma' department."

Noticing the uncertain grimace splashed across my face, she rolls her lush, mascaraed eyes. "Look, I'm not trying to braid your hair or force you to wear matching friendship bracelets or anything. I promised Palmer I'd make an effort, so that's what this is. Take it or leave it."

Her candor about the situation is something I can appreciate. We don't have to be friends, but we can do without being enemies.

"Okay. Thanks."

She nods before slinking back through the throng, satisfied at having carried out her one charitable deed of the night.

As Palmer and Mojo wrap up their exit walk, skipping merrily toward their getaway car—an antique roadster with tin cans and ribbon attached to the bumper, and a *Just Married* sign in the window that looks a whole lot like Leif's artistic handiwork—I spot the silhouette of a wheelchaired figure rolling away from the party. He moves up the curved walkway and toward the pitch-black beach.

Amid the shouts and the cheers and the waving, I steal away from the group and silently begin to follow.

CHAPTER FIFTY-SEVEN

I sneak behind my grandfather, deliberate and slow, unwilling to rush whatever comes next. No matter what happens, however this conversation goes, it likely won't end well, but I'm not deterred. Like a predator stalking its prey, I tiptoe through the night in the old man's wake, armed with the gun tucked into my purse—my one defense and consolation.

If Ambrose knows he's being followed, he doesn't show it for a second. He nears the beach and abandons his chair in the sandy dunes, and I'm momentarily shocked at seeing him stand, at seeing him *walk*. There's a limp in his movements, a swing in his gait, but he's undeniably mobile, more than I ever thought him capable of.

A trench forms in the sand where he drags his crippled foot behind him, all the way to the lapping shoreline. There, he pauses to stare at the endless ocean and beyond.

I emerge from my veil of darkness to join him by the sea.

"Ambrose." My voice rips through the silent atmosphere.

He turns his head in my direction, flashing me that signature winning smile, appraising me through the night with his swirling, marbled gaze.

"Is that my granddaughter?"

Something indefinable in my grandfather's expression—in his biting smile and barb-like eyes, in the puzzling darkness ticking beneath that aging skin—brings everything into sudden crystal-clear focus.

Willow's sea glass dangling from my neck is freezing-cold against my chest, like a sudden dousing of water, spilling ice into my veins. A confirmation of truth from beyond…from *her*.

Confirmation that beneath Ambrose's dashing exterior beats the heart of a killer.

Her killer.

"Yes," I say quietly. "It's me."

He opens his arms wide, inviting me in. "Meridel, darling. You're home!"

My response is deadpan—deadly. "This is not my home, Ambrose."

His grin slides downward as he lowers his arms, realizing I have no intention of hugging him, or even going near him. But then he catches himself, and that slippery smile finds its way back to his face.

He chuckles, the sound of it sinister, like a whispered threat in the dark. "If I didn't know any better, I'd think I was speaking to Laurel. She shares your rampant distaste for this island…and this house."

On this, we agree. "That's putting it mildly."

He turns his face from me back to the sea, as if I've bored him with my inane conversation. He changes the subject. "It was a beautiful wedding, don't you think? And this moon…" He lifts a hand toward the blanket of sky, where the bulging moon drips its silver-white glow. An unfeeling spectator to our tense exchange. "Marvelous," he croons.

Maybe Ambrose *isn't* blind at all. Appearances are never what they seem with him, and those gray-orb eyes, like the wheelchair and the smile, may just be another ruse. A means to disarm.

"How could anyone dislike a wonderful place like this?" he continues casually. "It's baffling that one could be so small-minded and provincial."

"Baffling," I repeat slowly, finding perverse irony in his word choice. "More baffling than what, exactly?" I dig my fingers into my clutch, feeling for the shape of the gun again. "More baffling than the senseless murder of a child?"

My statement slices through the night like a finely honed blade.

Ambrose turns to me, almost curiously. "You have quite a wayward imagination, Meridel," he complains, his brow layered in wrinkles. "What's this all about?"

The howling wind grows anguished and fretful, waves crashing like fists atop our feet. A storm looms over us to match the one battering my insides, the smell of impending disaster mingling with salt.

"I know what you did, Ambrose."

My grandfather's face takes on a veneer of bewilderment, as though my accusation has come completely out of left field.

"What *I* did?" His voice is impossibly soft.

I hate him with every last cell in my body, but I can't surrender to my own chaos, to the parts of me that yearn to tear him limb from fucking limb. I need to be smarter, sharper than that.

"To Willow," I clarify.

The world abruptly quiets when I utter her name, the wind and the surf falling still in tandem. All that's left are vestiges of the party in the distance, lightning flashes mingling with purple clouds, and my own thundering heartbeat rattling my bones.

My grandfather scoffs. "Meridel, whatever you *think* I did—"

"It's not what I think. It's what I know."

"And what do you know, exactly?" he asks. "What do you presume I did to that child? To my own daughter?"

"Don't play dumb with me." My voice is as brash as the fits of wind engulfing us again. "You know damn well that Willow wasn't your biological daughter. She was my mother's daughter. Your *granddaughter*."

Shadows fall across Ambrose's face as the moon takes cover behind a mass of storm clouds.

"But you were the only father she knew," I say, my anger mounting. "She was an innocent little girl, and you were supposed to protect her, to keep her safe. So I want to know why. Why did you do it?"

"Do what, exactly?" he finally snaps, testing me, pushing me to an irreversible point. There's no coming back from the place we're headed.

"Why did you kill my sister?"

After a long moment of stillness, Ambrose lets out a harsh sigh. "Is that the latest rumor flying around town?"

"I've seen the autopsy report," I counter. "Not the counterfeit one, the *real* one. The one you paid Alan Katz to conceal. Smart move. With the feds off your back, who would dare question you?"

"Please. This is utter nonsense."

"I know about the cane too," I add. "The one with the wolf's face. That was your weapon, wasn't it?"

Ambrose's face contorts with heat and aggravation. "I strongly advise that you let this go, Meridel. Casting aspersions on me won't amount to anything—"

"We'll see what the police have to say about that," I respond, gauging his shifting expression in the dark. "Tristen's got them on standby to arrest both you and your brother tonight."

"On what charges, exactly?" He laughs. "Is Tristen the one that's filled your head with all these preposterous theories?"

I glare at my grandfather in stark silence. He'd denied everything and admitted to nothing, leading us to an obvious impasse. I wonder how Tristen is faring with his father, if there's any chance it could be going better than this.

Ambrose clears his throat, as if to say he's finished with me and my abounding unpleasantries. As if this is all so beneath him.

"Well-meaning as your efforts may be, Meridel, these accusations are little more than misplaced delusion. It was the same case with your mother, and your grandmother before her. Insanity runs in your blood, I'm afraid, but it's no excuse for treating me like some common criminal."

He's an expert at pivoting the conversation to the thing I dread most, drawing out my deepest fears. The risk of losing myself to this island, of being fundamentally changed—twisted up by this twisted place—is the worst thing imaginable.

"I'm not insane," I growl. "And neither is my mother."

"You are well on your way," he retorts, taking a few menacing steps forward. "Supposing I am the savage killer you take me for, isn't this the last place you'd want to find yourself? Alone and defenseless, on the same dark beach where Willow died? Behavior like yours positively screams insanity."

My heart pounds as I unclasp my clutch and grab for Prescott's gun. "I am not defenseless," I say, holding the weapon down at my side. "Do not come any closer."

Ambrose freezes when he spies the glint of metal in the moonlight. "Oh no, Meridel. No, no, no…" He makes a deprecating *tsk-tsk* sound with his tongue. "Don't be rash, darling. I know that in this fantasy of yours, you think of yourself as some dauntless heroine, come to slay the dragon and avenge the fallen princess, or something equally as banal. But that"—he wags a gnarled finger at the gun in my hand—"doesn't make you the heroine. It makes you the *villain*."

The curl on his lip, a malignant little smirk, tells me this is all one massive game to him.

"Just tell me why you did it," I repeat.

A horrible crashing noise erupts from the Cliffmoor House grounds. Not a gunshot, more like the sound of rapid impact, like a car smashing full-speed into a tree. An onslaught of terrified screams burst in the distance. An icy jolt shivers down my spine as the screaming intensifies, the party spiraling out of control.

Something strikes me hard on the back—a painful collision that sends me toppling forward, face-first onto the dampened sand and barely clinging to the gun.

Grit blurs my vision, and I turn to find Ambrose's form closing in. Panting, lurching, he reaches for the gun. I fumble back in a panic, sand spraying up like a fountain over my head. I will my shaking fingers to get a firm grip on the weapon. Fueled by raw adrenaline, I rack the slide and point the barrel at my grandfather, my index finger lightly grazing the trigger.

The distant screams grow deafening, and I know that something awful is happening on the other side of that walkway. My mind pulls in every direction, stretching and twisting like saltwater taffy, utterly terror-stricken.

His dark shape towers over me, contoured by a milky sheen of moonlight. "You want to know why I killed your sister?"

The question comes in-between breaths, so low that I almost can't believe what I'm hearing.

At long last, an admission…a confession.

He drags himself closer and closer, looming like a skyscraper while I'm rooted in place—paralyzed, drowning.

"Willow is dead because my wife and daughters built empires of their lies. Time and again, they deceived me, all the while reaping the fruits of *my* wealth, *my* fortune. But all buried things rise to the surface eventually." He grins cruelly. "Just as the sea churns up the contents of its waters and splays them out on the coast for all to see, secrets can only remain secret for so long. And once those secrets are exposed, consequences must be enacted. Damages must be paid."

I keep the gun unflinchingly poised at his chest, despite the tremors stretching through every part of my body. At this range, even an inaccurate shot could be fatal.

"Don't misunderstand me, Meridel. I didn't dislike the child, but a man can only accept so much dissent—so much *disloyalty*—under his own roof. My first thought was to eliminate my swindling, two-faced slut of a wife. Virginia was, after all, the source of all the secrecy. But I knew I'd be the prime suspect if the beloved Ginnie Gold met an untimely end. So it had to be someone else, someone whose absence would hurt her beyond measure. Someone I could subdue without too much trouble. And on that summer solstice night, when Willow snuck off to the beach alone, I saw an opportunity. And I took it."

Piping, angry tears stream down my cheeks. I don't need to hear any more of this. All I need to do is pull back the trigger and let one single bullet fly. I can put a stop to this madness.

"I wasn't sure I could go through with it at first," Ambrose continues. "But when Willow turned around on that walkway, there was something about the way the moonlight shaped her face…" He shudders in disgust. "In that moment, the girl was a stranger to me, an uninvited interloper enjoying the charmed life I'd afforded her. She was identical to that Urban boy—that miscreant fleabag from the outskirts of town, the one who impregnated my Laurel. His was the face I saw in the moonlight, and I was instantly filled with hatred for the girl. It made my decision quite simple, in the end."

Sirens echo across the beach along with flickering blue and red lights—police descending upon the grounds of Cliffmoor House. The sharp sounds of people screaming and sirens wailing stab at my mind.

How will they know to find me out here?

"The only person who'd seen what I'd done was Florian, but I had no reason to worry about my brother," Ambrose goes on, undeterred. "He himself is no saint, and we share a certain understanding of things. I played the part of the grieving father, while Florian bribed the coroner. He pointed every gossip-monger and journalist in town to Urban's doorstep. He even jazzed up the story enough to provoke Kieran Blackbane's cultish delusions." He snickers, delighted by the horror story he'd authored. "Before long, the Brine was born, Halcyon Bay was on to its next great tragedy, and your sister was all but forgotten in the fray."

"Bastard," I choke out.

He ignores me. "My whore wife, of course, had some suspicions about my involvement. Oh, how it drove her mad, not knowing whether she shared a home—*a bed*—with a killer. When your mother moved away, Virginia felt she'd lost two children, and I watched her die a marvelously slow death, rotting from the inside out, consumed by her grief and her loneliness. Befriending ghosts, of all absurdities! It was exactly the outcome I'd always wanted, to watch Virginia cripple. To watch her *burn*."

Ambrose tilts his head down at me pitifully. "So you see, Meridel, your sister was no more than a necessary casualty. A pawn in a greater power struggle. A small fish in too large a pond, much like you."

"Shut up!" I scream, squeezing the gun so tightly that my sprained fingers begin to cramp.

"You must learn to curb those wild emotions of yours," Ambrose balks. "The world doesn't operate on love or compassion. All that matters is power, and what you're willing to do to keep it."

"You're wrong."

"Drop the gun and then tell me I'm wrong," he counters. "Because as far as I can tell, you and I are the same. We both want control, security, power. Deep down, you know that forgiveness is frailty, that mercy is weakness. That's why you won't put down your weapon—because you know you'd be a fool to. Because that isn't how the world works. You'd sooner shoot me than relinquish your power. And so we are exactly alike."

"I'm *nothing* like you."

"Prove me wrong, then," he goads, enunciating each word. "Put. The. Gun. Down."

"Shut up," I repeat, forcing myself to ignore his taunting. "The police are coming, and we're going to be right here when they do."

"Bloody hell. At least have the fortitude to shoot me yourself." He opens his arms wide, a sickly distortion of the hug he'd offered me moments ago. "Go on. Shoot me, granddaughter."

"No," I say through clenched teeth. "Shooting you is too generous. You're going to pay for all you've done, Ambrose. With every breath you take, every minute of every day, for the rest of your pathetic life, *you are the one that's going to burn.*"

My grandfather makes a bone-chilling smile, a ghastly flash of white perforating the dark. "You, my darling, are far more like me than you care to admit. It's a shame we didn't get more time together."

He lunges forward as I aim the gun left of his head, discharging a wide shot straight out to sea. The blast momentarily stuns us both.

Someone definitely heard that, I think triumphantly. *Someone must be coming to find me now.*

In a flash, Ambrose bowls into me with all of his might, his hands finding my neck and pressing me down into the sand.

"Clever girl," he growls, fingers squeezing above my collarbone, crushing my windpipe. "A clever little liar, just like all the others. But no matter. You'll join them shortly."

Unable to breathe or get a firm enough grasp on the gun to shoot, I lift my arm and bring the weapon down as hard as I can, pounding it against his temple. Ambrose cries out, his hold on me loosening, giving me the opening to clobber him a second time. He recoils from the blow while I kick against sand, writhing and wriggling out from under his weight.

Disoriented, I scramble to reset the gun, but Ambrose is faster this time, hurling himself onto my hand. There's a grotesque crunch in my wrist when he wrenches it out of my fingers, and instant, searing pain shoots up my arm.

He turns the weapon on me—the cold, black hole of the gun's muzzle level with my gaze—and smiles that winning smile.

A shot discharges. I scream, certain I've been hit...

But it's Ambrose's body that goes limp, a circle of blood spreading across his chest, saturating his elegant shirt in crimson. He crumples onto the sea foam, and the figure behind him slowly comes into focus.

Bram stands several feet away, a smoking pistol dangling from his right hand, his face unrecognizable. He seems clear, for once. Filled with determination.

"Bram, don't!" I call as he lifts the pistol again, but my voice is barely audible over the torrent of gunshots.

He shoots at Ambrose's body over and over again until the water and the sand and that heap of lifeless, misshapen limbs mingle and burn blood-red. Only after he's unloaded every single bullet, when the beach seems on fire with all that blood and death, does Bram finally drop the gun and sink to his knees. He doesn't look at me, despite my cries of desperation. He just stares out at the sea, as if in conversation with it— his purpose finally fulfilled.

A fresh peal of gunshots ring out in the night—two, four, six all at once—and Bram is hit now, his body collapsing onto the sand like a shapeless sack of potatoes.

"No!" I scream feebly, arms raised over my head. "Stop it, please!"

I crawl to Bram when the shooting ceases, tears running in rivulets down my cheeks. When I reach him, I see that he's been struck several times.

"No, no, no!" I cry, clutching fistfuls of his shirt. "Stay with me, Bram! Stay with me!"

Blood pours from his shoulder, stomach, and neck like a three-armed cascade. I apply pressure to the wounds, attempting to stanch the flow, but the blood gurgles up between my shaking fingers—Bram's essence spilling out of him onto me and this beach.

His lips curve into the faintest whisper of a smile. His eyelids flutter softly as if moved by the salty wind.

"It's going to be okay, Bram. It's going to be okay."

My promises emerge in a shivering blur of sobs, but I don't think he hears me, don't think he cares. He just smiles as the blood surges, like this is what he'd wanted all along. Like things are already okay, for him and for Willow. Things are finally okay.

His heaving chest slows, his gasps for air dwindling to shallow breaths.

"Bram?" I cradle his face in my hands.

"I see her," he croaks.

"W-what?"

"In your smile...I see her."

I'm transported back to that moment on the *Willow's Wind*, when we'd tossed our heads back like untroubled children, laughing fully as sheets of rain fell around us. I remember thinking it was some kind of miracle to see this broken man filled up with such uninhibited joy. The freedom and wildness bursting from him could only be matched by the sea. But maybe I'd been wrong.

Maybe the true miracle of that fleeting moment was that Bram had seen his daughter's smile again, had heard the peal of her laughter again—through me, in me.

"Bram," I choke out. My flesh hadn't been pierced by that deluge of bullets, but I feel myself shattering to fragments just the same.

"Smile." He wheezes the command between labored breaths.

"Smile and she lives. So smile again."

"I…can't."

"Find a reason, Dell," he insists. "Find a reason to always smile again."

In spite of the bone-crushing anguish that grips me, I do it. I reach for that source of pulsing, burning sunshine that's carved a home in my heart—the love that keeps me alive. Through a constant stream of sobs, I manage a tiny, watery smile.

With an exhale, Bram goes still in my arms, his expression peaceful, like maybe he's only sleeping. Resting.

"Bram?"

Panicking, I press an ear to his chest, a silent question to which there is no answer, no heartbeat.

"Wake up! Wake up!"

I shake him roughly, my fingers swiping at his cheeks, stroking his beard, grasping for anything, *anything.*

"Bram…please."

A legion of uniformed officers appear from the darkness, approaching the beach from the direction of Cliffmoor House, each of them wielding a gun.

They did this.

I droop onto his body, too exhausted to hold myself up on my own. "Bram…"

I weep for him, but he never stirs.

It's no use.

No use.

He's gone.

CHAPTER FIFTY-EIGHT

The beach fades as I curl into myself, eyes squeezed tight against the blasts of gunfire echoing maddeningly in the confines of my mind.

There's running and shouting and endless sirens as police and medics swarm, performing life-saving measures on Ambrose, on Bram, only to confirm what I already know.

He's gone.

Each time someone attempts to approach me, I scream and punch and kick until they give up and move on to more pressing matters. I know they won't tolerate my lack of cooperation forever. Eventually, they'll sedate me, force me into an ambulance, rush me to the hospital. I'll have to answer questions and endure their third degree. I'll have to defend Bram, make sure everyone knows what he did for me. The kind of man he was, in spite of a world that took him for a monster.

He's gone. He's gone.

I burrow deeper into my sandy hollow, withdrawing farther into my heartbroken shell. Fading, vanishing, dying among that chaotic rush of the living. I wish they would all just leave. Leave me alone, let me wash away with the surf, with Willow, with Bram…just let me go too.

Moments later, Hatch is there—a lifeline to keep me afloat and breathing, tethered to something good, something *real*. His arms wrap like a warm blanket around me as he scoops me up and folds me in, leading me up the beach, away from the red-tinged shoreline and the dead things tossing in the Sandspur waves.

I bury my head in his shoulder, breathing in the scent of his skin and the air of whiskey that perfumes his jacket. I feel more than hear the countless times he whispers a promise.

"I've got you, Dell. I'm here. Don't worry, love. I've got you."

I cling to those words—to *him*—like a prayer.

CHAPTER FIFTY-NINE

The door to Tristen's hospital room is ajar. A young attending nurse checks his vital signs, comparing the shifting pulses on a machine to the clipboard in her arms. I knock on the door frame and my cousin's dark eyes flit to where I stand at the threshold, shivering in my thin patient gown. He winks, inviting me in without words, and I slip inside and onto the corner armchair, absently spinning the medical band affixed to my good wrist.

A couple of minutes later, the nurse acknowledges my cousin with a small, sad-looking smile and bows out of the room quietly. That's how everyone looks at Tristen these days.

"You don't need to keep popping in here, you know," he murmurs before I can speak, his eyelids fluttering. "There's been no change."

"There will be." I sound more sure about this than I feel. "Once you get into physical therapy—"

"Therapy doesn't fix paralysis," he interrupts me.

After shutting me out of the attic, Florian had lashed out at Tristen, a confrontation that spiraled into a vicious brawl once he learned of his son's intentions to turn him over to police.

In an unbridled rage, Florian had shoved Tristen through the attic window. My cousin had plunged nearly four stories to what should have been his death, his body colliding—*splintering*—against ground. I'd heard it happen all the way from the beach.

By some miracle, the fall didn't kill Tristen, but the severity of trauma to his spinal cord came with lasting, and likely permanent, effects.

Meanwhile, my face-off with Ambrose had left me with a shattered wrist, a swollen neck, a bruised larynx, and a sprinkling of reddish-purple contusions along my chest and shoulders. On every count, I'd gotten off lucky, and I can't help but feel guilty about it now as I peer into the face of my bedridden, stitch-covered cousin.

He's completely immobilized before me, covered in more lesions than skin, with wires attached to every side of his freshly shaved head.

"You're doing that thing again," he mumbles irritably.

"What thing?"

"That pitiful smile thing. All the nurses and doctors do it too. Like I'm a three-legged kitten with some incurable disease."

"I am not."

He squints at me now, repressing a subtle, knowing smile. How he's capable of smiling at all after everything he's been through is a miracle all its own.

"When are they letting you out of here?" he asks.

"This afternoon, supposedly. But I'm not holding my breath."

I fold my legs beneath me and rub the goosebumps from my arms, steeling myself against the constant subzero temperatures at which they keep the hospital.

"Take one," Tristen commands, his eyes flitting to the stack of knit blankets laid out across his feet. "I don't need them."

"You sure?"

I'm still wary of my cousin's kindnesses, unsure of how to take them, uncertain which version of him is genuine. The snarky, calculating extortionist? The cold and detached combatant? The unappreciated savior avenging wrongs from behind the scenes? Had he fully outgrown his disdain for my mother? Had he made peace with his own cruelty? Did he ever get confused about it—muddled up in his mind by the many roles he played?

"I can't feel a thing, Dell, not even the cold," Tristen assures me, eyeing the blankets again. "Take one."

Careful not to disturb his legs, I slide the top blanket off the pile and spread it over my shoulders.

"Are the cops still harassing you?" he asks.

I shake my head. "I've been about as cooperative as I can be. And Dad's doing a hell of a job fending them off for me."

My parents were here within a day of being contacted by the HBPD. One minute I'd been resting, my good hand wrapped in Hatch's, and the next thing I knew, Mom sat in his place, concern and clarity replacing the grief in her eyes, looking more like herself than I'd seen in years. Hatch had filled Dad in on everything they'd missed, and he'd switched right into protective mode, stepping in with detectives, medical staff, and everyone else who walked through my door.

My heart had swelled at the sight of them in that gloomy hospital suite. I hadn't let myself feel how much I needed my parents over the last few months, how deeply I missed them despite pushing them away. So I let myself feel it all, let myself weep and scream and empty my heart out. And after I'd done that, after I'd been drained of every emotion imaginable, they were all still there—Mom, Dad, and Hatch— to reassemble my broken parts and stitch me back up.

"Are you still pissed over Bram?" my cousin asks.

I trace a finger down the edge of the blue cast on my wrist, not quite knowing how to respond. Truth be told, I am pissed. And sad. And resentful. And about a million other painful sentiments I can't verbalize or process.

I'd blamed the police after that night, blamed them for not getting to the beach in time to stop Ambrose, to keep Bram from doing what he'd done and forcing their hand. But all of it seems futile to dwell on now, and even worse to burden Tristen with when he's facing such unscalable mountains.

"If it helps, I think Bram knew what he was doing," my cousin offers. "He didn't go out guns blazing on some foolish whim. He killed the man who killed his kid, point blank. He had to know something like that wouldn't go unpunished."

I think back to Bram's calm demeanor on that beach, after he'd unloaded his pistol on Ambrose. He'd sunk to his knees at the foot of the ocean, swept up with relief. *Fulfilled*, I remember thinking, like at long last he'd finally done his fatherly duty.

"Bram did what he did knowing he'd pay a steep price. Either he'd spend a lifetime in prison, or he'd die for it. So maybe, on some level, it's better this way—"

"Don't say that," I cut him off swiftly.

Even if things had turned out exactly how Bram wanted, I'm not willing to admit it aloud. Nothing is 'better' about him dying. It's just loss, *terrible loss*, and I've had enough of death.

"All right." Tristen sighs. "Then I won't say it."

I follow his eyes to the open window, where the morning sky is laid out in pristine baby blue, spattered with cotton-ball clouds and slow-coasting gulls. It's picturesque, simple, sweet—worlds apart from life inside this dreary hospital.

Worlds apart from the life that awaits us both when we leave.

I gather the courage to ask him, "What about your dad?"

Tristen inhales deeply, his slow-rising chest the only perceptible movement in his body. "What about him?"

After the attempted murder of his son, Florian had managed to evade police and flee the scene, swallowed up in the chaos and confusion of the evening, the wolf cane disappearing along with him.

While an unconscious and critically-injured Tristen fought for his life, the HBPD and Coast Guard assembled search teams across land and sea to find and detain Florian, but their efforts came up dismally short. Reports later surfaced that a private jet had departed Halcyon Bay Airport in the dead of night, without clearance from air traffic control. Radar onboard had been disabled, and all that could be determined was that the aircraft was headed east upon takeoff.

Just like that, Florian had slipped away, leaving no trace behind for anyone to follow.

"Do the cops have any leads about where he might be hiding?"

Thus far, they'd been tight-lipped about the investigation, likely because they don't want me meddling, but I'm far from accepting defeat.

"They think he might be operating within our business network," Tristen says. "That he's being shuttled around by one of our partners. Someone he trusts. Someone with good reason to want to keep him out of prison."

"So if you provide police with a list of all the company's known associates, they can rule them out, one by one—"

"I already did that. But these are powerful people with deep pockets, and they know how to cover their tracks. If they want to keep someone concealed—if they want to make it look like my father vanished from the map—they can do it, no questions asked."

Before I can say anything to rebut his statement, Tristen adds quietly, out of nowhere, "I think he might've killed my mother."

I sit up straighter. "What?"

Tristen's jaw clenches then relaxes again. "My father hinted that there were *others*, like maybe Willow's murder wasn't an isolated incident for the Klyne brothers, but rather, the tip of the iceberg. I think he was trying to make me question what I knew, to make me doubt whether the long fight to bring him down is worth it."

"But you believe him," I say slowly.

"Maybe. I've always suspected that he had something to do with my mother's death. I don't think she overdosed in the shipyards alone. Maybe he orchestrated it, even if he didn't kill her himself."

This is a tough pill to swallow, but one we'd be stupid not to consider. Could men like Ambrose and Florian really kill once and never again?

"You said others…plural." My voice quivers with fear over where this path might lead. "How many potential *others* are we talking about?"

"I can think of at least one more," Tristen says. "Florian and Ambrose had a cousin who spent summers at Cliffmoor House back when they were all in grade school. Her name was Eribeth. One summer, an unfortunate mishap occurred. The cousins were all playing out in the garden when, allegedly, Eribeth fell from the roof of the guest house, and died soon after from her injuries." His lip twitches strangely, as if he's reliving a horrible moment in time. "If I had to guess, Eribeth's fall was as much of an accident as mine was."

"Wait, hold on. This all happened when they were kids?"

He frowns. "It's only a theory that the brothers had anything to do with it, of course. But you have to admit, the pieces fit."

My throat tightens. How far back did our family's depravity go? How long had the Klyne brothers harbored these murderous tendencies, this contempt for women? And, perhaps worst of all, how many more casualties lived on their deadly scoreboard?

I'm reminded of the spirit I encountered while staying in the guest house. Images of the broken-necked figure in the bathroom flick behind my eyes. I recall that uncanny feeling of numbness, of helplessness, when some unseen force nearly drowned me in the bathtub. Was that the presence of Eribeth? Was she the spirit that materialized for my grandmother years before too? The one that led her to Freya for answers?

"I passed this information onto my contacts in the police department, but I'm not sure they're taking it seriously," Tristen mutters.

"Why not?"

"Apparently, now that state police are involved, the HBPD no longer requires my assistance." Yet another shocker, considering all the work Tristen had put into this investigation and everything it cost him. "With the Brine torpedoed and Ambrose dead, they're confident they'll be able to apprehend my father without my help."

His sharp, black eyes roll off to one side. "I think they're trying to keep me from interfering. I guess I can't blame them. In my present condition, I'm a liability." A chuckle escapes him. "Their words."

This infuriates me. "Then *we* should go looking for him," I say fiercely, the statement spilling from my lips without a second's hesitation. "You and me. On our own. No police."

Tristen lifts his eyebrows. "Are you completely out of your mind?"

"Why?" I shoot back. "You've got plenty of money to fund a private investigation. And who better than the two of us? Who cares as much about catching Florian?"

Actually, if I were to accept the money Virginia left for me—something I'd put out of my mind long ago—then I'd have more than enough to finance the investigation *myself*. Using Klyne wealth to burn the Klyne name to the ground.

I can't think of a better use for my inheritance. Or my time.

"You're not thinking clearly, Dell."

"What's unclear about my thinking? After everything he's done, don't you want to see your father behind bars?"

"Of course."

"And do you have even the teensiest bit of faith that the cops will be able to make that happen without your help?"

"Not really, but—"

I raise a hand to stop him, knowing full well that whatever it takes to catch and arrest Florian, I'm willing to do it. Even if that means going around the police. Even if that means going around Tristen.

"Just think about it, okay?"

Tristen sighs. "Don't you want to be done with this?" Exhaustion weighs heavy on his tone. "Haven't you had enough?"

I have had enough. Enough of living in sheltered ignorance. Enough of hiding behind the farcical notion that I'm somehow separate from the Klynes and their world.

There's no way I'll ever be able to settle back into a serene and sequestered life in Woodbridge, pretending that I'm not intrinsically part of this—pretending I'm not one of them. I am. *I am one of them.* I can't run from it like Mom tried to do.

"Like it or not, I'm in this with you, Tristen. So think about it, please, because I'm not ready to forget. And neither are you."

He doesn't respond, but if I've learned anything about my cousin, it's that he's not one to resign himself to failure. Being restricted to a chair is a grim prospect for him to accept—and a bitter reminder of the depths of his father's evil—but it won't squash his resolve. He's acclimated to the darkness. It won't break him now.

I rise to my feet and shuffle to the doorway.

Tristen says, "Best of luck with the service tomorrow." He lowers his eyes. "Send Hatcher my regards too."

I nod and duck into the hospital corridor. Bram is the second father figure that Hatch would have to bury in a handful of years. The loss is more real for him than anyone. And though Bram didn't have any blood relatives left, he had family in *us*—the Seaborns and myself. We would grieve his passing, and we would feel his absence. We would miss him, even if no one else would.

My one comfort is knowing that Bram's story is bookended, tied together with heartstrings, tears, and blood. I'd like to think that he's with Willow now, that he'd gotten his closure, secured his peace.

I can't help but wonder what that must be like…and when the rest of us might get ours.

CHAPTER SIXTY

When Hatch asks how I'd like to spend my last night on the island, I tell him that I want to see it all.

"To remember," I say, an oversimplified statement that barely scratches the surface of this swirling of present and past, love and pain, in my veins.

Captain Patton offers to spend the evening on land, so Hatch and I get the schooner to ourselves. As we maneuver out of the seaport at sundown, I notice how gentle the sea is tonight—every bit the opposite of the angry, rushing waters that first brought me here. Short waves lap against the boat, tender as a soft swaying lullaby, almost so I can curl up inside of them and fall fast asleep.

We take a leisurely tour around the island, soaking up panoramic views of all of Halcyon Bay. It's like something from a forgotten storybook. The marinas, speckled in pastel boats and paper-white sails. The derelict lighthouse, perched and crumbling at the edge of the sea. The sea trumpet fields, circled in neon police tape. Cliffmoor House, desolate and ancient, looming from the Sandspur shore.

The mansion is empty now, save for its score of ghostly residents. As dusk settles over it, bathing the grounds, walls, and windows in shadow, it all feels haunted somehow. Haunted as I am, and all the others touched by it.

I watch for some shimmer of silver in the darkening water, some flicker of strange movement or shift in the currents. But all is calm, all is still, as if some great debt was repaid to the ocean, and all of its denizens, living and dead, rest easy beneath the surface tonight.

Though I can't see her, I pray that Willow is with me, in whatever form she may take. Siren, spirit, or sea foam—always, always my sister.

Per the reopened investigation into Willow's death, my parents are working with the HBPD to get her body exhumed, reexamined, and relocated to a cemetery of Mom's choosing, someplace closer to Woodbridge. She vows she'll never return to the island again, but she's come to accept that I must. That some gaping, unfillable part of me belongs here, inextricably linked to this mystifying place.

She said to me today, in that cautionary tone of hers, "You can only linger in hell for so long before you become flame or demon yourself."

I had to agree with this, and found myself wondering, *If I stick around long enough, which of these would be my fate?*

Hatch and I anchor somewhere in the distant ocean, and we settle onto the ship's bow under a clear night sky, gazing at the stars that shoot and race and fall.

He speaks of plans to visit Maine later this autumn, when the leaves are changed and the colors bursting, and I smile at the thought of it. Seeing his smile again, his cheeks made pink by the crisp wind, his forest eyes exploring the forests I grew up in, is an idea I can get used to. A future to look forward to.

"You thanked me," Hatch whispers against the shell of my ear, making me shiver with pleasure. "You thanked me for coming for you. Do you remember?"

My back is curled to his chest, his arms wrapped snug around me. I hum in response. I remember, of course. At the pier, after the fields.

"So long as you let me, Dell, I'll come for you," he says, lips pressing to my dewy skin again and again. "Wherever it is, if you're there, I'll come. Always."

For months, I'd toiled against this overwhelming sense of unmooring. Adrift from all that once claimed me, tossing like an aimless wave in search of everything and nothing. But in Hatch's arms tonight, I'm undeniably home, as if home were a feeling, or maybe a person, rather than a place.

"I'm here, Hatch," I murmur, my cheek resting against the solid warmth of him. "Tonight, I'm right here with you. And we'll find our way back when I'm gone. Always."

The next morning, Hatch accompanies me to the seaport, and we separate with a kiss upon my final boarding call. He stands dockside with his hands shoved in his jean pockets, squinting into the sunshine as my ferry pulls away from land.

I think of all I'm taking with me. The questions that fuel me, my relentless need for justice, and the love that has stubbornly taken root in my heart. At the center of it all is Willow—my reason for returning, answering the call in my soul. And now, Hatch—my reason for never truly leaving.

The waters of Halcyon Bay roll gently at the ferry's side, accompanying my departure like an old, familiar friend. I breathe in deeply, lungs filling up with the bitter, salty air that seems part of me now, fuel to my blood.

The island grows ever smaller behind me, fainter and fainter, until finally, it fades into a thick cloaking of fog.

ACKNOWLEDGMENTS

There are so many incredible individuals without whom this book would not exist. Nothing I say will ever be enough to sum up my gratitude or capture the full spectrum of my emotions, but nonetheless, I'll do my best.

To Ryan, my husband and endless love: thank you for never once doubting this journey. For urging me to keep at it, even on the cloudy days. For always being quick to pour me a drink, and for your depthless IT skills. In so many ways, you've given me my very own book-worthy fairytale. Maybe I'll write it someday.

To Mom and Dad, my lifelong champions and the greatest parents in the world: thank you for lifting me up so high that my feet barely touch the ground. You fueled every spark of creativity, encouraged every ambition, and raised a little girl with big dreams into a young woman with epic ones. I wouldn't be me without the two of you.

To Nicole, my sister in blood and soul: thank you for being my very first reader, my first critique partner, and my first fan. Gushing about literary things with you is one of my greatest joys. The world needs more author sisters, I think. Modern-day Brontës, if you will. So let's make it happen.

To the four of you mentioned above: thank you for believing in me. I love you *more*. Now it's in writing.

To the awesome publishing team that helped make this a reality: RaeAnne Betzelberger, for your editing prowess; Sandra Guerra, for your business savvy and unwavering support; Maria Spada, for your cover design wizardry. Thank you from the bottom of my heart.

To the beta readers who became some of my greatest friends: Vanessa Birkner, Hailey Brzoska, Daphne De Grandpré, and Alyssa Pressley. Thank you for loving this book at its earliest stage, for helping me see it through fresh eyes, and for singing its praises from the proverbial rooftops. I'm so glad the internet brought us together.

To my long list of writing companions (you know who you are): thank you for the daily laughs, the sprints, the infinite wisdom, and the encouragement whenever things got bumpy. You all taught me that writing doesn't have to be a lonely endeavor, and I'm forever grateful.

A special shout-out to my dear author friends: Vanessa Rasanen, Rachel Schade, Emily Schneider, and Emily VanderBent. Thank you for reading and applauding this story in advance, for tucking me under your wings and helping to guide me through the world of indie publishing.

To the family, friends, and acquaintances who asked countless times, "When can I read it?": thank you for your enthusiasm, I won't ever forget it, and I'm thrilled to say that the answer is now. Right now. *Finally*.

To the readers: thank you for taking a chance on this story, these characters, this strange island world, and me. I appreciate you so much, and hope to write many more books for you to enjoy.

Last but not least, to God, my heavenly Father and eternal source of Light: thank You for the gifts I've been granted. This dream was realized according to Your perfect timing, and that makes it all the more worthwhile.

Natalia Macias Lucia was raised on ghost stories, Cuban food, and sweltering summers in her native South Florida. She loves the sun, surf, and swampland almost as much as she loves writing, and when not dreaming up new book ideas, she can often be found by the ocean with her husband, family, and neurotic Jack Russell Terrier.

An avid reader with a lifelong dream of becoming a novelist, Natalia earned a bachelor's degree in English Literature from the University of Miami. She enjoys writing dark fairytales woven into contemporary life, filled with swoony romance, thrilling twists, and things that go bump in the night. *Girls of Salt and Sea* is her debut novel and the first book in the Halcyon Bay series.

Visit her online at **www.nataliamlucia.com**.

www.ingramcontent.com/pod-product-compliance
Lightning Source LLC
Chambersburg PA
CBHW031240310726
48971CB00004B/1110